Mid Witch Three

DJ Bowman-Smith

Illustrated by
DJ Bowman-Smith

Edited by
Anna Sharples

Copyright © 2025 by DJ Bowman-Smith

All rights reserved.

No part of this book may be reproduced in any form or by any electronic or mechanical means, including information storage and retrieval systems, without written permission from the author, except for the use of brief quotations in a book review.

For Paul

Foreword

Dear Reader,

Once again I must ask you to take the time to leave a review and/or star rating so others can find this story. Without your help the Mid Witch books will fall into obscurity.

I hope that you enjoy this next instalment of Lilly's journey into midlife and magic. Please join my mailing list for updates and news of upcoming books. You can find the link below.

Many thanks and lots of love,

Deborah Bowman-Smith

www.djbowmansmith.com

Chapter One

Ten o'clock and I've already got my washing on the line and two celebration cakes baking in the range. Time for a cup of tea. The sun shines through the kitchen door, so I plonk an old cushion on the step for me and throw a pile of blankets onto the path for Ink. The greyhound stretches out, her black coat gleaming in the May sunshine.

Maud, another of my witch familiars, is in the apple tree. Magpies don't sing; they clatter. I watch her stalk up and down her favourite branch. Queen of the blossoms. Claudia, my cat, emerges from the long grass of the lawn I can never bear to cut. This witch's opinion is that mowing hides the true beauty of grass and weeds. So many interesting and useful plants grow from a lawn if you let them. And anyway, I've got enough to do, and my cat familiar loves it.

Hard to see in the bright sunshine is Bethany Blackwood. Her ghostly presence is ever near, wafting about the garden. She often comes into North Star Cottage and watches me bake. I chat to her. It's company of sorts, but ghosts don't speak to the living.

I blow on my tea and take a sip. It's nice out here on the step in the sun, my familiars all around and the garden bursting into life. I should be grateful, happy and fulfilled. I have two delightful grown-up children and adorable twin granddaughters. I own my home, and now, with my cake baking business Fox Bake, I'm actually making ends meet. I've even got the hang of the witch stuff. Since I became a midwitch – well, let's just say I know my magical worth.

What bothers me is that I'm alone. Love never seems to stick. Probably because I'm cursed. Like my mother and all the many witches who lived at North Star Cottage before me. These days I'm too busy to care, but now and then, when I stop and take a breath, I feel the power of lost love. The lonely days cling to me and I wish that for this last part of my life there was someone to love who loved me back.

It's not about sex. Although I wouldn't say no. It's about companionship: having somebody on your side when things go awry. A partnership is what I long for. A partnership with cuddles. But it's no use moping about feeling sorry for myself. Best to face the facts and press on. Enjoy what I've got and be bloody thankful. I'm healthy. A few creaks and aches, but the HRT has softened the brunt of middle age, thankfully, and I have a job I enjoy, and I'm a witch.

Brew a love potion? Don't make me laugh.

I swig the rest of my tea and heave myself off the step. After a quick check on the cakes – they're doing fine – I get my secateurs and tramp through the grass to tackle the hydrangeas. Passers-by must think I don't garden. Not that many brave the potholes along Church Lane where North Star Cottage is the only dwelling. Actually, I'm a constant gardener, always pottering about while my cakes cool. Like my mother, I don't see weeds, just plants. The garden is my therapy, and chopping off the dried hydrangea heads, I'm happy again.

I fill a barrow until I hear Alexa in the kitchen. The cakes are done. 'Alexa, stop,' I say, washing my hands at the kitchen sink. I turn them out onto the cooling rack. A lemon sponge and a coffee cake made in a loaf tin. Both for Lady Wootton, who is having a 'small tea party for a few friends, darling' on the (short) lawn of Marswickham House.

I don't drive. Never learned and now I'm too scared to try.

So, all my baked goods need collecting. Her ladyship is sending a member of staff to pick up the cakes in the morning, and I'm half-expecting a liveried footman and a coach and horses.

While the cakes cool, I fetch a tape measure from my sewing box and measure the electric cooker. I never use it anymore, not now the old range works again. I need the space for a bigger fridge to keep my Fox Bake cakes cool and safe.

Online, I check dimensions and, because I don't trust myself, measure everything again. I have to make another cup of tea and re-check my bank account. My little cake making venture is going well and I really need this fridge. It's hard to concentrate with a ghost in the kitchen. Recently Bethany likes to float in front of me with a mournful expression on her pretty young face. It's very off-putting. I try not to get cross with her.

'Now come on, Beth. Just let me do this and then...' And then what? What exactly can I say to my ancestor, burnt at the stake on Fox Green? She wafts to one side, giving me the chance to call Marswickham Appliances and fix a delivery date.

The cakes are cool, so I get them decorated and then Ink and I set off to deliver chocolate brownies and scones to the Fox Tearoom and buy eggs.

Church Lane is cool and leafy and Ink trots back and forth, sniffing everything. The ghost walks beside me then floats under the lychgate of St Gutheridge and All Angels. She never comes to the end of the lane.

Mid Witch Three

At Fox Green, I deliver the baking and buy flour and an overpriced lemon. The eggs are also expensive. While I queue to pay, I read the notice board. Fox Lodge will open its garden to the public next weekend for charity; Grant must have found a new gardener. Mr Richards has Buff Orpington hens for sale. I look at the price tag on the egg box. Maybe I should get some chickens. The village fete committee is seeking volunteers and the Foxy Lady's Social Club is starting a book club on Thursdays at the village hall.

When I come out into the May sunshine, Ink has gone. That dog. I untie her lead from the ring on the wall and put it in my basket. I can't see her anywhere. Hard to lose a huge black greyhound? No. Happens all the time. That's the trouble with magical familiars – they get ideas of their own.

I whistle loudly through my fingers, which usually works a treat. I wait then whistle again. When she doesn't come running, I peer into the gift shop, the post office and the tearoom where she likes to scrounge for snacks. I scan the village green in case she's chasing birds or gone for a game with another dog. The space is empty. Then I glimpse a black shape slinking toward the pub. I whistle as loudly as I can and shout, 'Ink! Ink! Treats!' She doesn't even look back. The pub door opens and in she goes. Drat.

I march over the village green to the Fox Pub. As a rule, I don't like to walk on the grass, but my thoughts are full of stolen 'pie of the day' and this is the quickest way.

Halfway across, and the cold hits me - as if this bright day in May has become frosty February. I stand rooted to the spot as mist rises from the ground. No, not mist: smoke. I'm clutching my throat and choking for breath. Flames burst from the earth, scorching hot and loud. Above the rattle of the fire, an infant screams. Panic engulfs me, yet I cannot move.

'Lilly!'

Strong hands pull me free. Back into the sunshine. Back to life. I gulp in clean air and try to quell my fear as muscular arms embrace me.

'It's alright, Lilith,' Grant mumbles into my hair. 'I've got you.'

I break free of his grasp. The grass is brilliant green, jewel-studded with dandelions and daisies. Birds sing. Bees buzz in the clover. Everything is normal. Ink puts her cold nose into my hand.

Grant opens his mouth to speak, and I glare at him. We both know why I'm having a weird moment. This is the place where his family burnt Bethany Blackwood at the stake. A price she paid for being a witch and loving the wrong man.

'You okay?'

'Yes,' I croak, trying to pull myself together.

Ink is skipping about in the sunshine, chasing a butterfly.

'Lucky I was here to save you,' he says with a manly grin.

'It's you that needs saving, you arrogant fuck,' I say.

Grant strides back to the pub and ducks under the door without a backward glance. Who's he having a cosy lunch with, the bastard?

Chapter Two

Back at the cottage, I get the washing in and fold it onto the range to air. There's not much now I'm on my own. I can get away with two loads a week, easy. I make a pot of tea and check my cake-making schedule and try to ignore Bethany. These days I have to do everything through a haze of ghostly ancestor.

'Looks like we can have a day off tomorrow,' I say to Ink. 'If the cakes are collected early, we could pop out for a jolly.' Ink licks her food bowl and then lies on her pile of blankets by the range. An outing would do me good – but where? A walk on a different beach, perhaps? A wander around another village? Seems no point when you're on your own.

I check my cracked phone for any news from the kids. Nothing. I should contact them more, but I don't like to bother them. And anyway, what can I say? Made another cake, garden is full of useful weeds and here's another picture of Ink or Maud or Claudia.

I scrub a jacket potato for my tea. I live on them these days. They're simple, endlessly versatile – and I'm too lazy to cook for myself. Probably why I resemble a jacket potato. You are what you eat, or so the saying goes. Spud woman. That's me.

Bethany is spinning in circles. She knows this annoys me. 'What!' I say, tossing the spud into the oven.

She stops, folds her arms and taps her foot. This doesn't make any noise. My ghosts are quiet.

'I walked across the village green today,' I say. She hugs herself. 'I had a sense of what happened to you, Beth, and I'm sorry for what they did.' She drifts closer, her head bowed. A cloud hides the sun, and in the darkened room I see her more clearly. She's so young. A slip of a girl, fine-boned and pretty. She points toward the church. I've followed her there a few times now. But once I'm through the lychgate, she's gone. 'Bethany, I'm sorry. Truly. But there's nothing I can do. I can't fix the past. And I don't understand what you want in the graveyard.'

Ink woofs to let me know someone is coming.

'Is this Fox Bake?' says a middle-aged gent in jeans and a waistcoat when I open the door.

'Yes. Hi, I'm Lilith.'

'I'm just here on the off chance as I was passing, hoping to collect the cakes for Lady Wootton. But don't worry if I'm too early. I can come back tomorrow.'

'No, come on in. They're all done. Take a seat while I get them boxed,' I say. He steps into the kitchen. Ink gives his tan brogues a sniff, and he pats her.

'Hello, big dog. Is she a greyhound?'

'Yes,' I say, lifting the cakes from the fridge. 'Looks like you'll have good weather for the tea party.'

'All indications are positive.' He holds up crossed fingers. I get cake boxes from the under stairs cupboard, put them together and slide in the cakes. 'You've done that before,' he says, taking out his wallet. 'What do we owe?'

'Nothing.'

'Free cakes! My lucky day.'

'Lady Wootton paid online.'

'Ahh marvellous. Right then.'

'I'll give you a hand,' I say. We both carry a box.

'Lovely old place,' he says, peering into the witch ball hanging in the kitchen window. Today it has a misty blue sheen. 'Unusual thing,' he says. Outside, he stops on the path. 'You been here long?'

'Forever.'

'Used to ride ponies down Church Lane when I was a kid. Seems like a lifetime ago.' He has a friendly face. Amiable with nice crinkles around his blue eyes from smiling.

His silver Range Rover is in the lane. Two spaniels watch us from the boot. He opens the passenger door and sets the cake boxes in the footwell then stares at the cottage. 'I've been in your cottage before.' He points along the lane. 'Fell off my pony. Poor creature stumbled in a pothole. Came off, banged my head.' He rubs his temple and laughs. 'My brother and I thought a witch lived here, because sometimes there was an old woman in the garden in a black pointy hat. You know how kids make stuff up. We were scared. We'd started to believe our own nonsense. Anyway, this huge black lurcher came out with a woman. My head was bleeding badly, and she took us in.'

I'm fascinated.

'My little brother was crying, and the horses had run off.' His laugh is a deep rumble. 'Sorry. Ramblings of an old man.' He wipes his face with a cotton handkerchief.

'No, not at all. What happened? Was she a witch?' Ink wanders over and sits beside me, ears in the upright, most interested position.

'She was kind. Sat us in the kitchen. Gave us cakes and milk. Cleaned up my head.' He gazes at my wild garden.

'Toby, my little brother, he was all upset about the ponies. And you know what she said?'

I wait.

'Don't worry, the dog will bring them back. And when we left, the huge dog was here,' – he points at the gate – 'with the ponies.' Another big laugh. 'Haven't thought about any of this for years.' He gets in the car. 'Thanks for the cakes and the memories.'

'No problem.'

When the car has gone, Bethany is standing in the lane, hands clasped in a pleading gesture. Since the incident on Fox Green I'm sad for her. 'Alright, I'll come. But you've got to try and tell me what you want,' I say. She's already floated ahead.

'Come on, Ink,' I say and we follow the ghost. I've got odd shoes on. A pink plastic clog and a red welly. Not ideal, but few people come along Church Lane and there is only one service a month at the church. It's been a wet spring, and the potholes are rain filled. On the way, I pick cow parsley and buttercups. The sun is out again and I've lost sight of Bethany. At the lychgate I wait, squinting in the sunlight, trying to find her. She's gone, which is annoying. This happens every time. She annoys me until I come here and then she disappears.

'Come on, Inky dog,' I say, heading for the back of the churchyard where my ancestors are buried. I search for Bethany in the shadows of the ancient yew trees. Then I give up and put the wildflowers on Mum's grave. 'I met someone today who you helped when he was a boy. He fell off his horse in the lane,' I say, brushing away a few sticks and leaves before I walk to where the wall bulges out to encompass a group of older graves. Once these witches were outside the consecrated ground. Now the church wall enfolds them. One gravestone, small and crooked, has the north star scratched into the stone. I pull off strands of ivy and place a sprig of buttercups on the mound.

I'm listening to the birdsong and enjoying the peace when a cloud passes over the sun. I spot Bethany on the other side of the stone wall. She paces back and forth in the field, stopping now and then to glare at me.

'What do you want?' I ask.

She points at the grave, cradles her arms as if holding a baby.

'Yes. I checked the dates. This is your daughter, named after you. She started the shadow book.' I pat the headstone as she watches me.

Realisation dawns.

I scrabble around the headstones, tearing away ivy and scratching off lichen. There are a lot of Blackwood witches here. But not the first: Bethany Blackwood burnt at the stake on Fox Green all those years ago. My stomach churns, and I taste ash. There was probably nothing to bury.

'I'll get you a headstone,' I say. Is that what the poor ghost girl wants? Bethany has gone.

Chapter Three

I n the morning, I don't go out because Marswickham Appliances call to say they will deliver today. They're not able to say when exactly, but assure me they will fit my new fridge sometime before ten o'clock this evening. There is nowhere I need to be, so I don't mind.

There are a few rare spring weeds I want to dry. I take a basket and get picking. At the far end of the garden is the old chicken shed. It's overgrown with brambles, and I have to use my secateurs to get a proper look. Maud lands on the roof and wanders about. 'Any leaks?' I ask her. She hops onto my shoulder and pecks my ear. More aggressive bramble removal and a good tug gets the door open. Inside, the nest boxes and perches are beautifully dry. When I go into the kitchen for a mug of tea, I call Mr Richards and order some hens.

I'm really pleased. 'This is the new me,' I tell Ink and Claudia as I string the plants to dry over the range. 'Decisive, cake-baking witch – with enough free range eggs.'

Ink woofs softly. Someone is coming. I open the kitchen door to greet the tall, slim woman in a flappy long coat who is striding over the cobbled path.

'Is this Fox Bake?' she trills.

'Yes, hello. I'm Lilly.'

She holds out a leather gloved hand and we shake. 'So pleased to meet. Heard marvellous things about your cakes.' She steps back as Ink approaches for a sniff.

'Ohh, oh!' she squeaks as Ink presses her nose against her high-heeled boots and snort-sniffs. 'What a big doggy.'

'What can I do for you, Ms...'

'Tingle. Mrs Tingle.' She watches Ink saunter into the long grass then gets a leather-bound notebook from her shoulder bag. Finds the page. 'I'm hoping for a chocolate cake with cherries. Exotic and moist. With a juicy layer.'

'What sort of size were you thinking?'

'Very large, darling, sixteen slices and each slice beautiful.'

'When do you need it?'

'Day after tomorrow? Aren't you going to write this down?'

'I can remember, Mrs Tingle.'

'How much?'

I tot up the cost in my head and add a bit more because cherries are expensive. It will be a costly cake. When I tell her the price, she gives me a hard stare. 'We'll see how it looks, shall we?' she says.

'I usually ask for a deposit...' This is untrue, but there is something about her I don't like.

'Do you?' She arches an eyebrow, turns on her heel and stalks off. Ink pops her head out of the long grass when she reaches the gate. Mrs Tingle squeals and does a little leap in the air.

I start the chocolate cake then spend the rest of the day clearing out the chicken shed. By the time Ink woofs to tell me the fridge has arrived, I'm sweaty and grubby. I can't see a van in the lane, and I'm worried they've already gone as I rush to the cottage. Maybe I should have told them they would need to carry the fridge from the road.

There's a suitcase on the path. Maud flies into the apple tree.

My daughter Belinda is standing in the kitchen. 'Okay, love?' I say. She sits in her old place at the table, and I put the kettle on. She looks peaky.

'Tea and cake?'

'No thanks, Mum.'

I sit opposite and try not to jump to conclusions. She looks at her hands. The kettle boils and switches off.

'Do you mind if we stay here for a bit?' she says.

'No, love. Of course not.' The question 'why' hangs between us. It's a school day and my girl is a teacher. She never takes time off. Teaching is her life. Something is very wrong.

She dashes upstairs and I hear the bathroom door close. What has happened? Has their house burnt down? Is her husband, also a teacher, ill? Are the twins okay? Is it financial difficulties? Outside, Claudia hunts in the long grass and I grip my stumpy yew wand inside the pocket of the gardening coat. Please don't let them be ill, I pray.

Belinda returns and helps herself to a glass of water. 'I'm pregnant,' she says.

'Oh, darling!' I gush, moving in for a hug. She gives me a warning look and we sit at the table again. I know better than to ask questions.

'Brian has chucked me out.' She gulps some water. Her face is ashen.

'Didn't he want another baby? He'll come round. Some men don't like change,' I say, all soothing and reasonable and let's-sort-this-out.

She plonks down the glass and water slops onto the table. 'It's not his baby.'

'Oh,' I say, dropping a cloth on the puddle.

'It's the ski instructor's.'

'Are you sure? It might be his. Tricking Brian is not ideal, but keeping your family together seems a small price to pay for a bit of,' – I search for the word – 'duplicity.' She gives me her teacher's stare. Undeterred, I carry on. 'Does he have to learn the truth?'

'Of course he knows the truth. He can do the numbers, Mum. He's head of maths.'

Belinda lifts her handbag onto her lap and finds her phone. After some frantic scrolling, she tosses it on the table and stomps upstairs.

It's a group photo. Against picturesque mountain scenery stands my ex-husband, Mike, with his arm around Theodora Grimshaw. The bitch. My son, Jason, and Belinda are with a very handsome man who must be the ski instructor.

After returning from the bathroom, she goes to collect the twins from school, and I tackle the practicalities. I ask the shadow book for a morning sickness cure, and when I've got the herbs simmering in a pan, I lug the suitcases up the stairs and make the beds up. I haven't any food for an evening meal, apart from one jacket potato, so I message Belinda to pick up ready-made, heat-up pizza on the way home.

Chapter Four

The delighted twins race along the path shouting, 'Lillymar!' We play ball with Ink on the lawn, pet Claudia and feed treats to Maud the magpie. Then I sit with them while they do their homework. After tea, I give them a bath and snug them up in bed with a story.

Mid Witch Three

Belinda is in the kitchen working on her laptop when I return. I wash up, heat some of the morning sickness cure and ladle it into a mug. I don't say anything. Belinda can be very stubborn. I just put the mug by her side and hope.

I check my emails and cake-baking schedule then make a shopping list. Belinda shuts her laptop with a sigh. 'Honestly, by the time I've made lesson plans for the supply teacher, I might as well go in.'

'You're off work then,' I say, stating the obvious. She sips the herb tea. I say a silent prayer of thanks.

'Headteacher thinks I've got food poisoning. And it's half term next week. I don't remember feeling this sick with Amy and Sophie.'

'Every pregnancy is different,' I say. I didn't have morning sickness. Not that I remember. Did Mum give me something for it?

'I'm sorry.' Suddenly she's crying. Must be the hormones; she's never been a weeper. I move chairs so I can put my arm around her.

'It's okay, love. We can get through this.'

'Oh god, Mum, what have I done? I've ruined everything.'

I hand her a tissue from my pocket so she can blow her nose.

'Brian's a boring old fart. But we were okay, really.' She has a big sniff. 'I thought going on that trip with Dad would... I don't bloody know...'

'Make him miss you?'

'Something like that. And now his disappointment in me, it's,' – she has a big choking sob – 'it's crushing.'

I hold her tight, my heart breaking.

'It was all so neat and tidy. Both of us teachers. Nice dependable Brian. When we got jobs at Marswickham Primary, I thought we were sorted. Instead, it got boring. I wanted another baby. Can you be bored with someone and still love them?'

'Muummmy!'

'I'll go,' I say, dashing up the stairs. I settle the kids. Well, I leave Ink in bed with them and tell them to be quiet. In the kitchen, Belinda is splashing her face with cold water from the kitchen tap.

'Thing is. There's not enough money for one of us to get a flat. We need to sell the house. So I told him to stay there.'

'It's fine, love. You can always come home, you know that.'

'But, Mum, it might take ages to sell the house.' She dries her face on a tea towel.

'Don't worry. Stay as long as you need.'

'How am I going to tell the girls?' She starts to cry again and I hold her, wishing I had something wise to say. All I feel is grief for my daughter's loss.

'Brian says he's not leaving the school, but I should.' She sits and has a gulp of tea.

'Will you?'

'Yeah. I guess I'll have to, since it's all my fault.'

'It's not, though, love. Takes two to make a marriage. If he was making you happy, you wouldn't be...'

'Shagging random ski instructors?'

I clear plates into the sink.

'It's not as if we ever argue,' she says.

I want to say maybe that's the problem. I'm hardly a relationship expert with my dire track record, so I keep quiet. 'Just take your time about telling the kids.' Secretly, I hope they will work something out. Belinda sees through me.

'Don't be ridiculous, Mum. Boring Brian's not going to raise someone else's child.'

Ink and I sleep on the easy chair in the sitting room. I've put the twins in their mum's old room in the one bed, and Belinda is in the big bedroom. I've locked Jason's old room: my witch workroom. I'll worry about that later.

The sleeping arrangements need rethinking because the twins will need their own beds, and I have an inclination that Jason might be back. Last time I spoke with him, there were definite undertones of irritation with his wayward father, who he's been staying with.

As I try to sleep, I realise the fridge did not arrive. Oh well. Something else to sort out tomorrow.

Ink and Claudia breathe peacefully, and the house is still. I put my hand on Ink's smooth coat for comfort and cry quietly. None of this would be happening if it wasn't for the curse.

In my old dressing gown, I wander into the garden. It's a dark, damp night with no moon to light my way into the woods. But I have an urge to replenish my magical self from the blackwood trees. As I open the gate, Ink is beside me. When I'm sure no one can see us from the cottage, I snap my fingers for a witch flame to see by. Ink leads the way between the trees; the trail is different every time, and I have given up trying to remember.

A pair of luminous eyes ahead. The green-eyed fox waits on the path. We follow her to a blackwood tree which looms tall and dark into the night sky. I place one hand on the trunk. Even this strengthens me. Leaves softly fall. Some I eat. Others I put into my dressing gown pocket. Normally I wander about listening to owls and enjoying the night – the Blackwood is the one place I never feel lonely – but I hurry back in case I'm missed. At the garden gate, I thank the fox as she slinks away in the undergrowth.

Dawn is breaking and mist clouds the garden. Ink drinks from the birdbath and I listen to the first peeps of birdsong. Usually, I'm full of joy after visiting the trees. This morning my heart is heavy. My family is under a curse. Honestly, I never minded for myself; the chances of me finding true love are long gone at my age. But now my girl is here, her marriage in tatters, and I sense the weight of magical troubles.

'Bethany!' I whisper as loudly as I dare, and a pale presence emerges from the mist. The ghost usually joins me on these nocturnal wanderings. 'There you are!' She walks beside me. We are the same height. A short ghost and a short witch. 'I can't let this curse ruin my kids' lives,' I say. She's hard to see. 'I'll make sure you get a headstone. I promise. Can you help?'

She fades away and I'm left standing there like a bloody fool, as usual. That's the trouble with ghosts. They're rubbish at helping. Since my last altercation with the Allingshire County Coven, I have not neglected my witchy side. I keep the protection spells around the cottage fresh. Occasionally, I use a bit of magic to make the day easier. I've even invented a few spells of my own. I'm happy with my magical self, but I need this curse gone – and if it's the last bloody thing I do, at least I tried. My family's happiness is all that matters.

A light comes on in the cottage, casting a glow over the garden. 'Who were you talking to?' says Belinda in the kitchen.

'Oh, just the dog.' And the ghost.

She's peering into the kitchen cupboards. 'Got any more of that herb tea?' She looks better.

'I'll find it. Take a shower. I'll fix breakfast.'

Chapter Five

When Belinda and the twins have gone, I make a mug of tea and sit in the kitchen to get my breath back. I'd forgotten about the chaos of family life. Amy couldn't find her school shoes and Sophie was crying about a lost writing pen. It was all very dramatic.

Belinda drank more of the herb tea and wore her work clothes. I'm guessing she's going to have a word with the headteacher about the situation.

I open my old laptop and check my email. Marswickham Appliances would like me to rate my delivery. I'd forgotten about the fridge. I call and an automated message tells me the office is closed on Wednesdays. So I email and tell them the fridge has not arrived.

'It's probably still in a van somewhere,' I say to Ink. Then I do an online shop and get a slot for this afternoon, which is a miracle. I get dressed and tidy up and then stand in my witch workroom, wondering what to do. I don't want to reorganise my house and then find Belinda and Brian have settled their differences and she's moving back – or she's found a flat in Marswickham. Then again, this could go on for a while, and the sooner I get organised, the easier life will be.

On the table is my spell book – not the shadow book of the Blackwood witches but a book of my own. Recently I have devised new spells. Mostly to do with cake. Hardly ground-breaking magic, and I doubt anyone but me will ever use them, yet I'm happy. I still have Mouse's book, which I've read a dozen times and made notes from. I'll need to visit Allingshire County Hall, where he works as the witch librarian to return it. Maybe he can help with the curse. I lock the door and decide to leave everything as it is until the weekend.

I'm decorating Mrs Tingle's chocolate cake when Ink

woofs to tell me someone is coming. 'Let's hope it's the bloody fridge,' I say.

The man who collected Lady Wootton's cakes is walking along the path. I hope they were okay and nobody found a magpie feather in them. It could happen. Maybe that's a spell I should contrive – anti foreign bodies in baked goods.

'Marvellous cakes!' he says.

Thank god for that. 'So glad they liked them,' I say and wipe my hands on my apron. He's dressed as before: jeans, shirt, tie and a waistcoat. I wonder if he has a pocket watch and what he does at Marswickham House. Butler, perhaps?

'They were too good. Wondering if you had time to fix us up again? Garden Society afternoon tea and talk. Bit short notice – it's tomorrow.' He pets Ink as she sniffs his shoes. I've got enough on my plate right now and I'd like to say no. Then I remember the grocery bill.

'Come in, er...'

'Edward,' he says, extending his hand.

'Lilly.' We shake. His hands are smooth and warm. 'What do you need?'

'Nothing elaborate. Just a few morsels to have with a cup of tea. Scones, perhaps?'

'I can definitely help with scones.' I open the freezer compartment and bring out two bags of scones I have ready for the tearoom next week. 'What would you like, cheese or plain?'

'What a gem you are.' He has a nice smile. 'Too rude to ask for some of each?'

'Not at all. How many?' I sort the scones into boxes.

'This place has hardly changed,' he says, looking all around. 'Is this a witch jar?' he says, picking up a small bulbous glass jar full of herbs.

'Possibly,' I say, counting scones.

'Is it for sale?' he asks, turning the jar in the light. 'I love a curio.'

I take it from him and set it back on the dresser. 'No.'

'Was that your mother, then? When I fell off my horse?'

'Yes. Must have been.'

'Always meant to return and thank her. Never did. Even came back years later. The lady at the post office said she died. Always felt guilty.'

'Don't. She wouldn't have minded. Mum was kind,' I say.

I put one of my Fox Bake flyers into a box, close the lid and tell him the price. He takes a wallet from inside his waistcoat and leaves some notes on the table. I can see there is too much and get my purse from the dresser to give him change. 'No need,' he says.

We walk to his car, each carrying a box. 'What do you do at Marswickham House?'

He throws back his head and laughs. 'Probably not enough,' he says.

I'm not sure why he finds this so funny. 'Worked there long?'

'Too long.' Another loud laugh. He puts the boxes on the front seat. 'Thanks. You've saved my bacon.'

The spaniels wag their tails as he drives away.

I make another batch of scones. The grocery shop arrives early, and after I've had a chat with Noel, the delivery man, I pop the cherries onto the chocolate cake and box it ready for collection. I'm putting away the shopping when I hear, 'Ting-a-ling!'

'Mrs Tingle,' I say as she steps into the kitchen.

'Is this me?' she says, lifting the lid on the box with her name on.

I'm pleased with how this cake has turned out. It looks gorgeous and smells delicious.

'Oh,' she says, slipping on a pair of fancy spectacles and peering at it intently. 'I suppose it will have to do.'

I'm taken aback. People adore my cakes.

'Not sure this was entirely what I asked for.' She glares at me over the designer specs. 'You really should write down your orders.'

I'm worried she's going to leave the cake and go. Then she gets her purse out of her shoulder bag and counts out the exact amount of money, picks up the box and leaves without another word. Horrid woman.

To recover, Ink and I walk to the beach. The weather is warm. Ink is panting, and I have my coat over my arm when we get back. I'm so desperate for a drink of water that I only notice the suitcases in the kitchen when I hear Jason and Belinda arguing upstairs.

'This is my room...'

'No, Jason, it's not. You were at Dad's, remember?'

'Well, I'm back now and...'

Mid Witch Three

I close the kitchen door. Best not to get involved with your adult children's arguments. I feed Ink and make a pot of tea. There is a text on my phone. It's from Grant Fucking Rutherford. 'I think I've got your fridge,' is all it says. I take a deep breath and let it out slowly. Isn't breathing supposed to fix everything? Breathe and be grateful. Breathe and rid yourself of tension. Breathe and notice the small things. I stare beyond GFR's message and notice the cracks on my phone screen which resemble a tree.

Something else that needs fixing.

Chapter Six

Jason and Belinda try to be civil to each other at teatime for the sake of the twins. But the little girls are tetchy even though spaghetti Bolognese is their favourite. Funny how kids always pick up on any negativity. It's a nice evening, so I take them for a walk along

Mid Witch Three

Church Lane so Belinda and Jason can have another row in peace.

Sophie and Amy, reluctant walkers, are soon delighted because Claudia the cat trots between them with her tail in the air and Maud the magpie rides on Ink's back.

I catch a frog in the ditch and hold him for the girls to admire. Surprisingly easy to lure frogs and also moths. They seem to have a natural attraction to witches. The kids are happily chattering away and picking cow parsley for Mummy when I hear a car. I get everybody onto the verge and we watch the car bounce over the potholes. When I see who it is, I wish I was on the other side of the road so we could all duck into the churchyard. Bethany Blackwood is just visible in the shadows of the lychgate.

Grant stops his car beside me, and my heart lurches at the sight of him. Golden orts shimmer around his handsome face. I'm grinning like a fool.

'Why didn't you answer my text?' he says, pushing Ink's snoot out of the way. She has her front paws on the car door, tail whisking frantically.

He's right, I should have responded. 'Lot going on,' I say, glancing at the twins, who have found a puddle.

'Who are the idiots that got Fox Bake mixed up with Fox Lodge?'

'Marswickham Appliances,' I say.

'I'll give them a call and sort out when they can collect the bloody thing.' His face is stern. Even Ink has given up trying to cheer him and has returned to the twins. I touch his arm and my fingers tingle. Can he feel it too? This connection?

'So nice to see you,' I say softly, loving his dark eyes. He moves his arm away.

'Lilith...' he begins.

'Lillymar. Another froggy!' cry the twins.

'Catch him. Pop him in the ditch so he can find his friend,' I say and turn back to Grant. 'We need to talk.'

'No. No, we don't. Whatever you might think, you've got to remember I'm a thrall of the Coven.'

'I can free you,' I whisper.

'Lilith, I don't mean to be blunt, but everything that occurred... Well, it was just Coven business. Nothing more. Nothing less.'

'What about us?' I bleat.

'There is no *us*.' He turns to me, blank faced.

'But, Grant...'

'Time to face facts. You're a free witch and a Blackwood. We could never be together.' He's so fucking matter-of-fact I'd like to slap him. The twins are in the ditch shrieking with delight. 'Shouldn't you get those kids home before it gets dark?' he says.

'Shouldn't you fuck off before you get into trouble with your precious coven?'

He drives away slowly. Emotionless bastard.

Bethany folds her ghostly arms with a sneer. I ignore her and join the twins in the ditch. Dozens of baby frogs hop about in the warm evening. The kids' wellies are full of water, and they are both mud-spattered. I sit on the grass and watch them muck about. My heart hurts, which is annoying. That's always been my problem. I care for men more than they ever care for me. I'm not sure how much of this is because of the curse on my family or my stupidity. Either way, that curse needs lifting and Grant Rutherford is a two-faced bastard.

'Come on, girlies. Best get you home. Your mum will wonder where we've got to.'

We tramp back to the cottage. Sophie and Amy walk with Ink between them, resting their little hands on her back. Maud lands on my shoulder and gives my ear a friendly peck. Claudia is washing her whiskers on the gatepost and Belinda is marching toward us, a big scowl on her pretty face.

'For god's sake, Mum!' she cries. 'What were you thinking? Their pyjamas are covered in mud.'

Oh dear.

She stops at the doorstep and pulls off their wellies. A few small frogs hop into the long grass and Ink shakes, spraying everyone with ditch water. Belinda is furious with me while trying to be patient with the twins. I try not to laugh. Do the kids good to get back to nature.

Chapter Seven

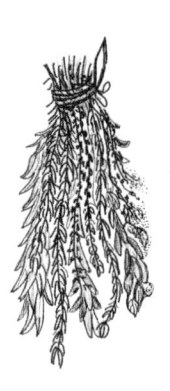

The next morning, Jason and Belinda are friends. They never fall out for long. There is no chance to discuss sleeping arrangements. They're too preoccupied with going to Belinda's house to collect some of her belongings after they drop the girls to school. I'm not sure the cottage can fit anything else in. But I keep quiet.

When they've gone, I sit on the doorstep star with a notebook and pen and make a rough plan. Not about bedrooms, although that will need to be addressed – no, the curse is my priority. These days I can think of little else. The current overcrowding and general unhappiness of my family will never improve unless I put the past to rest. If I fail, my daughter will spend her life alone or in unsuitable relationships. Something must be done. I haven't begun to consider if Jason is affected by the curse. I hope not.

The ghosts are no help so I must turn to the living. Grant Fucking Rutherford is not on my list. He's made himself perfectly clear where I'm concerned, and that's just fine. True, I'm a bit bruised and annoyed with myself that once again (at my ripe old age) I have fallen for an incompatible prick who doesn't love me. When this is all over, when I've got rid of this damn curse, I'm going to find a nice, sensible, loving bloke who actually likes me.

On the list, I have three people who might help: Mouse, the librarian at County Hall; Elaine Waters, who I consider my only witch friend; and Walter Cranford, the lawyer. I'm unsure if the old man is in the Coven but Mouse and Elaine are members

I ignore the breakfast washing up and the pile of laundry on the landing and go to my witch workroom, brushing my fingers over the wall to lift the locking spell I put on the door. Inside, my books, herbs and candles are where I left them. I often spend the morning in here pottering about with magic. Today I have other plans.

Ink settles herself on the couch bed, and I box everything and carry it into the loft. What began as a small suitcase and a few books is now a room full of witchy paraphernalia. Every item is useful and I don't mean to part with any of it. With some difficulty, I drag up the trestle table and chair. Then I find an old rug for the floor and a lamp I can hang from the rafters and clean the little round window in the eaves. By lunchtime I have a functional space and I'm pleased – except for one thing: Ink cannot manage the ladder.

I fold the ladder, shut the hatch and apply my locking spell. Jason's old room is clear; I've also lugged the sewing machine and much else into my once-empty loft. I clean the room and make the bed. Then I grab a bit of bread and cheese for lunch, settle Ink on some rugs in a sunny patch by the wall and wait in the lane.

I'm glad I've had a busy morning to take my mind off this afternoon. I check my watch and have a terrible urge to run into the cottage and hide when a small blue car comes bouncing over the potholes. The driver waves. No turning back now. I feel sick.

Len's Driving Academy car pulls alongside, and a surprisingly tall man in thick round glasses gets out. 'I'm Len,' he says, shaking my hand. 'You must be Lilly?'

'Yes,' I croak.

'Small bit of paperwork and we'll get started,' he says, reaching through the passenger window for a clipboard. We go through the questions while he arches his back. My hand shakes when I sign. Then he folds himself into the passenger seat and I stand there. Like a bloody fool.

'Do get in, Lilly,' he says, leaning over and opening the driver's door.

This is it, then. I'm finally learning to drive.

'Very good,' says Len. His round glasses magnify his eyes. I struggle with the seat belt and adjust the seat so I can reach the pedals. I'd like to open the window. It's a warm day, and he smells terrible.

'Have you had any lessons before, Lilly?'

'No, nothing. Not ever.'

His head is bent over, and he looks like a praying mantis clutching his clipboard. 'Very good. Absolute beginner, then. Often the best way. Nice clean slate. I'll go over the basics.' He tells me clearly how the car works. I obviously look terrified, so he assures me nothing can go wrong because he has dual control pedals. He moves his massive feet so I can see this car has, under a heap of crisp packets and paper coffee cups, pedals on both sides.

'Okay, then. Let's get this party started.' He hands me the keys. With a few more instructions, I drive off at a snail's pace. 'Very good,' says Len.

The little car crawls along Church Lane, lurching over the potholes like a lame horse. The car is as terrified as me. Bethany Blackwood drifts into the road as we pass the church. Automatically I swerve. Which is ridiculous. You can't hit a ghost. The car stalls.

'Sorry,' I say, 'thought I saw a...' I'm trying not to breathe in his body odour.

He turns with difficulty and looks behind us. 'What did you see?'

'A fox,' I lie, because that's how strong his stink is. Fox poo.

'Very good.'

When we reach the village green, the smoother road is like a silk ribbon. With his guidance, I drive around the green twice and stop the car.

'Very good. Okay, just a few preliminaries that we need to quickly check and then we'll be on our way again.'

I'm gripping the wheel and my palms are sweaty. We've been far enough, if you ask me. The thought of driving on an actual road fills me with dread.

'Now, Lilly, could you read the number plate of the car in front?' His pen is poised.

The car, some sort of jeep, is parked near the pub about twenty yards away. I lean forward. 'No,' I say. 'Shall I drive closer?'

He grins like I've cracked a huge joke, his pale bug eyes wide and expectant.

'I can't see it. I can see the car, though.'

Len taps his clipboard with his pen. 'Well, I'm very sorry, Lilly, but I assumed you met the requirements for driving and now I've ticked the box.' He scowls and brushes at the paperwork. 'Please get out of the vehicle.'

I gulp in fresh air. Has his smell clouded my vision?

'May I suggest an eye test before you contact me again?'

'Yes, of course,' I say as he folds his long limbs behind the wheel. 'So sorry. I didn't realise.'

'Would you like a lift home?'

'No. Thank you. The walk will do me good.'

'Very good,' he says, deliberately looking in the mirror and over his shoulder (twice) before indicating and driving slowly away. I sniff my jumper. Do I smell now? After I've bought a loaf and more eggs from the little shop, I wander home. Ink comes to meet me. I can tell by the look on her long hound face that something is wrong.

Chapter Eight

Total chaos. My new fridge freezer is in the middle of the kitchen, surrounded by bags of clothes and toys and a sack of chicken feed. Under the apple tree are two crates of hens, a bale of straw and a water dispenser. Jason and Belinda are shouting upstairs. The dog and I share a meaningful glance and go outside to say hello to the hens.

The six hens cluck contentedly, their feathers gleaming in the dappled sunlight. I didn't expect them so soon, yet I am ready. I stroke their backs with my yew wand and mutter a simple protection spell. Ink gives each a thorough sniff as I pop them into the coop. This is the first step of a six-step chicken wellbeing section I found in my mother's handwriting in the family shadow book. When all the birds are safe, I organise water, feed and straw and close the door. Then I get a basket and wander about the garden gathering herbs. After the terror of the driving lesson, it's nice to be outside. My phone chirps. Mrs Tingle has left me a voice message. She'd like a sixteen slice Bakewell tart with feather icing and strawberry – not raspberry – jam. No mention of the chocolate cake. She's placing another order, so it couldn't have been that bad. I message back the price.

Once I've tipped the herbs into the chicken run and watched the hens happily cluck over the greenery, I go into the kitchen to make tea.

'Some blokes dropped this off, and they completely ignored me when I said it wasn't ours,' says Jason.

'It is ours. For the cakes. They were supposed to take out the cooker and put it in its place,' I say.

'Well, that's bloody ridiculous,' says Belinda, stomping in and picking up a pillowcase of soft toys. 'We can't light the fire every time we want to cook something and it's going to be too hot in the summer.' She's using her teacher's voice. I'd like to argue with her, but I can see she's been crying. In fact, they both look like they've been crying. Kids! It never gets any easier.

Jason follows her upstairs with a bag in each hand. I start the washing up from this morning. Annoyingly, she's probably right about the cooker. It's okay when it's just me. I keep the range lit all winter and in the summer I light it on baking days. In between, I eat cold or toast. Quite a lot of toast.

'Are you sure you want chickens?' Belinda shouts. Sometimes she's just like her dad, Mike. I don't bother answering. I leave the dishes, pick up a box of toys and go upstairs.

'Have you two decided who's sleeping where?'

'I'm having the big room so I can set up an office. Got a new contract,' says Jason. He's already moved the furniture. From the bathroom, we can hear Belinda retching. Damn, I should have made her more tea. I'm a terrible mother. Ink stands outside the door with drooping ears. She's a sympathetic dog.

'What's the contract?'

'Allingshire County Magazine.'

'The free one?'

'That's it. I'm looking after their website.'

'That's great. Permanent?'

'Yep. Regular pay cheque. I'll get the rest of the stuff from the car.' Ink follows him.

'Which room do you want, Mum?' says Belinda when she finally comes out of the bathroom. She's very peaky, poor girl.

I sit on the bed in her old room. Can't remember when she stayed here last. Must be years.

'I thought I'd use the box room. What about putting some bunk beds in here and you have Jason's old room? There's space for a cot in there.'

She flops down beside me, and I put an arm around her.

'It's going to be ok, love. Why don't you see if Brian can have the kids this weekend? It will give us a chance to get sorted. I bet we can find some cheap bunk beds or even some free ones. We'll make them a lovely cosy room.'

'Have we got any pink paint?' she asks.

'I expect so,' I lie.

We clear out the box room. Jason finds some free bunk beds online and I call Any-Job-Steve, who collects them. We put the single bed in the box room for me. Steve assembles the bunks and fixes them to the wall and, much to Belinda's annoyance, takes away the old cooker and installs the fridge in its place. I explain I like my old range cooker, and I need the big fridge freezer for my cake business. Not that anyone's listening.

Any-Job-Steve comes back on Saturday and takes a van load of stuff to the charity warehouse. I decorate Amy and Sophie's room. No more subtle pastels for the bed-and-breakfast business I never quite started. It's Barbie pink or bust.

'Did you get this cheap because it's got the wrong label?' says Belinda, examining the paint tin. The label says primrose yellow.

'Probably,' I say. I should have thought about that when I

spelled the paint pink. She goes in Jason's room and shuts the door because of the fumes and gets on with filling charity bags with Jason's old clothes to make space for her own stuff.

Any-Job-Steve helps Jason with his home office space, repurposing old furniture for a desk and shelves. By Monday, everything is sorted. I have cleared out wardrobes and chests of drawers and now have bin liners stuffed with old clothes for the charity shop.

After a lot of herbal tea, Belinda is better and goes back to school, and Jason is hard at work in his office. The chickens are clucking about and the boundary spell I have placed around the garden is keeping them off the road and out of the woods.

I'm slightly behind with my cake baking, so I'm busy in the kitchen when Ink woofs. There is a man on horseback riding up the path.

Chapter Nine

I stand on the doorstep star drying my hands on my apron. It takes a moment to recognise Edward in his riding hat.

'Top of the morning to you, Lilly,' he says, dismounting

with ease. He's in long leather riding boots and black riding breeches. The horse snatches a bite of herbs from a pot beside the door. 'Monty! Really, he has no manners. I'm so sorry!'

'Don't worry,' I laugh as the horse munches appreciably. I expect he's come to order a cake. But no.

'I want to ride through those old woods. But I can't remember how to get in there. Or if it's still allowed. Used to be a public right of way when I was a boy.'

'Use my gate,' I say, pointing to the other end of my garden.

'If you don't mind?'

'No, it's fine. If you follow the trail to the right, you can reach the cliff path from there.'

'Ahh yes. I remember now. Want to come along? Is your giant hound okay with other dogs? You're probably busy.'

The sky is blue. It's a beautiful warm spring day and all my cakes are too hot for decorating. 'Yeah, why not? Ink's fine with other dogs. I have chickens...'

'They don't bother hens and cats.' He whistles, and the two spaniels splash through the big pothole, squeeze under the gate and run to greet us. The dogs do their greet and sniff while I pull on wellies.

'You're not going to lock up?' he asks as we set off.

'My son is upstairs working from home.'

'Ahh, boomerang kids. Glad I'm not the only one.'

'How far have you ridden?' I ask, opening the gate. The spaniels run ahead, and Edward leads the horse through.

Mid Witch Three

'Not far. I brought Monty in the horsebox and parked near the green. Hope nobody complains. I was on my way to the beach – then, on a whim, I got this idea to revisit my favourite childhood haunt. Which is perfectly silly. They say you should never go back.'

'They do say that.' I close the gate, and we walk side by side, Monty the horse clopping behind us.

'Always a bad idea to revisit places with good memories. I expect these old woods are half chopped down for buildings or fields.'

'No, they're just the same.'

'Sure?'

'Very. They're my woods.'

'Really?' he says, raising his eyebrows.

'Do all your kids live at home, then?' I ask.

'Just my youngest daughter, Collette. She has an erratic career. Modelling. One week she makes a fortune and the next, zero.'

Foxgloves bloom beside the path and we stop and watch the bees and listen to the birdsong. 'Do you ride?' he asks.

'No. I never learnt. Sat on a donkey once at a fair.'

He lets the horse snatch a mouthful of grass. 'I thought all little girls were horse mad,' he says.

'We weren't a horsey family. Too expensive.'

'Expensive!' He laughs. 'It's like throwing tenners into the wind!'

His dogs have run out of sight, and he whistles them back.

They hurtle through the undergrowth onto the path and then sit at his feet, good as gold.

'Now, boys, no disappearing. Stay close.' The spaniels quiver with excitement until he gives them a dog treat and then they scamper away without a backward glance. 'Kids and dogs. You just can't train them.' Ink saunters beside me. He holds out a treat for her. 'Apart from you, big girl. You're beautifully behaved.' Ink delicately accepts the treat. 'Not all dogs run off!' he calls out. There is no sign of the spaniels.

'Time for an upgrade?' he says.

'Upgrade?'

'From the donkey.'

He lets down the stirrups, plonks his riding hat on my head and tightens the chin strap. 'Safety first,' he says with a wink and cups his hands for a step. I don't hesitate. I let him boost me into the saddle and sit grinning like an idiot while he adjusts the stirrups and shows me how to hold the reins.

'He won't run off?' I say.

'Not a chance. Monty is far too lazy to run without being coaxed. Which is why he's fat,' he says, patting the horse's dappled neck.

He leads me through the woods. I'm so taken with the sensation and the sheer excitement of being on horseback that I cannot make conversation. Edward understands this and we wander along with Ink trotting ahead and the birds singing. When we come onto the cliff path and climb to the top, we stop and admire the view.

Dismounting is dangerous, and Edward holds me steady

when my feet touch the ground. My legs are wobbly, but I'm elated.

'Thank you.' I give him his riding hat and try to smooth my hair. 'That's two things off my bucket list in one week.'

'Glad to be of service.' He makes an elaborate bow. 'What was the other thing?'

'Driving lesson.'

'Ahh, covering all modes of transport. I like it. How did it go?'

'Not well.'

'You got caught speeding on your first attempt?'

'I can assure you, a snail's pace was maintained throughout. No, the instructor had run out of soap. Possibly deodorant as well.'

'Enclosed space on a warm day. Nasty.'

'Awful. But trying not to smell him took my mind off my fear.'

'Maybe that was his plan all along. Next time he'll be rose scented.'

'I like the smell of horses,' I say.

'Oh, nothing like it,' he says, blue eyes twinkling.

The cove is only accessible by the steep steps, so we walk on the cliff top and admire the sea. 'Beautiful up here,' he says, breathing in and looking at the horizon. 'Lots of sailboats out today.'

I follow his gaze, but I can't see anything. Then I remember I need an eye test.

The spaniels rush past and dive into some bushes. Ink

ignores them and lies on the grass. 'They are lovely. What're their names?'

'Sorry, can't disclose that. It's on a need-to-know basis.' He laughs. His phone beeps, and he hands me Monty's reins and wanders away to take the call. I pat the horse's dappled neck while he grazes. His coat is grey, white and black, like a stormy sky.

'You're a lovely creature,' I say, threading my fingers in his coarse mane. A few loose strands come away. Automatically, I twiddle them into a ball and put them in my pocket. That's the trouble with witchcraft – everything is useful.

'So sorry. Have to make a dash for it, I'm afraid. Trouble at the House.' He throws the reins over the horse's neck. Monty is suddenly alert. Head up. Ears pricked forward. 'Feel awful running off. Will you be alright?'

'Don't worry. I walk here most days. I'll take Ink down to the beach,' I say. He kisses my cheek, which surprises me, and mounts the horse with practiced ease.

'Sure you're alright?'

'Sure.'

He whistles and the dogs bound through the long grass, carrying a large stick between them. 'Leave it!' he cries good naturedly. 'We have enough firewood.'

'Thanks for the ride,' I say as he canters away with the dogs (and their stick) following.

'Come on, Inky dog. Might as well have a refreshing paddle since we're here.'

Mid Witch Three

After the beach, we go home. Jason is making sandwiches in the kitchen while having a video call on his phone. I leave them to it, give Ink some dog biscuits and then drag the recycling bag from the bin, in which I find the Eyewear Warehouse free eye test voucher.

Chapter Ten

The following week I'm so busy baking cakes – Mrs Tingle ordered three – and trying to cope with the sudden impact of family life, I have no time to think about magic or anything else. Practical tasks enslave me.

Laundry, cooking and trying to keep up with the mess is all-consuming.

The herbal tea is working wonders for Belinda's health, but not her foul mood. It can't be easy teaching in the same school as her soon-to-be ex-husband. Brian ignores her and the staff are taking sides. She should leave, or at least put the girls into a new school. She's furious and the twins are tetchy, no doubt picking up all the tension. They're asking why Mummy and Daddy aren't friends anymore. I can't explain because they haven't been told. As usual, I'm piggy in the middle.

Jason is happy working on his new business, but I'm not sure it's healthy, him being on his own all day. He doesn't go out, which I suspect is because he has no money. I can't help. Money is tight.

The hens are delightful at least. Sophie and Amy have named them and they are getting tame. No eggs yet, though.

On Friday, Belinda gives me a lift to Marswickham on her way to school. She's grumpy because I insist on bringing Ink. We have a small, quiet row in the kitchen while the twins brush their teeth and find their reading books.

'Just leave the dog here. Jason will look after her.'

'I'd rather she came, love. Jason is busy.'

'Busy playing video games.'

'She'll be fine in the back with the girls. Or I'll sit with the kids and Ink can be on the front seat.'

'She needs a doggy seatbelt. And I don't need the girls all covered in dog hair and paw prints.'

'She won't make a mess,' I say, 'and I promise to get her a seatbelt today.'

Belinda lifts her stacking box of books and teacher resources. I reach to take it off her. 'I'm pregnant, Mum, not incapable,' she hisses.

'What's pregnant?' asks Sophie, snatching something from the top of the box. It's a foldable shopping bag, which she flaps open.

'I'll tell you tonight,' Belinda says sweetly. 'Go and fetch your sister.'

'A banana!' laughs Sophie, waving the banana-shaped shopping bag around the kitchen. Belinda looks furious. 'Can I have it?' says Sophie.

The banana, half peeled, has a cheeky smile and a speech bubble that says, 'Always wear a condom!'

'Mummy bought it for me,' I say, taking it from her and shoving it into Big Bag. 'See if you can find your sister.'

'She's on the loo.'

'Go and knock on the door and tell her to hurry up,' I say. Sophie skips off.

'Can you believe Brian left that bag in my pigeonhole?'

I actually can't, but I don't say. Brian always seemed so – mild.

Sophie and Amy are suddenly here, shoes on, lunch boxes and book bags in their hands. 'What good, organised people you are!' I say. We make our way to the lane where Belinda's little car is parked. I take the box from Belinda. 'I'll put this on my lap,' I say, balancing Big Bag on top. Belinda scowls. The twins shriek with delight as Ink sits between them. We check the kids' seat belts and get in.

'Why do you have to have such a big dog? Why does she have to come everywhere with you?'

Hard to explain to your non-magical daughter that a weird coven would like to control me and I'm safer with my familiar. I can't imagine ever telling her I'm a witch.

The twins chatter happily to Ink. I watch Belinda scowling as she drives. Like Mike, she hates not getting her own way. She's going to have a few arguments on her hands when her daughters begin to find their own personalities.

She drops me off at the top of the high street in Marswickham. It's barely 8 o'clock and nothing is open, so I take Ink for a stroll by the canal. It makes me feel guilty to admit, but it's nice to be alone. I sit on a bench with my notebook while Ink has a good sniff. Away from the chores, my thoughts turn to magic. In particular, the curse. All the people I need to get in contact with are in Barrington. I was going to take the train there after collecting my HRT from the chemist and my eye test, but I've arranged to meet Cressida. She contacted me last night and said she had exciting news. Curse breaking will have to wait another day.

Eyewear Warehouse is already busy when I arrive for my 9 o'clock appointment. The girl at the reception desk takes my name, and Ink and I stand in the waiting area. I'm glad they're not funny about dogs.

Forty-five minutes later, a young man calls, 'Lilly Blackwood?' even though I am the only person waiting. 'Could you leave the dog outside please?' he says. 'I have an allergy.'

'Ink, wait,' I say, giving her a warning glare and tying her to a chair leg – not that this will make any difference. 'No funny business,' I whisper in her velvet ear.

'I meant outside,' says the lad, pointing to the street.

'She'll howl. She has anxiety issues.'

He's still pointing to the street.

'She's a rescue,' I add.

He relents and I follow him into the consulting room and get onto the huge chair. He sits beside me at a desk. Prods his keyboard.

'I'm Rodney. I'll be your Eyewear Warehouse optician for this eye consultation.' He sounds like he's reading from a script. He checks my address and postcode and adds my email and telephone number. 'When was your last eye test?'

'When I held a wooden spoon over my eye,' I say. This is lost on young Rodney. 'They probably don't check kids' eyesight like that anymore. After the eye test, they searched our hair for nits. Happy days.' I laugh. Rodney looks horrified.

'How many years ago was this?' he asks.

'About a hundred,' I say.

Rodney's hands hover over the keyboard as he gazes at the screen. 'Um...' he says. Poor lad needs to tick a box and I'm not helping.

'I've never had an eye test. This is my first one.'

He types a short sentence. 'You've never had glasses?'

'Just reading glasses. Two pairs actually.' I fish them out

of Big Bag. Neither are in a case. One is fixed with sticky tape. He takes them between finger and thumb.

'These are your glasses?' he says, holding them up and squinting at them. 'From the chemist?'

'Supermarket.'

Oh dear. Rodney is not impressed.

The eye test takes ages and I'm worried Ink is making mischief. Rodney is not chatty, but he is thorough. When he pronounces I need glasses, I'm not shocked and climb out of the chair. 'Let's start you off with some bifocals. They take a while to get used to, but it's definitely the way forward as you'll be needing to wear them all the time.'

'All the time,' I repeat.

'Yes. I'm amazed you've not noticed your eye deterioration sooner.' He gives a slip of paper to a woman. 'Melanie will assist you. Thank you for choosing Eyewear Warehouse,' he says and goes back into his little room before I have the chance to speak. When they get robots to do this job, people will hardly notice the change.

Ink is no longer in the waiting area. I'm not surprised.

'Have you seen my dog?'

'What dog?'

I pick up Ink's lead. 'The big black one that was at the end of this.'

She shakes her head, face blank. I stuff the lead into Big Bag. 'Don't worry,' I say.

Melanie helps me choose a cheap pair of spectacles from the economy range and makes an appointment in two weeks to get them fitted. I give her the voucher, which she scrutinises. Her spectacles suit her perfectly. I expect mine will make me look old and unfashionable. Hey-ho.

'So sorry. This is out of date.' I pay and try to ignore my brain telling me how many celebration cakes this has cost.

On the street, I search for Ink. Everything is calm. Sauntering people enjoy the spring sunshine. A few pigeons peck at the pavement. No sign of a magical greyhound causing trouble. On the other side of the road, a group of people stand in front of a shop window. I cross over and join the crowd.

'Clever marketing stunt,' says a man. I push in so I can see. In the sunny window of the furniture store, Ink sleeps. The window display depicts a child's room: there's a toy train on a mat, with picture books and puzzles strewn all around. Ink lies on a pink fleecy bedspread among an array of soft toys. She's on her back with her legs in the air, blissful doggy grin on her long hound face, legs twitching in time with her dream.

I edge past the onlookers and go into the shop. The window is boarded off from the shop floor. There must be a door that the window dressers use.

'Can I help you?' A suited gentleman glides over.

'Erm.' Should I tell him my hound is snoozing on one of his beds?

'Madam?'

'He's next,' I say, pointing to a man with his hair in a bun.

'May I help?'

'How much is that dog in the window?'

'So sorry, sir, but the soft toys are for display only.'

I scurry away and continue my door search. Ahh, here it is. Not so much a door – more like a hatch. The window dressers must be hobbits. I crouch down. There is no handle, just a keyhole. 'Ink, Ink!' I whisper, not wanting to draw attention to myself.

The shop assistant and man-bun come closer. 'I can assure you, sir, none of the soft toys are alive.'

'Mate. I'm telling you, there's a massive fucking dog asleep on one of your beds.'

'If this is some kind of scam! May I inform you we have high end security cameras!'

'Mate! No scam. Get outside and take a peep.'

'Ink! Come here NOW!' I hiss.

Nothing. I give the door a push and then a little magical shove, and it opens. I crawl in. Twenty people are watching my dog sleep. Her tail beats the bedspread. I clip on her lead as she rolls over. 'Come on!' I say. A normal-sized door opens at the far end of the display. I can see the shop assistant and man-bun peering in. Ink and I crawl out the hobbit door and run.

At the chemist I'm told I must leave my dog outside. 'Absolutely not! This dog must remain at my side at all times,' I say in my best haughty older woman don't-fuck-with-me voice. He steps back like I've slapped him and says no more. Ink and I queue at the prescriptions desk.

'Sorry, you'll have to have an owing note,' says the young girl, handing me the paper bag.

I check the contents. 'There're no patches.'

'That's right. National shortage.' She's already smiling at the next customer.

'But I need them.'

'Sorry. Please come back in a week. Probably best to phone first.'

'But I've almost run out.'

She disappears into the back room. Great.

Chapter Eleven

Ink and I have a picnic in the park and then walk to Cressida's flat. I buzz the door and she's there. She must have been looking out for us. 'You can only come in if you've got cake!' she says, laughing her throaty laugh.

'Homemade shortbread,' I say, holding up a paper bag.

'It'll have to do.' She crushes me in a bear hug and then does the same to Ink. We all feel better for this and follow her up the stairs to the smart flat she shares with her partner, Jayne.

Ink wanders about and has a good sniff then settles onto a rug for a doze. Cressida makes a nice big pot of tea.

'Come on then. What's this news?' I say.

She can hardly stop grinning. 'Two things.' She stirs the pot. The anticipation is killing me. She chuckles. 'Jayne and I are getting married!'

I leap up and so does Ink, and we all hug again. 'Have you got a date?'

'July twenty-fifth.'

'This year?'

'No, next year. Nothing big. Just family and a few friends. You'll come?'

'God yes.'

We talk wedding plans, and I offer to make a wedding cake. 'Anyway,' she says, pouring the tea. 'You know that poetry book of mine?'

'*Poems to Make Your Fanny Laugh?*'

'Exactly. Jayne took it upon herself to enter it into the Allingshire Literary Festival and it won Best Newcomer Award and a small grant.'

'Wow, that's great. Well done, you.'

'Can't honestly believe it.'

I press her to read me a few of the poems and they are clever and hilarious, as expected. I chat about driving lessons, blokes arriving on horseback and the chaos of family life. By the time I leave, I'm much happier.

Ink and I walk to Marswickham Primary School so Belinda can give us a lift home. We wait by the teacher's car park at 4.30pm, as arranged. She's late. Better not text her. She's probably in a meeting or has forgotten – or there is some parent–teacher issue. I sit on the wall and watch as the teachers get in their cars and leave. Brian bursts out of the staff door, his face bright red as he chucks his bags into the boot and bangs it shut. He sees me and half-lifts his hand in greeting then gets in his car and drives away.

Eventually Belinda arrives with the twins. Both are crying and Belinda looks like she's on the verge of tears. We all climb into the car. The twins are happy to have Ink to cuddle. Belinda doesn't speak.

We all try to carry on as normal. I have made a lasagne, which helps, and Jason, realising something is wrong, leaves his desk and baths the twins while I chat to Bel over the washing up.

'One of Miss Trim's kids told Amy that Brian and I are getting divorced,' she says, slamming a plate into the rack.

'Miss Trim, who teaches year three?' I say.

'Yes, and her son is in year two.'

'The kids will cope better if you tell them what's going on.'

'Brian says he's not ready.'

'Love,' I say, taking a glass she's drying off her before she breaks it. 'I know you feel guilty about your situation and you're trying to keep the peace with Brian.'

'Oh god, Mum! You don't understand!'

She's about to stomp off. That's the trouble with kids. Just when they could benefit from your advice, they don't want to hear it. 'Belinda!' I say. 'Just listen for two fucking minutes. I understand. More than you think.' I point at the chair and she sits there scrunching the tea towel.

'Sometimes you've got to realise that men can manipulate you in subtle ways. Brian is angry. Understandably. But by refusing to tell the kids what's going on, he's just being a selfish bastard. They need to know so they can deal with their situation. Right now they're confused and unhappy.'

Big tears drip down Belinda's cheeks. 'I just thought,' she says, wiping her face with the tea towel. 'I just thought that maybe him not wanting to tell them was because really he wanted me back.'

'Or it could be because he's angry. He feels slighted, and he wants to make you suffer.'

She opens her mouth to speak. I hold up my hand. 'He may not be doing this consciously. But trust me. He's being a shit, and it's time to do some serious thinking. If you ended up having a fling with what's his name, obviously you weren't happy. It takes two people to make a happy marriage.' And I should know.

Belinda examines the tea towel. 'It was just a drunken fling. I wasn't massively unhappy, just... bored.' She has another cry. 'God, I'm sick of feeling sorry for myself,' she says, tearing off a sheet of kitchen roll and blowing her nose.

'It's okay, love. Rich pattern of life.'

'We hadn't had sex for about eighteen months. I wanted another baby, and he said we couldn't afford it. I'd come off the pill. So whenever I made a pass he was like not until you go back on the pill. He can be very stubborn, couldn't even get him to use a condom.'

'And what about what's his name?'

'Vito.'

'Vito, what about him?'

'He's always up for sex.' She smiles.

'No, I mean, have you told him he's going to be a father?'

She tears the kitchen roll into strips. 'No, Mum, I haven't.'

'Maybe you should.'

She nods.

I reach over the table and take her hands in mine. 'You'll get through this. You're a strong woman. You just have to decide what it is you want.'

'I want everything to be like it was,' she wails.

'Do you?'

'No.'

'Then you've got to take control, love. Don't spend your life like me, letting everything happen to you. You decide how this goes. And stop fucking blaming yourself for everything.'

Chapter Twelve

In the morning I stand in the garden in my dressing gown with a mug of tea and a pocketful of salt. Birds sing in the trees. There's no wind, and this early the sun is a beautiful band of orange in the sky. Ink snoops beside me

Mid Witch Three

as I sprinkle salt around my boundary and mutter spell words to keep us safe. When I've completed the circuit, I go through the gate, around a massive pothole and into Church Lane.

North Star Cottage is chocolate-box pretty if you don't mind a little dilapidation and an overgrown garden. It looks idyllic if you are unaware of the troubles within: my discontent adult kids dealing with the fallout of magic they would not believe in if I told them. I banish the Coven's lurking threats every few days, and I always wear the sea glass in its pouch around my neck to keep me safe from their hexes. Ink and I walk along the lane, first one way and then the other, pacing out a protection symbol. When I have finished, I can see my own orts – traces of magic – glowing in the dawn light like a fallen rainbow.

At this time of year – late May – I love the early morning when the natural world is waking. There's so much energy in the air and new plants growing. The trees are drawing their sap, and when I press my palms on the yew tree's knurled trunk, my fingers tingle. The yew tree that guards my garden gate is ancient. Old magic lurks within it – generations of witches have held the wand that came from this tree. 'How can I get this sorted out?' I say, pressing my forehead onto the bark. 'How can I lift this curse and make them happy?' The tree keeps its secrets.

I let the hens out of their coop and throw them some grain. How nice they are, clucking and scratching about the garden. Still no eggs, which is disappointing because the grain is quite expensive. Perhaps I'm doing something wrong. On a whim, I call Mr Richards for advice.

'Everything would be so much better if you had a nice reliable cock, my darling.'

You can say that again.

'Got a lovely-looking fella here you can have. I'll pop him round when I'm passing.'

'How much will he be?' I ask. Absolutely no money.

'How about a ginger cake?'

'Deal.'

I sit under the apple tree, look up at the blossom and listen to the bees. Ink sniffs the hens, who are untroubled by her morning inspection. Then she lies with her head in my lap. Maud floats down from her branch and settles on my foot to preen her feathers. Claudia washes her whiskers on the doorstep star.

I'd like to stay here today in the peaceful garden. Plant some spring vegetables. Practise a little witchcraft. But I must go to Barrington. I've decided to see if Elaine can help; she seemed to know a lot about our two families – the Rutherfords and the Blackwoods. Then I'm going to the witch library at County Hall to return Mouse's journal and see if he can answer a few questions. It's not much, but it's a start.

For now, everyone in the cottage sleeps and we are safe. I rest my head on the tree and close my eyes, listening to the garden and the distant pulse of the sea.

I doze off. Then Jason is shouting, 'Mum!' and I leap up and run into the kitchen.

Jason smiles at his phone. Thank god nothing is wrong. I glance at the wall clock; I've slept half an hour and now I'm all behind on the morning jobs. I set about making packed lunches.

Jason blabs on. 'Mum! You're not listening. You've gone viral!'

Upstairs, the twins are awake and so is Belinda, by the sound of the yelling. Jason waves his phone in front of my face. 'It's Ink. Look!'

I put down the cheese grater and put on my reading glasses.

'That is her, isn't it?'

'Yes. That's her. She, er, went off yesterday when I was getting my eyes tested.'

Jason is delighted, and it is pretty funny. Someone filmed her in the furniture store's window and posted it on social media. She wanders around the display, sniffing the toys and shelves, and then gets onto the bed, twirls around, flops down and rolls onto her back. The perfect picture of comfort and contentment.

'Did you get into trouble? What did the furniture shop people say?'

I don't need to answer because Belinda and the girls are getting breakfast and Jason is showing them. Even Belinda is amused. And when Ink comes in from the garden, the twins pet her and tell her she's famous.

I scoot upstairs to use the bathroom and get dressed while they eat breakfast. I want to catch an early bus. No more lifts from Belinda; I can only handle so much stress. I don't faff about because I'm in a hurry. Pair of jeans that seem clean enough from the back of the bedroom chair. Flowery shirt and a comfy grey (goes with anything) cardigan. I stand in front of the mirror to tie up my hair and do that thing where you tuck the front half of your shirt into your jeans. The jeans are baggy. Mum jeans, they call them. They make me look fatter, and I call them bum jeans, because that's basically what I am in them: a fat bum. Is the shirt tucking better or worse? The shirt is too long and lumpy, and I should probably take a minute and make a smoother job, but there's no time.

As Belinda and the twins leave, I don't ask what she plans to do about telling them. I've said my bit, and that's all I can do. I give Jason instructions about which cakes are getting collected today, show him where each is in the big fridge and set off with Ink.

We walk to Fox Green so I can drop a bag of scones into the tearoom and then take the bus and the train to Barrington. After the inevitable delays, it's late morning when I arrive at Elaine's flat. I'm debating whether to come back when it's not so near lunchtime when the door opens and there she is.

'Hi, Elaine!' I call, all smiles. I expect her to be happy to see me.

'Lilith Blackwood,' she says. Her face blank. Not a shred of warmth in her voice.

'So nice to see you!' I'm still grinning. I've obviously caught her at a bad time. Maybe she's late. She's smartly dressed in a tweed skirt and a purple jacket that matches her hair. Her Poorbrook House lanyard is around her neck. 'I can see you're busy. Just wanted to have a chat…'

Elaine walks away, and I follow. I hope she's alright. 'Elaine?'

She stops and turns, and I scrutinise her face for a silencing spell. I can't see anything. 'I thought we could have a catch up?' I say. 'What's wrong?'

'You made your choice, Lilly. I tried to make you see reason. Turns out you're just like your stupid mother.' I've never heard her raise her voice before. It's surprisingly loud.

'Elaine, I'm sorry you feel this way,' I whisper.

'I tried to help you. Make you see sense. But no!'

My mouth is open.

'You've made your choice. You don't want the Coven. Well, we don't want you either. Please don't bother me again!'

Elaine has always been pro the Coven, yet her reaction is hurtful. Until now, she's been kind. I'm stunned.

Elaine grasps me above the elbow. 'Have I made myself clear?' she says, squeezing my arm and glaring at me. 'Don't come here again,' she says, digging in her fingers at every word.

I watch her walk away. A short, purple-haired witch who used to be my friend.

Chapter Thirteen

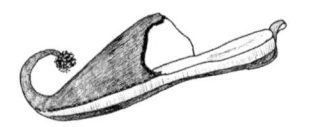

Shocked by Elaine's reaction, I take Ink to the park. It's a warm day, and after a stroll – and, yes, a little cry – I pull myself together and find a bench in the sun. Ink and I eat our picnic and she settles on the grass for a nap. While she sleeps, I consider the best way to get into

County Hall without being noticed. I rub my arm where Elaine grabbed me. I'm going to have a bruise. How horrid she was. If Elaine feels this way and I thought she was still my friend, then what might those in the Coven who actively dislike me do?

'We'll have to be careful,' I tell Ink. She lifts her head at the sound of my voice. I'm sure she knows what I'm saying.

I consider sneaking through a side entrance but decide against it. Hiding in plain sight is a safer plan. After some research on my cracked phone, I discover tours of County Hall begin on the steps at 2pm. Sure enough, as we cross the road, a small group waits. I hang around with the tourists. As the clock on the tower strikes two, a man dressed in the doublet and hose of a medieval gentleman steps through the door and takes a bow. The tourists, many of whom are Japanese, bow back and some applaud.

'Lords, ladies, peasants and vagabonds, welcome to Allingshire County Hall, the historical beating heart of the biggest county in England,' he booms. Another bow and he fastens back a door and the tourists file in, showing him their tickets. I don't have a ticket, but some everyday magic on an old receipt does the trick. 'Gather round, gather round and learn the incredible and shocking story of Sir Henry Broderick the second,' bellows the tour guide, standing beneath a huge oil painting of a man on a prancing horse. Ink and I slink up the stairs.

I have the rare ability to see orts – the colours of magic. Some people glow with magical ability; others leave wisps of mist as they pass. Mouse, the librarian, can also see them and has made a lifetime study of their meanings. I've read Mouse's journal four times since he leant it to me. I have not dared return it until now.

Ink walks ahead; she's already slipped her lead. On the carpet, the orts of many witches swirl. We round a corner. It's very quiet now. I put my hand over the sea glass, which hangs in its pouch under my clothes. The feather within is the Coven's mark – it was on my mother, and she removed and encased it within the sea-kissed glass. No idea how she did it, but carrying it keeps me safe from the Coven, tricking the forces that search for free witches into believing I belong. Even so, there are witches here who could recognise me as an outsider. Ink nudges her nose on the library door, and I hope there is no one in there. I should have worn a disguise.

The library is still and empty. Dust motes mingle with fading orts in the sunlight from the tall windows. Relieved I'm alone, I go to the table where the Coven's Grimoire rests. Usually, Ink waits by the hidden door for Mouse. Today she lies on the hearthrug next to the unlit fire. I'd like to ask the Grimoire a question, if it's alright with Mouse. Has he turned against me like Elaine?

'Mouse,' I say, tapping on the bookcase where the hidden door is. He never comes out immediately, so I wait before tapping again. 'It's me, Lilly. I brought you some shortbread. Homemade.' Ink stays where she is. If he was in there, Ink would be beside me, tail wagging. He always comes out for baked goods. This librarian has a very sweet tooth.

He must have popped out, so I turn my attention to the Grimoire, placing my hands on the ancient spell book. A few pale orts puff from the pages as I open the cover. 'How may I lift the curse on my family?' I ask.

Pages flutter and stop. My pulse quickens. Could this be the answer?

Putting on my reading glasses, I lean closer. Tiny writing in the centre of a blank page reads, 'Who are you?'

I touch the book again. 'I am Lilith Blackwood,' I say.

BANG! The book slams shut.

'Even their Grimoire dislikes me,' I say, stepping back. Ink stands and stretches. She's right: we should leave. I put the shortbread and Mouse's journal on the table. They're not safe there, though: anyone could come and take them.

'Ink, can you open this door?'

Ink has another stretch and sniffs the bottom of the bookshelf. If she can't open it, I will come back another day. County Hall gives me the creeps. If Ink can open the door, I can leave Mouse's book safely in his office and never come back. Chances are the librarian wants nothing to do with me, either. This is much less confrontational.

'Ink,' I say, hooking a finger under her collar because she's ambled off. 'Open this door for me. There's a good girl. Then we can get out of here and I'll take you to the big pet shop for treats.'

Who knows how much a dog understands? Even a magical dog? It's ever a conundrum. I pat the bookcase. 'I need to go in, Inky dog.'

She gets the idea and steps forward. When she bops her long snoot on the bottom shelf, the bookcase swings inwards. We walk in and the door closes softly.

I expected an office. This is more. Mouse lives here. The space is large and dimly lit by high, narrow windows. Bookshelves encase the room. In an alcove is an unmade bed. Red Turkish slippers and a night shirt lie on a mat by a cold fireplace. Clothes and stacks of books cover the floor, and there's a half-eaten meal on a round wooden table. More telling: there are no orts. The smoke-like wisps that are Mouse's magical signature are absent. 'He's been gone a while,' I say to Ink. She's lying where the door is. Even from this side, it looks like a bookcase. She puts her head on her front legs, ears pricked, listening. I stand still. Someone is coming.

In the library are footsteps. Heels click on the parquet floor and stop. I recognise that step. My frenemy, Theodora Grimshaw, is speaking on the phone. 'There's no one here. Another false alarm,' she says. 'Yes, I'll check.'

Ink leans on the bookshelves. She's keeping the door shut. 'No, it's still locked. He's not been back,' says Theo. More footsteps. Ink waits, teeth bared. Thank god I brought her with me.

'I don't bloody well know. Could have been anybody.' She minces off. We wait. I take my lead from Ink. When she relaxes and those hooked fangs are no longer on display, I breathe a sigh of relief.

Obviously, Mouse left in a rush, taking only the books and belongings most important to him. I wander around his

Mid Witch Three

home. A low door leads to a Victorian bathroom, and there is a tiny cooking space behind a screen. I search for another way out and ask Ink to 'open' as I pat the shelves.

'What did he do to piss off the Coven?' I say as we leave the way we came. I keep his journal and, on a whim, stuff the Turkish slippers into Big Bag.

Chapter Fourteen

I want to run, but that would only draw attention, so we walk at a brisk pace and trot down the sweeping staircase. Hot, I strip off my cardigan and drape it over Big Bag. The entrance hall is empty, and we make it outside unseen. I never want to go to County Hall again.

Mid Witch Three

The sun is shining, and I've had enough of the lumpy shirt and I'm still too hot, so I pull it free. To hell with fashion.

There's a café on the corner of the road and I could do with a pot of tea while I decide what to do next. I stop by a grassy verge so Ink can have a pee. The next minute she's wagging her tail, and her face is all happy-dog-pleased-to-see-you. Oh no, I hope it's not Grant Fucking Rutherford. He lives in Barrington. I've seen him jogging in the park. I just want a peaceful cup of tea, but there's no dissuading Ink in a sociable mood.

'I thought it was you!'

'Edward!'

'Well, I recognised Ink,' he says, petting her.

Yes, that's me. Forgettable woman. Memorable dog. Then again: beautiful dog.

'You are a good girl,' he says to Ink. 'Couldn't bring my boys into town. Far too scatty. Lovely day.'

'No horse then?'

'Difficult to park them. Fancy a cup of tea? I've got an appointment but I'm early. The little kiosk is open in the park.'

'Okay.'

We walk to the park. There's still a lump in the top of my jeans. I give my shirt another tug to make sure it's free.

At the kiosk he buys us paper cups of tea, and we sit on a bench. I get out the shortbread I made for Mouse.

'Do you always have homemade shortbread and exotic slippers in your handbag?'

'Always,' I say, giving Ink a dog biscuit.

'Sorry about leaving you on the clifftop the other day. Terribly rude.'

'It was fine. We had a paddle. Did you get the, er, problem sorted?'

'There's always something only I can fix – or so they think. Yes, all okay again.'

He doesn't mention what exactly, and I don't press the matter. He talks about horses and dogs and I tell him about my chickens not laying and that I'm getting a cockerel that will cost one ginger cake.

'Love ginger cake. Mind you, this is delicious,' he says, brushing sugary crumbs from his clean-shaven chin.

'Have another piece,' I say, reaching for Big Bag.

'God no. If I have any more, I'll eat the bloody lot. Your husband, does he struggle with his weight?'

'I'm divorced.'

'What, actually and completely divorced?'

'Yes.'

'Must be nice. Marriage can be such a mess. If you ever wanted to sell that, erm,' – he makes a circular motion with his hands – 'ball thing in your kitchen window I could give you a good price. I have a penchant for curious objects.' He looks at his watch.

'No, it was my mother's. Sorry.'

'Right. Must get going. Be just like me to arrive early, forget the time and then end up late.'

As we walk out of the park, the lump in my jeans slips

down my leg. 'It's been so nice to see you again,' he says, passing a hand through his thick grey hair. Most blokes his age are thinning out. I push thoughts away about running my fingers through it.

'It wouldn't be any trouble.'

'What?' I'm not listening.

'Another horse ride?'

'Be lovely,' I say.

'It's the only way to wear the dogs out. Little blighters.'

I can't concentrate on what he's saying. The lump is now above my knee. Must be a fucking sock. I resist the urge to look down and draw attention to it. 'I'm going this way,' I say, heading in the opposite direction.

'Me too,' he says, catching me up. Across the road, more tourists wait for a guide on the steps of County Hall.

'Always mean to go on one of those tours. Really should explore what's on your own doorstep.'

'Absolutely,' I say. That's it; the sock has dropped. It's going to fall out of the old bum jeans. All I can do is ignore it.

'Went on a midnight guided tour in York. Absolutely fascinating.' We cross the road. 'Maybe we should do something like that?'

'Great!' Great. The sock has left the bum jeans, and no one has seen.

Edward stops. A tourist has caught us up. He and Edward exchange a few words in Japanese and then the man is unravelling something in his hands.

'He says you dropped this.'

The Japanese man bows and presents me with a large pair of red knickers.

All I can do is bow and take them. Edward says a few words to him. They bow and the man leaves. I stuff the offending knickers into Big Bag. My face is burning.

Of course, we don't acknowledge what just happened. We ignore it and carry on in silence.

'Well, this is me,' says Edward outside an office block. 'See you soon, Lilly,' he says, bowing and giving me a wink.

Ink and I walk to Cranford, Holstein and Wigg, the solicitors. I half hope that Walter will not be free. My nerves are jangled, and if the train wasn't so expensive I'd leave this for another day.

Jean is reading the free Allingshire County Magazine when I go in. She's so engrossed it takes the old woman a moment to notice me. 'Oh, Lilly. How lovely to see you! Have you read this?' she says, tapping the cover with the end of her specs. 'Mabel and Green did a fashion photo shoot at Marswickham House.' She pets Ink, who has gone around the desk to say hello. 'Just go on up. About time he woke up!' She laughs.

I knock, and when there is no answer I open the door. Walter sleeps in one of the wing chairs by the fire. Ink and I creep in. I sit and Ink lies on the hearthrug. The old man's study is overly warm. Soon we are all asleep.

The chink of teacups wakes me. 'Ah, the restorative powers of an afternoon nap,' Walter says, passing me a steaming cup of tea with a biscuit on the saucer. Ink has her head on the old man's lap so he can pet her. The curtains are drawn against the sun, and in the dim light I can see his orts. I've not noticed them before. They shimmer, smoke-like in shades of blue.

'What can I help you with, Lilith?' he says, giving Ink a neck scratch so she pulls a funny face.

I drink more tea and eat the biscuit to fortify myself. 'That's just it. I'm not sure if you can help.'

He turns in his chair and changes his specs.

'Try me,' he says.

'I'm trying to find a way to lift the curse on my family.'

'From the Rutherford witches?'

'Is there another?'

'No. Not that I know of.'

'That's a relief.'

'Well, Lilith, I'm sorry to say you're not the first Blackwood witch who wanted to break this spell.'

'Did Mum try?'

'Fanny tried, and your grandma, Gwen. Have a go, but remember, many witches have failed at this. You might instead have to,' – he rubs his chin – 'find a way to live with it.'

Walter's crinkles reflect his good nature. Laughter lines from a life well lived. We gaze at each other. His smoky orts frame his face like a halo.

He heaves himself up, grasps his walking cane and hobbles to a bookcase. Swapping his glasses, he peers at the spines. He looks older today, if that's possible. A little more bent. A bit more shaky.

'Ahh, there you are.' He pulls out a slim notebook and returns to his chair. I plump his cushions for him and put a rug over his knees. I know what his strange orts mean and I hope Mouse is wrong. Tears prick my eyes.

Walter hands me the notebook. As I take it from him, he puts his hand over mine. 'I've had a long and happy life, Lilith. If you can see my death shimmer, that's okay. It's time. Ninety-two is long enough and I'm glad we got to meet in the end.'

He lets go and leans back, staring into the fire. 'Your mum was a clever witch. She stood up to the Coven. Lived her own life. And although we could never truly be together, we had a relationship of sorts. So you could say she defied that bloody curse as well.'

Reality is dawning. Walter realises this and pats my knee. 'I'm your father, Lilly. And although your lovely mum and I could not share our lives, I loved you both from afar and did what I could.'

For a long time, I hold his hand, enjoying the truth of his words. We sit in companionable silence.

'Have a read and pop back in a few days and we'll thrash out a few ideas. Do my old brain good to do a bit of problem solving.'

I flip the pages of the notebook.

'It's all the things Gwen and Fanny tried. And some stuff your great grandma did.'

Mid Witch Three

I must look defeated because he adds, 'What you've got to realise is that you possess abilities they didn't have. You're a midwitch. You can see orts.'

'And ghosts,' I say.

'And ghosts! Well, that might help.'

'Probably not.'

'Notoriously unpredictable, so I've heard.'

'And there's something else.'

His eyes twinkle. I can imagine him young. 'Tell me,' he says.

'I can sense truth or lie.'

'A rare gift indeed. Maybe you will be the one to mend the past.'

'I'm going to have a bloody good try.'

'That's the spirit. You're very like your mum. She never would take any shit from anyone.'

This side of my mother is at odds with my memory of her. She was always so peaceful. Passive even. Yet the more I learn about my identity, the more of hers is revealed. I only knew one side of her and never met the no shit troublemaker others knew.

'And there is something else that you aren't considering,' he says, snatching me from my thoughts. 'You have one of their familiars.'

Ink lies on her back enjoying the warmth. 'That's the Rutherford's dog. Course I knew her a generation back. Interesting that she's swapped over to the Blackwoods.'

'Why has she done that?'

'These creatures have wisdom we can't comprehend. But it's a good sign and is probably to do with you and the Rutherford boy. What's his name?'

'Grant,' I say, slightly shocked that Walter knows this. 'He's very pro the Coven...'

'But you still like each other. And it's another good reason to get this curse lifted.'

'I'm not bothered about that. I just want my kids to have a happy life.'

I give him the rest of the shortbread and we have another cup of tea while I talk about his grandchildren and great grandchildren. I'm reluctant to leave. When I finally pull myself away, he sees me to the door and we hug for ages, trying to make up for lost time.

Chapter Fifteen

O n the train home, I don't read the notebook. I stare out the window and think what a strange day I've had. Elaine's aggressive rejection – my arm still hurts – Mouse's disappearance and then Walter.

Who is my father, apparently. It's a lot of information to process.

I'm not sure what I should do about Walter. Ask him to North Star Cottage so he can meet his grandchildren and great grandchildren? Carry on as before, with him as my friendly magical solicitor, nothing more? Truth is, I can't imagine calling him 'Dad'.

Then there is the flirtation with Edward. Errant knickers aside, I think he likes me. And I like him. He's interesting. If nothing else, I'd like to know why he speaks Japanese.

The days are getting longer, and although it's gone seven when we get off the bus at Fox Green, it's still light. The birds are singing, and Bethany Blackwood stands under the lychgate as we walk past. I raise a hand in greeting. She watches from the shadows, arms folded. Maybe that's her problem – and mine: Bethany Blackwood does not want me to lift this curse because the Rutherfords would be free of it too. I can't blame her. If I'd been burnt at the stake, I'd probably be angry hundreds of years later.

'The ghosts don't want to help,' I say to Ink as Maud alights on my shoulder.

The cottage is quiet, which is unusual these days. In the living room, Belinda sleeps in the easy chair with Claudia. She has one hand on the cat and the other on her small bump. It's the first time I've noticed her pregnancy. She looks beautiful, and I make a silent promise to the unborn babe that I will get this curse mess sorted before he or she arrives.

I feed Ink and search the fridge for a snack. There are

dishes draining beside the sink, so they must have eaten. I make toast and tea, glad of the quiet. Jason is out and the twins are with their dad.

When I've finished, I check Belinda. It's getting dark, and she's awake, staring out at the garden. It's so unusual to see her unoccupied. She's always on the go: marking books, making lesson plans, ferrying the twins here, there and everywhere. I sit on the end of the easy chair near her feet. 'Alright love?' I ask.

She sits up, and I wait. 'Had a bit of a run-in with my headteacher and Brian.'

'Okaaay.'

'Brian won't answer my texts or calls. He's just about cut me off since this happened. But you're right, Mum. We need to talk and move on. For the kids' sake, if nothing else. Anyway, I cornered him in the photocopying room at first break and broached the subject of telling the girls.'

Claudia jumps off her lap and wanders into the kitchen. 'And you know what the bastard said? After all his posturing about not telling them yet, and these things need to be carefully done, and we need to find neutral space and tell them together. But not yet. Not in term time.'

I can guess.

'He's fucking told them.'

'What a bastard,' I say.

'Exactly. He's told them without me. And now he's got them this weekend.'

There is nothing I can say. These things are always messy.

'And that's not the worst of it.' She's always been a keep-it-bottled-in type. I pat her leg for encouragement. 'The headteacher has asked me to leave.'

'Can he do that?'

'Not really. But he has. He says our marital strife has downgraded the atmosphere in school. Pompous shit. To be fair, this was after Brian called me a whore at the staff meeting.'

'What did you say?'

'To Brian or the headteacher?'

'You pick.'

'It wasn't good. Everyone was making tea and finding a seat for the staff meeting. It was all normal. After our altercation by the photocopier, Brian had gone back to ignoring me. I was washing my safety mug, and he said, "Get out of the way, whore."'

'He actually said that?' I can't imagine Brian acting this way at all.

'I should have ignored him. He only said it quietly. Nobody heard.'

'I hope you told him to fuck off,' I say.

'Worse.' She looks at her hands. 'I said, "You can't blame me for being desperate for a shag."'

I laugh, and she does, too. 'God it was awful, Mum. I said it really loud. And he goes, all hurt and quiet, but by this time everyone is listening: "You can't have everything your own way, Belinda." God, I was so mad. I said, "Just because your libido is fucking nil doesn't mean that I have to spend the rest of my life celibate, you selfish, dickless wanker." And that's when the headteacher took me into his office.'

'Not both of you?'

'No, just me. Golden boy Brian must remain untarnished by his harridan wife. He'll be deputy head at the end of the year if the rumours are true.'

'That's awful, love.'

'So grim. Anyway, the headteacher and I had a bloody good talk. He's got an NQT lined up to take my place. He's agreed to giving me a good reference for a teaching agency. And there's something else.'

'Go on.'

'It sort of involves you. If I start supply teaching, then getting the kids to school will be a problem. I thought I'd move them to Foxbeck Primary.'

'Then I can walk them in for you. That's a good idea. But what does Brian say?'

'He actually agrees. The girls are getting picked on and he can see a fresh start would be better for them.'

'Good he agrees on something.'

'He also said,' – she pauses for dramatic effect – '"At least I won't have to see you and your bastard every day."'

We both laugh because what else can you do?

'He's so enjoying being the wronged husband. The shit.'

I'd like to say a few choice words about Brian, but it's wiser to stay neutral just in case they get back together.

'A bloke came by with a bird,' she says.

'A bird?'

'He said you ordered a chicken. I gave him the cake with his name on.'

'The cockerel came. That's great. Apparently, it will get the girls laying. Where is he?' From what I've read, they have to be introduced to the hens gradually.

'Dunno. In the garden somewhere. He didn't seem to like being in the box.'

Oh dear.

The next few days are a whirlwind of activity, and I have no time for dealing with ancient witch curses. Everyday life is enough to contend with. Foxbeck Primary are happy to have the twins, and Belinda gets a maternity cover job – the irony is not lost on us – at a school in Barrington. My only magic is to sew a few friendship and luck charms into the lining of Sophie's and Amy's new book bags when no one is looking.

The good news is that the cockerel has fitted in seamlessly. The hens are quite happy and the fine feathered fellow prances around enjoying the garden. He's uppity if anyone goes near his ladies and the twins have named him Cocky. Jason calls him Cocksure. I just want some eggs.

Jason is going into the office for the Allingshire County Magazine two days a week. Which will do him good. Give him some human bloody contact. Belinda will take him into Barrington with her on Mondays and Tuesdays. And the big plus is I get the gift of free time at home alone once I've walked the kids to school.

Chapter Sixteen

I'm keen not to waste a precious second and work at getting everything out of the way to be free when Jason goes into the office. I bake, cook, clean and get the bus to Marswickham to collect the rest of my HRT and my new specs. 'So sorry, no dogs,' says the young woman at the opticians.

'She's a therapy dog in training,' I say, hoping Ink will take the hint and magically put on her disguise. She doesn't, but the girl lets her come in. Ink and I sit in the waiting area. My bum has hardly touched the seat when a smartly suited middle-aged woman glides over.

'Mrs Blatewood?'

'Blackwood.'

'Ah yes. Follow me.'

She's in kitten heels and sheer tights and she looks more like a glamorous flight attendant in her uniform than a colleague at Eyewear Warehouse.

She ignores Ink and we sit opposite each other at a small desk in a corridor. 'I'm Ophelia and I will be your Eyewear Warehouse specialist today,' she says, taking the new specs from their packet. She holds them up. 'These are the correct glasses?' she says.

'Yes. I think so.' Honestly, so much has gone on I can't really remember anything about them except that they were from the budget section.

'Just the one pair, Ms Boldwood?'

'Blackwood. Yes. Just one pair.'

She taps at a calculator and then scrolls her iPad. Her fingernails are a delicate pink. 'For a small upgrade, you could order from our designer range. We have a special offer on this week.' She turns the iPad to face me. I see the price and repress a flinch. 'Now you need glasses full time, it's advisable to have more than one pair. It's what we recommend at Eyewear Warehouse.'

Before I can say no, she minces off to the display area and returns with a small tray of spectacles. I open my mouth to protest. Too late. She has applied the first pair to my face. 'These are from our High Wear Eye Wear range. The perfect blend of fashion and practicality.' She holds a mirror up. 'A fabulous range of spectacles that will take you all the places you need to go.'

Why does everyone sound like they're reading from a script these days? What happened to good old-fashioned conversation? I don't bother looking. I can't afford them. With all my family living with me again, I'm wondering how I'll be able to pay for the utilities. Designer specs are low on my list of priorities.

'They are very nice. But just the one pair today, thanks,' I say, handing them back.

She leans slightly forward. 'But these suit you so much better than the cheap ones,' she whispers.

I whisper back, 'But these are the only ones I can afford.'

Her glasses are marbled grey and white with a Holly Brasse logo. They suit her perfectly.

With a heavy sigh, she puts the economy specs on me. 'Mm, yes. Your ears are very uneven,' she says, wiggling the glasses. She takes them away for adjustments and I pet Ink. It takes her three trips to compensate for my crooked ears. When she's satisfied, she hands me the mirror.

I look around the room. My god, everything is so clear like

a freshly washed window. Have I really been staggering around in such a blur?

'How do they look, Mrs Blockhead?'

I peer in the mirror. 'Ghastly,' I say, and I'm not joking. Her face lights up and she reaches for the tray of High Wear Eye Wear. Quickly, I jump up before she drags me into another sales pitch.

It's Wednesday and the Marswickham chemist shuts in the afternoon. I need to get a move on. 'But I can see really well now and that's the main thing.' I give her a big smile and head for the desk.

'Could I interest you in prescription sunglasses? We have an economy range,' she says.

'Are they as ugly as these?'

Ophelia is flummoxed, I can tell. 'I'll just pay for these,' I say.

Ink and I hurry along the high street toward the chemist. I didn't think having new glasses fitted would take so long. Now I wish I'd collected my prescription first.

Behind, I hear running footsteps and I step aside so that whoever it is can pass. 'I knew it was you!' cries the jogger. Oh hell, it's the man from the furniture shop. He's so out of breath, I can't tell if he's angry or not. He mops his brow. 'I just wanted to thank you. Since she showed everyone how comfy our beds are...' He dabs his eyes with a tissue. He's on his knees and he has his arms around Ink, who wags her tail politely. 'We were thinking about selling up. But now... Sales haven't been so good since the eighties.'

Mid Witch Three

He stands and shakes my hand. A small crowd has gathered around us – well, around Ink. She's enjoying her celebrity and has slipped her lead (of course) and is cruising around everyone's legs so they can pat her. Daft dog. A few people film her on their phones. Eventually, we go on our way.

At the chemist, an athletic security guard is locking the door with a huge bunch of keys. I smile and raise my hand. She smiles back and I fully expect her to let me in. Especially since it's not twelve o'clock yet. She fastens the top lock.

'I need to collect a prescription,' I say, pointing at the small queue waiting at the prescription desk inside. She smiles again. Ahh, now she understands. Nope, she turns away. I tap on the glass. 'It's only ten to twelve!' I cry. She shrugs and walks off. Bitch.

I'm so annoyed sparks gather at my fingertips as I watch her march off. Then I have an idea. 'Ink, open the door. Good girl.' She loves a spot of mischief, and the door is open in seconds.

'I'm so glad you've got it,' I say when I'm handed the white bag after the young chemist has checked my address. 'Couldn't cope with boomerang kids, seven-year-old twins, my daughter's unplanned pregnancy and discovering who my father is without it.' The chemist is wide eyed. 'It's HRT,' I add, by way of explanation. He scuttles away to enjoy his afternoon off. 'Maybe I shouldn't have said all that out loud,' I say to Ink as we wait in another queue to be let outside. Security woman takes her time. She's mumbling something into a walkie talkie on her shoulder.

'No dogs in the store!' she says, pointing at Ink.

'Better let us out then!'

Slowly, she unlocks and opens the door to set us all free.

Once the errands are bossed, I take Ink for a stroll along the canal. It's peaceful by the water with the trees all fresh in their new leaves. I sit on a bench and call Len's Driving Academy and leave a message informing him I now have glasses and I'm ready to resume my lessons. Surprisingly, he calls back straight away. I almost expect him to say that he will not be teaching me to drive because I'm far too dangerous. But Len has nerves of steel and, after some negotiations, he suggests a lesson this afternoon. Turns out he's in Marswickham and can collect me.

'It's probably for the best,' I say to Ink as we finish our walk. 'Means I haven't got time to get myself worked up.' Then I realise I didn't mention the dog.

By the time I've found the side road, Len's Driving Academy is already parked and Len is leaning on the car, eating. 'Ahh, Lilly!' he says, wiping crumbs from his chin and screwing up a paper bag. 'All sorted with the new lookers!'

I touch a hand to my specs. I'd completely forgotten I was wearing them. 'Sorry I forgot to mention the dog,' I say.

He bends down from his great height to pet Ink and she helps herself to a few flakes of pastry on the front of his shirt. 'You'd like a car ride, wouldn't you, girl?'

He checks I can read the numberplate of a parked car,

and then Ink is on the back seat and I am putting on my seatbelt. He scrunches the paper bag into a ball and tosses it into the footwell with the other rubbish and folds his tall frame into the passenger seat.

Then it hits me. The smell. Oh, my god, the smell.

I drive slowly around a housing estate. The roads are smooth and quiet and I concentrate on his clear instructions and not his body odour.

'Very good,' says Len encouragingly. 'Now indicate left. Very good. Look both ways – and again.' It's worse today. Body odour and garlic halitosis.

'Could we open the window?' I say.

'Yes, good idea. I think your dog has farted,' he says, pressing a button. I wish she had – it would improve the smell. The windows roll down and I gulp in the clean air as we trundle along. I can see Ink in the mirror. She's put her head out the window, sensible hound. I'm so busy concentrating and trying not to breathe, the lesson is quickly over. I pull up near the curb.

'Very good,' says Len, shifting in his seat and peering down at me with magnified eyes. 'Have you started studying for the online part of your test?'

'No, not yet, but I will,' I say, leaning back in the hope his halitosis will sail past my nose and out the window. It doesn't. I unbuckle my seatbelt.

'I'm happy to drop you off at Foxbeck,' he says and starts a long explanation about learning the highway code. Ink leaps through the window. She's had enough.

'Must hurry, dog needs a walk.' Out I get. In the fresh air and standing well back, we organise next week's lesson time. When he's gone, I walk behind Ink and admire large expensive houses with short mown lawns and neat, colour-coordinated flowerbeds. Blossom Hill is the posh part of Marswickham. I had a school friend who lived here and I'm trying to remember her name and which house when Ink hops over a low wall into a garden.

Chapter Seventeen

'Ink!' I hiss. 'Come back here!'
    Ink is oblivious to my pleas. With nose to the ground, she sniffs the vast striped lawn in ever-increasing circles. The house is palatial. White pillars and a long conservatory on one side. 'Ink! Come. Good girl,' I

call, rummaging in Big Bag for a treat. She can smell something exciting. Nothing short of a piece of cheese is going to get her back now. I find a broken dog biscuit and wave it about.

'Look what I've got,' I say encouragingly. Ink lifts her head, looks at me, lowers her head and *runs*. That's it. Now I am going to get into trouble. A dog sauntering on your lawn and leaving can be overlooked. A huge black greyhound doing zoomies – not so much.

There's something about a wide space with a smooth surface that sends running dogs crazy. Ink races back and forth. There is no point trying to dissuade her when she's having a mad run. I sit on the wall and wait.

The house looks empty. It is the middle of the afternoon. Most people will be at work. Ink slows down. Perhaps we will get away with it. At last, she lies on the lawn. Tongue lolling. Big doggy grin. I walk over, clip on her lead and give her the biscuit. 'Come on, you daft dog. Before you get us both into trouble.'

The front door opens. There stands Grant Fucking Rutherford. Great.

He walks over the lawn barefoot, buttoning his shirt. 'What are you doing here?' he says.

'I was about to ask you the same question,' I say, petting Ink so I don't have to look at him.

'I'm visiting a friend,' he says, tucking his shirt into his suit trousers. He's got lipstick on his neck.

'A friend with benefits?'

'You could say that.' There is not a trace of mirth in his voice.

'Well, I was walking past, and Ink fancied a zoom on your friend's lawn,' I say. His golden orts shimmer in the sunshine. Bloody man.

At the sound of her name, Ink rolls on her back. Grant obliges her with a tummy rub. The dog does nothing to dispel his annoyance. 'You shouldn't be around here looking for me,' he grumbles.

'You arrogant shit. You honestly think I'm here because of you? I was having a driving lesson, and this is where I got dropped off.'

Ink stands and shakes. I'm left holding the lead. 'Now come on, Inky dog. Time to go.' I clip on her lead. Again.

'Since when did you need glasses?'

'Since I had an eye test.'

Grant opens and closes his mouth. I'm about to leave with as much dignity as I can muster when the friend with benefits walks across the lawn carrying a mixing bowl. Her black negligee fans open as she moves, revealing tanned legs and flat gold mules. Her waist long, dark auburn hair floats in the breeze. She has the sort of features that are always attractive. No resting bitch face here. 'I thought she might like a drink,' she says with a perfect, white-toothed smile. Gracefully, she places the bowl on the grass.

He's fucking a storybook heroine.

We watch the dog lap. When she's quenched her thirst, the woman pets her. 'You are so beautiful and so fast,' she says, stroking Ink's head. 'So sorry, I'm Rebecca.' She holds out her hand. Her eyes are green. Of course they are.

'Lilly,' I say, putting my battered gardener's hand into her softly manicured palm. She holds me with both of hers.

'Lilly! I've heard so much about you. Why don't you come in for some tea?'

'No,' says Grant loudly. 'I'm sure she's got *something* to do.'

'Don't be a grumpy old shit,' says Rebecca. 'We could all do with a drink.' She winks at me, and I smile at her. She takes me by the elbow and leads me toward the house. Ink wanders off to sniff the flower beds, and I drape the lead around my neck.

A butler holds the front door. 'Could we have some tea on the terrace, please, Roger?' she says. The hall is marbled and cool. An antique chandelier glints above a table with a billowing vase of flowers. They look too perfect to be real, but they are.

'Beautiful flowers,' I say.

Grant leaves us and goes up the stairs two at a time.

The terrace has wicker furniture and a view of sweeping lawns leading to a swimming pool. Rebecca covers her legs with the black lace as she sits. 'So, you're the Blackwood witch,' she says.

I'm taken aback. Is she a witch? I've not noticed any orts apart from Grant's. 'I'm not one of you. A witch,' she says, guessing my thoughts. 'G and I go back a long way.'

The butler places a large tea tray on the table. Silver pot.

Cups and saucers. Sugar lumps with silver tongs. How fascinating.

'Would you like something to eat?' she says. The butler hovers.

'No, thanks. I didn't mean to disturb you.'

She chuckles and pours the tea. 'Delightful to meet you. Really.'

The butler returns with a plate. 'Would the hound like a few morsels?' he asks me.

'She's always hungry. Thank you.' Where is Ink? She's gone. Dreading what she's getting up to, I put my fingers in my mouth and whistle. It comes out louder than I intended, but Ink hurtles across the lawn and sits in front of Roger, the butler, one paw raised.

'Just a few slivers of roast beef,' he says, putting the dish on the patio.

'That was brilliant!' says Rebecca.

'Absolute fluke, she usually ignores me.'

'I meant the whistling. I've always wanted to do that. Got this dream of hailing a taxi on a busy London street.' She laughs, and it's not put on. She's genuinely friendly. And so compelling. I'm glad he's found a nice woman. I'm happy for them.

'It's easy to do, just takes a bit of practice,' I say.

She scoots her chair nearer. 'Show me.'

When Grant returns, Rebecca is attempting to whistle using her fingers – and Ink, having galumphed her snack, is sitting in front of us tipping her head to one side every time she makes a sound. Ink's face is a picture of dog puzzlement and we're both laughing.

'I should get going,' says Grant. He's dressed: shoes, jacket and tie.

I look at my watch. 'Oh, my god. The twins. So must I. Got to collect my grandchildren from school. I'm a bad grandmother. I'd totally forgotten. Thank you for the tea,' I blab.

'Come and visit again soon,' she says.

'I'll give you a lift,' says Grant.

At the front door, the butler has Grant's overcoat and his laptop case. 'Thanks, Roger,' he says.

Rebecca stands on the stairs. 'I'll practice my whistle. Until we meet again.'

We all watch her climb the stairs, hips swaying, red hair swinging.

'She's amazing,' I say as Grant settles Ink on the back seat.

'Which school?'

'Foxbeck Primary.'

'You drive.'

'What?'

'You can drive.'

'No.'

'So you weren't having a driving lesson?'

'You still think I came here to find you? You really are an arrogant prick.' I get my phone out. 'I was having a driving lesson. I made him drop me here because…'

'Because what?'

'Because he stinks.'

'At teaching you to drive?'

'No. He's actually very patient and clear with his instructions. He's got body odour. It's terrible. Ink jumped out the window.'

Grant roars with laughter. 'Not Smelly Lenny,' he says.

'The same.'

'Come on, hop in. Don't call a taxi.'

'You've met him then?' I say, getting in.

'Not exactly. A lad at the office had the misfortune of learning with Len.'

'What did he do?'

'Wore some very pungent cologne and passed first time.'

'I'll try that.'

'That's great you're taking lessons, though. Do you good. Bit of independence,' he says.

'I'm independent. I just don't drive. Try not to be a patronising git.'

My phone is on my lap. He points at it as he changes gear. 'You ought to get that sorted out. Use the new one.'

'What new one?'

'I thought you won a phone in the raffle at County Hall?'

'Oh, that.'

'Don't tell me you've given it to one of your kids?'

I don't see what business it is of his. The phone is still in a foil gift bag on the kitchen dresser. I stare at the trees. Blossom Hill Road is living up to its name.

'I went to see Mouse at the library. Had a book of his...'

'You shouldn't go there,' he says, casting me a glare as he stops at a junction.

'It was fine. I'm fine.'

'It's not safe for you. Not anymore.'

'It never was.'

He drives slowly along another road with opulent properties. 'Don't go there again,' he says.

'Mouse wasn't there.'

'He's got more sense than to get involved with a free witch,' he says, turning into the high street. 'Give me the books. I'll see he gets them.'

'I don't mean he didn't come out. I mean, he's gone.'

Grant has a small, condescending smile. Git.

'I went into his rooms. Looks like he left in a hurry. The place was a mess.'

'You did what?' He pulls the car over and stops, his patronising smile replaced by a dark frown. Anybody would think he cared about me.

'Lilith,' he says, his voice very deep. He's struggling, and I can also see the binding spell over his face.

'You want me to take that off so we can actually have a fucking conversation?'

He shakes his head, and we drive on.

'I just thought you ought to know about Mouse. Something's not quite right.'

At the end of the high street, he turns into the main road. I read an article in a magazine that the way you drive is how you make love. Figures. Grant knows what he's doing and is very controlled, but he's not against a burst of speed now and again when necessary. While I can't drive. The thought makes me laugh.

'You think it's funny,' says Grant, waving a hand over his face.

'I was laughing about something else. No, I don't think the way the Coven treats you is funny. I think it's bloody well wrong. When you're brave enough, come and find me and I'll set you free of their marks. Then you can lead your own fucking life.'

'It's not as simple as that,' he says darkly.

We don't speak to each other after that. He drops me off outside the school. I thank him curtly for the lift and get out.

Chapter Eighteen

Bumping into Grant has done me good. Really it has. That hope that we'd get back together when I get the curse lifted has gone. His story book heroine has made me realise women like Rebecca actually exist in real life. Who knew? I cannot compete. Not on any level. She's beautiful, obviously wealthy, posh, younger than me and, as much as I'd like to loath her, I can't, because she's nice. Facts must be faced. I'm a middle-aged menopausal old hag who lives in a tumbled-down cottage (that dislikes men) with a mischievous dog, a moody cat, a magpie and a clutch of hens who are incapable of laying eggs even with the addition of a very handsome cockerel. Add in boomerang kids, dodgy finances, a few ghosts, cellulite and a centuries-old family feud and no bloody wonder he's with that delightful woman.

I'm digging a vegetable patch. And yes, I'm having a cry. Usually, I plant veg wherever I can find a gap. This makes it hard to find a cabbage when you need one, so I've decided on a designated vegetable area. I can't bring myself to plant in rows. North Star Cottage doesn't do straight lines. I'm planning clumps of cabbage, potatoes, carrots and runner beans.

Maud sits on the spade handle while I strip off a layer. It's early morning, everyone is out and this is my first Monday alone. I have a cake cooling for tomorrow, and when I've planted my seedlings, I'm going into the loft to conduct some witchy business. It's going to be a good day.

I'm behind the cottage. No one can see me. I strip off my shirt, which is cooling bliss. I'm not sure if it's a menopause thing. The HRT has stopped the hot flushes, but if I move around, I'm boiled. If I'm still, I'm frozen to the core. I guess drugs can only do so much when your thermostat is broken.

I dig on. Fuck it, I'm still too hot. Off come the jeans.

Digging in wellies and my bra and knickers is liberating. Ink lies on my heap of clothes. That's what I like about dogs: they never go, 'What are you doing?' – they just join in.

I'm on my knees planting seedlings while Maud and two of the hens hop about for grubs in the newly turned soil when I hear, 'Need a hand?'

Edward stands beside the bean sticks.

'Oh hi,' I say, pulling my shirt from underneath Ink. I'm not sure what's more embarrassing: that I'm practically naked or I'm covered in mud.

'Just getting some veg in,' I say.

'Nasty bruise,' he says. I touch my arm where Elaine pinched me. Horrid woman. I put on the shirt, but it barely covers my fat bum.

'Dangerous job, gardening.' And witchcraft.

'Nice day for it. These are doing well,' he says, pointing at the beans. They are already curling around the sticks.

'Let's have a cuppa,' I say, walking toward the cottage and trying to act normal. Tricky with a magpie on your shoulder and muddy knees. I hook my boots off on the doorstep.

Edward is already in the kitchen looking at the witch ball. 'Sure you don't want to sell this?' he says, patting it with his fingertips.

'No, sorry. It was my mother's.' And all the witches' that came before her.

'Shame. Fascinating thing. I brought two horses,' he says.

'Oh.' I'm surprised he has come back after the knicker

business. I thought the chat about going for a ride was, well, just chat.

'Oh no, or oh yes?'

I laugh. 'Yes, why not?'

'You might need to put some clothes on. Saddles can chaff. Although, if Lady Godiva is your thing...' He raises an eyebrow.

'Give me two secs. Help yourself to tea.'

I get cleaned up and attired in jeans and a sweatshirt and return to the kitchen in record time to find Edward pinned by the range, shaking a wooden spoon at the cockerel.

'Your bird doesn't like me,' he says.

Cocksure has his wings spread and is standing as tall as possible. I do the same – spread my arms and shoo him from the kitchen.

'Sorry, he's a cheeky bird.' I pull on my wellies and take my tea outside.

'You're good at doing spontaneous stuff,' he says.

'Always best to seize the day.' Which sounds good, but the reality is I'm going along with this because it means I can avoid dealing with my magical difficulties. If I was a conscientious witch, I'd turn handsome Edward away and get on with the day I planned. Then again, why not go for a horse ride?

We carry our tea to the gate where the horses and dogs are tied. I say hello to the excited spaniels and give them a dog biscuit from my pocket.

'This is Matilda, your trusty steed,' Edward says, patting a small brown pony. We leave our tea mugs on the gatepost, and he gives me a riding hat. 'This should fit you better,' he says, doing up the chin strap. Our eyes meet. Yep, he definitely fancies me. Even in budget specs.

After some instructions and a little flirting, we get mounted up. Matilda is on a lead rein, and she plods along behind Edward on Monty. Ink and the spaniels are already in the woods.

It's incredibly peaceful. Edward turns in his saddle to smile at me. I'm grinning and I can't stop. What's nice is he just lets me enjoy the moment. Doesn't make inane chat. So I'm left to soak up the unfamiliar sensation of being on horseback. The other thing I notice is he doesn't make me run before I can walk. Literally. Plodding is enough. Good man, Edward.

On the clifftop, we dismount. My legs are like jelly, and we sit on the grass looking out to sea. The spaniels are careering about, but Ink is ready to relax. She flops beside me with her head in my lap and closes her eyes.

'Thanks for this. Always wanted to ride. Never quite got around to it,' I say, taking off the riding hat.

'Life gets busy. And it's my pleasure.'

'Are you going to tell me the spaniels' names?'

He laughs. 'Well, I'm not sure,' he says, laying back in the grass and squinting at the sky. 'And anyway, they don't know what they're called.'

'Of course they do.'

'No, really. They don't have a clue. Cheese!' he cries. 'Lots of cheese for naughty dogs!'

The dogs tumble through the grass and sit before him, expectant. 'Sorry boys, I lied,' he says, giving them some dog biscuits, which they snaffle in seconds and run off.

'Maybe I'll tell you if I can ask you something. Two things actually,' he says, turning on his side to face me.

'Okay. But what if I agree to whatever it is and then I don't like your dogs' names?'

'You won't like the dogs' names. That's a given. Because it will reveal that I am nothing more than an old fogey.'

'Fair enough,' I laugh.

'So,' he says, taking my hand and kissing it. 'Lovely Lilly, will you go out with me?'

I'm actually quite shocked.

'It's outdated to ask, but...?'

'Yes. I'll go out with you, Edward.' Unexpectedly, I'm filled with joy. How nice. This is just what I need. A charming, courteous old-fashioned man.

'So the other thing was: will you come to a boring party with me? I warn you, it's going to be impossibly dull. Full of pompous twats like me.'

I agree to be his plus one, and we chat about this and that. I'm surprised he doesn't kiss me. That's my trouble. I've been with too many men who are what my mother would have called *fresh*. Edward is a gentleman and so I shall behave like a lady. I'm guessing he's not a shag on the first date kind of guy, and that's ok.

I check my phone for the time.

'We should get going,' he says, guessing my thoughts. He helps me mount and I take him a different way along the public footpath through the fields. I'm not on the lead rein. Edward has assured me that Matilda will just follow behind Monty.

'Such a lovely day. I'm surprised how different everything looks from horseback,' I say, watching the spaniels run together over the field.

'Different perspective, I guess. Higher up.'

'So, what are their names?'

He reins Monty back, so we are riding side by side.

'I hope this doesn't change anything,' he says with mock gravity.

Ink stops on the path ahead. She lowers her head, steps back. Something is wrong. A shadow seeps over the grass, although the sky is clear. The shadow darkens and I reach for the sea glass around my neck. It's not there. Rushing has made me careless. I don't even have my wand. The horses sense it too and Monty shakes his head and puts his ears back. I need to be on the ground. I take my feet from the stirrups and dismount. Without Edward's help, it's not a pretty sight. I land on my arse. Matilda tosses her head and gallops away. Edward is trying to control Monty, who wants to bolt. I kneel with my hands on the earth and breathe in, bringing the power of nature into me.

The shadow draws slowly nearer, a dark stain with grasping tendrils. It's the biggest hex I've seen. Even if I had a frog, this could not be tricked into a jar. Once I would have been afraid, but I am a different witch these days. I dig my fingers into the ground and mutter a counter curse. The witch language is now familiar on my tongue. They make sense to me, these ancient words. It takes magic to understand them, and I do. The hex shrinks back and moves toward Edward. He's behind me and I'm aware he's dismounted and is trying to calm his horse. I force my magic under the earth. I'm strong. Stronger than this shit they keep sending.

The hex shrinks. It rolls back as I stand and raise my muddy hands to the sky. 'I am the Blackwood witch. This land is mine. Be gone.' The hex flees. A light breeze rustles the grass and then everything is normal again.

Behind me, I expect to see Edward shocked and appalled. It's not every day you witness a witch in action. But he's too busy trying to calm Monty, who has stopped rearing up and is now shaking. Poor creature. Ink is close beside me, thank god.

'Alright, it's alright,' he says in soothing tones.

I pat the horse's neck. 'It's okay, Monty. You're safe now.' I let a little magical energy filter through my fingertips and the horse sighs.

'I'm so sorry,' says Edward. 'Matilda's never thrown anyone before. Something really spooked them.'

'I just lost my balance,' I say, because it's clear Edward has seen no witchcraft. Just as well. Will I tell him what I am? This is not a question I have the answer to right now. Other problems are more pressing.

The spaniels trot along the path together and greet their

master. I notice they don't run off again. 'Trouble is, Matilda has one fault,' says Edward. 'She's hard to catch. If you need to get back, that's ok.'

The horse is nowhere in sight. 'She won't come if you call?'

He laughs.

'Can you bring back the horse?' I whisper into Ink's neck. I'm never sure how much she understands or what she can do. Edward said my mother's dog found their horses. Ink bounds away and soon returns with Matilda trotting behind her. I catch her bridle as soon as she's near. Now Edward stares as if seeing me for the first time. He's going to have questions, and I'm not sure I'm ready to answer him. Whether I'll ever be ready.

'You have a way with animals,' he says.

'Always wanted to be a vet,' I say.

'What stopped you?'

'Had a baby.'

Edward advises we ride back, so we do. The cottage is safe. My hens have eaten some seedlings, but apart from that, all is well.

Edward says he needs to get going and I'm secretly glad. If I'm lucky, I will get a few hours to myself before I need to collect the twins. In the lane I hand him the riding hat. 'I'm sorry about today,' he says.

I hook my hand around his neck and kiss him. He might be on some slow burn thing, but turns out I'm not. And let's face it, at our age, who's got the time? He kisses me back.

Nice. A nice kiss. Nothing weird. Not earth shattering, but nothing weird and I can work with that.

Afterward, he looks at his feet. 'I wanted your first proper ride to be magical,' he says.

I hold his face. 'It was,' I say, standing on my toes to kiss him again. 'Very magical.'

Chapter Nineteen

I don't waste any time. As soon as he's gone, I find the sea glass in my veg patch where it fell when I had my practically naked gardening moment. Then, armed with a pocketful of salt and my mother's stumpy yew wand, Ink and I walk along the field and apply a protection spell to the earth. After that, I settle Ink for a nap in the kitchen, make tea, bread and cheese and head to the attic.

The loft is as I left it, only dust covered. Which tells the story of my witchcraft – neglected. Life gets in the way of the things you want to do for yourself. I put my mug of tea and a jute bag that I'd hidden under my bed onto the table.

Honestly, I don't know what to do and I need inspiration, witchy inspiration, to strike. First out of the bag are the Turkish slippers. Mouse had surprisingly large feet for a short man. The slippers are red and well worn. I slide my fists inside and sit there with my eyes closed and wonder what happened to him. Is he safe and happy? After examining the slippers, I set them aside. I hoped they might provide a clue to his whereabouts. I'm none the wiser.

Mouse's journal about orts, I return to my shelf. Next, I consider the notebook Walter gave me. He's my father. This is such a strange thought, and I can't quite get my head around it. If I'd asked Mum, would she have told me? Now that I know, I am unsure what to do. Discovering your parentage in middle age is an odd thing. A part of me wants to ask him over to meet the kids. Another part of me wants to leave things as they are.

I swig my tea and promise myself to worry about Walter/Dad later. The curse is my priority. Jason and Belinda are not magical, and if I don't get this sorted before I die, it could go on and on, affecting generations.

In the notebook, my mother and grandmother kept a list of the spells they tried. It's clear they were working together –

two witches' magic is better than one. I can imagine them boiling potions and collecting ingredients. There was not much they didn't try. Herbs, crystals, hag stones, roots from the yew tree. Even hair from the Rutherford Boy is listed. Some of the spells they cast are simple, others complex and time consuming.

Fascinating as the notebook is, I am no closer to solving the curse. I pack up, close the loft and walk with Ink to collect Sophie and Amy from school. I touch my hand to the sea glass around my neck as I follow Ink along Church Lane.

The notebook has given me a glimpse into Mum and Grandma's magic. This is nice, as I never witnessed their abilities. I have memories of them that in hindsight now speak to me of witchcraft, but I never saw them cast a spell or heard them talk about magic.

Bethany Blackwood is lying inside the lychgate. She's always in here these days, resting in the place where once a coffin would have waited for burial. I stop and look in on her. 'How are you, Beth?'

She folds her arms across her chest and stares at the roof. This is Bethany's problem: she bears a grudge. I complained about her constant presence, and now she ignores me. Not that communication was ever easy – life and death are reluctant bedfellows – but at least before she tried to communicate. Now she just cuts me dead, literally.

'I found out Walter Cranford is my dad,' I say. Her face is expressionless. This news is not important to her. 'I'm still trying to get the curse lifted. It would be best. There has been enough unhappiness.'

Bethany has gone. Ghosts do that.

'She's still mad at me,' I say to Ink as we continue along Church Lane. Could Mum see ghosts? She never said. Did she make a spark when she snapped her fingers?

Waiting at the school gates, I decide to visit Walter so I can ask him what my mother could and could not do. He's probably the only person who can tell me. If nothing else, it will bring me closer to the witchy side of my mother.

The next day, I get more witchy stuff done. It's raining and chilly, so I light the range and hang the never-ending laundry around the kitchen to dry. I decorate a cake with chopped chocolate and fondant vegetables for Foxbeck Allotment Society's 50-year anniversary then make scones and a Bakewell tart for the tearoom and a large baked lemon cheesecake for Mrs Tingle. After sticking a casserole in for tea and a jacket spud in the oven for my lunch, it's up to the attic for witchcraft and it's only 10.30am. Plenty of time, as I don't need to fetch the twins because Belinda is having a scan this afternoon and will get them on the way home. Also, it's pouring with rain, which stops me from getting distracted with gardening.

In the night when I couldn't sleep, I made a list. First item: does GFR (Grant Fucking Rutherford) know what his family tried (if anything) in regard to lifting the curse? I don't fancy talking to him, but some problems are bigger than my personal emotions. I call the estate agents and ask to speak to him, but he's not in the office today. When will he be back? Not until next week. I imagine he's spending time with the lovely Rebecca.

Next item: arrange to meet Walter for a chat. I organise my driving lesson so that Smelly Lenny will drop me off in Barrington.

Edward calls me – actually calls – and we have a nice chat. Tomorrow he's taking me out to lunch. How very civilised.

Cressida calls for a chat, which always cheers me up. I wish I could talk through my witchy problems with her. Then I go through my Fox Bake admin, make a to-do list for the following week, check who has and hasn't paid and order more cake boxes.

Admin done, I take out the notebook and have another look in case I've missed something. I cast a revealing spell upon it to be sure nothing is hidden. Then I sit drinking my tea. It's very hard solving a magical problem when you don't have a clue where to begin. I write a list of the sorts of spells Mum and Grandma Gwen tried. Potions, lots of these. Witch jars. Fire (and candle) spells. Crystal magic and a plethora of spells and chants cast on moon-filled nights.

Once the ghosts showed me my mother with a spell jar. At the time, I thought she was stirring the old curse. I never believed it. Now I think what they were showing me was her trying to lift the curse with a witch bottle. This is why I believe the ghosts can't help: it is too easy to misconstrue what they try to impart.

Mid Witch Three

I doodle on some scrap paper then Google some stuff about lifting curses – and learn nothing new. In the kitchen I eat my jacket potato while Ink sleeps beside the range. At least the dog's happy. She likes a cosy day on her blanket bed when it rains.

My next problem is what to wear to lunch. I've never had a formal lunch date with a bloke before. Unless fish and chips in a plumber's van counts. Edward has asked me not to bring 'the long-dog' as he calls Ink, explaining that it's not dog friendly and, here's the thing, the restaurant is smart casual. 'Great,' I chirped. Now to face the harsh reality. What the fuck is smart casual?

I Google the problem. Absolutely no help at all. Lots of pictures of young folk in taupe linen shirts and jeans or flowing summer frocks. Smart shorts and blouses. Everybody is slim. Not one helpful picture of a middle-aged hag resembling a jacket potato.

Upstairs, I search through my clothes and Belinda's. Claudia lies on the bed and watches me try things on. 'It's a big ask. I'd prefer casually scruffy. Or smart and outdated,' I say, pulling on a flowery dress. If my boobs didn't look like they were trying to escape, this would be ideal.

I try a longish black skirt. The waistband is too tight, but with the top button undone and a loose white blouse, it's not too bad. Classic black and white. Smart. Yet casual. Perfect.

I'm just giving it a press in the kitchen when Sophie and Amy burst into the kitchen. 'Lillymar! Guess what!' they squeak. Sometimes it's hard to follow which one of them is talking. I move the iron to a safe place and give them a hug.

'Okay, slow down. What is the fantastic news?'

'Bridesmaids,' pants Amy, grabbing her sister around the waist.

'She wants us to do it.'

'In lilac.'

'Just us, nobody else. It's a special occasion.'

Belinda comes into the kitchen with a stacker box of exercise books. Her face, in contrast to the twins' glee, makes my heart sink. The scan!

I take the box while she gets her wet coat off. Amy and Sophie have already kicked off their school shoes, and they escape me and their mother while also leaving us holding all of their things.

I hang the coats over the range to dry. Belinda sits heavily, puts her head in her arms and cries. I hold her until she gets herself together. 'I'm being stupid,' she says.

'What's happened, love?'

'Brian's parents are retaking their wedding vows.'

I'm so relieved it's nothing to do with her scan that I almost laugh. Belinda's face is a mixture of sheer fury and sadness. This is no laughing matter. I put the kettle on. 'And they're having bridesmaids?'

'It's going to be like a full-blown wedding. Church, flowers, reception.'

'Really?' I say, thinking of the spell I cast on John and Mary, for their happiness. My feelings are mixed. I'm glad they've reconnected, and I'm delighted my spell worked, but their timing is a bit off. Maybe I should cast the same sort of spell on Belinda and Brian? It worked on his father. I try to remember what I did exactly.

'Mum!'

I re-focus on my daughter.

'Will you?' she says, fixing me with one of her angry frowns.

'What, love?'

'Take the girls to this damn wedding thing. I just can't face it. Apparently, Brian is going to *give his mother away.*'

'Ick,' I say.

'So ick. What's got into them? They used to be so *normal.*'

I think I know.

'I can't believe she did that.'

'What?'

'Mum, have you heard a single word? I told you. She came to the school gate and met the girls and just asked them to be bridesmaids. I didn't really have any choice in the matter.'

'You can't say no.'

'Well, not now I can't. Not now the kids are all excited.' She pushes away her tea. 'It sounds stupid, but it's like she's rubbing my nose in her happy marriage. God, I'm beginning to sound like a bitter old cow.' She blows her nose.

'How was the scan?' asks Jason, breezing into the kitchen.

'Fine,' she says, lifting a handful of exercise books and slamming them onto the table.

Chapter Twenty

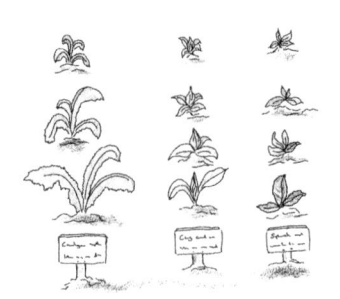

I decide to walk the twins to school and do the chores before getting ready for my lunch date. Don't want to be all sweaty when Edward collects me.

The twins are so busy playing bridesmaids that getting them to school on time is hard work. We're almost late. I avoid

Mid Witch Three

all the school gate chit chat and rush home. Cocksure has got out into the lane. Every time I try to catch him, he attacks me, and no amount of arm spreading and strutting – you have to pretend you are a bigger bird apparently – makes any difference. He's a confident creature and he's having none of it. In the end I have to fetch my family shadow book and ask it for a remedy for an angry bird. Instantly the book answers with a song for soothing. The witch words are simple to learn, and with my fingertips on the page I hear the haunting melody. Armed with this new magic, I march into the lane, locate Cocksure, who is rummaging in the ditch, and sing him a song he can't argue with.

'You're not the first belligerent male who's lived at North Star,' I say as I carry the sleeping bird and put him safely under the apple tree. After that, I put another protection spell around the gate and one across my kitchen door to stop him strutting where he shouldn't. This takes over an hour and I run upstairs for a shower. My timing is all wrong; Jason is hogging the bathroom with the best shower. I use the other to get washed and dressed in and make sure I have the sea glass around my neck and a bit of lipstick on. Hot and sweaty, I dash into the kitchen.

Edward is chatting with Jason. I faff about finding shoes, Big Bag and a cardigan in case it gets chilly. Then persuade Ink to remain behind, which is something my magical familiar disapproves of. As I tuck her into bed, I give Jason instructions about lunchtime walks, the allotment cake which is being collected and Mrs Tingle's cheesecake and remind him he's getting the twins from school. Ink gives me a searching look with her big brown eyes. Jason is also giving me a funny look, like he can't believe his old mother has a date. He's all smiles and cheer, which is weird.

'Shall we?' says Edward, holding the door and bowing as I sling Big Bag over my shoulder.

'Yes,' I say. I can't wait to get out of the kitchen and just be me. Not somebody's mother or a witch. For a couple of hours, I want to be Lilly and nobody else.

'Sorry, this is a bit of a drive. Thought it would be nice to get off the beaten track,' he says as we set off.

He's wearing trousers and nice shoes. A check shirt and no tie. He is indeed smart and casual. And very clean. I look casual and hot. Not 'hot' like the women on Google search. I'm the wrong temperature.

We chat, and he tells me horse stories from his childhood. 'Do you have any siblings?' he asks when I've finished chuckling about him and his brother standing on their ponies' backs to scrump apples over a fence; it went well until the horses moved and his brother fell into the orchard.

'No, just me.'

'Were you lonely?'

'No. Lots of friends over. Mum had an open house policy. And we had dogs and cats.'

'And you've always lived there?'

I give him a potted history of my life – omitting witchcraft and ancestral curses. He gets the acceptable version of events. I even make my divorce sound like a mutual parting.

Mid Witch Three

We arrive at a country hotel about an hour outside Barrington.

'Wow, Ruddington Manor. Always wanted to come here,' I say. Then wish I hadn't because he probably thinks I'm a peasant now. It's raining, so we dash in under his umbrella.

Inside is all vintage chic. Mismatched floor tiles. Wellington boots in different sizes by the door. Huge stone fireplace with a coat of arms above.

A waiter leads us to a window table and plucks away the reserved sign. Casually yet expensively dressed customers are a contrast to the smart staff in long black aprons, white shirts and bow ties. The waiter holds my chair and tucks me in. How nice.

'What do you fancy? There's brunchy breakfast stuff or actual lunch food.' He hands me two menus. Everything sounds delicious.

'Now what I'd like is a dirty great fry up,' – he pats his stomach – 'but I've got to be good.' We choose eggs and avocado on sour dough with crispy bacon. And tea for two. I gaze out the window where a peacock strolls over the wet lawn and rest my chin in my hand. In the morning rush, I forgot to check my face. I only epilated everything yesterday, but I can feel a hair. I'd like to touch my chin and upper lip for the telltale spikes of middle-aged growth. Obviously, I don't want to draw attention to any hairs. But something must be done.

Edward is beginning another of his stories. Something

about a lost peacock and a Jack Russell dog. 'Would you excuse me?' I say, getting up.

The ladies' room has vases of flowers, tissues and cotton cloths to dry your hands on. How very civilised. In the mirror (antique, gold frame, speckled) I can see the offending whisker. The new glasses make everything horribly clear. The hair is so long and white I'm surprised I haven't tripped over it. And it's not the only one. It has friends. Several fucking friends.

As soon as abundant facial hair for women becomes fashionable, we will all be so much happier. Big eyebrows are in. It's only a matter of time.

I rummage in Big Bag for tweezers. Must have a pair in here somewhere. I've certainly got everything else. However, the bloody tweezers are not forthcoming.

I tip out Big Bag onto the carpet. It's the only way. Working quickly before some smart casual woman comes in, I put everything back: animal-themed ponchos for unexpected rain, mints, tissues, emergency HRT, hairbrush and spare socks. Banana-shaped, condom-themed shopping bag. Panty liners and phone chargers. Sweaty old lipsticks and plenty of fluff and old receipts. My yew wand. Herb bundles. Seven hag stones and various crystals. Big Bag has double the stuff now I'm a midwitch.

At last, I have the damn tweezers in my hand. I leave the rest of the contents on the carpet and get plucking before anyone comes in. Outside are women's voices, posh and shrill. I've never ripped out my facial hair more quickly. No time for wincing or examining the fruits of my labour. Out the fuckers come. As the door swings open, I'm on my hands and knees, picking up the rest of my stuff, ready to laugh and say I dropped my handbag. Silly me.

Two women, one smart in a navy button through dress and the other casual in riding clothes (or is that fashion?) go into the cubicles. I check my face again while they pee and have a loud conversation about a woman called Rachel. Apparently, she's a 'complete slut, darling'.

I'm about to leave when I notice my phone has slid under the sink. Lucky I noticed it. Smart and Casual, who really hate poor Rachel, wash their hands. I don't fancy grovelling about on the floor with them watching my fat arse, so I wait. The women dry their hands on the cotton towels and then hand them to me without so much as a glance. Can't blame them.

I drop the used hand towels into the wicker laundry basket and retrieve my phone. Damn. The cracks have spread: no more tree, just a mass of lines. I'm going to have to change it.

Lunch is delicious, light and tasty, and Edward is easy to talk to – or, more accurately, to listen to. He has a lot of amusing stories.

'Can't believe you've never been here.' He's forgone dessert, so I must do the same. Nobody wants to eat fattening food on their own. 'Would you like to stay?'

I laugh and sip my tea. Actually, I can't imagine myself in

a place like this, but Edward is entirely comfortable. Some people fit in anywhere.

'Shall we take a stroll? They have a lovely walled kitchen garden you'd like.'

'I'll just pop to the ladies first.'

I'm trying a little hand cream and thinking what a nice day I'm having when in walks Theodora. We stand like rabbits caught in car headlights. Both of us stunned. Theo gets herself together first and pastes on a sickly smile. '*Love* your outfit. You could get a job here, darling,' she snipes and flounces past me into a cubicle.

'Oh, fuck off,' I say and march out.

In the entrance hall Edward is chatting to Mike. Oh god. Edward has already seen me and smiles. No chance I can dart out a side door into the vegetable garden.

'Lilly, have you met our plumber extraordinaire, Mitch Turner?' says Edward, all bonhomie. 'This is Lilly Blackwood.'

'We've met,' I say.

Theo arrives and links her arm through Mike's. 'This is cosy. Here for brunch?' says Theo. She fits right in: haughty voice, long white cashmere cardigan, string of pearls, designer jeans and trainers.

'We've eaten,' I say.

'Just off for a garden stroll before the rain starts again,' says Edward, walking away.

They go into the restaurant, and we help ourselves to

wellington boots. Outside, the sun is bright on the wet garden. 'Sorry, didn't want to get bogged down chatting.' He holds my hand. How sweet.

I don't say anything. I'm just glad to be outside.

'Oh god, now you think I'm an awful snob,' he says, giving my hand a squeeze. 'It's not that I don't want to socialise with the plumber chap, it's just that he's, well...'

'What?'

Edward laughs. 'Don't get me wrong, he's an excellent plumber. Managed to source all sorts of modern vintage to fit in with the old place. But I've always found him to be a bit of a prat.'

He leads me through a hedge arch into the kitchen garden. 'Please don't tell me I've insulted your friends.' He pulls a face of mock horror.

'No, they're not my friends.'

'Did he do your bathrooms at the cottage?'

'He did.'

'But you loved him and gave him lots of tea and cake?'

I did love him, once.

'He's my ex.'

'Ahh. He was *your* plumber!'

We burst out laughing.

Edward doesn't press me for details of Mike. He's had my potted history and is happy to leave it at that. We enjoy the garden, which is so unlike mine: all neat rows and labels. None of these plants will ever forget their names. When it spits with rain, we sit on a bench in a cute summerhouse. No one else is braving the weather. Edward puts his arm around me, and we kiss. Politely at first and then with a little abandon. It's nice and I forget about Mike and Theo. Almost.

The rain slows and a young couple, arm in arm, wander into the garden. 'We could get a room,' says Edward, arching an eyebrow.

I laugh.

'Seriously. Why not? Bit of afternoon delight, do us good,' he says. I like the twinkle in his eye.

'What, here?'

'Absolutely here.'

'Be expensive...'

He holds up a hand. 'My treat. And to be honest, I'm curious to see if you have a bruise on your arse where my horse chucked you.'

That's what I like about Edward. He's funny.

We wander back into the hotel, and he has a chat at the reception desk. Moments later, he has a key, and after we've climbed the red-carpeted stairs he unlocks the door and lets me go in first. It's a beautiful room. A bay window with a seat. King size bed with a flowery canopy and about a thousand cushions. A pair of comfy chairs in front of a fireplace. I'm in a romcom sponsored by William Morris.

Edward kicks off his shoes and closes the frilly curtains. Takes off his jacket. I put on a smile. If only my sex drive was so easily obtained. I dodge into the bathroom, make use of a free toothbrush and have a pee, then stare at my reflection. I'm about to have decadent afternoon sex. Why aren't I excited? What I'd really like is a nap among the cushions.

Edward is lying on the bed – clothes on. I lie beside him and he rolls over so we face each other. We kiss. It's a nice kiss. Not sloppy, bit of tongue, quite pleasant. He slides his hand up my leg and I'm glad I'm not wearing tights and that my underwear, while not exactly sexy, matches and is not threadbare.

I undo his shirt and slip my hand over his shoulders so he takes it off. Unexpectedly, Edward has curly ginger chest hair. This makes me want to laugh. He interprets my little gasps as passion and redoubles his efforts. His hand is in my knickers (I've got rid of my panty liner and the sea glass charm). He rummages about.

Not a clue.

Unzipping his trousers, I reciprocate. I do have a clue and Edward is on his back moaning while I stroke him. We take off our clothes and I fetch a fancy bottle of body lotion from the bathroom. I squirt some on both hands and apply it with an easy stroking motion and a gentle twist. Edward is at my mercy. Head back. Eyes closed. I flutter my fingers over his balls. His pubic hair is soft and also ginger. 'Oh, Lilly!' he mutters.

This is a hand job I learnt online when I believed better sex would keep Mike at home. To be fair, it worked for a while. But Mike is the type of bloke who is never satisfied for long. Another pump of Ruddington Manor Hand and Body Spa Lotion and a quickening of pace and Edward comes. His ejaculation shoots out at an alarming speed, and I'm glad I have the foresight to face his foreskin in his direction and not mine. The spunk lands in his chest hair. Peaches and cream.

Chapter Twenty-One

We get ourselves cleaned up and under the sheets. He's soon asleep. I extract myself from his embrace, and he rolls onto his back. Unusually, he doesn't snore. I would have loved a good nap and an orgasm if I'm honest, but these things are increasingly about timing when you get older. I listen to the rain pattering on the window.

A few creaks come from the adjacent room. Sounds like they are getting into bed. I'm surprised a luxury hotel like this has beds only a wall apart. Noises of classic bonking ensue. Edward sleeps on and I bite the duvet, trying not to laugh. The couple stop. Then they continue. Faster and faster and there is something about the grunting and the rhythm that is oddly familiar. The strangled groan at the end confirms my suspicions: Mike and Theodora.

What are the bloody odds of listening to your bastard ex-husband fucking your oldest frenemy in a country hotel of an afternoon? Slim odds is the answer. It's the curse that perpetuates my awful sex life and wrecks any chance of romance. I've got to get this sorted or my kids will have a lifetime of shit coincidences and crap sex. Also, I'm sure Edward and I could get it together when bad magic no longer hangs over me. In the shower, I resolve to keep my relationship going with Edward because, deep down, I know the reason it's not perfect is not actually his fault. I towel myself and slap on something called Ruddington Manor Soothing Spa Gel for face and neck. The bruise on my arm where Elaine pinched me is now a shade of green. I apply spa gel to it, but I suspect nothing short of witchcraft is going to cure the mark she's left. Dressed, I sit in the window seat and wait for him to wake. He's a nice man. He doesn't even snore. I'm going to make this work.

When he does wake, he takes me for afternoon tea, which

we have on the lawn. It's delightful: a silver cake stand with tiny sandwiches and scones; an old-fashioned tea pot and pretty cups. I dread Theo and Mike suddenly appearing. But they don't.

'This has been like a mini holiday,' says Edward, dabbing his mouth with a linen napkin.

'Yes, nice to forget everything for an afternoon,' I say.

Edward drops me home. As I get out of the car, he catches my hand. 'Lilly,' he says, kissing my knuckles, 'thank you. You've made an old man very happy.' We both burst out laughing at his mock sincerity. 'Seriously though. I'm sorry it was over so quick. It's, er, been a while.'

I kiss his cheek. 'See you soon,' I say.

Ink hurtles along the path to greet me with her skinny wriggle dance and lashes me a few times with her tail – I deserve it for leaving her behind; she's been worried sick – all accompanied by a low, deep growl: her special hello for me.

Belinda and Jason are sitting at the kitchen table eating cheese and biscuits. In the sitting room, the kids are laughing at the telly.

I give Ink a piece of cheese. She takes it to her blanket bed to nibble.

'Is that my old waitressing skirt?' says Belinda, looking up from her marking.

'Probably.' I pull the foil gift bag from the dresser, take out the phone and give it and my poor smashed one to Jason. 'Could you do whatever it is you do to phones so I can use the new one and keep my contacts?'

'Beyond your skill set, Mum?' says Jason with a grin.

'Totally.'

He unboxes the new phone. 'This is fancy,' he says.

'Won it in a raffle.'

'No kidding,' says Belinda, taking it off him. 'You've got the poshest phone in the house now!' She laughs.

'Speaking of posh – how was your afternoon, Mum?'

'Lovely,' I say, filling the kettle.

'Mum had a hot date with none other than Lord Wootton.'

'Bloody hell, Mum. How long has this been going on?' says Belinda.

'Quite a while,' says Jason with a big smirk. 'He's been taking her riding. I wasn't sure it was actually him, but I got a proper look at him today.'

'He's not Lord Wootton. He's Edward...' What is his surname? 'We're just friends.'

Jason gets a copy of the Allingshire County Magazine and flicks to the society pages. 'Yeah, it's him alright,' says Jason, pushing the magazine across the table. 'I did the page layout. Charity ball at Marswickham House. Is that where you went, to his place?'

The society page has a large picture. There is no mistaking a smiling Edward. He looks handsome in his tuxedo with his arm around Lady Wootton. She is wearing a tiara and a full-length silver sequin evening dress which shows off her slim figure. Around them the great and good of Allingshire County raise champagne flutes. Lovely.

Mid Witch Three

'Mum, you okay?' says Jason.

I turn away. Pour water into a mug. No matter that both my children are grown adults. I can't bring myself to discuss the vagaries of my 'relationships' with them. It's too odd.

A cry from the sitting room sends Belinda to see what the twins are up to. Upstairs, I sit on my bed with my mug of tea. How stupid am I? He's Lord Wootton. Everyone knows this. Except me, apparently. And he's married. The picture of him is etched on my eyeballs, all happy with his glamorous wife. I bet she doesn't get mistaken for staff. There's a reason married men don't wear wedding rings. They're bastards. On the other hand, I'm cursed.

Chapter Twenty-Two

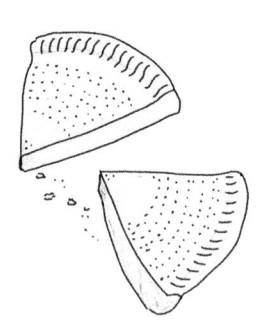

I fill the kitchen sink with hot, soapy water and add a few sprigs of bay, rosemary and sage. Then I take down the witch ball for a wash. Even magical things get dusty. As I wipe the mercurial surface with a soft cloth, Maud hops onto the draining board and cocks her head on one side

Mid Witch Three

to watch me. I place the football-sized bauble on a towel, and she pecks the surface like a budgerigar. Silly bird.

Inspired, I clear the kitchen window ledge, tend to the red geranium and give everything a good wipe. After I've cleaned the window, inside and out, I hang the witch ball and put everything back. Then I admire my slightly tidier clutter. The witch ball gleams in the sunlight, its surface clear and bright like the still summer morning outside. It's a beautiful day. Blue sky. The birds are singing, and the cottage is peaceful. Amy and Sophie are at school. Belinda is at work and Jason is out because he's taken a day off.

I'm in a cleaning mood because I'm mad about Edward. It's not that he's deceived me. More that I've deceived myself. I told myself a story that he worked at Marswickham Hall and left it at that. I suppose I should be flattered that a member of the landed gentry fancies me – a peasant in a cottage. Maybe that's my appeal. The main problem is that he's a married man – and I've spoken to Lady Wootton on the phone and she sounded, well, posh obviously, but also very nice. Is she aware he's a philandering bastard? Whether she knows or not, I don't want to be a part of this. I've spent my life being second best. I'd rather be on my own than let this happen again. When I pluck up the courage, I will tell Edward exactly that. Thanks, but no thanks. Pity because I do like him. He's nice company, and I'm sure we could get the sex together if we tried to do it before a big meal and not after.

I water the geranium and Ink woofs softly from the doorstep where she is lying in the morning sun. I hope it's not

Edward with a pair of horses. I need a few days to mull things over.

Hobbling along the cobbled path is Walter. A large car drives away behind him and he raises his walking stick in greeting.

'Walter!' I say, taking his arm and helping him over the doorstep star. He taps it twice with his stick and settles into a kitchen chair.

The short walk has left him breathless. He mops his brow with a spotted handkerchief and nods as he looks about and smooths a hand over the wood of the table. His orts are ghost pale.

I make a pot of tea and put a plate of shortbread petticoat tails on the table.

'I'm sorry to bother you…' he begins. Ink puts her head on his knee and he pets her with an arthritic hand. He looks weary.

'It's lovely to see you,' I say and mean it.

'Nothing's changed,' he says, smiling at the kitchen.

I stir the teapot while he wrestles with his memories.

'Don't mean to intrude, my darling. But time is short. I thought I'd bring forward our meeting. Do still come next week. If I'm still alive.' He laughs.

I reach over and take his hand. We sit there for a while. Can you feel love in a touch? I believe I can, warmth with a soft fizz seeping into my skin.

Walter coughs politely into his handkerchief. 'Do you still

have that old copy of *Mrs Beeton's Cookery and Household Management?*' he says.

'Yes, I do.' I get up to find it on the dresser. Maud leans over from her perch to see what I'm up to. Nosey bird. I give him the old book.

'Marvellous,' he says and pats it. 'Much safer now.'

I pour the tea and pass him the sugar.

'So, was the notebook any help?'

'Not really,' I say.

'No, I didn't think it would be. At least it gives you a starting point.'

'Yes, I made a list. Although that doesn't mean that I can rule out the type of spells they tried.'

'Exactly. Might just need a different version.' Walter adds two heaped teaspoons of sugar and stirs thoughtfully.

'I was wondering what my mother and grandma could do. Magically.'

'Ahh well, I can tell you about Fanny. Not much about her mum, other than she was good with plants and potions.' He sips his tea. 'Fanny was a seer, as you know. Her sight wasn't the usual hit and miss, open to interpretation type. Your mum had a rare, clear sight. Which is why I'm here. She always said that you were the witch to free the curse.'

'Did she?'

'Indeed.'

'Might have been helpful if she'd seen how.'

His eyes crinkle. 'You're very like her, you know.'

'What else could she do?'

'She could cast accurate spells. Usual stuff. Love potions. Basic healing. She had familiars, like you. That old dog, Rufus. A hare in the woods. She renewed her magic from the blackwood trees, as I imagine you do.' He closes his eyes, remembering. We sit in silence for a while, filled with thoughts of my mother.

Walter puts a biscuit on his plate and admires it. 'She also baked these.'

'Mum's old recipe.'

He takes a bite and chews appreciatively. 'And she confounded the bloody Coven. Lived as a free witch despite their meddling.'

'What about you? Are you a Coven member?'

'Once,' he says, pulling back the sleeve of his jacket to show me a scar.

'She freed you?'

'She did. But that's a story for another day. Tell me again what you can do. My memory is not what it was.'

I snap my fingers and make a small flame. 'I'd been lighting the fires for the longest time without acknowledging that this is not exactly normal.'

'Witchflame,' says Walter.

I snap again. Click. Coloured sparks float in a cloud between us. We watch until they fade away. Walter's mouth hangs open. 'I can see orts and ghosts. And sense truth or lie.'

'That's a lot of rare gifts, Lilith.'

Claudia saunters into the kitchen from the garden and rubs against his legs. 'How many familiars?'

Mid Witch Three

'Ink, Claudia the cat. And the magpie.' I point to the dresser. 'She's called Maud.'

'Nothing in the woods?'

'Oh yes. There is a green-eyed fox. I see her now and again.'

'You are a powerful midwitch,' he laughs and shakes his head.

I want to ask about him. Does he have familiars? What can he do? But Walter says, 'Let's start with the ghosts. What do you see?'

'I see the ghosts of my ancestors. In particular, Bethany Blackwood.'

'Fascinating. What do they do? Tell me everything.'

I describe my encounters with the ghosts, including Bethany Blackwood and how she is. By the time I've finished telling him, it's lunchtime. I make us sandwiches.

'I'd like to visit your mother's grave, if it's no bother,' he says, pushing his plate away. He hasn't eaten much, and he looks exhausted.

'Yes, but first a nap,' I say.

Walter does not protest and lets me tuck him into the easy chair in the sitting room. Claudia curls up beside him in the sun.

When he's asleep, I close the door and set about making a potion. I put a pan of water to boil and Ink and I go herb gathering. When I'm in the garden snipping leaves and rootling up seedlings, I see him through the window. He sleeps peacefully, one hand on the cat. I stare, searching for some familiarity in his features to match my own. There is nothing I can recognise. No one would realise we are father and daughter. Oddly, I find this disappointing.

Walter sleeps well and does not wake until the potion is cooling in jars. 'Well, that smells good,' he says, tottering into the kitchen and sitting at the table.

'Drink this,' I say, handing him a mugful.

'It's a long time since a witch made me a cure,' he says, taking a sip.

'I can't cure old age. But it should make you more comfortable.'

I busy myself with kitchen jobs until he's finished. Then we go to the church. A folded wheelchair is propped by the gate. I settle him into it and put a blanket over his knees. Claudia appears as from nowhere and jumps onto his lap. The old man folds the edge of his rug over her as if they've been lifelong friends.

Chapter Twenty-Three

Church Lane is dappled with lacy shadows from the trees. I push Walter carefully around the potholes, stopping now and then to pick cow parsley, buttercups and red clover for the grave.

'She liked weeds the best,' he says, holding the bunch.

'I'm the same. Never can see the value of one plant over another.'

St Gutheridge and All Angels is pretty, the churchyard frothy with cow parsley and meadow sweet. Ink waits under the lychgate to be let in. 'Hello, Bethany,' I say out of habit.

'You can see her?'

'Right here,' I say, pointing to where the ghost lies on a raised stone slab where coffins waited for burial in times of old.

Bethany folds her arms and glares at Walter as I lift off Claudia, help him out of the chair and hand him his stick. Claudia jumps back onto the chair, glares at the ghost, turns a circle and curls into the warm spot.

'This is my father, Beth.'

'Fascinating,' says Walter. 'Does she speak to you?'

I open the gate and hold it for Walter. 'No. But she listens.'

Ink trots off for a good sniff. 'Is she coming with us?' he says, looking behind.

'No. She never comes into the graveyard.'

'You'd think that's where you'd find a ghost.'

We walk slowly along the stone path, Walter's stick tapping as we go. He stops beside the large raised tomb of Sir Galahad Thornbury, pushes a trail of ivy away with his stick and reads aloud. 'Lilly, Lilly. Lovely Lilly. White in the sunlight. Pure in the morning dew. Sweet perfection the whole day through. Yet I love thee best, sweet Lilly, when your blooms are bright from moonlight.'

Mid Witch Three

Walter dabs his eyes. 'Gave your mother a book of his poetry once. Well, that's what we did in the olden days. No internet memes back then. Love was a serious business.' He chuckles.

He leans on the headstone at my mother's grave. Bobs his head. 'Hello, my lost love,' he softly says. Lips mutter words from the living to the long dead. I give him the flowers and leave him in peace.

Ink is at the far right-hand corner at the back of the graveyard, where the wall curves out to encompass the witches' graves. On the edge by the wall a patch of forget-me-nots grows. I pick a bunch, adding cow-parsley and dog roses. Walter finds me there.

'So this is her, Bethany Blackwood,' he says as I place the flowers on the grave.

'Yes and no. I thought so at first. But this is her daughter, named after her mother.'

'Who was burnt at the stake?'

'That's right. That young woman – the ghost I see – looks very young. She has no headstone that I can find.'

'Interesting,' says Walter, rubbing his chin. 'Did you realise your Grandma Gwen's mother organised this?' He points at the curving wall.

'No,' I say, fascinated.

'Fanny told me all about it. That's why they bought the church and the surrounding land, so they could bring the family into the sanctified grounds.'

'Were they doing it because they were trying to lift the curse?'

'She never said. But it wouldn't surprise me. Shall we go in?'

Inside the church, sun shines through the stained-glass windows, making coloured marks on the worn stone slabs. The door creaks shut behind us as we wander up the aisle. We sit on a pew and gaze at the window. 'Supposed to be ten magpies but I can only ever see nine,' I say. Funny how churches make you whisper.

'Ahh yes. Fanny showed me the hidden fellow. Now where are you?' He changes his spectacles, rests his hands and chin on his stick and stares.

Behind us, the door creaks and Ink pads in. She wanders up the steps to the altar and lies on the carpet there. I don't bother calling her off. There's rarely anyone here. I check my watch; soon be time to fetch the twins from school.

'What can you do? Magically speaking,' I ask.

'Me? Oh nothing much. I was just a thrall. Like most fellows.'

'But you have orts.'

'Faded now, I expect.'

I don't say anything.

'They used to be golden. Or so someone told me once.' He smiles, lost in his thoughts. Then: 'Ah ha! There, do you see? On the bottom of the saint's robes. Is that it?'

I take a picture with my new phone and enlarge the image. Sure enough, there is magpie number ten. 'Always

Mid Witch Three

good to solve a puzzle before bed,' he says. As we take a stroll around the church, he asks, 'You've checked your lost witch is not interred here?'

'Yes, I checked. And the burial records here and for the parish. I just assumed that there wasn't much left of the poor girl. But I thought I'd have a headstone made for her. Put it with the family. She's the only one missing.'

'I don't think the Rutherfords would leave the charred remains of a known witch to fate,' he says.

'I need to meet the twins from school. Why don't you come with me, stay for tea?'

I settle him in his wheelchair, with the cat on his lap. 'Is she still there?' he asks, peering into the shadows of the lychgate.

'No. She's gone now.' We meander along the lane, avoiding the potholes.

'I think that's the problem. She can't get into the graveyard. And she waits, posing like a corpse. You need to find your ancestor's remains and give the poor soul a funeral and a fitting memorial.' He tilts his head back to look at me.

'You think they have her ashes, then? The Rutherfords?' I say.

'It wouldn't surprise me.'

Which means I'll have to speak to GFR. Great. At the end of Church Lane, the road smooths and I manoeuvre the wheelchair onto the path. Other parents and carers are making their way toward Foxbeck Primary. 'They don't know about magic,' I say.

'Noted,' the old man says.

Amy and Sophie come tumbling over. They do seem so much happier at this school, which is a relief. At least something is going right.

I've been so busy thinking about my troubles with witchcraft I have not had time to overthink introducing Walter to the children. 'This is Amy and this is Sophie,' I say as the identical girls gaze up at the old man. 'This is Walter. He's your great grandad.'

Walter holds out a hand and they shake.

'You're very old,' says Sophie.

'Very true,' says Walter. Claudia pops her head up from beneath the blanket.

'You've got the cat!' says Amy. 'She normally never likes anybody.'

'I think she fancied a ride,' says Walter as Claudia settles herself into a comfortable ball and Walter tucks her in.

I turn the wheelchair and we set off for home, Ink trotting beside us.

'We're nearly eight,' says Amy. 'How old are you?'

'Nearly ninety-two,' he says.

Tea is shepherd's pie. Belinda and Jason are somewhat amazed to be introduced to Walter – my father.

'How did you find each other? Did you use that Family Reunited thing?' says Jason.

'Something like that,' says Walter.

As I watch him with my kids and grandkids, I'm sad for time lost. He's nice. Even at nearly ninety-two, he's funny,

Mid Witch Three

easy to talk to and interested in others. I can see why my mother liked him. I like him too.

Over the next few days, Walter and I chat on the phone. He likes to call me at coffee time, which for him is 10.30am. It's a relief to have a magical friend. And oddly, although I have known him for so short a time, I am beginning to think of him as my father. I tell him about Mouse, who I am worried about. He says he'll ask around. We talk about Mum, magic and, of course, the curse. Walter has a theory. He's sure finding Bethany's ashes is key.

This is good, because I think I know where they are.

Chapter Twenty-Four

On Friday, I'm making a wedding cake. I have the largest tier baking in the range and I'm splitting the fruity mixture between a medium and small tin when Ink woofs. Four celebration cakes are being collected today and Ink does not get up from her blanket bed outside the door. She just wags her tail. I'm surprised to see Edward rush into the kitchen.

'Fuck!' he says, brandishing a large bouquet at Cocksure, who is strutting up and down the doorstep looking for a fight.

'Edward,' I say. I'm pleased to see him. Which is annoying. I've been ignoring his messages.

'For you,' he says, putting the flowers on the table.

He waits while I sort the cakes, get them in the oven and ask Alexa to time them.

'Lilly,' he says when Cocksure has gone to check on his hens and he has my full attention. 'I've been a complete prat and I'm here to apologise.'

I open my mouth to speak, but he holds up a hand. 'The sex was rubbish, and I should have made more effort. Especially as it was our first time.'

'Edward...'

'No, there's no excuse. You think I'm a selfish lover and I don't blame you. But if you give me a second chance I'll...'

'Edward, it's not about the sex.'

'...make it up to you.'

'You're married.'

'You know I'm married. You made cakes for my wife.'

'Well, that's just it. I didn't realise who you were. I thought you worked at Marswickham House.'

He roars with laughter. I take off my apron, hang it on the back of the door and lean on the sink. Suddenly he's serious. 'I never meant to deccive you,' he says.

'Yes, I realise that, but even so. You are married so I don't know how you can ask me to be your girlfriend.'

'Felicity and I have an arrangement,' he says.

'Oh, I've heard that before. You arrange to see other women and she has to turn a blind fucking eye.'

On the dresser, *Mrs Beeton's Cookery and Household Management* slides to the edge.

'The arrangement is we both see other women. Felicity is gay.'

I push the book back into place. My fingers tingle. 'So, if I ask Lady Wootton about your extra-marital affairs, she'll introduce me to her girlfriend, will she?'

Edward starts to say something. I point to the door. 'I'd like you to leave,' I say.

He's too gentlemanly not to comply and goes outside. 'Lilly, I understand you're mad. But it's the truth. It's common knowledge. Or I thought it was.'

I'm pointing at his car in Church Lane. 'Edward, it's been nice. But I've had a bellyful of crap from men and I'm not about to take any more. Give these to your wife.' I hand him the flowers.

'I'm not lying,' he says, looking genuinely hurt.

'Oh, piss off, Edward.'

He wanders toward the gate dejectedly until Cocksure chases him off the premises. When he's gone, I'm quite pleased with myself. I'm a midwitch and I'm not taking shit from anyone. The Coven or the landed gentry.

Mid Witch Three

'Who needs men?' I say to Maud. She's not listening. She has her head under her wing, asleep.

Unlike my love life, Fox Bake is doing really well. I'm busy all day with my little venture, baking, decorating and chatting with people when they collect what they've ordered.

When I go to meet the twins from school, Edward's bouquet is beside the gate with a note: 'SORRY'.

I can't bring myself to chuck them in the ditch – where they belong. I carry them to the church. Bethany frowns at me as Ink and I pass under the lychgate. I put the flowers on Mum's grave and stand in the peace and quiet. Bethany drifts beyond the wall, a white shape barely distinguishable in the haze of cow parsley.

The evening disappears in a whirl of homework and bath time, arguments and laughter, washing-up, bedtime stories and cleaning school shoes for tomorrow. I tiptoe around Belinda, who is tired and irritable, and console Jason, who is bored and frustrated being stuck in the family home.

I need a full night's sleep and a bit of a lie in, if I'm honest. Nevertheless, I set the alarm on my phone for midnight. It's the only thing I can think to do.

When the alarm bleeps under my pillow, I am less than enthusiastic about getting up in the middle of the night. I throw on jeans and a sweatshirt. Ink follows me downstairs with a puzzled look on her long hound face. She harrumphs when I put on the gardening coat and my back door trainers. Like me, she would rather be in bed.

As I hoped, it's a moonless night. There are no streetlights on Church Lane, but my eyes soon become accustomed to the dark. Ink shakes off her sleepy self and trots beside me, ears pricked, nose in the air.

I'm not afraid of the dark. Never was, even as a child. Yet recent events make me hold the yew wand in my pocket and check I have the sea glass charm around my neck, just in case. I look for Bethany as we pass the church. The ghost whose ashes I seek would be useful. Then again, I am not so sure she wants the curse lifted.

Fox Green is empty, and the cottages around the edge sleep. Ink and I wait in the shadows. When I'm sure we're alone, we walk out to the centre of the space and stand where I never tread. In the blackness, I pace back and forth until a distinctive chill rises from the ground into the soles of my feet. A chill that becomes heat. Burning heat.

I mutter a protection charm to keep us safe and the heat dissipates as I kneel on the grass and take my gardening trowel from my pocket. Recent rain makes removing a square of turf easy. I push the fingers of one hand into the soil beneath. In my other hand, I hold the wand and ask it to find Bethany's earthly remains. I speak in the language of witches, the words melodious and familiar. The wand vibrates and then is still. Nothing.

I replace the square of grass, press it down with my foot and sigh. The chill of a troubled soul brushes my cheek. One and then another. In the darkness the ghosts of women, burnt and then forgotten, writhe about me. My focus has always

Mid Witch Three

been on my own ancestor: one witch who was murdered here. I never gave a thought that there might have been others.

I hold out my arms and greet them. Snap my fingers and send coloured sparks into the cool night air to show them I care. These are my sister witches. Their fate would be mine if I lived in different times. The writhing spirits calm and weave among the coloured sparks. It seems to soothe them, and I hope they feel acknowledged.

In the witch tongue I tell them that, somehow, I will make a memorial here, that they will be remembered. Fox Green is crowded with the wandering ghosts of women.

Chapter Twenty-Five

The next day, sitting under the apple tree so Jason cannot hear my witchy chat, I speak to Walter about my night escapade.

'Good idea to check there first,' he says.

'What do you think the chances are that I can get a memorial erected on Fox Green?'

'I'll investigate,' is all he says.

After the call, I lie back in the long grass and watch Maud hop about on her favourite branch. Already small apples are forming, and I sense a shift in the seasons. Summer is here. Ink lies with her head on my chest. The birds sing and the sky is blue. Really I should get up and get the house cleaned before the weekend, hang the laundry out to dry.

I'm asleep when Ink woofs. A woman is standing over me.

'Don't get up, darling. I'd love to join you.' With that, she kicks off her shoes and lies next to me. 'This is the most perfect tree. If this was my garden, I'd lie here too. Do you lie here a lot?'

I can't help but laugh. 'Yes,' I say, leaning up on one elbow to see her. These days I check everyone I meet for magical energy. I can't see orts, nor can I sense anything 'other' about her. Apart from her very posh, born-in-the-blood accent.

'I'm Felicity. Felicity Wootton.' She reaches over and we shake.

'Lilly,' I say.

Oh god. Has she come to tell me off for (almost) bonking her old man? Or does she just want to order a cake?

'I've come for a little chat about my husband,' she says, sitting up and hugging her knees.

Here we go.

'Eddie's been telling me all about you ever since you two met. He absolutely has a thing for you. So I've come to explain. We have an understanding.' From her leather shoulder bag, she takes out her phone, scrolls and then shows me a picture of herself and another woman. 'This is Fiona. She's my companion.'

I just sit there staring at her.

'Edward and I got married young, and you know how it was in our day. Gay was not something one talked about. Or acknowledged. Anyway. I'm not going to go through my long and tedious journey of self-discovery. But the long and the short of it is that Fiona and I are a couple, and Eddie does his own thing too. We put on a united front for the press and we are the best of friends. Always have been.'

I still haven't said anything.

She gets up with the ease of one who attends fitness classes. Felicity looks younger than me. I'm not sure whether she is or if she's had some 'work' done to her face. Or is it the result of a lifetime of expensive face creams and beauty treatments? I struggle to my own feet, which involves rolling my fat self onto my knees and heaving myself up using the tree trunk for support.

'I love your garden. Are you doing No Mow May? So good for the bees.'

'Would you like a cup of tea?' I say.

'Gosh, that would be lovely.'

In the kitchen, I switch on the kettle and wash some mugs. There is laundry everywhere at various stages: airing, dirty, clean, ironed, waiting to be ironed. A huge mound of dry school uniform is on the table waiting to be sorted. I sweep it into a laundry basket, and we sit.

'Of course, these days nobody cares whether you're gay or straight. Thank god.'

'Why don't you marry Fiona?'

'If we were living in a storybook,' – her laugh is a posh girl's hoot – 'of course I'd divorce Eddie and wed the woman I love. But real life is complicated and, if I'm honest, being Lady Wootton is part of my identity. I'm not prepared to give up my title.' She drinks down her tea and stands. 'There's a magpie in here, darling?'

'That's Maud,' I say.

'How jolly. Oh, I meant to give you this. Eddie says he's asked you, but I thought I'd bring the formal invite. Something to prop on the mantlepiece, if nothing else. Do come.' She hands me an envelope embossed with a picture of Marswickham House. 'Change your mind about Eddie. He's one of the good guys,' she says, air kissing me on both cheeks.

I watch her stride down the path, climb over the garden gate, leap over the pothole and then (without opening the door) vault into a vintage open-topped car. The woman is a gazelle.

The invitation is for Marswickham House Summer Sunshine Ball. The dress code is Black Tie and ladies are requested to wear 'gowns of sunshine yellow'.

'Was that Lady Wootton?' says Jason, suddenly appearing at the kitchen door. Sometimes I forget he's here. He looks over my shoulder. 'You've been invited to the ball. Oh my god, Mum. How exciting.'

I'm not sure I'm excited right now. Confused more like.

'Saw the photos from last year. It's literally *the event* to get an invite to,' he says.

I tip the laundry back onto the table and start pairing school socks.

'Lovely day! How are you all?' It's Martin the Mouth, the noisier of our two postmen. Jason takes the stack of letters and a small parcel from him.

'We're good, thanks. Any news?' says Jason, because he likes to poke the bear. Martin needs little encouragement for gossip.

'Strange news,' he says, lowering his voice. 'Last night, people saw ghosts on Fox Green.'

'Really?' says Jason.

'Two sightings. Mrs Peacock at Rose Cottage and Mildred at Milldean. Both reckon they saw floating shapes after midnight.'

Jason hands me the mail and walks Martin to the gate.

'Might suggest it to the editor,' he says, when he returns to the kitchen. 'Allingshire Ghosts. Be good for the October issue. We start that next week.'

I'm opening another invitation. I can guess what it is from the purple envelope.

'What's that?' he asks, filling a water bottle.

'John and Mary's wedding vow retake thing.'

Mid Witch Three

He pulls a face like he's smelt something bad. 'Do I have to go? They're not my in-laws.'

'It's up to you, love.'

'Then no. No thanks.' He takes his water upstairs to his bedroom office.

I stare at the invitation, which smells of violets and has a scalloped gold embossed edge and purple roses. It's like some Victorian love letter. The invite has not included either Jason or Belinda. It just says, 'Lilly plus one.'

The state Belinda is in, I don't think she'd be thrilled not to be invited even though she's said she's not going. I shove it into the kindling basket.

Chapter Twenty-Six

M y mum always said, 'Money isn't everything. But it's a bloody nuisance if you haven't got any.' For now, I'm making ends meet despite having all the kids, and their kids, at home. Turns out people will pay quite a lot for celebration cakes. And the orders keep coming. Mrs Tingle is an awkward old bag, but she orders a huge cake at least once a week, sometimes more. Funny that she only has disdain for my baking. The jam was far too sweet. Not sure about the amount of vanilla. The sponge was less than perfect. Every cake is thoroughly criticised. But she's a regular customer and pays cash, so I smile at her derision and write down the next order.

Driving lessons have proved too expensive. I called Lenny and told him I'd have to start again at a later date. He sounded quite upset on the phone, and I had to reassure him I was happy with his instruction and that I'd definitely have lessons with him again, as soon as I was over my current family crisis.

Without the expense of driving lessons, I have a modest sum left over this month. This is good because suddenly I need to purchase a yellow dress. Or should I say *gown*.

Edward and I had a long chat on the phone and we are now 'back together', which is nice. I think. He is keen to see me today, but I have put him off until this evening. I need to go shopping without delay.

Barrington is bustling with tourists. Ink and I head to the posh part of town because I have a voucher for Mabel and Green Ladies' and Gentlemen's Outfitters.

I've put a summer dress on for the occasion and I've cleaned my boots. Summer footwear is the scourge of the middle-aged woman. Old toes don't like straps, and my poor feet can't cope with anything other than stout footwear if I'm planning on taking more than ten steps.

'Never been in here,' I whisper to Ink.

'Welcome to Mabel and Green,' says a smartly dressed woman.

'Do you mind the dog?'

'Not at all,' she says. I half wanted her to say no so I could go back where I belong. At the cheap end of town.

The shop is lovely, though. Soft music, a delightful smell and the clothes are gorgeous. I flip through the rails and try not to look like an amateur. The prices are fierce. I can't imagine affording these sorts of clothes and actually wearing them on a daily basis.

'Can I help?' Another shop assistant sails over. I may be wrong, but is she dressed in the smart casual style? I think she is. She observes me, her assessment quick and accurate. No designer labels. Poorly shod. Overlarge handbag of indiscriminate origin. Hair like a witch.

'Just browsing?' she asks in a tone that suggests I leave this refined establishment immediately.

'Yes. Thank you.' I have a voucher. I will not be put off.

She glides away, and I move to a different rail, Ink sleek and beautiful beside me. 'You're gorgeous,' I say, patting her smooth head.

A group of women come in. The shop assistant turns her attention to them and I relax and get on with the job in hand – find a yellow evening dress. There is a long pale lemon skirt in flowing silk. I hold it next to me. It is tiny. I find my size and move on. Flared evening trousers with white daisies on a yellow background. I like the Abba vibe. The only other garment that is the correct colour is a gold sequin jump suit for women who are tall and like to strip naked every time they need to pee. I leave it.

Salvation is found at the back of the shop on a sale rail: a bright yellow full-length dress in soft fabric. The price tag shows several reductions. Must be my lucky day.

The shop assistant is too busy helping customers with more potential than me, so I go into a changing room and pull the heavy curtain. Ink lies on the carpet with a sigh.

The changing room has all round mirrors. I can see myself from every angle. Not a pretty sight. I put on the lemon skirt. 'Does my bum look big in this? Certainly, Madam,' I say. Ink is asleep. Next, the trousers, which come in size S, M or L. I'm not that fat. I've gone for M. That's me – I am middle-aged and I have a medium amount of middle-aged spread. Or so I think. Can't even get them over my medium fat thighs.

I pull the frock over my head. The material is slippery-soft and delightful against my skin. The shape suits me. A scooped neckline gives a glimpse of cleavage. Three-quarter sleeves are good for the fat wobbly arms that greet middle age, and the shape – voluminous sack – is my kind of dress.

But the colour is not flattering. It's doing something weird to my skin tone; I look ill. I turn in the unforgiving mirrors. It skims the flab in a flattering way. It's not my shade, but I'm sure I'll be okay with a bit of makeup and maybe some beads in a different colour.

I take it off and check the price tag. Crucially, I can afford it.

At the counter, a different shop assistant peers at my voucher. I half expect him to say the sale rail is exempt from extra discount. But no. Another 20% is knocked off the price. What a bargain. He wraps the dress in tissue paper, puts it in a box and then a paper bag carrier with ribbon handles. 'Enjoy your dream wear, Madam,' he says when he hands it over. I'm posh.

From a normal shop, I purchase tights and underwear and then head for County Hall. I touch my hand to the sea glass charm around my neck. Ink has a collar that I have modified, small pockets on the inside containing many protective items. Her winter coats are full of such things, some added by me and others from the witches who loved her before I did. Coatless, in the hot weather, I worry about her.

My plan is to go to County Hall and, if I can get in, explore Mouse's living quarters. Maybe ask the Allingshire County Coven Grimoire a few choice questions about the whereabouts of Bethany Blackwood's remains. Then I'll visit Walter.

I cross the street and take a shortcut to County Hall along a narrow alley so Ink can walk in the shade; the pavements are already getting hot. Halfway, I wish I'd stuck to the high street. This is bin alley. We mince around a massive heap of stinking refuge and disturb a few sea gulls feasting on rancid scraps. The gulls fly to the rooftops and wait. Ink sniffs and I hold my breath as I tiptoe around puddles where ripped bin bags ooze and regurgitate their unspeakable innards.

'Come on, Inky dog,' I say, trying to discourage her from getting too involved. She's enjoying the pong.

Suddenly, she stops and stares. I follow the hound's gaze. At first, I think it's GFR walking quickly toward us. My heart does an annoying little flip, which I ignore. It's his brother, Barry, in a pale linen suit.

His dark grey orts puff from his feet as he walks. 'You're to come with me. Coven business,' he says.

In the shade, I search his face for a binding spell and see none. Barry is reputably a powerful witch. He's not a thrall like Grant. Six feet apart, we regard each other. Witches don't pick fights because they sense each other's strength. My magical energy is dominant. I know this. Yet I feel defenceless. Backing down is my default. Isn't that what nice women do? Give in?

'I'm not a member of your Coven. Or have you forgotten?'

'No, I've not forgotten, witch of the Blackwood.' He spits the last word.

I go to walk past. He steps to block me and Ink growls. 'You want nothing to do with us, yet you meddle in our affairs.'

Like his brother, he's a big guy and I'm aware of my vulnerability here in this shaded alley, alone with my dog.

'What are you on about?' I say, trying to get past him.

Barry steps closer. A bead of sweat trickles from his brow. 'What gives you the right to set Mouse free?' he hisses.

Ink's hackles prickle under my hand. 'What?'

'Mouse has fucked off because of your meddling. The Coven will hold you accountable.'

It's strange how two brothers can have such similar features yet be so different.

'I don't know what happened to Mouse,' I say, trying to keep my voice even and calm.

'You Blackwoods, you're all fucking liars. And while I've got your attention,' he says, so near his breath is hot on my cheek, 'leave my brother alone.'

'Barry, we need to put aside our differences. If we work together, maybe we could get the curse lifted?' I step back and something squelches underfoot.

'You're a conniving bitch, just like your mother. Stay away from my family and my Coven.'

His Coven?

Ink snaps, teeth bared. He sneers and mutters something to Ink, making her freeze. At the end of the alley, people are walking in the sunlight. If I call out, will they ignore me or come to help? He looks down on me, in every sense of the word. 'I can't believe I fucked a hag like you.' He stalks off.

'Don't worry, I didn't feel a thing,' I shout. 'Your cock's much smaller than your brother's!'

He turns on his heel and strides back. Face contorted, fists clenched. Ink is still motionless. 'You fucking bitch,' he says, raising his hand. Instinctively, I'm turning away, raising my arms for protection. All thought of magic gone. I'm a defenceless woman about to be hit. My arm throbs where Elaine grabbed me.

The blow never comes. His fist bounces as if he struck a sheet of plastic. Unbalanced, he staggers. Ink comes to herself and leaps at him. On her hind legs, she is tall. Front paws land on his chest and send him sprawling into the grime. Ink stands on his shoulders, hooked fangs bared. They are nose to nose.

'Come on, darling,' I say softly. 'Don't play with garbage.'

Chapter Twenty-Seven

A fter that, I amend my plans and go straight to see Walter. Today I am going to meet him at home. He lives in a tall town house with a view of the park. A woman lets us in. 'You must be Lilly! Come in, come

Mid Witch Three

in. I'm Lisa. He's in the conservatory.' She points down the hall. 'Walter! Wake up! Your guests are here!'

Walter is cosy in a wicker armchair with a rug over his knees. His tartan slippers with zips up the front remind me of a womble.

'You're early,' he says, easing himself up and putting on his glasses. 'Something happened?'

I nod and glance at the door. His shakes his head slightly. We must wait until Lisa has gone.

It's different now I know who he is to me. We sit holding hands.

'Lunch,' says Lisa, carrying in a tray of sandwiches. She gives a bowl of water to Ink, and we all eat together. Lisa talks about this and that. I'm not really listening. I'm looking at Walter's orts. They have a bit of colour today, less smoke more silver. I think my potion has improved his health. I will make more.

When Lisa has gone, I tell him about Barry. Well, not what I shouted after him. Just the bit about Mouse and how he stopped Ink and then tried to hit me but couldn't.

Walter peers at me intently. 'When you met him, did you sense his strength compared to yours?'

I press my lips together. I have an idea what he's going to tell me. It's what I've been saying to myself all afternoon.

'No point knowing you're the stronger witch and then not having the guts to use your power.'

I nod and he grasps my chin before I have the chance to look away. 'It's time to stop being apologetic, Lilith. You're a powerful midwitch. Possibly the most capable witch for decades. But you've got to own it. Believe in your abilities.'

He lets go, and I dash a tear from the corner of my eye. He's right, of course. I must get a grip.

He pats my arm. 'Someone put a protection spell over you. That was nice.'

'I think it might have been Elaine,' I say, rubbing my arm. Then I tell him about my strange encounter with her.

'She knew you'd face danger.'

Ink gets up, stretches and gives me a hard stare. I pick up the rug she was lying on and move it into the sun. She settles herself and wags her tail twice.

'I looked into the Mouse situation. Nobody has any idea where he went. Or why. He's been a tethered thrall for as long as I can remember,' says Walter.

'Tethered?'

'The Coven doesn't like to use the word prisoner, but that's basically it. For some misdemeanour or another, he's been detained at County Hall as the librarian.'

'So why leave now?'

Walter's eyes twinkle. 'Someone must have given him the means to escape.' He raises his eyebrows.

'I never gave him anything,' I say.

'Must have been something.'

'No, nothing. Well, the books I borrowed. I'd take him a cake or two.'

Walter chuckles. 'I bet he was thrilled.'

Mid Witch Three

'He seemed to like them, yes.' Everybody likes my cakes. Except for Mrs Tingle.

'Never occurred to you where he got his magical energy?'

'No.'

'You're an old woman and a young witch. No wonder the Coven fears you. Sugar, Lilly. Mouse needed sugar.'

'I'm glad he broke free.'

'Yes. Me too.'

'What I don't understand is why Barry doesn't want the curse lifted. Surely it would be better for everyone?'

'Ahh, that's the trouble with the Rutherford boy. He doesn't like anything getting in the way of his own ambition. If he lets you start rummaging about in his affairs, who knows what you'll find?'

'Like what?'

'It's just a hunch I've always had. Although since you've told me about Grant's orts and the binding spell, it seems to me I'm more right than wrong. But it is still a theory.'

I'm all ears. 'Tell me.'

'Ever wondered why Grant has those golden orts and never seems to have any actual power himself?'

'You think Barry takes it from him?'

'It's just an idea. But some witches, they don't have an actual energy source so...' He waits while I fill in the gaps.

'They have to take it from someone else.'

'Bingo.'

I make us a fresh pot of tea. The kitchen is old and

homely, like North Star Cottage. My mother must have come here, which is a comforting thought.

In the conservatory, Ink is standing perfectly still with one leg raised. I set the tea tray down. Walter hands me a scrap of paper. A word of witch language is scrawled across it. 'Say that,' he says. I do and Ink is herself again and seemingly untroubled by the experience.

'Now say this.' He hands me another scrap and I say that word. Ink, sniffing the milk jug, is once again a statue. I free her using the other word. Ink continues her doggy investigation, and Walter calls her to him and gives her a treat. 'The trouble with Ink is that once she was a familiar of the Rutherford witches. So they know the words to hold her still.'

'Grant did that a couple of times to her. Will it work on other familiars – these words?'

'No, each animal is specific. You'd need intimate knowledge.'

'So how do you know?'

'Oh, let's just say I'm very good at magical guesses. Remarkable that this dog swapped allegiance. Never heard of that happening before.'

He doesn't drink his tea. He dozes off and I take the cup and saucer from his hand and tuck in his blanket. Sleep shows his years. His breathing rattles and his grey orts settle upon him like mist on water.

I wish my mum had told me who my father was so that I could have got to know him. Someone to guide me in times of trouble. Another magical to confide in when I became a midwitch. Even somebody to negotiate her early death would have helped. Sadness clogs my throat, and I have a quiet cry while my father sleeps.

Chapter Twenty-Eight

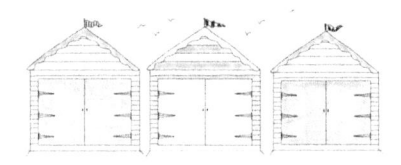

When Ink and I return to North Star Cottage, it's late in the afternoon. It's been a long day and I'm glad I don't have to collect the twins, who are spending the night with their grandparents. There is a message from Edward. I'd forgotten I was seeing him

Mid Witch Three

because my thoughts are full of witchy mysteries. His text says, 'Pick you up at five. Bring an overnight bag.' Winky face emoji.

What I'd like is a nap on the easy chair, followed by an early night. I have absolutely no buzz of excitement regarding sex with Edward. I don't fancy him. Not really. I'm not repulsed by him – I'm just not bothered. It's like an old relationship, not a new one. Maybe I'm just tired. When we get to know each other and form a connection, things will change.

I get my act together, shower, put on a nice dress and a cardigan and pack a small holdall.

I knock on Jason's door. No answer.

On the whole I don't come in here. I've read that the best way to get along with your boomerang kids is to give them plenty of space and privacy. I half expect to see him neck deep in a sea of mess. On the contrary, he's all organised. Bed neatly made. Room tidy. He's sitting at his desk by the window. Four large screens surround him, and he seems to be in the middle of a video game about a dragon. He's wearing headphones, so I tap him on the shoulder.

'Alright, Mum?'

'Just letting you know I'm out tonight.' I hold up the bag.

'With the Lord?'

'With Edward, yes.'

'You still seeing him then?'

'His wife's gay.'

'Yeah. Sometimes they go down the club. Her and Fiona.'

'I'm taking Ink. And there's a spag bol in the fridge if you're hungry. A woman called Wendy Hall is collecting a chocolate cake tomorrow. I've left a note. Could you put a wash on in the morning?' I'd like to interrogate him about these bloody video games. Shouldn't he be doing something more productive with his time? His phone bleeps, which saves me from starting an embarrassing chat.

Ink and I wait for Edward in the lane. He's bang on time and all smiles.

'Can I bring Ink?'

'I've got my two varmints,' he says. 'One more won't make any difference.' The spaniels are in their dog crate in the boot. I put a blanket on the back seat, although the car is filthy, and clip Ink in. I'm relieved and so is she, by the look on her face. Hard to explain that I need my magical familiar with me.

The front seat is slightly less grubby. Edward begins a story about a horse and a greyhound, but I'm asleep before we reach the end of Church Lane and don't wake until the car stops.

'So sorry. You must think I'm terrible company. Bit of a busy day.'

'No no. Sleep on, sweet princess.'

Hope I wasn't snoring.

We're in an empty car park on a clifftop. The sea is calm and the most beautiful blue.

'This is one of my favourite places,' says Edward as we get out.

The dogs streak about, sniffing, and we shoulder our bags.

Mid Witch Three

I look for a building. There is none. 'Hope you don't mind roughing it. Thought we'd spend the night in the beach hut. It's a bit of a walk.'

Penstel's Cove is a mixture of sand and stones. Sea pinks blow on grassy tufts and it is completely deserted. Six pastel beach huts stand in a line. Postcard perfect.

'Keep meaning to come and give the place a coat of paint,' he says, dropping his rucksack and unlocking the doors. 'If you don't fancy sleeping here, I can take you home no trouble. It's a bit rustic.'

'It's lovely,' I say.

Inside is a basic kitchen with a gas camping stove and a sofa, which I assume pulls into a bed. He drags deck chairs and a table onto the decking, and we laugh at Ink who is doing zoomies on the sand while the spaniels try to catch her.

'What are they called? You never did say.'

'Laurel and Hardy. But they also answer to cheese and biscuit. Make yourself comfortable. I'm going to fill up the water,' he says, holding up a canister.

I sit and watch the sea and breathe. This is just what I need. Bit of ozone to calm my soul.

'Should have told me. I would have brought my costume,' I say when he hands me a glass of wine.

'Oh, I shouldn't worry. Never anyone here,' he says, raising his eyebrows.

'Don't the other huts get used much?'

'Honestly, I don't get down here much these days, but when I do it's generally deserted. We got the hut when the kids were small. It was a little community then. All the kids played together. Happy days.' He's filling a pan with water.

'I bet. How many kids have you got?'

Edward laughs. 'You don't Google people, do you, Lilly?'

'Never occurs to me. Can I help?'

'No. Three girls. Two flown the nest. Collette is at home when she's not in London.'

'The model?'

'That's right. Blessed with her mother's good looks. But mostly the place is like a morgue now they've more or less gone.'

I think of my own family chaos and suffer a twinge of guilt that I'm so overwhelmed now they are all back again.

'Any grandchildren?'

'Not even an inkling.'

The dogs return, lap water and flop onto a blanket. I take off my shoes and socks.

'Off for a paddle?' he asks.

'No,' I say, pulling my sack dress over my head. My thought was to swim in knickers and bra. But fuck it. I used to be a nude model. Off they come. Edward can't believe it.

'You're sure this beach is deserted?' I say, fastening my hair in a clip.

'Who cares?' he says, stripping off.

Two minutes later and we are clutching each other as we negotiate the stones in bare feet. The tide is out, and we run when we meet the sand. The sea is further away than I realised, and I hope no one is watching my flabby arse from the clifftop.

Then again, I don't care. It's good to feel the breeze on my skin. I slow to a walk, mostly from vanity. The joggling run of middle-age is even less pretty wobbly bum naked. Edward's cock likes the sight of me, by the looks of things.

'Fucking hell!' I cry. The sea is freezing cold.

Edward, possibly in a fit of manly pride, dives in headfirst.

'Don't tell me the water's lovely!' I say, dithering and splashing myself.

'I'm not going to lie. It's awful. Don't do it!'

Laurel and Hardy have come to the water's edge to bark at us. I take the plunge. Well, I sort of sink into the water, followed by a long-necked swim. Don't want to get my hair wet. I'm not that spontaneous.

We swim about, yelping. Then he's next to me. Skin on skin, which is incredibly warm. We have a kiss. Nice. Also, warm and salty. His hard cock is pressed between us. He's kissing me with a proper passion now. He moves down my neck nibbling and biting and sucks my nipples, which are supersensitive in the cold.

I check we are alone then wrap my arms around his neck and my legs around his waist. A bit of fumbling and he's inside me. Sea water on double duty, providing lubrication and making me light as a feather. We bounce around. Edward groans softly. It's not like the movies. All I can do is slide up and down. It's all very gentle. What I need is him throwing me on the sand and giving me a good pummelling. My middle-aged fanny needs a bit of vigour to wake it up these days.

'Oh Lilly,' breathes Edward. I lean back, hoping to get a better angle. No. Can't feel a thing. But the sky is very pretty as the sun goes down.

'Oh Lilly,' he says again. This time not in a sexual way. Two people are strolling slowly along the beach. Honestly, I'm glad of the distraction. When they've gone, maybe I can persuade him to finish the job in the beach hut. I start to get untangled, but he holds me tight and takes a step back so we are neck deep. His ardour softens.

The couple are taking their time picking up bits of driftwood. When they spot us, the woman raises a hand in greeting and we wave back, all polite and British.

'How's the water?' shouts the bloke.

'Lovely when you're in!' Edward calls back. Then says into my neck, 'Inside a good woman.'

I can't help but giggle. And just for fun, I reach down and clasp his balls. He hardens up again. The couple walk on, arm in arm. When they have their backs to us, Edward attempts a bit of a thrust. We almost lose our balance. I want to laugh again, then realise that my absent ball fiddling is absolutely hitting the spot as far as he's concerned. He shudders as I make soft sex noises in his ear and quicken my tickling. Boom. With a strangled grunt, Edward is undone.

'Oh fuck,' I say. The couple, who I thought would be

making their way along the cliff path by now, are unlocking a beach hut.

'Ah,' says Edward as we untangle ourselves. 'This might be tricky.'

We watch as they faff about putting out deck chairs and a fire pit.

'Any chance that dog of yours is trained to fetch beach towels on demand?' he says.

'Not a chance.' Ink is watching the proceedings with interest from her blanket. 'What about Laurel and Hardy?'

'They just think everything is a joke,' he says.

We watch the shore like a pair of chilly hippos. 'We have two choices,' he says. 'Wait until it's dark, which will be in about twenty minutes. Or brazen it out.'

I'm properly cold now. Shivering, teeth chattering. The couple go into their beach hut and draw a curtain over the doorway. 'Hurry,' says Edward, grasping my hand. 'They must be getting changed for a swim.'

We rush quickly and quietly over the shingle. Behind our own curtain we cling together, shivering and laughing. He has towels, and when we're dressed and wrapped in blankets, he makes us hot chocolate. The other couple are already in the water and are swimming athletically back and forth. They wave as they stride back to their hut. No hanky panky for them. We watch the sunset and eat the posh picnic he's bought.

In the night I lie awake listening to the soft lap of the sea and the snuffle of the sleeping dogs, who are in bed with us. We've laughed and chatted. It's been romantic and fun. Pity we're not in love.

Ink snuggles nearer and I rest my hand on her sleek head. She settles her chops and sighs. I sigh back. We do that, Ink and I – share a sigh. But where hers is one of contentment, mine is frustration. I'm tired but I cannot sleep. If I lie here, I'll fidget and wake everyone up. Extracting myself from dogs and man I creep outside.

The tide is in, and the calm sea reflects a full moon. Ink and I sit on the shingle and enjoy the night. I wrap the blanket around us both and think.

When Barry attempted to hit me, I'd forgotten I was a midwitch. Old habits die hard and I have had a lifetime of feeling second best to the men in my life. I squeeze my arm where the tingle is. Elaine wasn't trying to hurt me. She was protecting me. I need to see her. Soon.

Then I lie back, do a bit of moonlight bathing and doze off.

'There you are!' Edward is smiling down at me.

'Lovely beach,' I say.

'Breakfast?'

'God yes, I'm starving.'

I don't think he has a clue I've been out here all night like the mad witch I am. I am better for a moonlight bath, though. Ink and I walk to the toilet block, and when we get back Edward is frying bacon over the camping stove.

Mid Witch Three

'Smells delicious,' I say, rummaging in Big Bag for the plastic tub with Ink's breakfast in. Laurel and Hardy are too interested in the smell of bacon to interfere with kibble. They wait side by side like perfect angels watching their master.

We sit on the deck chairs with steaming mugs of tea and eat the eggs and bacon, balancing the plates on our knees. 'Sorry, there's no toast,' he says.

'It's wonderful. Absolutely delicious.'

'Always nice to have the two f's,' he says, taking my plate.

'Two f's?'

'Fuck and a fry up.' He laughs.

We chat while Laurel and Hardy chase up and down the beach. Ink lies on her rug and watches them with mild disdain.

'Thanks for this. It's been lovely,' I say when we pack up.

'Sorry it's been so bloody cold.'

'Can't be helped. Great British summer.' I laugh.

'Ahh, now, meant to have said. Madly busy until the weekend. Won't actually be able to see you again until the ball.'

'That's fine.'

'You are still coming?'

'Absolutely. I have purchased a very yellow dress.'

'Good. Can't pick you up...'

'That's fine.'

'Not really. But I have to be there hosting, and from experience I know there will be a small crisis – possibly several –

on the night that will need sorting. Felicity takes these events very seriously. I will send a car to collect you,' he says.

'There's no need.'

He puts his arms around me and hugs me to him. 'Let me take care of you, Lilly,' he says quietly. How sweet.

It's sweaty work lugging all the stuff back to the car. The hot day we could have done with yesterday is happening now. We leave the car doors open to cool the interior while we load our stuff and take in the view. Then we catch Laurel and Hardy, who are not keen on leaving and require a cheese bribe to get them into the car.

'Drop you home?' he asks as he drives away. It's still only eight in the morning.

'Are you going home – back to Marswickham House?'

He sighs deeply. 'Duty calls, I'm afraid. Got a big meeting with my estate manager. Then Felicity and I have planned to get our heads together about the next phase of our renovation project. Never an easy task.'

'Could you drop me off at Poorbrook House on the way?'

'No problem. Get the dog walked early. Good plan. How will you get back?'

'Meeting a friend,' I say.

He drops Ink and I in the visitors' car park. A quick kiss on the lips goodbye.

'Thanks for the beach hut mini break,' I say.

'See you at the ball.'

'God, I feel like Cinderella.'

'I will send your horse and carriage for seven thirty. Stay

Mid Witch Three

the night if you like. It's a creaky old place, but no ghosts as far as I know.'

That will make a change then.

Laurel and Hardy gaze forlornly from the back of the car as he drives away.

Chapter Twenty-Nine

Poorbrook House is not open to the public until ten, so I take Ink for a walk. It's been years since I came here helping on school trips when the kids were small. I follow another dog walker through a gate and over a

Mid Witch Three

field to the woods. The sun is already hot. It's going to be a scorcher. In the cool of the woods I try to get my thoughts together.

This is an absolute whim; I'm not sure which days Elaine does her volunteering, so she might not even be here. If I find her, will she speak to me? She was certainly hassled last time. She might act like the Coven is always right – but beneath the surface, Elaine knows they are corrupt.

The walk around the garden perimeter and over a few fields doesn't take long. It's ages until the house opens, but I'm determined to see Elaine; even if all I manage to do is thank her for the protection spell, it will be worth it. I find a bench and message Cressida to see if she fancies a chat. Seconds later, we're having a video call and I have to turn the sound down because she's laughing so loudly about my exploits with Lord Edward.

'Have you seen the photo shoot they did at Marswickham House?' she says when she gets her breath back.

'No,' I say, slightly bemused.

'Can't remember which magazine. Maybe it was in the weekend papers. Anyway, the place looks amazing. You'll have a fab time.'

She tells me about her wedding plans and then has to go.

The café, located in the stable yard, is opening, so I buy a tea and sit at a table outside. It's quiet. Staff and volunteers are busy sweeping paths, cleaning windows and making everything ready for the tourists.

This is a silly idea. I won't be let into the house with Ink. And I assume Elaine volunteers as a room guide inside. I put my coffee cup into the recycling bin and wander along a gravel path past the gift shop. Poorbrook House looms ahead. Pale stone walls and marble columns. Funny to think that Grant Rutherford's ancestors lived here, when they were known as the Ruffheads.

I follow the path into the formal gardens beside the stately home and ignore the 'No dogs beyond this point' sign. Ink sniffs the neatly planted flowerbeds. It's then I see pink orts on the path. They are pale wisps above the pea gravel. I follow where they lead – around the side of the house, down some steps to an oak door marked 'private'.

I try the handle. Locked. 'Ink, open the door,' I say. Nonchalantly Ink threads down the stone steps and bops her nose on the door, and in we go.

I expect disused servants' quarters not open to the public. Or a storeroom full of dust and boxes. Instead, a busy kitchen greets me. The staff of Poorbrook House are enjoying breakfast at a long table before their working day begins. A few heads turn as we enter, but they take no notice of us.

'Ahh, there you are!' It's Elaine. She bustles over and leads me into the room by the elbow. 'Welcome to Poorbrook. So glad you made it! How was the traffic? Would you like something before we start? Tea, coffee, pastry?'

'I'm fine, thank you,' I say. She walks off and I follow.

'This dog?' A thin man with a clipboard blocks our way.

'I did tell you, Eric,' says Elaine, smiling and lightly touching his arm. Eric frowns, and Elaine stands aside to introduce me. 'This is Lara Baywater. She's come to examine the fifty-second archive.'

Eric holds out his hand and we shake. 'Erm,' he says.

Elaine continues: 'Remember, I said she can come today, but she needed to bring her dog. Either that or we'll have to wait another month to get the papers verified.' Again a light touch on his arm.

'The dog?' says Eric. The conversation at the breakfast table has stopped and I am aware that people are looking and listening.

'The lame dog, Eric.' Elaine smiles patiently.

He faces me.

'Yes, so sorry,' I say. 'She can't be left on her own. Vet's orders.'

Everyone stares at Ink who, with drooping ears, stands with one front paw raised.

'That's why you told her to use this door. So we can go straight to the archives,' says Elaine.

'Yes indeed,' says Eric as Ink limps past on three legs.

Elaine leads the way through a low door and into a narrow corridor. 'This place is like a maze,' she says. Her hair is pale green today to match her skirt and jacket. She's a colour-coordinated witch. I'm a salt-covered witch in a faded sack dress, carrying two bags. I certainly don't look like the academic Elaine is trying to pass me off as.

She unlocks a heavy, panelled door and we go in. The door swings shut behind us and Elaine pulls me into a hug and then pets Ink. 'You are a clever girl,' she says. Ink glances at me sideways. Sometimes I'm sure this dog is laughing at me.

We go deep into the room and sit at a table between tall shelves packed with wooden storage boxes. Beside a dust-covered window is a ragged armchair where Elaine's cat Oscar watches.

'I'm so glad you found me!' she says.

'I thought...'

'Oh, it was tricky. That day you came over, I'd spotted two familiars on the roof – corvids – and there was a rat I didn't like, lurking in the shadows. Can't be too careful. The Coven has eyes and ears everywhere.'

I pat my arm. 'Thank you for this. Barry tried to hit me...'

'He's such a hateful bastard,' she says, and we laugh. I tell her what happened and when I get to the part where Barry landed on his arse in the bin alley, she smiles and leans back as if she's eaten a hearty meal.

Ink has finished sniffing about. She goes to the armchair and the animals touch noses. 'Do you always bring Oscar with you?' I ask.

'Recently, yes. It's much too dangerous to go about without your magical familiar these days.'

Does she bring the cat in a bag or does Oscar walk on a lead like a dog? I don't have time to satisfy my curiosity because Elaine has questions. 'So,' she says, leaning closer and lowering her voice to a whisper. 'Do you have it?'

'What?'

'The ACC's Grimoire.'

'No. Why would I have it?'

Elaine stares at me. Her pink orts swirl around her in a cloud.

'I went to the library. Needed to give Mouse back a book he lent me. He wasn't there, but the Grimoire was,' I say.

Elaine shuffles in her seat. 'When? When did you go?'

I tell her the date and she gets a diary from a large shopping basket.

'Mmm interesting. The book you saw was a decoy. I think it took a few days to notice it was missing. And, of course, by that time Mouse had long gone.'

'You think Mouse took it?'

'Possibly. But you realise the Coven is placing the theft at your door?'

'Why would I even want it?'

Suddenly, I'm not sure whose side she's on.

Behind her, Ink and Oscar are cuddled up in the armchair. This is surely a good sign. Even so, I reach out and put my hand on her arm.

'You think I took it?'

'Yes. Why else would you free Mouse?' I feel the truth of this statement.

'I didn't free Mouse. Well, not intentionally. And I don't have the book.'

'Really?' She looks into my eyes.

'Yes really. Is that why you let me in, because you're on the Coven's side?'

'The Coven. It's complicated. You think it's black and white, good or bad. But I've been a member since I was a girl, and in those days it was more good than bad.'

'And what do you think now?'

'Pains me to say it, but it's more bad. A lot more bad.'

Truth. I fold my arms.

'It's why I wanted you to join us. It needs someone with enough power to restore balance. From the inside.'

'Someone to ward off the bad guys.'

'Exactly,' she says.

'Two things. I'm a bit old to do any hero shit, and even if I was twenty years younger there's not much I can achieve as a Coven member because then they'd be controlling me.'

'Many of us thought you'd be our salvation,' she says.

'Not this old witch.'

Elaine shakes her head, her mouth a hard line. I'm just glad she's on my side and she's still my friend.

'I'm sorry about the bloody Coven and Mouse. But I don't think there is anything I can do about it.'

'So why are you here?' she asks.

'The curse.'

'Oh, that old chestnut.' She looks at the ceiling. 'If you're too old to tackle the Coven, surely you're too old to be worrying about true love?' My family curse is not important.

'It's not me I'm worried about.' I tell her about Belinda, the baby and the whole fuck up that is my family.

'If you get this curse lifted, you do realise this might not sort everything out? Real magic is not like it is in story books: everything sparkles and improves; everyone lives happily ever after.'

'Even so,' I say, 'I've got to try to give them a future.'

Chapter Thirty

Elaine waves at a cupboard, which opens. Inside is a tea-making station. With another flick of her hand, the electric kettle switches on. Two tea bags hop into two mugs. Sometimes I love magic.

'Haven't got any milk,' she says, patting her stomach.

Mid Witch Three

'Need to lose a few pounds.' When we both have a hot tea, I tell her my theory about Bethany, the grave – or lack thereof – and all the witch ghosts I saw on Fox Green.

'My mother was a spirit seer,' she says when I've finished.

'Really?'

'Mmm. Not very reliable. The dead.'

'So I've gathered.'

'She saw many spirits. And the ones on Fox Green.'

I have a sense of relief. I'm not the only one who's seen them. Elaine gets a half-eaten packet of biscuits from the basket.

'Her theory was we mistakenly think they are on our side. We misconstrue what they seem to communicate because we are trying to make it fit into our living world. But those that float between realms are troubled souls, wounded by their past and unable to make sense of or forgive the wrongs done to them.'

'Can't blame the Fox Green witches.'

'No. No, most living witches are daughters of survivors. Women they didn't manage to burn.'

'I've tried to ask Bethany what she wants.'

'My mother used to say it was no good asking them questions. We see ghosts as pale images, but when they look at us it's like they're staring into the light.

'In other words, they're blinded.'

'Something like that.'

We sip our tea and munch biscuits. Ink is having a doggy dream. The whimpering seems apt. 'I approve of what you're trying to do,' she says. 'Acknowledging these wronged women may well settle their souls. It might not lift the curse, though.'

'Even so, I think I should try.'

'Where have you searched for Bethany's remains?'

'St Gutheridge and my woods. Fox Green.'

'Did you try Fox Lodge?'

'No, but I will. Although I never sensed anything when I was there.'

'And that's how you think you'll find these remains? If they still exist. On a hunch?'

'I think I'll have a sense of her. Bethany Blackwood.' We've spent enough time together.

'Not sure that'll work. The way my mother did it – connecting with the lost, as she called them – was with something they owned. Something that mattered to them. That way you had a halfway link, if you like, between now and the past.'

The fried breakfast has done nothing to quell the mid-morning hunger. I'm having trouble not eating all Elaine's biscuits. 'I always thought you volunteered in the house, showing people around the rooms. Tour guide stuff.'

Elaine puts the mugs back in the cupboard and searches through a draw. 'Only sometimes. Mostly I'm down here documenting the archives. Or trying to. Poorbrook has a lot of space and there are all sorts of historical papers from city houses that got dumped here for safekeeping during the war. When I say dumped, I mean it. Most of it is unlabelled.'

'Ever find anything special?'

Mid Witch Three

Elaine isn't listening. She brings out a lanyard with a visitor's pass attached. 'First things first. You might as well look for her here. Since it once belonged to the Ruffheads.'

Ink lounges in the armchair. 'Don't worry about her. She'll soon come and find you if something is wrong.' She spreads out a map on the table and explains where we are and how to get back in with the key code.

Poorbrook House is vast. Map in hand, I wander through the rooms, trying to detect Bethany's remains. I've left my bags with Elaine, but I have my mother's yew wand in my cardigan pocket in the hope it once belonged to Bethany. I don't find a thing. When I get back, Elaine lets me walk among the archives and other rooms not open to the public. Nothing happens.

Aware I'm incredibly scruffy and covered in sea salt, I decline lunch in the café. 'At least you can tick this place off your list,' she says, hugging me goodbye. Ink and I catch a bus from Brook Lane.

Back at North Star Cottage, normal life resumes. I get washed and changed into a clean, flowery sack. Tackle some laundry. Attempt to tidy the kitchen. Light the range so I can cook something. Rush to collect the kids. Supervise homework. Get them bathed and stuff them in front of the telly because I need a break. Then I make us all macaroni cheese and bake chocolate chip cookies for the tearoom and us. Everyone is always in a better mood when they're well fed.

Belinda gets in just as I'm setting the table. Her expression is grimmer than normal. 'You okay, love?'

'Brian's seeing someone else.'

Oh dear.

'A science teacher from the comprehensive.' She plonks her stacker box on the floor and lifts out a bundle of exercise books. 'Where's my bloody pen!'

'Sit down, love. I'll find it.'

Ink puts her head in her lap, and she bursts into tears. As big tears land on Ink's black head, she twitches her ears but doesn't give up trying to comfort her. She's such a kind dog. I hand Belinda some kitchen roll and a glass of water. She's off tea and coffee.

'Maybe he's having a fling to even things out.'

More sobs. 'She's moving in with him.'

I don't say anything else. I know from bitter experience it's best to say nothing – because every word of comfort will be unhelpful.

She gets her phone and picks at it. Slides it across the table. A social media post shows a young woman moving boxes from a car into what was my daughter's family home. I stop myself from saying something like, 'Maybe she's a lodger?' Which is good because at the end of the clip she and Brian are on the doorstep smiling with their arms around each other. Belinda drinks some water and tries to get herself together.

That's the trouble with the modern world. Too much information. It would be enough just hearing your estranged husband has a girlfriend. These days you see a whole video with captions and background music. Can't be good for anyone's mental health.

She wipes her face with the kitchen roll and Ink has a shake and goes back to bed. From the living room comes a peal of laughter from the twins. 'Why do you let them watch so much telly!?' she says.

Because I'm knackered, love.

Alexa beeps. 'Alexa, stop,' I say and lift the bubbling mac and cheese out of the range. At least I've got something right.

Chapter Thirty-One

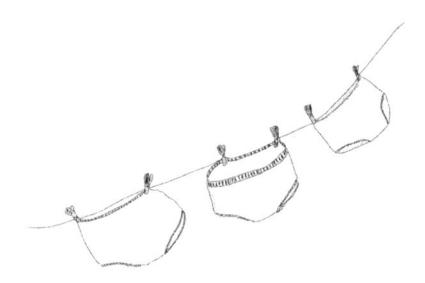

The next day after I've walked Sophie and Amy to school, dropped cookies and scones into the tearoom and bought more eggs (I don't know what's up with those chickens) I rush back to the cottage for a much needed sort out.

Mid Witch Three

The chaos of family life is a tidal wave of mess. When Belinda and Jason were small, I kept my head above water. These days I'm sinking. The last time I dealt with kids, I was young and there were fewer of us. Now I have five lots of food and mess and endless laundry.

It's a beautiful day and we're all in good health, I remind myself as I tackle the chores. An hour later, I've tidied up and put the vacuum round and I'm pegging washing on the line. Oddly, this is a chore I take quite seriously. It's probably a mark of my generation, neatly pegged laundry. Similar items grouped together as if they could not dry properly otherwise. Shirts all in a row. Then t-shirts. Three of my flowery frocks blowing in the breeze. A few tea towels. If I misjudge and find an item that needs to be with its group, I shuffle everything along so it can be hung where it belongs. Can't possibly have a pair of pants in the middle of a row of school dresses.

Mum said it was important to do it properly or people would think your house was messy. Funny really that she was a stickler for regimented washing lines when the cottage is, was, and probably always will be in a state of perpetual disorder.

The younger generation doesn't care. No, they hang items as they come to hand any old how. Shirt, towel, sock, frock, pair of jeans. Then I have to sneak out and do a bit of laundry organisation.

Maud likes to keep an eye on the proceedings and flits from the top of the line prop to the edge of the laundry basket. Last are my knickers. I remember when they were one-peg items. Skimpy little things that dried in a puff of breeze. Now my knickers require two pegs so the wind can blow through. Not for me sexy silk or bum-splitting thongs created from fabric so delicate a man could snap them with his strong hands – if need be. 'I'd like to see a bloke try to destroy these bad boys,' I say to Maud, who is eyeing the shiny buttons on Belinda's cardigan.

Ink woofs; someone is coming. A woman has spotted me and is wading through the grass (it's almost hay) toward me.

'Cooee!' she calls, arm raised, full of cheer. My heart sinks. It's Mary. It must be two years since I've seen my daughter's mother-in-law. She's had a makeover, lost about half her body weight and her hair is now long and blonde. It has a plastic sheen in the sunlight.

'Lovely day!' I call out.

The 'lawn' has proved too great an obstacle for Mary. She stops and bats away a few flying insects that have flown out to greet her.

'I just wondered if we could have a quick word,' she says, looking for her feet.

I peg the last of my knickers – Christmas themed with sprigs of holly. 'Come this way, there's a bit of a path.'

Ink, excited to have a visitor, runs. She's fast. Leaping left – zoom – then right – zoom.

'What's it doing!' shrieks Mary, clutching her clutch bag.

'Just letting off greyhound steam. They need to do that now and again. It's a pent-up speed thing,' I laugh.

Mid Witch Three

Ink wizzes past us and dislodges a particularly large bumble bee, who lands on Mary's lacy pink summer dress.

'Oh, oh!' she cries, flapping.

'Come here, friend,' I say to the bee. Mary is too busy shrieking to notice I'm speaking witch. Then again, it probably sounds like a weird mumble to the untrained ear. The bumble bee understands and lands in my hand.

'It's alright, Mary,' I say, showing her the bee in my palm: a perfect ball of fuzzy yellow and black. 'I have her here.'

Mary's mouth is open, and her pencilled eyebrows lift a fraction. I wade through the hay and set the bee on a peony flower. 'Thank you for visiting,' I whisper to her.

Mary dashes to the safety of the kitchen. 'So glad I caught you on your own. Is Jason out? He's living here now, isn't he?' Her tone makes the situation sound like a failure.

'He's upstairs. In his office. Working from home.' Playing video games.

'How, er, convenient.'

'You're looking nice,' I say and mean it. The pink suits her.

'Oh, I'm fabulous. Ever since I went on the HRT. It's been an absolute game changer.' She flicks her blonde hair. It doesn't look quite real. 'John says it's taken twenty years off me. You should try it.'

'I'm on it.'

'Oh. Well, it affects people in different ways.'

'Tea?'

She still looks surprised. Must be Botox. 'No, thanks all

the same. Really can't stop. I'm meeting the girls at the book shop café.'

I put the kettle on anyway.

'The thing is, I was wondering if you got the invite. To our little do?'

Ink comes in and laps water so loudly that we have to wait. At last, she stops and gazes at her treat tin. After the zoomies she thinks she deserves a biscuit.

'I did get it, thank you.'

'Must have misplaced the RSVP,' she says, fixing me with a wide-eyed, surprised stare. I try not to glance at the kindling bucket behind her where the purple invite sticks out. I hadn't thought to reply.

'Sorry, been so busy.' I wave a hand at the kitchen, intending to show a thriving cake-baking business, not the breakfast battle and my laundry problem. I open the dog treat tin and take out a biscuit. Ink is dodging side to side to see where I'll throw it.

'You will be coming, Lilly?'

I throw the biscuit. Ink leaps and snaps it in mid-air. Chomp! Mary teeters in the kitten heels and gasps. Her face is immobile.

'Why don't you sit down, Mary,' I say, ignoring Ink, who is wiggling for another treat. I clear her a space, lifting a Lego house from the chair and dropping it in the sink. It's covered in modelling dough and needs a wash. I grab Jason's breakfast bowl, mug and plate and chuck them on the draining board and wipe the table while pushing all else to the side: my laptop, two shoebox cars, the unopened post and a large jug of cow parsley and buttercups, which are doing a magnificent job of adding to the mess.

Mary sits gingerly. Ink sniffs her hair then pokes her nose deep into the blonde curls and snort-sniffs. Mary is on her feet again. Ink sneezes.

I steer Ink onto her blanket bed and toss a rug over her.

'What's on your mind, Mary?'

Mary sits, pink handbag on her lap like she's on a train. 'Well I, we, were so hoping you could come to our wedding vow renewal. It would mean a lot.' She smiles. Not easy when your face is frozen. I give her a mug of tea, which she pushes away.

'Not sure you noticed on the invite. But I didn't really want— What with the situation— Be difficult, and I, we, just want a happy, joyful day. Because that's what it's all about, celebrating our long and happy marriage. So obviously having Belinda there in her current condition— Well, it would spoil the photos. And to be honest, Brian's still very angry.'

I take a sip of tea.

'That's the thing about Brian. Sooo like his father. Faithful as the day is long. My John has never strayed.'

I take another sip of tea and try not to think of last Christmas when John and I had a jolly good bonk. Several good bonks in actual fact.

'I can't wait for you to see the twins' dresses. They are absolutely adorable. From Mable and Green. You should go there. They have the most scrumptious clothes.'

'It is a lovely shop,' I say, still thinking about her husband's faithful cock. At its best.

Mary smiles. Well, she's baring her teeth at me. 'These special days rush by and we don't want to be distracted. Lovely as they are. Adorable. But small children, they need taking care of. Sometimes they can get tricky.'

'You want me to keep an eye on the twins?'

'Well, yes. I thought it would be better than hiring a nanny.'

'Yeah.'

'I knew you'd understand,' she says, getting up, little pink handbag like a shield between us. 'I could ask Brian, of course. But you realise it's a bit difficult. What with him in his new relationship. Don't want to make a big deal out of the baggage from previous marriages.'

I suppose you can say what you like when your expression never changes.

I toss her tea into the sink a little too violently. It splashes over the Lego house onto my t-shirt. I'd like to tell her she's an old bitch. But it wouldn't change anything, so why bother?

'Now, must fly. Mustn't be late for book club.' I walk with her to the garden gate. Her car is in the lane. 'So glad that's all settled. I'm going to give you the dresses so you can get them organised before the church.' She opens the boot and hands me two identical frocks in plastic wrapping and a large box. She taps the box as I take it off her. 'These are the flowers. Silk. So much easier than dealing with the vagaries of fresh flowers. I'll leave the shoe buying up to you. Children's feet grow so quickly. Don't want them growing out of them before the big day. I've seen some simple ballet pumps in that little shop in Market Forrington. Can't think of the name. I'll send you the link.' She air kisses me, hops in her car and drives away with two chirpy toots of her horn. Lovely.

The bridesmaid dresses are frilly, flouncy and lilac. I hang them safely on the back of my bedroom door and put the box of flowers on top of the wardrobe.

Jason finds me standing on a chair. 'Was that Mary?'

'It was. She needs me at the wedding to take care of the twins.'

Jason helps me down. 'She's always been a bitch, Mum. Don't let her get to you. God, these are a horrible colour. Do you think the blushing bride will be in purple?'

'I really don't care.'

Her words about Amy and Sophie being 'baggage' make my blood boil and my fingertips tingle with pent-up magic. I've never liked Mary with her bitchy undertones. If the twins didn't absolutely adore this whole bridesmaid–wedding vows nonsense, I would insist that they not go. But what can I do? For the sake of two little girls who just want to wear a frothy dress, I can curb my distaste for a day. But one thing is for sure: I must get on with sorting out the curse. For all our sakes. The irony is not lost on me; I cast a spell to improve John and Mary's love life, yet I cannot mend the troubles my family faces.

'Probs won't be back until tomorrow,' says Jason. He has a

holdall at his feet and a car horn beeps in the lane. There is no time for questions. He's gone.

I'm scrubbing the Lego when I hear a strangled cry from the garden. Ink stands on the doorstep watching Edward run away from Cocksure.

'Lilly!' he gasps, hiding behind the apple tree. Trying not to laugh, I approach the cockerel, arms outstretched, and hum a few bars of the soothing spell. It's enough to send the bird into a daze so I can scoop him up and pop him in the chicken run. Edward comes out of hiding, dusting himself off.

'There's only one thing you can do with belligerent cocks,' he says, making a wringing motion.

'He's new. He'll settle down.'

'Just had to see you,' he says, catching me around the waist and kissing me. It's a good kiss. The best yet. I'm glad Jason is out and not watching from the cottage.

Edward is trying to grope me, but all he manages to do is rummage around in my apron pocket and I laugh. 'Come on,' I say, leading him inside and unfastening my apron ties.

'Are we alone?' he says as I close the kitchen door, leaving all the animals outside.

'We are. Fancy a...'

I don't get the chance to say anymore because Edward has me pinned against the dresser with his hand up my skirt. There's no way he's going to find easy access to my big knickers, so I wiggle them off. He doesn't hang about. Moments later, he's got his corduroy trousers around his ankles, and I have his cock in my hand. We kiss and fondle each other.

Mid Witch Three

Mrs Beeton flies off the shelf and lands on the floor with a bang.

'Bloody hell,' says Edward, one hand on his heart. We laugh then move away from the dresser and carry on the proceedings with me bent over the kitchen table. Entry is difficult. I keep forgetting I'm an old hag and not a moist young thing. No matter. I swipe some hand cream from the kitchen window and smooth a glob onto Edward's cock. He shudders and makes a little moaning sound. I guide him inside and he gets to work, with some really nice deep thrusts that have me hanging onto the table and sighing with pleasure. This is great. I knew we'd get it together. Edward leans over me, hot breath on the back of my neck.

'Oh Lilly!' He stops and shudders and, once again and all too soon, it's over. Inside me he is still hard, and if I could have a little more action, I too could find release. I lean into him, wriggle my pelvis, clench my vagina. But Edward is slumped on top of me – he's asleep, and soon so is his cock.

It's not exactly the most comfortable position – sprawled over your kitchen table with a bloke asleep on your back. I nudge him with my elbow. 'Edward!'

'Ting-a-ling!'

'Who's there!' mumbles Edward.

I grasp the kitchen roll and shove a few sheets in his hand and some between my legs. Seconds later, Ink opens the door, and Mrs Tingle stands on the step. I'm washing my hands at the sink and Edward, bollock naked from the waist down, is sitting at the kitchen table.

'Lord Edward,' she trills. There is so much laundry in my kitchen, she doesn't notice the Lord's trousers and Y-fronts on the floor, nor does she realise he's holding a tea-towel over his credentials due to all the coats, bags and school uniform hanging from the back of every chair creating an effective modesty shield.

'Top of the morning to you,' he says as I fetch her sixteen-slice lemon drizzle gateau from the fridge. 'That looks delicious,' says Edward when I lift the box lid to show her. She giggles as if she made it herself. Is she going to take a seat and have a chat? Ink ambles over for a sniff and she throws the money on the table and lifts the box high. Ink helps her out by sniffing her ankle socks and sandals and then putting her cold, wet nose on Mrs Tingle's bare leg.

'Ew,' she says with a visible shudder.

'Watch the step...' I say.

'And the vicious chicken,' says Edward, but Mrs Tingle has already trotted away.

Chapter Thirty-Two

There aren't many blackberries ripe in Fox Lane. But there are a few and it's the only way I can be here without causing suspicion. Fox Lane only leads to Fox Lodge.

Ink sniffs about while I pick. We make our way along the

brambles until I have a plastic tub almost full and the high metal gates loom. No car has gone past, and Fox Lodge – Grant and Barry Rutherford's old family home – is still and empty. I hang about and keep an eye on Ink. She is happy. After the incident in the alley, she will let me know if Barry Rutherford is near.

'Right, come on, Inky Dog. Time for an investigation.' She wags her tail. 'Open,' I say, patting the gate. I'm not sure she can do electronic gates, and I'm about to see if I have the number for the keypad from when I worked as a gardener here, when the gate creaks and swings slowly open. My heart quickens. Should I do this? Then I think of Belinda. 'I just want everyone to be happy,' I say to Ink as we walk in.

I can't see any orts on the path, and the house is dark and quiet. Ink waits by the kitchen door. 'In we go,' I say, and she bops her nose on it and the door opens. Muddy after scrabbling around in hedgerows, I leave my short wellies on the doorstep with the blackberries. Then I check Ink's paws are dry and we go in.

It's not the first time I've accidentally on purpose broken in here. This doesn't make it any easier. Wand in hand, I creep around the kitchen. The Aga is cold, which could mean it's off because it's summer or that no one is expected to stay. Grant has a flat in Barrington, although I've never been there, and his brother lives in London. Their old family home is a relic of their past they don't really want yet cannot bear to sell. I check each quiet, dusty room with Ink at my side. 'Search for Bethany,' I say to her. She sniffs the carpet and gives me a quizzical look – one ear up, the other down. She doesn't understand, poor dog.

I'm convinced I will find Bethany here. Elaine sent me an email with a lot of attachments about witch remains. Even ashes are steeped in residual magic. Some cultures create shrines for dead witches, believing their power is still potent. Definitely not something that would be left lying around or carelessly disposed of.

In the hall, I try not to get distracted by the photographs on the grand piano. I still can't see any orts, so no one has been here for a while. This gives me confidence to go upstairs. The paintings are as I remember. The one of me has gone, which is a relief. It's been replaced by a turbulent seascape.

Ink has lost interest and is lying on the landing. Was this a favourite spot when she was the Rutherfords' dog? It's a good vantage point. The landing window has a view of the front gate, and another window shows the back garden. She's keeping watch, sensible dog.

I concentrate on my task. Outside, I was a blackberrying witch. In here I am a magical detective searching for my ancestor. The rooms are neat and musty. I try to be quick and thorough, but I've no idea what I'm doing. I just hope the wand will... do what exactly? Ping like a microwave oven? Vibrate? Light up? I'm probably going to experience nothing more than a vague sensation. Even so, I feel along walls and around the old fireplaces and poke under beds and in cupboards.

The last room is Grant's.

Easing the door open with my foot, I look at the four-poster bed. Did we 'make love'? Or was it just sex? I get a move on, step into the room. My portrait is on the wall. I stare at my naked self, sitting on a chair with Ink's head on my knee. He must have kept it for the dog.

First, I check the four-poster bed, moving the wand over it like I'm a metal detectorist while the weird carvings of animals watch with beady eyes. The chest of drawers, dressing table and cupboards all draw blank. Nothing is in the bathroom.

This is the last room in Fox Lodge. I was so convinced I'd find something today I actually can't believe I have found nothing. Maybe it's in the garden.

I lean on the window ledge. I love this garden with its mellow brick walls, wisteria arch and old standard roses. The lawn is short and the box hedge tightly clipped. The Rutherford brothers must have employed a new gardener. Ink is outside, sniffing along the edge of an herbaceous border. She chooses a sunny spot on the lawn and flops down. Greyhounds. They're always on the lookout for a nice warm place to have a nap. Smiling, I turn back to the room.

On the mantlepiece a candle burns. How strange. I hadn't noticed it before. A white candle in an old-fashioned holder – the sort people used before electricity. My first thought is suspicion. Obviously, it's witchcraft. It wasn't there a second ago and I'm sure I am alone here; Ink wouldn't wander off for a nap otherwise.

Maybe I should just blow it out before I leave. As the

thought crosses my mind, it topples over, bounces on the tiled hearth and lands on the rug. I scurry to pick it up. Too late. Flames streak out, and in seconds the armchair is on fire. This happens so fast. The fire spreads across the carpet as if it's been soaked in petrol. The roar is deafening as the curtains ignite. I run for the door. A wall of flames stops me. The windows are unreachable; only the bed in the centre of the room is untouched. Climbing onto it, I cling to a post. Outside, I can hear Ink barking. Thank god she's safe. I try to get a grip. Not easy when your heart is pounding. I have my wand and, turning a circle, I spell some sort of barrier between myself and the flames. I fancy it stays back, although the room is blazing. Wallpaper curls in molten strips. The ceiling creaks. I hope the four-poster will keep me safe when it caves in.

Kneeling on the bed, I'm aware my phone is in the back pocket of my jeans. I take it out and call the fire service, but I have no signal. Moving around, I get one bar and try again. No joy. I poke at my phone in desperation. There's a thing on the bottom of the screen that says 'emergency'. I press that and I hear a ring tone. Who am I calling? The police, perhaps. One of the kids?

'Lilith?'

It's Grant Fucking Rutherford.

'Your house is on fire!' I wail over the sound of the burning.

'What?'

'It's burning down. Call the fire service.'

'Lilith, calm down. Where are you?'

'On your bed!'

'My bed?'

'Yes! Fucking Fox Lodge. It's on fire, you idiot. Do something.'

'Don't move. Draw a circle around you. Use your wand...'

'I've done that,' I say.

He's gone. I'm crying and I didn't even realise. The bedspread is thick and green, and I wrap it around me in the hope of protection and shut my eyes. I can't bear to see this beautiful house burn. It's all my fault. I should never have come. Outside, Ink howls. Poor dog. Grant will look after her. Mundane matters concern me. Who will ice a cake for tomorrow? The poor twins will be at school with no one to collect them. My daughter – how will she cope with her troubles without me? And the fucking curse! If I end up burning like my sister witches, the curse will go on ruining the lives of those I love.

I'm sobbing loudly – great wails of sorrow for fucking EVERYTHING – when Grant appears at the bedroom door. I screech out something or other. It's too dangerous for him to be here. And surely the entire house must be on fire by now.

He walks into the room. Through the roaring flames. Am I imagining this?

Then he's beside me, in the clearing where the flames cannot yet come. With outstretched arms, he calls to the inferno in the witch language, turning and speaking the words again and again. As he does, the fire abates. Flames shrink to nothing and disappear.

Then he takes me into his arms, lies on the bed and gathers me to him, cradling my head and holding me tight.

'It's all right. I've got you,' he murmurs into my hair.

It takes me a long time to stop shaking. I'm suddenly so tired. Then Ink leaps onto the bed, cold nose on the back of my neck. She rumbles her happy growl. We sit up and pet her. She lies on her back. 'You are a beautiful girl,' says Grant, rubbing her tummy.

Only then do I realise the room is not burnt to shreds. I'm wide eyed.

'It was spirit fire,' he says.

I slide off the bed and walk around the room. Point at the mantelpiece. 'There was a candle,' I say, totally bewildered.

'It was just an illusion spell.' He pushes Ink to one side and gets off the bed. She remains, legs in the air. Big doggy grin. She's in heaven.

He takes a log from the fireplace. Mutters a word and the wood flares alight. Automatically, I step back and I'm worried he'll burn himself.

'It's just a spell,' he says, taking my hand. I know what he's going to do. Every instinct goes against playing with fire. Then our hands are in the flames. Nothing. No warmth or pain. He stops the spell and tosses the unburnt log into the grate.

'You must think I'm a fool,' I say.

'No. If you've never come across it before, it can be scary.'

Especially when your ancestors were burnt at the stake.

'Ever heard the expression "no smoke without fire"?'

I nod.

'That's where it comes from. But it should really be "no smoke, no fire". What can you smell, Lilly?'

'Nothing.'

'Next time, have a good sniff. I'm surprised Ink's reaction didn't make you realise it was fake. She knows about spirit fire.'

'She was in the garden.'

'Ahh. Then she couldn't get back in. Probably because you stopped her.'

'Did I? I was glad she wasn't in here.'

'That'll do it. Come on, you and I need a cup of tea.'

In the kitchen, I sit at the table. 'Sorry, no milk,' he says, placing a Spode mug in front of me. His golden orts shimmer around him. He looks well. Then again, he got here pretty quickly – he must have been enjoying some quality time with the very lovely Rebecca.

'Why have you cast such a weird spell in your bedroom?'

'Why were you in my bedroom, Lilith?' he says, eyeing me over the top of his mug. I'm so embarrassed my cheeks are aflame. And they *are* hot.

Ink comes into the kitchen and Grant fills a bowl of water for her.

'My brother likes to set these little fires. It was his childhood trick.'

'Your brother's a shit.' I can see the binding spell over his face, fine as cobwebs over his mouth. I won't mention it. We both know I can see it and that he won't let me remove it. So fucking annoying.

'He is. But the fire was just an accident.'

'Accident! I could have died of shock.'

'It's just to keep intruders out.'

I put my mug in the sink. 'Then why do I have the distinct feeling that it was directed at me?'

Ink opens the door and goes outside. Finds a sunny patch on the lawn and stretches out.

Grant takes my hand and leads me into the garden. He's so confusing. I want to hold his hand, and I also want to slap him.

'He knows,' says Grant as we admire the vegetable patch. He frowns, rubs his arm where the Coven's mark is. 'He knows, Lilith. Barry knows you're searching for the burnt witch.'

'Do you have her? Is she here?'

He shakes his head. Manages one more word. 'Lost.'

As he speaks, his orts fade and I fancy he's in some pain. Emotional and physical. I reach to touch where the mark hurts him. I only want to soothe. Abruptly, he turns and marches back to the house.

I catch him up. 'Let me take it off you...'

'No!' Soft Grant has gone, and arrogant bastard is back.

'Be free of it. Of them. Not for me. For you.'

'Then what? What the fuck have I got? No Coven, no family? Probably no job, if I'm honest. It's not as simple as you think. You should go. Don't come back. It's not safe for you here.'

I cry as I walk along Fox Lane, a lot of emotion overspilling from multiple sources. I didn't find the burnt witch when I was so sure she was there. And now I can't fix anything. I've been frightened out of my wits by magic I didn't understand or realise existed, and I've made a bloody fool of myself – again. And as for Grant... I don't even know where to start about him. My feelings are a confused mess of anger, indignation and some other shit which I suppose is love, but I'm not going there. Definitely not going to think about how he held me on that ridiculous bed when I was frightened. Like he really cared.

He drives slowly past me in his big car, his face a stone. My fingers tingle with irritation. I'd like to do something. Cause a flat tyre, have a bird shit on his windscreen. I remind myself that I am not a vindictive witch. Instead, I give my nose a good blow and pat Ink, who leans against my legs in sympathy. 'Good girl,' I say.

We make our way along Fox Lane and I pick more blackberries. I have time to kill as it's not worth walking all the way home and then having to walk back again to get Amy and Sophie. Much better to go straight to school.

Even picking two more punnets of blackberries at a slow dawdle, I'm too early. I sit on a bench outside the still locked school gates and wait. There is no one here, so I call Walter and tell him what happened. When I've finished rambling on, Walter says, after his customary long pause, 'Interesting to consider what exactly young Mr Rutherford is trying to achieve with his fire spell. He's always keen to show the magical community that he's a powerful witch.'

'But you don't think so?'

'Well, he is. Spirit fire is no beginner's spell. And as you describe it, it sounds like it was quite a show. But the thing about being old, Lilly, is that you remember people before they got so big for their boots. And I remember little Barry trotting after his big brother. And when he was a spotty teenager. He was an arrogant little shit then, if I remember, even though his magic was weak.' He pauses and I wait. A few mums with toddlers and babies are chatting by the school gates now.

I lower my voice. 'So, what do you think he wants with Bethany's remains?'

'There's no doubt Barry's power is stolen. If you ask me, he's going to use the burnt witch for his own enhancement. And there's something else.'

'What?'

'You're the only one who can stop him.'

Chapter Thirty-Three

'Marswickham House Midsummer Ball! Bloody hell, you're going to the social event of the year. Are you excited?' says Cressida.

'Terrified. What exactly am I going to say to people?'

'Don't sweat it. Just be yourself,' she says, plonking mugs

of tea on the kitchen table. She's come over to help me get ready. I need an expert to transform me into a well-groomed woman of substance. This might take a while. I could do with a fairy godmother.

Cressida peers at my hands, which, like my feet, are soaking in a bowl of soapy water. I've already bathed and epilated my whole body – legs, arms, face. Especially the face. Cressida has wound my hair onto large rollers. Everything has been well moisturised, and I've trimmed my nose hair in case I get chatting to someone shorter than me.

Cressida gets to work on my battered hands. She doesn't moan about the state they're in and I'm grateful for that. Eventually, after a good scrub, file and a small battle with my cuticles, Cressida paints my stubby nails. Blue. I'm not sure about the blue.

'It will look nice with the yellow. Don't worry,' she says, shaking a bottle of topcoat.

'Don't think I've ever had this much nail polish on in one go,' I say.

I hold up my hands and toes and admire them. It is a pretty blue with a subtle sparkle. Cressida has done a lovely job, but there's no disguising my gardener's hands and welly-boot feet.

'Now,' says Cressida, leading me into the sitting room and depositing me on the easy chair. 'You're to sit here and no moving for an hour.'

'An hour!' I've got stuff to do.

'Yes. One hour. Anyway, it will do you good, a little rest.' She puts my mug beside me and an old magazine on my lap.

'Thanks. They look amazing.'

'Sorry, I've got to rush off.'

'Enjoy the wedding planner.'

Cressida looks at the ceiling. 'This wedding gets bigger every day.' Picking up her massive box of cosmetics, she says, 'Alexa, one hour.'

'One hour, starting now,' chirps the bot.

She's right, I do need a nap. It's been a busy morning; getting my old self party ready is no small task, and I've baked a cake – a nice chocolate and cherry sponge ready for Mrs Tingle to collect this evening. My overnight bag is packed and I only need to brush my hair and put on my very yellow frock. It's nice and quiet because Belinda and the twins are staying with friends. I'm asleep before Claudia has turned round three times in my lap.

The smart speaker wakes me up. I'm groggy with that horrible feeling when you need more sleep. Like trying to quench a thirst with a thimble of water instead of a pint. I put my specs on then take them off and polish them on my shirt. The rollers are sticking in my head, and I'll be glad to take them out. I swing my legs off the easy chair and admire my nicely painted toes.

Outside, Ink walks past in the long grass. On her back – yes, her back – is the chocolate and cherry cake. Am I still dreaming?

I tap on the window. 'Ink!'

Mid Witch Three

I've never known her to steal food before. Ink has done some strange things as befits her magical status – yet she is still a dog, and dogs must not eat chocolate. 'Ink!' I cry more loudly.

Upstairs, I can hear Jason speaking. He must be on the phone, so I don't bother calling for help. In the kitchen I put on a welly and a pink crock and pursue her.

'Ink, come here. Good girl!' She ignores me and walks carefully on. Can't be easy balancing a large celebration cake on her narrow back. She stops at the gate into the woods. I'm doing the jiggly middle-aged run. Grotty dressing gown flapping. Boobs bouncing. I'm not built for speed. 'Ink!'

The gate opens. Of course it does. She slinks into the woods. I put my fingers to my lips and whistle. All I get is a flustered blowing sound. In the woods, I stand on the path and call her. She's gone.

I need my wand and run to the cottage. Wand in hand, back I go. The wand is no help. Cross and indignant, I hurry along the path we normally take. Why can't things run smoothly? I just want to put on my frock in peace and be all ready and composed. My lift is in twenty minutes. And that cake is getting collected tonight and there is no way I will be able to make another in time, magic or no. 'Ink! Come back here, you naughty dog!' Mrs Tingle is going to kill me.

I stop and listen, hoping to hear her. Birds sing and the breeze rustles leafy branches. Suddenly, I'm filled with foreboding. What if she's eaten it and is lying somewhere unseen in need of a vet? I love her. I need her. 'INK!'

I'm crying now. All the nice mascara and foundation Cressida so carefully applied is on the move with my tears. What should I do? I'll have to get Jason to help me. I head for the cottage.

There she is.

Ink trots toward me. I'm on my knees checking her long snoot and inside her mouth. Did she eat it? I can't see anything or smell chocolate on her breath. I'm so relieved I don't care about the bloody cake. I'll just have to call Mrs Tingle and tell her what happened. Well, a version of it.

My stumpy yew wand is in my hand. 'Don't suppose you can tell me the time?' I say to it. Late. That's what it is. Kneeling on the path hugging my dog, I have another cry because I'm so relieved the daft creature is unharmed. 'What have you done with the chocolate cake?' I say and she gives me a sideways glance that shows the white of her eye. 'Ting-a-ling is my best customer. I hope you realise that,' I say, wiping my face on my dressing gown. Black mascara and foundation everywhere. She trots ahead along the forest path as if we are out for an evening stroll.

A small figure waits under a tree. I'm so shocked I nearly fall in the brambles.

'Mouse!?'

Ink greets him with a nonchalant tail wag. He's holding my cake and hangs his head in shame. 'I'm sorry, Lilith, for stealing your food.'

I step closer to the cake. It's untouched. 'I was going to bring this back. Honest. I can see it's special.'

I take the cake off him. 'What are you doing in my woods?' I say. Although the answer is obvious, really.

'I had nowhere to go.'

'Well, you can't stay here.'

'Yes. You're right. I'll pack up my tent and leave in the morning.'

'I mean come in the cottage. You can't stay out here. That's ridiculous.'

'What about the Coven?' he whispers.

'Fuck the Coven.'

Mouse laughs. 'That's the spirit, Lilith Blackwood.'

'Don't stay out here. It gets chilly at night,' I say, walking toward the cottage with the cake.

Mrs Tingle waits outside the kitchen door. 'There you are!' she says, looking at her watch.

'Lovely evening,' I say, all bright and chirpy.

'Is that my cake?' Subtext: why are you wafting about in the garden with it?

'Yes. So pleased with this one. I was just photographing it for Instagram,' I lie.

She gives me a suspicious glare and then stares at Mouse. I walk past her into the kitchen. 'Let me pop this into a box for you.'

Mrs Tingle is, for once, speechless. Mouse waits outside, clasping and unclasping his hands. A tiny figure in a long black coat. His shoes are pointed and his hair is long and straggly. He looks like he's escaped from a gothic horror novel.

It's only when Mrs T is mincing down the path with her

cake that I notice Mouse's orts. In the library, they were a pale grey mist. Now they shimmer blue and silver.

'Come in,' I say.

He shakes his head and remains where he is. 'I shouldn't have stolen from you,' he says.

'It's fine, Mouse. You were hungry and there's no harm done.'

He still won't come in.

'Touch your hand on the star. That's what people do.'

'Can't I just stay in the woods?'

A limousine pulls up in the lane. I'm not ready for the party and I can't think where Mouse could sleep. Even if he is tiny. North Star Cottage is already bursting at the seams. Mouse hugs himself as he watches the liveried chauffeur get out of the car. I hold Mouse's sleeve and pull him into the kitchen. He's such a small, frail man, it's not difficult. His beady eyes are bright and fearful, like a captured bird.

Jason comes into the kitchen. The chauffeur stands in the doorway and politely removes his cap. I'm aware Mouse and I both check if he has any orts. He doesn't.

'I've come to collect Lilith Blackwood,' he says.

'I'm, er, not quite ready. Small, er, crisis...' I say, looking down at myself. One welly and a pink crock. Mud, leaves and smeared make-up all over my bedraggled dressing gown. Hair in rollers.

'That's quite alright, Madam. Take your time. I shall wait in the car.'

'No. Come in. Have a cup of tea. Something to eat?'

He hovers in the doorway and pats Ink, who is sniffing him. He looks hungry. Not as hungry as Mouse, but hungry.

'This is my son, Jason. He'll make cheese toasties.'

Jason scowls at me. I give him my best mum glare. Ink wags her tail. She likes the word 'cheese.'

'This is Mouse. Friend of mine who's come to visit.' Mouse takes a bow. It really is a long time since he was out in the real world.

'Harold,' says the chauffeur, and also bows.

Jason's mouth is open.

'Mrs Tingle has collected her cake. There's a fresh loaf in the bread bin, and treacle tart in the fridge,' I say.

Chapter Thirty-Four

When I return to the kitchen forty-five minutes later, Jason and Harold are having a lovely chat. There's a good smell of toasted cheese and everyone looks happy and well fed. Mouse is blissfully munching chocolate chip cookies.

Mid Witch Three

'You look lovely, Mum,' says Jason. I give him a twirl and the big yellow dress flaps pleasingly around my legs.

Harold stands and puts on his cap. 'Shall we?' he says, taking my overnight bag.

The limousine is spectacular. Smooth leather seats and curtains at the windows. There is a selection of alcoholic drinks in little bottles and crystal glassware, of course. I don't touch anything.

'Sorry I kept you,' I say.

'Thanks for the sandwich.' He smiles at me in the mirror. 'Would you like some music? Drink?'

'No, I'm fine thanks, Harold.'

He nods and the glass partition glides up.

I try to enjoy some peace. Cressida's blue sequin evening bag is on my lap, tiny and sparkly with a strange bulge because I've stuffed my yew wand inside.

Annoyingly, I'm filled with trepidation. What if I'm the only one – having missed some vital memo – in a yellow dress? What if there is formal dancing like waltzing? I've no idea how to do anything like that. And I'm staying the night so no chance to sneak off early. I should have brought smarter clothes to wear in the morning. I've just chucked in a pair of jeans. And I'm so late.

Soon, we are winding along the tree-lined driveway to Marswickham House. Once through the trees, the house appears surrounded by sweeping lawns and clipped topiary. Expensive cars queue up and drop guests at the front steps. Turns out I'm fashionably late.

People are drinking champagne on the lawn in a cloud of yellow dresses. Then I realise I'll have to get my grotty holdall and carry it in. I'll leave it in the boot to save myself the embarrassment. Harold drives past the front entrance and takes a small road to the back of the house. The screen between the seats glides down. 'I have informed his Lordship that you have arrived, Madam,' he says.

'Please, call me Lilly,' I say.

'In that case, I've told Eddie and he's on his way to meet you.' He laughs. The door opens automatically, and I get out. Harold already has my holdall. I want to tell him to chuck it in the ditch.

My stomach is acidy. I should have eaten a snack. Edward, in a yellow bowtie, skips down a flight of stone steps. 'Gorgeous,' he says, kissing my cheek, tipping the driver and nodding at another member of staff who's appeared from nowhere to take my bag.

'Come on,' he says, hooking my hand over his arm. Inside is a small hallway. Doors with brass labels say things like Estate Manager and Housekeeper. Another door leads us into a marbled hall. There's a double sweeping staircase festooned with a garland of yellow flowers. Huge oil paintings. Marble statues. And I thought Fox Lodge was posh.

Guests chat, drink champagne and eat canapés. A string quartet plays *Eine Kleine Nachtmusik*. Edward stops beside a young man holding a large tray of drinks. 'What would you like?' he asks.

'Erm...?' An anti-acid tablet is what I'd like. I take a flute of champagne. He does the same, smiling at his guests. Everybody looks fabulous. And very yellow. For once, I'm not out of place.

'Good mix of people,' I say, admiring everyone. A tray of canapés floats past. I could do with a few slices of topped toast to settle my stomach.

'Yes, I think so too. I like a mix of ages. Good to have some young ones strutting their stuff. Otherwise it would just be us old fuddy duddys and we'd probably end up going to bed at ten with a cup of warm milk.'

'You must know a lot of people.' Stupid thing to say.

'Not really. Some are friends of either Felicity or myself. Some of the young ones are my youngest daughter's crowd. She's not embarrassed by her parents at a party. I'll have to work on that. And the rest... absolutely no idea. They're paying guests.' He leans closer and whispers in my ear, 'The proceeds from which will go toward modernising the septic tank.'

'Lovely.'

'Don't tell them.' He laughs. 'They think they're here to boost their social standing. But the truth is, they're here to fix my shit. Have you been to the house before?'

'No. I think the kids came on a school trip once.'

He scrunches up his face. 'Ew. School trips.' He pretends to shudder.

We're laughing now and I'm beginning to think this evening might be fun after all. 'Are they awful?'

'Even worse than my own kids.'

I imagine he has a few stories to tell about this, and I wait. Instead, he leads me into a group. 'Come and meet some people.' He lowers his voice again. 'Not cesspit funders.'

He introduces me to a group of well-dressed folk. It's a lot to take in, so I mumble banalities and hope for the best. I expect they will forget me immediately anyway. Another couple join us, and Edward introduces himself.

'John and Mary, how lovely to meet you! Have you met Lilly Blackwood?' he says with his hand on the small of my back. My daughter's in-laws are gobsmacked.

A tall waiter in a white jacket tinkles a bell and announces that dinner is served. Bifold doors slide open and the yellow clad visitors filter into the ballroom. Felicity glides over. 'Lilly!' she exclaims. 'So glad you came.' Her dress is sapphire blue, tight fitting with a fishtail skirt. We air kiss and her perfume, expensive and lovely, wafts over me.

She takes Edward by the arm. 'Duty calls. See you later,' says Edward with a wink. I watch them weave through the throng like royalty. They greet a few lucky guests as they go, then disappear through a side door.

The woman on my right wears a velvet strapless gown. 'Love your dress. Where did you find it?' she says. 'I had such trouble tracking down something yellow. Not exactly the colour of the season.' She gives the dress a hitch.

Mary steps closer to listen over the string quartet. John looks elsewhere. It's the first time we've met since we had an ill-advised yet pleasurable secret shag at Christmas.

Mid Witch Three

'I found it in Mabel and Green,' I say, and stop myself from mentioning the sale rail.

'Really? How clever. Never seem to get on with the high street. So much easier to shop online and then return what you don't want. Which is most of it.' She brays with laughter.

'Oh I do the same,' says Mary. 'Much safer.' She smiles down at me. 'I always like to have a choice. Even on the day I often change my mind. I'm very mood driven when it comes to clothes. Aren't I, darling?' She's wearing a yellow satin jump suit and very high heels. John looks like he'd run away if she wasn't clutching his arm. Proprietorial or a necessary precaution because of the heels?

'Exactly right. I'm just the same,' says the woman in velvet.

'Did you bring something else to wear?' asks Mary.

'Oh no. I'm a one dress at a time kind of woman.' All I can afford.

'Pity. You do realise you're wearing a nightie,' says Mary loudly.

More braying laughter. 'I knew I'd seen it before. Mabel and Green's Dreamy Nights photo shoot. It was in the County Magazine. What fun you are!'

'Saves time later, I suppose,' says Mary.

We saunter toward the ballroom. John looks at his feet. Mary hisses in my ear before she abandons me, 'Please don't come to our wedding vows ceremony in your nightclothes, Lilly.'

Absolute bitch.

Chapter Thirty-Five

The ballroom has a table seating plan in a large gilt frame in the entrance. There are thirty-four tables. I'm on thirty-four. Edward is far away at the other end of the room and I take my seat like an unwanted wedding guest. A pillar obscures most of my view.

Mid Witch Three

Soon I'm joined by three young couples. They all know each other and are already quite drunk. To give them their due, they introduce themselves and we exchange a few pleasantries, and then they forget me and get on with their evening.

I gobble a ping-pong ball-sized bread roll to settle my stomach. Football-sized is what I need, so I steal my neighbours' from both sides. Serves them right for sitting with their backs to me. Acid calmed, I try to enjoy myself anyway. The flowers are very pretty: balls of yellow chrysanthemums suspended from the ceiling over each table. The food – a choice between chicken or fish – is nice because I haven't had to cook it. Chocolate brownies make dessert and then coffee and mints. All very tasty, really. And while I've been sitting here alone, I've hatched a plan. I will order a taxi and leave.

I'll say there was a small crisis at home. Question is which crisis to pick. The strange witch librarian living in my woods. Hens that won't lay eggs. A dog that steals cakes. My grown-up son who plays video games all day and a daughter who's accidentally pregnant. Picturesque cottage that dislikes men. Oh, and I'm a witch and none of my family knows because I'm too scared to tell them.

Edward stands and dings the side of his wineglass. The buzz of conversation stops and he makes an amusing speech, judging by the bursts of laughter and spontaneous applause. Here at the edge of the room, it's hard to hear.

Guests leave the ballroom by a door that leads into the garden, and lanterns show the way along a path mowed into a wildflower meadow to a huge marquee where music plays. Along I go in my big yellow nightie. Might as well have a look.

Inside, I find a seat at the back and watch the dancing. I'm well camouflaged against the yellow silk interior. No sign of my date and I'm entirely confused by the music, so I creep out.

This midsummer night has a magical haze. An enormous moon rises above Marswickham House, and the garden has an ethereal glow. I wander along a path between herbaceous borders, white Marguerite daisies shining in the half light. The scent of mock orange blossom fills the air and lilies gleam in the moonlight.

Through a hedge arch, a pond reflects the moon's face as clear as a mirror. I kneel on the stones and dip the fingers of one hand into the water. With the other, I hold my wand inside the sparkly bag and make a wish. I whisper a witch's prayer for the protection and happiness of my family – words murmured by my mother whenever the moon was full, that I never understood until now. It would be nice to light a small fire and burn some herbs. It is the summer solstice, after all.

Then I see Bethany Blackwood.

She stands beside a yew hedge and watches me with pale ghost eyes. It's been weeks since I saw her anywhere but under the lychgate. Has she followed me here?

'Bethany?' I whisper. She moves away through a rose arch and over a lawn then glides through a croquet match in full drunken swing. No one sees her but me. I follow past a throng drinking cocktails on the terrace and into the house. Jacketless men play a game of billiards, bow ties loose around their necks. Women lounge about chatting and drinking on antique sofas. Like bits of lemon peel at the bottom of a glass. They are all too busy having fun to notice me. Bethany waits by a door on the other side of the room.

'Hello, buttercup,' says a deep, familiar voice. I turn and there's Grant. All golden orts and smiles. He's quite drunk.

I don't get a chance to speak. He holds me, warm hand on the side of my face, the other around my waist, pulling me close. Dark eyes gaze into mine. Then he kisses me. Full-on passion like before. My mind says no, but my body is a traitor. I'm kissing him back. Hands around his neck. Pressing myself against him. I'm only vaguely aware that the men are cheering.

When he lets go, we're both breathless. Another raucous cheer from the blokes and a few lewd suggestions. A blush, a hot flush, possibly both, creeps up my neck to my face. Not just a woman in a nightie. An embarrassed woman in a nightie. Great.

'I'd like to propose a toast!' says Grant, picking up a champagne flute. The men cheer and some stand and raise their glasses.

I can't imagine what he's going to say.

'This. This woman—' He teeters. Grasps the back of a chair for support. The women have stopped chatting. Everyone is watching. 'This woman is—' He takes a gulp of champagne. A few people from the terrace are standing in the doorway. I'm drawn to the one face I recognise. Barry Rutherford.

'This woman is the—'

Barry strides toward us. I grip my wand through the sequin bag. Rebecca, in a shimmering gold dress, glides over and takes Grant's drink away.

'Come on, honey. Time for bed,' she says. 'Take the other side, darling,' she says to me. I do as she asks, and we manoeuvre him through the door. Two big fellows dressed as waiters (but who are probably bouncers) emerge from the shadows of the hall.

'I'll take care of my brother,' says Barry, blocking the way.

'I've got this,' says Rebecca.

'Buttercup!' says Grant with a drunken smile. Then his legs give way and the two guys who were hovering nearby move in to help. They carry him like a sack of potatoes into a library and lay him on a couch. Rebecca puts a cushion under his head and gets her phone from her handbag. In the hall, I can hear a security/waiter bloke mumbling into a walkie talkie.

A cold fake fire burns in the grate. Barry's dark orts mingle with the flickering faux firelight. 'What the fuck are you doing here?' he snaps.

Grant is holding my hand, his grip warm and firm. I try to extract myself, but he's holding me tight. How embarrassing.

'I thought I told you to leave my brother alone.'

Grant sighs and moves our hands over his heart.

'Why don't you fuck off, Barry,' says Rebecca. She walks

smoothly across the room and murmurs to the security guard. Her dress is molten gold, cascading behind her like pools of liquid sunlight.

When she returns, I'm still stuck. It's like we can't let go of each other. Which is ridiculous. I'm about to start apologising to Rebecca – for the kiss and this, whatever this is – when Barry starts.

'Don't speak to me like that, you filthy whore,' he says.

'Why not leave before this all gets out of hand,' she says, calm and cool.

I give Grant's hand a tug. Nope. He's still got me.

'I thought I told you to stay away from him,' says Barry. It takes me a moment to realise he's speaking to her and not me. He lunges at her, but she scoots out of his way behind a wingback chair beside the fire. 'You repulsive bitch,' he says.

Rebecca's laugh is a tinkling stream. 'Only because you can't afford me,' she says. Barry makes another pounce. He's quicker than he looks. I flick my sequin bag at him and he bounces back as if he's been hit by a blast of air.

Now his anger is on me. I can do magic: no problem. But I'm slow. What I need is a magical self-defence class, if there is such a thing. Barry charges and grasps my wrist, twisting my hand behind my back. Now I can't use my wand. And, worse, his face is inches from mine. His breath smells of whisky and his dark eyes glint with malevolence. 'You dare to use magic in a public place in front of a non-magical. The Coven...'

'Don't threaten me with your corrupt Coven. I'm a free

witch, and unless you want the whole of Marswickham House to learn that magic is real, I suggest you let go of my arm and fuck off.'

Angry sparks fizz at my fingertips and my rainbow orts swirl around the room. Barry's stare wavers.

A shrill note slices the air. We both turn to Rebecca, who has a finger and thumb in her mouth. She whistles again, even louder this time, and seconds later a massive bloke jogs into the room. He assesses the situation and has Barry in a headlock before he can utter a word.

'Could you escort this twat off the premises, please, Pete?'

Pete walks away with Barry's head under his arm. I tap Grant's hand gently with my sparkly bag and he lets me go with a sigh. He's out cold.

'Are you alright?' we say together and then laugh.

The bouncers/waiters return. 'He's in the blue room. Would you like us to take Mr Rutherford up for you, Madam?'

'That would be most kind.'

Rebecca takes me by the arm. In the hallway people are gathering ready to leave. The large front doors are open, and expensive cars crunch on the pea gravel.

'No thinking about leaving,' says Rebecca, reading my mind. 'When the paying customers depart, the party truly begins.' She leads me in the opposite direction through a set of doors into a large dining room where a buffet is set out. She hands me a plate. 'Men. They really are so much trouble. Sorry about G. I should have kept a closer eye on him.

Mid Witch Three

He's been in a state since he saw Eddie with his arm around you.' As we file along the buffet, she loads her plate and mine.

'I'm sorry,' I blurt.

'For what? Smoked salmon?'

I nod. 'For the whole kiss thing. It was...'

Rebecca is laughing. 'Come along, darling. Let's find a quiet spot so we can eat and chat.'

In the garden, strings of lights sparkle in the trees, and chairs and tables are set out here and there. Soft music plays. She picks a table set apart. 'There was a kiss?' she says, shaking out a linen napkin. 'Good. I told him to kiss you. I didn't think he would. Edward might not be too pleased.'

She's so beautiful even at this time of night. Can't think why he's kissing me. I've lost the thread of this conversation. I was going to apologise for my appalling behaviour.

She pats my hand. 'He loves you. You do realise?'

'Rebecca. What exactly is your, er, relationship with Grant?'

Another peal of laughter. 'Just as Bastard Barry said. I'm a whore, darling. Although I prefer the term "lady for hire".'

I wipe my glasses on my nightie. Put them back on. Nothing seems clearer.

'G has, er, certain needs. But I suppose you know about that. Being a witch yourself.'

'Yes.'

'We've known each other for years. He's complicated. That brother of his is a piece of work and there's something very odd about their relationship. He never tells me anything about that side of himself. Apart from a few basic facts.'

The hulking form of her bodyguard hovers on the edge of the gathering. She smiles at him and he nods. 'Thanks for teaching me to whistle. So useful if I can't get my phone to play ball. I used to carry a whistle, but now Pete the Meat's happy. He likes to keep me in earshot.'

'Do you take him everywhere with you?'

'Every girl needs a faithful pet to protect her,' she says, arching an eyebrow.

Suddenly I'm starving.

Chapter Thirty-Six

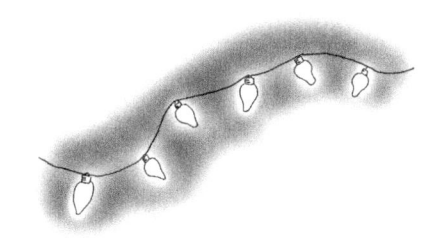

I'm glad I stayed. This part of the evening is less formal. Guests kick off their shoes and dance on the lawn. Rebecca and I sit in companionable silence and watch the party. Edward reappears. He gives me a wave as he networks with his guests. A joke and a chat here, a shake of a hand and a slap on the back there. A man born to social situations.

'Have you been seeing Lord Edward long? Or is this a new thing?' asks Rebecca.

'Not long.'

It's clear she has a few things she'd like to say, but Edward is here. 'Ahh, ladies,' he says, pulling up a chair.

'Lovely party,' says Rebecca.

'So much easier when the weather behaves.'

'Not like last year,' she says.

'We had a thunderstorm fit for a horror movie. I was still damp a week later,' he says. He's friendly but something is off. No doubt he's heard about Grant's drunken kiss.

'House looks divine. Love the new lighting,' says Rebecca. There are strings of white lights everywhere: in the trees, on the house and looped on poles over lawns and flowerbeds.

'Allingshire Symphony Orchestra next week. Our first outdoor concert. All Felicity, of course. I never have an idea outside of the farm.'

We admire the house, which is skilfully lit to accentuate the architecture. Bethany Blackwood hovers in an upstairs window. I ignore her.

Rebecca crosses her legs. Such a subtle flirtation. Edward tries not to stare at her ankle and her dainty feet in red-soled sandals.

'I hear there was a spot of bother,' he says.

Here we go.

Mid Witch Three

'The Rutherford brothers had another fight,' says Rebecca.

'I heard he clutched you in the billiards room,' says Edward, studying the wine in his glass. Yes, he is a bit peeved.

'He was drunk. I'm alright.' I can still feel Grant's kiss and his hand grasping mine.

'Such naughty boys,' laughs Rebecca. 'We put G to bed and Pete sent Barry home.'

'Oh, you brought Pete the Meat?' says Edward with a laugh.

Rebecca nods toward the terrace where the huge man stands beneath a potted palm. 'That's me,' she says. 'Ever cautious.'

'Right, must continue my social duties,' he says, smiling amiably, but he avoids my gaze as he leaves.

'Do they argue a lot?' I say.

'The brothers? Only when G gets drunk. Which happens about once a year. Although we might get two fights this year. Christmas is usually a trigger.'

I'm all ears, but Pete steps from under the potted palm and gives Rebecca a nod. 'Sorry, darling, but I must go.' The gold dress cascades as she stands.

'You're not staying?'

'No. I'm off to Paris for a few days.'

Work or pleasure, I wonder. She shimmers over the lawn and every man stares.

I sit alone and observe the party. It's thinning out. People must be going to bed – or leaving. I search for Edward as I walk back into the house.

'Can I help you, Madam?' A tall butler glides out of nowhere.

'Looking for Edward.'

'I believe his Lordship is taking a moonlit dip in the great pond,' he says.

I have a brief mental image of Mr Darcy in wet breeches.

'Would Madam care to join him? Or shall I show you to your room?'

'I'm really tired,' I say truthfully.

'Very good, Madam. Right this way.'

The room is so big even the enormous bed appears small. I'm so tired I hardly register that my clothes, such as they are, have been put in the wardrobe. My toiletries are in the bathroom. Must be nice to have staff.

I brush my teeth, clean off my makeup, slather my face in a cream optimistically named 'eternal youth' and wriggle out of my underwear, keeping the offending nightie on. The bed is vast and soft and the nightie is very comfortable. Sleep claims me instantly.

I wake much later and lie still. A quietness has descended on Marswickham House. The party has ended. Edward has not joined me, and I'm unsure if I'm disappointed or relieved.

In the half dark of the summer night, my eyes soon adjust. I see the unfamiliar shapes of furniture and patterned wallpaper. Sleep is what I need. I'm always ghastly after a late night as it is. Then I have the prickling sensation of being watched and slide my hand under my pillow for my wand.

'Edward?' I say, sitting up.

Not a sound.

'Hello?'

I decide I'm being silly, and I'm about to switch on the light when Bethany drifts into view.

She waits by the door, a determined look on her little ghost face. Obviously, she wants me to go with her. She won't give up.

I slip on trainers and a cardigan and grab my wand – because you never know what life will throw at you, even at this time of night. Wand in hand, I follow Bethany along the hallway. She's in a hurry, and I hope she doesn't get me lost. Marswickham House is vast and creepy in the dark. Which is ironic – as I'm following a ghost. We pass through rooms I saw at the party then up a flight of backstairs. The door at the top is locked. Bethany folds her arms and twirls around and around. She knows this annoys me. A quick spell opens it.

The room beyond is dark. Tall windows are tightly shuttered, so I click my fingers for a flame to see by. Packing cases and tea chests fill a long narrow room. Dust sheets cover the furniture, and there are stacks of paint pots and decorating equipment. A room on Edward's restoration list. He has spoken about opening the Tudor part of the house to the public. The wooden floor creaks, and I have the sense the old place is aware of me.

Bethany hovers ahead, her youthful face pinched in

concentration. Somewhere an old clock ticks, steady as a heartbeat. She darts behind the stacked antiques, and I thread my way between the boxes. A shimmer of white takes me to her. She points at a tea chest, nailed shut. I hold my flame to the label: 'Curiosities collected by Lord Horatio Wootton – 1804–1810'. Bethany's pale hands caress the lid.

If I was a hero, I would not hesitate. I'd pry off the lid and find the urn containing her ashes. For that is surely why we're here. But middle age sensibilities grip me. I can't just break open a box in someone's house and pilfer one of their antiques.

Can I?

In the darkness, the ghost is vivid. She's so small and delicate. So young. She clasps her hands at her breast.

'I'm going to look. That's all,' I say, and slowly she nods once.

I fold open a window shutter to give enough moonlight to see by and put out my witchflame. Then I run my wand around the lid and mutter a freeing spell. It's good for knots and stuck jam jar lids. Twice more I speak, and one by one the nails loosen and pop free. I slide the lid off. The chest is full of sawdust, and I brush some aside, expecting to find an array of small objects that a Victorian gentleman would have collected. I delve deeper and deeper. Nothing. Then my fingertips find an object. It's big and heavy. I nearly crick my back heaving it out.

It's a carved casket, the lock welded shut. It's bound by metal strips – and more. I kneel with my hands upon it and perceive the spells of other witches. Their voices whisper down the ages, 'Keep away.'

This is her. The corporeal remains of Bethany Blackwood. I recognise her presence within just as surely as I see the ghost before me. Glued on the lid is a tatty label. In the moonlight, I read the words, 'burnt witch'.

Not even a name.

Chapter Thirty-Seven

I'm so enraged that Bethany is reduced to a curiosity, middle-aged sensibilities are forgotten. I steal her.

Another spell from the household magic section in my family grimoire – this one for locating hidden objects – finds me a sack trolley.

Mid Witch Three

With the casket safely on, I put the lid on the box, close the shutter and leave. As I bump my load down the stairs as quietly as possible, I tell myself that this is a sensible thing to do. No one will know and it will save me having to explain to Edward why I need him to give me an old casket containing the remains of my ancestor. This way may be a little dishonest, but it keeps my witchy self a secret and, most importantly, keeps Bethany from Barry's immoral grasp.

Finding a side door, I leave the sack trolley in a flower bed and return to my room for my belongings. I'm quick. Well, as quick as a flat-footed, slightly overweight midlife hag can be.

In the garden, the dawn chorus begins and the sky lightens. It would be beautiful if I wasn't shit scared and boiling hot. I hurry over the lawn in the general direction of the road and stop beside a lush herbaceous border to catch my breath. From here, specimen trees hide the house. I'd be so much better able to cope if I was wearing a bra. And some knickers. Behind a clump of delphiniums, I reinstate my underwear.

Lord Wootton keeps his walls in good repair, and it takes ages to find a gap where a tree has fallen on the boundary wall. I stagger over the rubble with the sack trolley to the road and call a taxi.

The tired taxi driver doesn't ask questions. I suppose they see a lot of weird stuff. Middle-aged old bag in a nightie on a country road with a loaded sack trolley and an ugly handbag is probably the least of it.

At North Star Cottage, Ink hurtles down the path to greet me and Maud perches on the casket, which is not helpful.

Exhausted, I carry it into the cupboard under the stairs and hide it with old coats and dog blankets. What's really weird is the sensation of heat; I examine my hands, expecting them to be burnt. But I'm too tired to think, and I flop onto the easy chair. Ink joins me and we sleep.

What seems seconds later, Jason is nudging me awake. 'Mum! What's that smell of burning?'

I'm woozy. 'Oh, it's probably just...' I eye the cupboard in case smoke is curling under the door. It's not. 'Probably a bonfire,' I say as he heads into the kitchen.

'Bloody stinks,' he says.

When he's gone, I crawl into the cupboard and check for fire. No fire. Good. Might need to find a better hiding place until I can arrange a burial, though.

'Would you like some toast, gorgeous?' Jason is talking to the dog. I dash upstairs for a shower before the morning chaos.

After I've dropped the twins to school, I call Walter as I walk along Church Lane. He doesn't say much. I think he's a bit shocked.

In the early afternoon I'm back on the easy chair having a tactical nap before the twins need collecting. The whole place is a tip. Or, more accurately, a laundry. With Jason lurking, I couldn't hide the casket in my attic room, so I've hidden it in the secret cupboard and left the bedroom window open to dispel the smoky smell. I've scrubbed some jacket potatoes for tea because that's all I can think of. Edward has not been in touch, even though I messaged him a thank you. I suspect he is more pissed off about the kiss than I realised. Probably why he politely ignored me all night and did not join me in bed. Am I bothered? I'm not entirely sure.

I expect to sleep; I've been up most of the night. Instead, I lie there listening to Claudia purr and Ink's gentle snore. I've found Bethany's earthly remains and I should be pleased, or at least relieved. But now I have more problems. A headstone and interment are the physical practicalities. More pressing is what else needs to be done to lift the curse.

Jason clatters down the stairs, making Maud, perched on my foot, spread her wings in alarm. 'How was the party?' he says, getting a coat from the cupboard under the stairs.

'Nice,' I say.

'Off out. See you later...'

'Back for tea?'

'Don't wait up!' The door slams and he's gone.

Now I'm alone in the cottage, I'm wide awake and the casket beckons. Ink, Maud and Claudia streak up the stairs ahead of me. They know exactly where I'm going and wait outside the secret door in the back bedroom. Bethany, who I have not seen since last night, wrings her hands.

I brush my fingers over the wall and the hidden panel slides open. The walk-in closet is chock full. I drag the casket into the room, Walter's warnings about not opening it ringing in my ears as if he stands beside me: 'Curiosity killed the witch,' were his exact words. My heart beats and sweat prickles my armpits.

I kneel on the carpet and place my hands on the dark

wood. The strange carvings press against my palms – something inside wriggles to be free. I close my eyes to sense the magic of other witches. A group spell. So many enchantments, like the layers of an onion, have kept it hidden and tight shut for hundreds of years. A jolt of recognition and a deepening of the power. What was once a locking spell becomes a curse aimed at a Blackwood witch. Faded voices whisper in my head, 'Be gone.' But I can't stop now. Not when I'm so close.

Bethany hugs herself by the door. There is something about her face that reminds me of my granddaughters. The curve of her cheek, the tilt of her nose. A family resemblance that cannot be denied. I owe it to her, to all of us.

I take my wand out of my pocket and a few leaves from the blackwood trees and speak the spell word I need to free the binding. It works. Even though I've used the simplest spell, the physical lock clicks open. The metal ties drop away and the binding spell releases with a sigh. I swallow and slide off the lid.

A body. Even bound in layers of cloth and leather, she's still tiny. And I know it's her. I recognise her magic – even in these charred bones. Bethany is a part of me, and I am a part of her.

'Bethany,' I whisper, placing my hand over her heart.

Here she is. Intact. I thought I'd only find ashes. And if a body, I expected it to be violated. I've read how witch remains were driven through with iron spikes or crushed beneath stones. This body was interred with love. Around her are packets of things she liked in life. I don't need to open them to learn their contents – simply placing my wand on my forehead activates my third eye. I see everything. A cotton dress dyed with woad, bright as a summer sky. A corn dolly woven for the infant child she would never see grow up. A lover's knot bound onto a hag stone and a gold wedding ring tied on a ribbon around her neck.

Beside me, the ghost hovers, brighter than I've ever seen her. So much magic is instinctual if you trust it. I reach my free hand to the glowing ghost, my other still over the heart, and in one shuddering flash the two become one.

I know deep within myself that at last she is at peace, and more – part of the curse is lifted.

I stay for a long time with her, my mind full of visions of her life. I see North Star cottage as it was then: a small two-room dwelling in deep woodland. What I learn is love. Bethany was once a lively girl full of laughter and magical spirit. I'm so incredibly happy I've found her. Then I cry for this lost member of my family and the unfairness of life.

When I pull myself together, my knees are protesting and my neck is cramped. I slide the lid on, shove the casket back inside the secret closet and close the panel with a sweep of my hand. The small room is oddly empty without Bethany, and another wave of sadness hurts my heart. Ink puts her snoot into my hand, and I pet her sleek head.

I've been so engrossed, it is only as I start downstairs that I hear banging. Someone is knocking on the kitchen door. I hurry, Maud on my shoulder, dog and cat at my heels. It's loud and someone is shouting my name with some urgency. God I hope the kids are alright.

Ink gets there first and opens the door. Two police officers stand on my step. My heart sinks. Jason. Belinda. The twins. Oh my god, there must have been an accident. I grip the door to brace myself for bad news.

'Ms Lilly Blackwood?' says the policewoman.

'Yes.'

'You're under arrest.'

Chapter Thirty-Eight

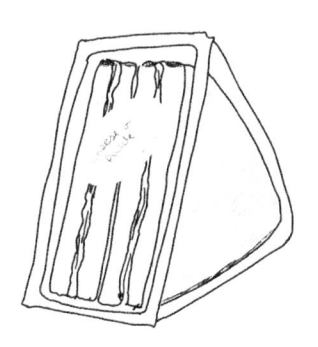

I sit on the hard bed in the police cell and stare at my hands, the fingertips slightly blackened from when they took my fingerprints. I'm in a daze. It's all been a bit of a blur. All I could think of when I was being driven to

Barrington was who was going to collect the twins from school. To be fair, they let me make a phone call, and I left a message with the office at Belinda's school. Obviously not mentioning that I was getting arrested for theft. I hope Belinda assumes I'm just off for a fling with Lord Wootton.

Oh my god. Edward. I pace up and down the small space. Metal door with a hatch and a spyhole. Toilet and tiny sink in the corner and a bed. No window. No clock. No Big Bag and no phone. It is very clean, though, and I have been given a large paper cup of water.

Why was I so stupid? I'm sure I could have spoken to Edward and made some sort of arrangement. Bought the casket off him fair and square. Pretended I had a crazy passion for ancient witch remains. Or told him the truth. After all, Rebecca is not a witch, but she knows about us.

Without my wand and the pouch I always wear around my neck to ward off hexes, I'm vulnerable. Especially in Barrington. Any moment, I expect a dark stain to seep beneath the door.

Eventually, a policewoman comes in. 'Lilith Blackwood,' she says, checking her clipboard.

'Yes,' I say.

'Sorry about the delay. So busy today!' she says, as if I've been queuing in a coffee shop.

She looks at me for the first time. 'Lilly!'

I made a cake for her mum's fiftieth. Lemon sponge decorated with sugared violets. Wendy sits beside me on the bed.

Mid Witch Three

Neither of us can believe I'm here. She checks her notes. Clears her throat. 'We can take you for questioning right now. Well, in about twenty minutes. And that might be the best thing. There's obviously been a misunderstanding. They think you were caught on a security camera stealing. A quick chat to put things right?' She looks at me and smiles. I don't smile back. Or say anything. What can I say?

'Or we can organise a solicitor for you. But they won't be here until tomorrow. Or you can appoint your own representation.'

'I'd like you to call my solicitor.' My dad.

Without a clock or phone, I'm disorientated. I'm given a sandwich, which I can't eat for worry. I lie on the bed in a stupor. What will the kids think? Will I be put in prison? Will I have to tell them the truth about myself and, if so, what will they think? Well, I know what they'll think. Belinda will assume I'm delusional, and Jason will barely register the news before returning to his video game.

There is a tiny camera in the corner, which I find very disconcerting. It makes me refrain from weird witchy stuff like clicking sparks from my fingers. A simple spell would open the door. Another bad idea. I must wait for Walter. He'll have a plan, won't he?

Eventually, sleep takes me. Not surprising; I've been up all night stealing. I don't know how burglars do it. When the door lock clicks, I'm dreaming. I jump up at the sound. Different police officer this time: middle-aged fellow who looks like he was asleep too. He takes me to a room and, after a brief wait, Walter hobbles in on two sticks. I have a pang of guilt. Poor old Walter. This is the last thing he needs. On the contrary, he is bright eyed and smartly dressed in a green three-piece suit with a daisy in his buttonhole.

When we're alone, he reaches over and pats my hand. 'Well, Lilly, you'd better tell me everything that happened at Marswickham House.'

I tell him my foolish tale and leave nothing out not even the kiss and the altercation with Barry. How embarrassing.

Walter has his usual think and I wait. 'I thought you had a thing for the Rutherford boy,' he says at last.

'It's complicated.' My love life is not really what I want to discuss.

'I bet. Especially if you're seeing Woolly Wootton.'

'Woolly?'

'Sheep farmer. The two houses go back a long way. The Rutherfords had the cloth mills and the Woottons provided the wool.'

I rest my head on my arms. I don't think I can take another family feud.

'Both sides have a version of events. In a nutshell, the Rutherfords owed money for the wool and couldn't or wouldn't pay. They say they couldn't because of a bad debt. Lost ship taking cloth to the Americas. Anyway, let's just say they never really made it up. The Woottons gave up on the cloth trade and exported lamb meat for considerable financial gain. They were early adopters of refrigerated ships.' Walter steeples his fingers.

'So why did they have Bethany?' I say, wishing we had a nice pot of tea.

'Now this is interesting and not common knowledge. A few generations later, the Rutherfords, to curry favour, gifted them a number of curios. The Woottons were avid collectors at the time. So Bethany must have been part of the collection. She could have been given in all innocence.'

'What! The Rutherfords not know what was in that casket!'

'Exactly. Which is why I suspect it was included in the gift in the hope it would bring the Woottons bad luck. Either that or the Rutherfords hoped that giving it away would free them from the curse.'

'But the Woottons – they seem to be okay?'

'Money is their problem. They're always teetering on the edge of financial disaster. Only this year, Eddie was in the office considering his options for selling. And I think he would if his wife was not so attached to the old place.' Walter raps his knuckles on the table. 'Which is good for us in our current situation.'

I can't think how any of this helps. One of his walking sticks slips from its resting place on the edge of the table and I catch it before it hits the floor.

'Witch reflexes,' he says as he takes it off me. 'I've sent Joan over to his Lordship with a fat cheque. People short of money are always easy to deal with.'

'But I can't let you...'

'Don't be ridiculous, child. I'm a wealthy man, and all of it will be yours soon, anyway.'

'I don't like the sound of soon,' I say, and suddenly I'm crying like the big idiot I am.

'Now come on,' he says, pushing himself up and hobbling around to me. We hug. 'All these long years I've been denied helping you.' He chuckles. 'What's a father for if not to get his kid out of jail and buy her a corpse?'

We're both laughing now. It does all seem faintly ridiculous.

He taps on the door with his stick. Gives me a card from his wallet. 'I anticipate you'll be out first thing in the morning all charges dropped. Joan is a very persuasive woman. You'll be rattled. Ring my driver and she'll take you home. I hardly go anywhere these days. It'll do her good to do some work.'

Early next morning, the door opens. Wendy is all smiles. 'You're free to leave,' she says. I follow her to a desk where a young officer reunites me with my personal belongings. Big Bag is in a big plastic bag and the contents are in another. Some items are bagged and labelled. The pouch with the sea glass reads, 'magic charm'. They're right about that. I take it out and put it on with relief. My wand label reads 'piece of old wood'. Half right.

'Well,' I say, hefting Big Bag on my shoulder and signing for my stuff. 'Glad that misunderstanding is all sorted out.'

Wendy and the officer exchange a knowing glance. She's

still grinning. And I realise this is not friendliness, it's curiosity. I stand there like a fool.

'The exit is that way,' she says, nodding to a helpful arrow on the wall.

'I'm free to go? Yes, thanks.'

'Seems like it,' she says.

I follow the arrow. Their voices echo after me: 'That's the last cake I'm ordering off her. Bloody weirdo.'

Chapter Thirty-Nine

It's so early the shops in Barrington are not yet open. I wander along hoping I don't look like I've spent the night in jail. My legs are wobbly, I feel grubby and I could do with a mug of tea, some toast and a good cry. Not necessarily in that order.

Mid Witch Three

My phone is flat. So no chance of contacting Walter's driver for a lift home. I hope the kids aren't worried. There's a small scruffy café that looks closed even though a sign on the door reads, 'Come in, we're open'.

I go in, sit in a booth and plug my phone into the charger. Seconds later, it's pinging. Here we go.

Belinda wants to know where I am and when I will be back. Nothing from Jason. He's oblivious these days. I must have a chat with him soon about wasting his life. There is a text in shouty capitals from Edward: 'WE NEED TO TALK'. Sounds ominous. Nothing from Grant Fucking Rutherford. Then again, he's probably still hung over or gone to meet Rebecca in Paris.

'What do you want?' A young woman with no expression stands by the table.

'Tea, please.'

'Eating?'

'Er...'

'Breakfast food, yes?'

'Er, yes.'

A cardboard menu is propped between the salt and pepper, but she's already gone. I'm too knackered to choose, think or argue. Let miss grumpy bring me breakfast food, whatever that may be.

My phone bleeps. It's Walter. 'Can you talk?'

'Yes,' I say, looking at the empty tables.

'Good. You're out, I take it.'

'Yeah I'm out. Just having a cup of tea in a café round the corner.' Can't bring myself to say, 'from jail.'

'Pleasant.'

'Not really,' I say, twiddling a pot of plastic grass that looks like it belongs in a fish tank.

'No, the café. Are you in Pleasant's?'

I check the menu. 'Yes.'

'Sit tight. I'll be there shortly.'

I doze off, I'm so bloody tired. Walter and the food arrive together. Unlike me, he looks great. Yellow waistcoat, natty tie with moons and stars on, rosebud in his buttonhole. White hair neatly parted. Face closely shaved. I expect my own chin hairs need attention. I refrain from touching my face for tell-tale spikes; it will only distract me.

'You want Food?' says the waitress as she plonks a fried breakfast in front of me, then a metal teapot and a chipped white mug.

'Food and coffee and something extra for my furry friend.'

Things must be worse than I thought. I'm stroking my chin as Walter reaches into his briefcase and lifts out a rat.

'I don't think you've met my familiar,' he says, putting the creature on the table between us. The black and white rat regards me with shiny black eyes.

'Hello there,' I say, offering the little fellow a small crust of bread.

'His name's Atlas. Obviously.'

It's then I see that the rat's markings resemble a map.

Mid Witch Three

Atlas takes the crust, examines it, puts it down and then wanders about for a sniff.

'Come on, eat up before it gets cold,' he says.

I take a bite of sausage and remember how hungry I am. A fried breakfast is not what I should eat but is exactly what I need. Soon Walter's breakfast arrives. 'Ahh, death on a plate.' He smiles. 'Just what the doctor ordered.'

The waitress returns with a saucer of sliced fruit and an espresso cup of water, which she sets before Atlas the rat. 'He's looking well,' she says, stroking him gently. 'How old did you say he was?'

'Gosh, hard to remember. Must be twelve now,' says Walter with a twinkle in his eye.

We watch Atlas tuck into his fruit while we eat. 'You come here often then?'

'Generally, once a week. More when the weather is bad. We've been regulars since I discovered Gerda prefers animals to people.'

Atlas takes a sip of water and then sits on his haunches to give his face and whiskers a wash. 'Is he twelve?' I ask.

'Who knows? I've had him since I was a lad. One of the blessings of witchcraft – our pets don't die, and they can do useful things.'

I wonder what Atlas can do, but Walter moves our plates to one side and lifts a yellow legal pad from his briefcase.

'Unfortunately, we've run into a few glitches regarding Bethany and Lord Wootton.'

'Go on,' I say, suppressing a sigh.

He taps the pad with his fountain pen. 'Turns out Lord Wootton has big plans for Bethany.'

'Like what?'

'He's planning to make a feature of the witch's remains. Use it as a tourist magnet. Apparently, he has a whole witch-themed attraction prepared and is a keen collector of magical artefacts.'

'So, he's not selling,' I say, remembering Edward's intense fascination with objects at North Star Cottage.

'No. Not even persuasive Joan could get him to change his mind. She offered a substantial sum of money, but he thinks keeping Bethany would be better for the future of Marswickham House in the long term.' Walter lifts a knitted woolly hat from his case and puts it on the table. Atlas climbs in and curls up for a nap.

'Except he hasn't got her. I have.'

'He was adamant that he will press charges against you if you don't return the casket intact,' says Walter, giving Atlas a pat.

'I've already opened it.'

'Ahh. That does complicate things.' His deep frown suggests there's something more. I wait.

'Barry Rutherford is involved.'

'He's wasting his time. I already reunited the ghost and her remains. The curse is nearly gone. No question about it.' I can't help smiling at the memory.

'That's good.' He loosens his tie.

'He can have the casket. I'm sure it can be restored. But

her body needs to be buried with dignity. In the graveyard with the rest of us.'

'I agree. And you could probably persuade your boyfriend to make the right decision. But now Barry is involved, it's a lot more complicated.'

'Complicated how?'

'Turns out Barry has been enlisted as an expert.'

'An expert in what?'

'The history of witchcraft and magic.'

'What bollocks.'

'Indeed. Nevertheless, he has Edward's ear in all matters concerning the museum, and he's telling him that without the burnt witch the entire project will be useless.'

My fingers tingle with irritation. 'I'll tell him the curse is over…'

'I don't think he cares about the curse. He wants Bethany to enhance his power. That's for sure.'

Atlas is blissfully asleep. Lucky rat.

'There's a lot of ancient magic in that corpse,' I say.

'Keep her hidden. Let me have a think. It's always better to let things lie for a few days so everyone can cool off. Maybe Edward will change his mind if you speak to him.'

'And explain Barry is a complete dick.'

'Exactly.'

The problem is, they might both be complete dicks.

Chapter Forty

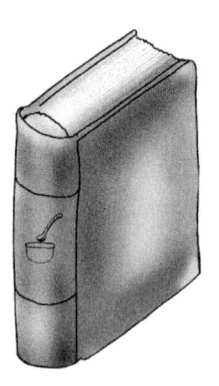

Hilda, Walter's driver, takes me home. She drives the old Bentley smoothly and wordlessly. Soon I'm asleep. I'm still asleep when she opens the door and pats my leg. I've keeled over on my side clutching Big Bag, dribbling all over the leather upholstery. She reaches out a huge hand to pull me up, her face blank. No doubt she's seen it all. I hope I wasn't snoring.

It's only after I've thanked her and watched the car bounce over the potholes along Church Lane that I realise a car is parked outside the cottage. Edward's car. Here we bloody go.

Walking up the path, I wonder where my familiars are. They normally greet my return like I'm a conquering hero. Especially Ink. Apart from a few chickens pecking around the yew tree, my homecoming is unheralded. Maybe Jason has taken Ink for a walk. There's always a first time.

The kitchen door is open, and Jason and Edward are sitting at the table having coffee.

'Mum. Where have you been?' Jason says, folding his arms.

'Oh, erm...' I say, suddenly aware what a mess I am. Ink is lying across the doorway to the rest of the cottage. Her tail thumps the ground. I know exactly what she's doing: she's guarding Bethany's remains. There's no way anyone is getting past her. Clever dog. She flops her head down – giving a perfect impression of a hound relaxing. But one ear is cocked. 'Good dog, Ink,' I say as I step over her and head upstairs.

'Mum!' calls Jason. I ignore him. Must have a minute to myself before I face any deep conversations regarding the dead body I've stolen and hidden in my secret closet.

I take a quick shower and tie my wet hair into a ponytail, brush my teeth, epilate my moustache and slap cream on all areas. Then I pull on clean jeans and a shirt. With a dash of lipstick, I'm ready to face the music.

Jason passes me on the stairs. 'Come on, Mum,' he whispers. 'I've got work to do!'

Unlikely.

Jason holds my arm. 'He's been here bloody ages. Have you two had a row or something? He seems pretty agitated. He was convinced you were upstairs and insisted on looking for you. Well, he tried, but Ink got shirty so he thought better of it.' I bet he did.

'It's fine, love. You get on. I'll tell you about it later.' Much later.

'And,' he says, lowering his voice, 'I think there's someone living in the woods.'

I pat his arm and scoot past. Mouse is tomorrow's problem.

In the kitchen Edward is rubbing his head. *Mrs Beeton* is on the floor at his feet. 'That book just fell off and hit me,' he says, checking his fingers as if expecting blood.

'It does that,' I say, picking it up and returning it to its place on the dresser. 'Tea?' I fill the kettle.

'No, thank you. Lilly, I don't know what came over you. But you need to give the burnt witch back.' His voice is deep and commanding.

'I can't,' I say, facing him.

'Now look here.' He slaps a palm on the table and stands. 'I've had quite enough of this nonsense. Whatever you're playing at, it stops now. Do you hear me?' I haven't seen this side of him or heard him raise his voice. A pulse beats on his temple and his cheeks are red. Ink places herself between us and curls her lip. They're both so much less cute when they're angry.

'Calm down, Edward,' I say. Oddly, I am perfectly relaxed. I make a pot of tea and we sit at the table. Ink gives herself a shake.

'Why is Barry Rutherford involved?' I say.

'I'm asking the questions,' he says. Pompous arse. I pour the tea and push a mug toward him with the sugar bowl. He looks at it like it's poison. Clears his throat.

I sip my tea and wait. He huffs a sigh.

'Fine,' he says. 'I was at County Hall with my proposal for an extension to the west wing for the museum when Barry approached me. We had a chat, and he expressed an interest in historical witchcraft, so I showed him my collection. He's been trying to purchase the burnt witch ever since.'

'Her name's Bethany.'

'Who?'

'The burnt witch. Her name's Bethany Blackwood and she's my ancestor. That's why I took her.'

Edward laughs. Which is annoying. 'That's funny, because Rutherford seems to think he has a claim on it too. Some cock and bull story about owning the artifact and that it was stolen from Poorbrook House. He even had some pretty impressive documents to furnish his argument.' He puts two heaped sugars into his tea and stirs.

My head is buzzing. If Barry gets hold of Bethany, it won't be good.

'So you see,' he says, taking a sip of his tea, 'you're not the only one who wants it.'

'Her.'

'Her. It. Bethany. Whatever. The point is not what or who, the point is that you've taken – stolen – something that does not belong to you.' He looks me squarely in the eye. No doubt in that gaze. Lord Wootton clearly believes he's in the right.

'Why not let me keep her remains and you have the casket?'

'No, no, no! It's got to be authentic, or it won't work. Rutherford suggested much the same. But sooner or later the public will find out the truth. It only takes one expert to recognise the casket's been opened for it to lose all credibility. For any of this to work, it's got to remain intact.'

Oh dear.

Edward dabs his angry, sweaty face.

'But she does belong to me. She's part of my...'

'No. No more nonsense. I've invested a lot of money in this project. Felicity and I have been working around the clock promoting the concept of Witchy Marswickham. She's even managed to get the BBC documentary department interested. It's not just about us, it's about providing work. Promoting tourism. It will be very good for the village...' He diverts into a story about how he went to an auction in Scotland to purchase a fifteenth-century cauldron.

Mid Witch Three

While he talks, I'm trying to decide how much I will need to tell him in order for him to let me keep Bethany. Will he cope if his material interest in witchcraft becomes reality? Will he be delighted to meet a real witch or will he be horrified? Does he collect his 'artefacts' because he likes the idea of witches or because he is drawn to his fears?

'So I hope that makes my position clearer,' he says, smiling now. Edward is used to talking himself out of trouble – or is he just used to being listened to?

I stand and drop my mug into the sink. I think I'll start with the curse. If he's interested in witchcraft, he must be a little superstitious. Maybe I can persuade him.

Ink skitters across the kitchen doing her skinny wriggle. Grant Fucking Rutherford is standing in the doorway.

Chapter Forty-One

Grant looks awful. You'd think he'd spent the night in the county jail. He stands on the threshold and I'm about to invite him in when Edward leaps up, even redder in the face.

'What the fucking hell are you doing here!' he bellows.

Mid Witch Three

Grant takes a step back. *Mrs Beeton* goes for another strike and misses. Edward is already out of the door.

Grant holds up his hands as though Edward is pointing a gun at him. 'I'm not here to make trouble,' says Grant, casting me a glance.

'You're always fucking trouble,' says Edward.

Ink and I stand on the doorstep star. I'm not entirely sure what to do. The two men are inches apart, glaring at each other like a couple of sumo wrestlers. Oh my god, are they going to come to blows? Edward takes a step back and faces me.

'The burnt witch needs to be returned by six o'clock this evening or you'll be hearing from my lawyers,' he says, face like a tomato.

Grant swings a punch at him. Edward ducks. Grant is furious and swings again. Edward is light on his feet, fists raised, bouncing on his toes like he's in a boxing ring. He stabs his fist into the air inches from Grant's face. It would be funny if it didn't look so dangerous. Grant dives in for another punch and Edward hits him. Bash. Straight in the face. Grant is cursing, staggering, punch drunk.

I scream, 'Stop!' Ink barks. Cocksure struts about, loving it.

Grant goes in for another punch. He misses and Edward strikes again. Crunch. Grant falls into the shrubbery. This is too much for Cocksure. He flies at Edward – let's be fair, the bird has never liked the man – and feathers fly. Where Grant failed, the bird succeeds. Edward runs down the path, screaming and flapping. In the lane, there is a lot of commotion as he fights off the cockerel to get into his car.

'That bird needs shooting!' cries Edward from the car window as he examines his scratched hands.

'Fuck off!' is the only thing I can think of to shout.

'Six o'clock and I'm...'

'Cock-a-doodle-dooooo!' Cocksure – he's always got to have the last word.

Edward drives off with a wheel spin. Prat.

Cocksure perches on the gatepost and flaps his wings.

In the shrubbery, Grant staggers to his feet. I help him into the kitchen and give him a clean, wet tea towel to hold over his bleeding nose. I cradle his head against me. 'Put your head back. That's it. I'll make you something for that black eye,' I say. Then I get busy gathering the herbs I need, putting a pan to boil and adding wood to the range.

He sits there quietly. Ink rests her head on his knee and gazes at him adoringly. No matter that he lost the fight. He's her hero. Annoyingly, I feel the same. Although I'm surprised. Not at my repressed feelings for GFR but that he lost. Out of the two of them, I would have put my money on him. He's fitter, taller, stronger.

Pan on the boil, I lift the tea towel and check on the bleeding. Looks like he's going to have a nasty bruise. 'Why are you here?' I ask.

'Two reasons. Well, three really.' He holds my wrist with a gentle grasp.

'Reason one?' I say, ignoring my quickening pulse.

'I saw the news.'

'The news?'

'You're on the news, Lilly. I suppose that shit thought it would be good publicity for his Museum of Witchcraft.'

I reach for my phone.

'Don't,' he says, 'it'll only upset you.'

'The second reason?'

'I needed a good witch to make me a poultice for this.' He lifts his shirt. The whole of his left side swirls with a deep blue bruise. 'I had an argument with my brother. Again.'

I put my hands on his flesh. A dark spell is cast upon him. 'You realise he's an absolute bastard, right?'

'I guess I had it coming.'

'He's your brother. He has no right to do this to you.' I give his flesh a good sniff. 'Yes. I think I have a counter spell for this. Hang on,' I say, finding an empty jar under the sink.

One side of my garden is shaded and damp. It doesn't take me long to lure a frog into the jar.

'This is going to hurt,' says Grant when he sees what I've got.

'It will, but not for long. I could make you a poultice instead, but that could take a week to get the hex off you.'

'It's fine. Get it over with. You already think I'm useless.'

'Stop feeling sorry for yourself and lift your shirt.'

Grant does as he's told as a loud cheer rings out from upstairs, followed by a stamping of feet. 'What does your son do up there all day?'

'God knows. Now hold this jar on your stomach. That's

it.' I grasp the green frog in one hand and roll my wand down Grant's torso like he's a lump of pastry. The hex mark writhes like angry snakes. Grant grips the arms of the chair and grimaces. I wave the frog over the hex and it follows. When the frog is on top of the jar, the hex flicks inside. A deft twist of my wand and the lid closes. Dark swirls spin inside, trying to escape.

'You're very good at catching hexes,' he says as I set the frog on the doorstep so she can hop free.

'I've had a lot of practice lately. Come on. You need a lie down. Get your strength back.' He doesn't argue and lets me lead him to the easy chair, where I tuck him in with Ink and apply the poultice to his face.

'What will your son think?' he says.

'Nothing. He's used to living in a madhouse.' I kiss him then. Long and slow.

'Thank you,' he says.

'So what was the third reason?'

'You know,' he says, falling asleep.

Chapter Forty-Two

Cocksure is roosting on the gatepost. Head on his back, sun making his feathers gleam. I can't leave him there; he'll terrorise the postman. Humming his soothing song, I lift him down, tuck him under my arm and pop him beside the doorstep in a patch of sun. He ruffles his feathers and settles himself for a nap. Then I check for eggs in the henhouse. Not a single one. Shame. I really need to do something about these hens. But right now, it's the least of my worries.

'Is that the estate agent bloke in the easy chair?' whispers Jason when he wanders into the kitchen at lunchtime.

'Grant,' I say.

'Mum, so many suitors,' he says, grinning and closing the kitchen door quietly. He doesn't ask about the fight. Too busy having a virtual fight to notice two old blokes boxing on the lawn. I cut some bread for sandwiches. The young: they miss so much.

'Belinda was trying to get hold of you,' he says, making us mugs of tea. I'd seen the missed calls, but it's always hopeless trying to call her back. Teachers have to lock away their phones. It's the strange new world we live in. I've sent her a message, and whatever it is will have to wait until she gets back.

'Any idea what's wrong?' I say.

'Brian came over last night,' he says. 'I looked after the girls while they went for a walk.'

I'm about to ask how that went when Jason's phone rings. He answers straight away, grabs his sandwich and tea and disappears upstairs to his 'office'. I sit at the kitchen table with my lunch and check my messages. Good job I do. Mrs Tingle wants a Swiss roll and chocolate cupcakes by 6pm. Best press on with the jobs.

Mid Witch Three

By the time Grant is standing in the doorway, I'm rolling up the warm Swiss roll on sugared paper.

'Smells nice in here,' he says.

'Better?'

'Thank you.'

I make him tea and give him a sandwich. He reads yesterday's paper as he eats, and I beat buttercream. It's comfortable with him here. Which is annoying.

'You should go on Bake Off,' he says when I give him one of the warm cupcakes. I always make extra.

'Don't think magic is allowed.'

'Do you put spells on them, then?'

'Sometimes. Sometimes not. Depends.'

'On what?'

'Finish your cake and you'll find out.'

He looks at the last morsel of cake in his hand and laughs. 'Have you thought about what you're going to do?'

'Edward's not having her back.' I drop my wooden spoon in the sink with a clatter.

'Can I see her?'

I notice he doesn't say 'it' or artefact.

'Jason is upstairs. But I'll tell him to collect the twins from school so we can have some privacy.'

He checks his watch and returns to the paper. He looks better, but he's going to have a black eye, and I can see the gag Barry puts over his face. A mesh of fine lines, delicate as a cobweb. Bastard. Absently, Grant rubs the Coven's mark on his arm. It looks sore and angry, the tattooed feather ragged and worn. It gets like that when he's not behaving. I'd like to reach over, wind the cobweb from his face and pluck the feather from his arm. It would be easy to do. I'm that strong a witch. But having the power does not mean I should use it against another's wishes. GFR has made his position clear: he's not about to give up a lifetime's identity and belonging for me. His family, even though they are fucked up, come first. Hey ho.

I take Jason a cake and some tea and inform him of his errand. He pauses the game and lifts one side of his headphones. A large purple dragon looms on the large screen as I set the mug and plate at his elbow. God only knows what he's up to. Not work, that's for sure. As soon as I've sorted out my current crisis, I'm going to focus on him. Because one thing is certain: my boy has lost direction.

Grant helps in the kitchen with the washing up. Seems like we are destined to be 'just good friends'. How nice. I try to dispel images of us shagging – real and imagined.

While I decorate the cakes, he frowns and fiddles with his phone. Something's up. 'What?' I say.

'Suppose you might as well see this.' He pushes his phone toward me, and I wipe my specs on my apron. There I am. Yellow nightie flapping, dashing across the lawns of Marswickham House, pushing a sack trolley. I look demented.

'Where's this?'

'Social media. Local news.' His scowl deepens.

Mid Witch Three

A dollop of butter icing falls to the floor. Ink saunters over to clean it up.

'Does it say it's me?'

'No. Not quite.' He shows me the screen again. The caption reads, 'Woman in a nightgown makes off with historical artifact.'

'How the fuck do they know it was a nightie?'

He shrugs. 'Everyone knew. It was the talk of the party. "Who's that woman in Mabel and Green Dreamwear?"'

'How awful.' I'm still holding the piping bag, and Ink is sitting bolt upright in front of me, hoping for another treat.

'Mabel and Green did a big photo shoot in the grounds of Marswickham House.' He taps his screen and shows me a collection of glossy magazine covers, all featuring a skinny model cavorting about in a field of buttercups in that nightie.

'Is that Edward's daughter, Collette?'

'Yes. She's been the face of Mabel and Green for two years.'

'You're very well informed,' I snip.

'Rebecca.'

Rebecca. Figures. If you have a glamorous friend (with benefits) of course you know what's going on.

I carry on piping the cupcakes and Ink sighs and returns to her blankets on the sunny path outside the kitchen door. Poor dog.

Eventually Jason leaves and I give him the scones for the tearoom, a list of groceries I need from the little shop and some money to buy the twins an ice cream. That should keep them gone for an hour at least.

As soon as Jason is through the gate, Grant and I go upstairs, Ink on our heels. I open the secret closet and pull out the casket. The straps trail. The lock is clearly broken.

'You're going to have to mend it before you give it back.'

A great blob of a tear rolls down my cheek. I dash it away, kneel beside the casket and lift the lid to show the tiny body wrapped inside. 'But I've only just found her, and Bethany, the ghost, she looked so happy and relieved.' I'm crying and trying to find a tissue in my apron pocket. Ink whimpers and puts her nose in my ear. I wrap my arms around her.

'We'll have to put something else inside. Seal it up again. Do you think you can spell it back together?' he says.

'Probably,' I say, wiping my face with a scrap of loo roll.

Grant looks about the small room. 'Is the ghost here now?'

'She's gone.'

'Gone where?'

'If I knew where ghosts go when they stop being ghosts, I'd have the secret of life.'

He smiles at me, and suddenly I'm so glad he's here.

'We need to weigh her. Make sure she's replaced by something of the same weight,' he says.

I go into the closet but all I can find is an old leather suitcase. I tip out the clothes and bring it over. Grant has fetched the bathroom scales. We weigh the casket with her in, and then I carefully lift Bethany out and place her in the suitcase with her mementoes. It's easy to see now that she was interred in a foetal position. 'They must have cut her down before she was burnt. Perhaps she died from the smoke,' he says.

'Or one of her witch sisters ended it before she could suffer,' I say. Seeing her there, I can't stop crying and Grant holds me. 'I don't know why I'm so upset,' I say.

'Of course you're upset. She was a member of your family. It doesn't matter that she lived so long ago,' he says, squeezing me tight. I rest my head on his chest. It's unfair when a man who just wants to be friends has a 'come to bed smell'. I pull back. Making a point of not looking into his dark brown eyes, I go to the bathroom and blow my nose. Take some deep breaths.

In the bedroom, Grant is weighing logs. When he's found the right one, I wrap it in a bathmat that's seen better days and place it in the casket. 'Just give me a moment,' I say, checking my watch. With any luck, Jason is letting the girls eat their ice creams on a bench beside Fox Green. That can take a while.

I dash around the garden with my snippers, getting the plants I need. Rosemary for remembrance. Sage, bay and lavender for protection. I tie the bunch with dried grass from my 'lawn' and wish there was time to make a witch bottle. When everything is in the casket, I light a black candle, eat some blackwood leaves and cast a spell to close the locks and clasps as they were before. Then I stroke the casket, adding wards to keep out intruders. They will whisper dark threats that will discourage those who'd like to open it. Even a non-magical person will have a grim sense of foreboding if they meddle with the fastenings. And if someone does open it? Nothing will happen. I'm not that sort of witch.

Grant lays the suitcase containing Bethany in the secret closet and I close the door. 'What will you do with her?' he asks.

'Bury her in the graveyard at St Gutheridge, I suppose.'

He shakes his head. I see the binds that control his speech tighten. He can't explain why.

'I know what you think,' I say. 'You think there is a very good chance of someone digging her up.'

He almost nods.

'I won't do it yet. She's safe here for now.' And the ghost is happy at least.

I'm annoyed by the way sweat beads his forehead. Even shaking his head has cost him. My fingers tingle with the urge to pluck the bind off. But we've been through this before. 'Your brother's a cunt,' I say, heading downstairs.

Grant carries the casket. Deliveries are tricky when you don't drive. I'm about to ask him if he could return it for me, when there is a commotion at the garden gate. Vans and cars are arriving and people are getting out of their vehicles and focusing cameras and video equipment on the cottage.

'I wondered how long it would take them,' he says, closing the door so they can't see in.

We watch from behind a curtain. A woman in wide-legged trousers and expensive trainers minces around the pothole and tries to open the gate – it remains firmly shut.

Mid Witch Three

She fiddles with the bolt and a bloke tries to help. Before I can catch her, Ink hurtles down the path and does her best impression of a mad and dangerous dog. She stays behind the gate, snarling, head lowered, and paces back and forth in a menacing manner. The reporters move back onto the road and stand in a huddle.

One brave soul thinks he can tame her and steps closer, holding out a piece of food. Ink sniffs. Approaches the man slowly. We can hear him speaking softly, telling her she's a beautiful dog. He leans over the gate and holds out the morsel. Ink wags her tail and goes closer. Everybody is smiling.

'It's cheese,' he says to his colleagues. 'All dogs can be tamed with cheese. I always carry some with me for times like these. Watch and learn, guys. Watch and learn. Good girl. Hear you are.'

When she's inches from the man's fingers, she leaps at him – a snarling, frenzied beast. The man, clutching his heart, falls backward into the pothole. The cheese flies out of his hand. Ink jumps and catches it in mid-air, no problem. No way my magical dog is going to waste a good lump of cheese. Bless.

Two reporters help the bloke up. He's mud-covered and shaken. Some of them are putting their stuff back in their cars, but a few stalwarts remain and position themselves on the other side of the lane. Probably because they feel safe from the dog there. Which is true. They are safe from the dog. The chicken – not so much.

Cocksure strides down the path, vengeance in his little black eye. He's pulled himself to his full height, feathers fluffed and tail plumes quivering. Cocksure has no qualms about not hurting the reporters. He's got hens to protect. He flies over the gate and the spell on the ground that is supposed to keep him in. Letting lose a blood curdling squawk, he attacks.

'Fucking Hell!' someone cries. A few brave ones attempt to shoo him off with their notebooks and mobile phones. I've spent the best part of a year arguing with this belligerent bird. Only a soothing witch song will calm him, and I'm not singing.

One by one, the reporters decide this story is not worth any bloodshed. When they've driven away, Cocksure settles on the gatepost. This time I leave him there.

'Would you like me to return this?' says Grant, patting the casket at his feet.

'Could you? Thanks,' I say. We walk together along the path and check the lane, but they've all gone.

I pet Ink, give her a dog biscuit and put a few sunflower seeds on the post for Cocksure.

'That's one mad bird you've got there,' says Grant, putting the casket in the boot of his car.

'Which is why he fits right in,' I say, giving his gleaming plumage a stroke. I watch Grant drive away. When his car has gone, I see Jason and the twins cavorting along, having a lovely time. Jason chases them through the gate.

'We had ice cream, Lillymar,' they cry.

Mid Witch Three

'Yes, I can see you're full of sugar,' I laugh.

Ink greets them gently; they pat and hug her and run off for a game of ball.

'Did I miss anything?' says Jason.

'Not a thing.'

Chapter Forty-Three

I set about my evening tasks. Box the cakes ready for collection. Make the kids' packed lunches for tomorrow. Cook a shepherd's pie. Tackle the laundry mountain; an impossible task – that mountain is too high – but I deal with the clothes that are in the kitchen, the pile waiting to be washed, the pile that needs to go upstairs and the ironing. Good to keep busy and not let this business with the reporters get to me. I tell myself it's most unlikely that Belinda will see me on the news – she's too busy and Jason is too immersed in his virtual life. But if they do, I have a story ready of a drunken dare that got out of hand. Mostly I try not to think about Grant – and fail. Bloody bloke.

Magic seems far from reality as I deal with the chores. A piece of me hopes that all this has not been for nothing. I'm sure most of the curse lifted, but what that actually means for me and my family is unclear. Will it be weeks, months or years until our bad luck regarding love and relationships abates? Or has the damage been done and is in fact irreversible?

While the twins do their homework, I stand at the kitchen sink and watch the hens pecking beneath the apple tree. It's such a lovely summer evening. Warm and breezy. Peaceful. I hope Edward isn't going to turn into a vindictive bastard over this. If he opens the casket, he's going to be pissed off when he finds my grotty bathmat and a log. I put a finger on the witch ball hanging in the window so it spins gently and gaze into the depths of the mercurial surface, hoping for an answer. Edward wanted to buy it and maybe I should have been more suspicious concerning his interest in witchy artefacts. His interest in me may have had a motive. But that's me: too bloody trusting.

In my back pocket, my phone vibrates. It's Belinda.

'Mum! Where have you been? I've been trying to get hold of you.'

'What's up, love?'

'I'm going to stay out tonight.'

'Okay, love.'

She lowers her voice, which means she's still at school. 'Brian came over...'

'Jason said.'

'Anyway. We've been talking. He's asked me out on a date.' She laughs.

'Well, that's good...' I'd like to ask questions.

'Thanks, Mum. See you tomorrow.' And she's gone.

It's funny how when your children are in a happy relationship, you like their partner. But when the relationship changes, you go off them. Nearly every private conversation with Belinda (out of earshot of the twins) is about Brian and his faults. At this point, I'd be happier if she was seeing someone new. If they get back together, I will have to forget that he is dull, stubborn and an inadequate lover. Tricky.

While I've been musing, the twins have sneaked off to watch TV. I pack their books into their school bags and put them by the door for morning and hope they've made a good job of their homework because I have no energy to check it over. I set the table for tea and make a salad.

I like this time of year when the kitchen door is always open. When Ink woofs and a car pulls up in the lane, I expect it is Mrs Tingle for her rose-themed cupcakes. Instead my son's ex, Jonathon, is walking up the path. He stands on the doorstep and looks at his feet.

'Is Jason in?' he says as if he's a kid asking if my boy can come out to play. Well, I liked him once too, but Jason lost his job and was broken-hearted when they split up. I've a good mind to say he's out.

'Come in,' I say.

He smiles and steps over the doorstep star.

'Take a seat. I'll get him. Probably got headphones on,' I explain. Really, I want to warn him who's here.

In his room, Jason is totally engrossed, as usual. A large blue dragon lumbers across his three screens. I tap his shoulder. He moves a headphone to one side so I can impart my news: 'Jonathon is here.' Why am I whispering?

The effect of my words is electric. He whips off the headphones and jumps out of his enormous office chair in one swift movement.

'What? Where?'

'In the kitchen.'

'Go down. Tell him I'll be there in a minute,' he says, peeling off his snoopy t-shirt and running into the ensuite.

Jonathon is petting Ink. 'I think your dog really likes me,' he says. Ink is wagging her tail because she's having her ears scratched. She's just being polite. If she really likes you, she does the skinny wriggle dance. Ink saunters off and settles on her blankets in the evening sun outside the door. She's not keen on you, mate, and neither am I.

'Hi!' says Jason. Cool as you like. Clean shirt, subtle whiff of aftershave. They hug. I go to check on the twins. They're quite happy. I tidy up the sitting room.

'Just going out. See you later,' calls Jason from the kitchen.

I refrain from shouting, 'When will you be home and shall I save you some shepherd's pie?' Not being an annoying mother is a tremendous strain.

After Ting-a-ling collects her cakes (pity the cupcakes weren't bigger but they will have to do), the twins and I eat. No point waiting. Then I get them bathed and in bed early. I remember how hard it was to sleep on light summer nights when I was a child, but they are tired and soon settle. I sort out the kitchen, fetch the washing off the line and shut up the hens.

It's been a strange day. After a soak in the bath and a quick check on the secret contents of my secret cupboard, I go to bed expecting to sleep. I don't, even though I've done all the sleep hygiene nonsense that sleep experts recommend: warm bath, no screens, measured breathing, relaxing thoughts, lavender on my pillow, blah blah blah. I'm too busy fretting about the kids. Are Jason and Belinda having a horrible emotional time with their exes? It's true what they say: you're only as happy as your most miserable child.

When Ink woofs to let me know someone is coming, I'm fast out of bed, peeping through the curtains. Jason is walking up the path – alone. I pad downstairs.

'Everything okay, love?'

'Yeah,' he says, drinking from the kitchen tap – a bad

Mid Witch Three

habit he picked up from me. He wipes his mouth on his arm. 'Weird, isn't it? I used to dream of him wanting to get back together.'

'Is that what he wanted?'

'Pretty much. He didn't exactly proclaim undying love. Just that he thought it would be nice if we gave it another try.'

I wait. Ink saunters past, brushes against Jason as a hello. The kitchen door opens, and she goes out for a pee. Jason doesn't notice. He's looking in the fridge. 'Can I eat this?' It's cold mac and cheese. I hand him a fork.

'What did you say?'

'You know what, Mum, I'm over him. Absolutely no point going back. He's a nice guy. But it's done. Thanks, but no thanks.'

'Well, that's good,' I say, relieved he's calm and happy.

'And his mother is an absolute witch,' he says, squirting tomato sauce on the leftovers.

Chapter Forty-Four

In the morning, I walk the kids to school and clean the fridge. Belinda is still not back. I hope she's not having a stressful time. Jason seems fine, though. Good he knows what he wants. Just because love comes knocking doesn't mean you have to accept it as if you only have one option. I'm proud of him. Wish I'd had his presence of mind when I was his age.

While pegging out washing, I try to organise my thoughts, such as they are. Each problem clamours for attention. Where to start? As far as I know, Mouse is still living in my wood, although I haven't seen him, and I hope he's alright. Maybe I'll take a walk with Ink later. I haven't called Walter because I'm worried about telling him I've returned the casket with a bathmat and log inside. When Belinda re-appears, I'll visit and take him a thank-you cake. Also, I haven't heard from Edward. Did he receive the casket and is he happy now? I bloody hope so. The police haven't come for me again and nor have the reporters – so with any luck that part of the crisis is settling down. No news from GFR, but I wasn't expecting any. Like other men I've cared for in my life, he has a habit of turning up when least expected, getting me in a tizzy and then fucking off without a word. Hey ho.

Mrs Tingle has left a long voice message. She wants a red velvet cake and something with an orange tang. I can't face any baking today or Mrs Tingle's demands. She only collected bakes yesterday. She can't possibly need more. She'll have to wait. Perhaps I should get a sign for the gate: 'Away on witchy business. No cakes today.' Actually, that's not a bad idea.

I sit on the grass under the apple tree with the washing basket on my lap and begin pegging underwear and millions of little socks onto one of the five multi-peg devices I own. This one is octopus shaped. Ink flops beside me and Maud lands on the washing line, making it sway. It's a beautiful day. Hot but not too hot, with a light, carefree breeze. If only I could emulate the weather.

From here, I can see the bedroom window where Bethany is hidden. It's the big problem that I can't get my head round. Grant pretty much told me that Barry will dig her up if I bury her at St Gutheridge and All Angels. I will have to wait until this has all died down. It's not as if she's rotting or anything. She can stay there safely enough. The trouble is, she won't be truly at rest until I find a safe place for her. My phone chirps and I fish it out of my apron pocket.

'Lilly?'

'Speaking.'

'It's Joan. From the front desk at Cranford, Holstein and Wigg,' she says.

'Oh hello,' I say. From the tone of her voice, something is wrong.

'Walter asked me to call you if... Well, my dear, I'm afraid he had a bit of a turn late last night and he's in hospital.'

'Oh no. Is it bad?'

'Hard to say, my lovely.'

I'm speechless. I need to be with him. Right now.

'I don't like to presume, Lilly. But I could send Hilda.'

'Oh yes. Yes please. Send her now if she's free. And thanks. Thanks for letting me know.'

As soon as I ring off, there is a message from Belinda. She's staying with Brian tonight. That is good news, just not right now. Right now, I can't cope with grandma responsibilities.

Chucking the laundry to one side, I run into the cottage, Ink hot on my heels. Jason is oblivious as I dash into his room. He jumps when I tap him on the shoulder. 'What's up?' he says, moving his headphones to one side and not taking his eyes from the screen.

'I've got to go out. Belinda's staying with Brian. Could you get the girls?'

Jason faces me. Pulls off the headphones. 'You okay, Mum?'

'It's Walter. He's been rushed into hospital.'

Bless him, he's on his feet giving me a hug. 'You go, Mum, I've got this.'

I wait in the lane for Hilda with Big Bag. When the vintage Bentley pulls up, I hop into the front seat. Poor Ink stands at the gate, ears drooping. I've tried to explain the situation to her, but how much does a dog, even a magical dog, understand? She knows that something is wrong, that's for sure. Ideally, I'd like to take her. But she won't be allowed in the hospital, even in one of her disguises.

We drive in silence to Barrington Hospital. Hilda is not one for a chat at the best of times. She drives smoothly through the traffic, but her mirrored sunglasses cannot disguise the fact that she's been crying. Her orts are pale purple and wispy.

She drops me at the entrance. 'Text me when you're ready,' she says.

'Aren't you coming in?' I ask.

'I don't do hospitals.'

Because my brain is like a sieve, I've written 'Level 5, Sunset Ward' on the back of my hand. In the lift, I stand next to an old man holding a wilting bouquet.

'Martha's favourite. Yellow roses,' he says, frowning at the cellophane wrapped bunch. A big sticker declares, '7 day guarantee'. They don't look like they'll last the next seven minutes.

'How is she?' I ask, as if I know her.

'Not so dusty. She'll be alright.'

The lift opens. We step out. The old man looks at the drooping bunch. 'I should have bought the chrysanthemums. Always last a long time, chrysanths. I think these buggers are done for.'

'They'll be fine when they've had a nice drink. Roses are always thirsty. Here, let me. Which bed?'

He points to his wife, who has already spotted him and is waving. I take the flowers and head for the nurse's station. A nurse sends me to a visitors' resource room, where I find a cupboard full of containers and choose a large cut-glass vase. When the cellophane is in the bin and the flowers are in water, I mutter words of witchy encouragement and bring them to a glory they never had. The trouble with me is that when I start this sort of thing, I can't stop. Before long, my wand is out of Big Bag and I'm casting a big fat spell. The bouquet I deliver to the old man and his wife is magnificent: two dozen buttery yellow roses, scented and magical in a gleaming crystal vase. I set them on the nightstand and beat a hasty retreat before they ask questions, none of which I can answer.

Walter is alone in a side room wired to a plethora of machines. I pull up a plastic chair and hold his bony hand. He's very old, but it seems crazy that he's lying here unconscious. So small and frail in a floral hospital gown. White stubble on his chin. So short a time ago, he was full of life, sharp of mind and smartly dressed. Flower in his buttonhole.

'Please don't go. Not yet,' I whisper.

'He's nice and comfortable,' says a nurse, bustling in, checking a few of the machines and adding notes to a clipboard hooked on the end of the bed.

'What happened?' I ask.

'Are you family? We can only tell family,' she says, not unkindly.

'I'm his daughter.' Oddly, it isn't strange to say it.

'Walter is getting on a bit. He's had a turn that's left him in a coma. We're not sure what exactly happened. His heart seems fine. He's not had a stroke, which was our first fear...' She frowns at her patient. 'We'll probably give him a scan tomorrow. Get to the bottom of it. Has he had a turn like this before?'

I'm blank. How can I say that we've only just met? 'No,' I say, hedging my bets. She pats my shoulder and leaves.

I have a little cry. Then root through Big Bag for a packet of travel tissues. My hand brushes my wand, and I feel a vibration. It's slight, but it's there. A buzz in my palm when I hold it. I pull the blind at the window and switch off the light, ease the door closed with my foot and stand there in the gloaming. Now I can see the colours of magic.

Walter's orts are a gentle silver mist clinging to his prone body. I'm no expert, but they look strange, as though tangled with another's. I put my wand in the mist and twist, pulling out a dark thread. It licks and flicks, trying to hold onto Walter.

'No. No more. Off you fucking come,' I say, dragging the wickedness from him in a deadly strand. When the last comes free, Walter splutters. Is he waking or dying? The machines are bleeping and nurses rush in. I stand by the wall and pray. Please don't let him die. Please don't let him die.

What seems like ages later but is probably only a few minutes, the danger is over. Breathing tubes are removed and Walter blinks and coughs. He mouths my name when I'm allowed near enough to hold his hand. Soon he is asleep again.

'We've given him a gentle sedative and a painkiller,' says a nurse reassuringly. 'I think your dad is out of the woods.'

When I'm alone with him, I take my wand from Big Bag. Now they have lost their purpose, the black threads are fading fast. I place my fingertips over them, sensing the magical signature. I know who did this to Walter long before he's standing in the doorway.

Chapter Forty-Five

I remain where I am, holding Walter and my wand tightly. Barry is smiling.

'I wondered how long it would take you to lift the hex,' he says.

A wave of anger flows through me. His face pales. I count

to ten. Magical rage is so dangerous, it's important I get control of myself. It would be so easy to hurt him; I'm so much stronger and he knows it. Lucky for Barry, I'm not that witch.

'He's an old man. You could have killed him! You bastard!'

'What, Walter? He's as tough as old boots, even if he is getting complacent in his old age.'

'If You Ever...'

'Let's not get ahead of ourselves. It was just a warning to you, Lilly. Just a little warning to let you know how serious I am about the burnt witch.'

'She's been returned. Go see Edward.'

'Oh, I already did. Lord Wootton is delighted. He won't be so pleased when I tell him the body is gone.'

I point my wand at him, and he holds up his hands in supplication.

'Put it away, Lilly. You're not about to hex me in a hospital.'

'What better place to get hexed?' I say, raising my brows.

He takes a step backward. Good. You should be afraid of me, you fucker.

'The burnt witch belongs to the Rutherfords and you need to return it or this will seem like you had a pleasant day.'

'She, not it. And no, she does not *belong* to you. So why don't you fuck off,' I say.

'Just remember when everything goes wrong: I warned

you.' He speaks with such malice I shudder as he strides away.

A nurse bustles in to check on Walter. She reassures me he is stable and suggests I return in the morning. Suddenly, I remember Hilda is waiting in the car park. I drop a handful of herbs and a hag stone into the nightstand drawer and put a protection spell over my poor old dad. 'I'll come back tomorrow,' I say as I kiss his forehead. He looks peaceful now and his orts have settled into their normal silver hue.

Hilda brushes off my apology when I find the old Bentley in the car park. I tell her what happened in the hospital as we drive home. She grunts and grips the wheel tightly. 'Hate that Rutherford shit,' she says when I've finished. Hilda is a woman of few words. Back at the cottage, I ask her in for food, which she declines.

My familiars are here to greet me. I kneel on the path to hug Ink and then scoop up Claudia and put her on my shoulder so she can purr into my ear. Maud rides on Ink's back as we enter the kitchen. Jason is washing up.

'How was he?' he asks.

'Oh, not too bad.' Considering he was hexed.

'I've failed to get the kids to bed,' he says, dipping his head toward the living room where the TV blares.

'Oh no worries. Friday, thank god.'

'Did some reading practice, and I managed to get Sophie to eat something green. We walked Ink along the lane. Everybody came.' He looks up at Maud, who is preening herself on top of the dresser. 'Good job we don't live in a built-up area. People might think we're eccentric.'

'Bathed?'

'Rinsed in the shower.'

'Good enough.'

'Saved you some pasta bake.' He's a good lad. Even if all he does is play video games all day. I slump at the kitchen table while he takes a dish out of the range. I'm about to tuck in when Amy dashes in.

'Lillymar! Come and see! You're on telly.'

Oh god.

Jason and I stand behind the sofa where the kids are squirming around. 'Lillymar's on telly ha ha ha!!'

A smartly dressed reporter is interviewing Edward and Felicity. They are standing on the lawn in front of Marswickham House. On the left is some footage of me dashing along with the sack truck in that bloody nightie. I switch it off.

'Come on, you two. Time for bed.' Reluctantly, they trail upstairs.

'What were you doing?' says Amy.

'Oh, it was just a party dare. Bit of nonsense.' I try to force a laugh.

'The man on the telly says you were in a nightie,' says Sophie.

'Well, it was nighttime.'

'What were you stealing?' says Amy.

'A box. We were playing a party game, and I had to take the box to…'

'Who won the game?' says Amy.

'I'm not sure. We were all a bit drunk.'

'What was in the box?' says Sophie

'No idea,' I lie. 'Come on. Teeth.'

Dental hygiene fields some of their questions, but as they tumble into bed, Amy fixes me with a firm stare. 'Have you been naughty, Lillymar?'

'A bit,' I say.

Story time settles them down, and because it's so late, they are soon asleep. I go downstairs to eat my cold pasta, expecting Jason has returned to his online life. No such luck. He's in the kitchen, lips pursed, arms folded, waiting for an explanation like an angry wife.

'What really happened?' he says.

I stuff my mouth full. Is it time I told him the truth about myself? I take a gulp of water. At some point, they will need to know. Hard though to tell your son that you're a witch without sounding like a delusional nutter. I could show him the truth of it, the sparks I make with a simple snap of my fingers. Will he understand it is magic, or will he think me some kind of freak? That's not even starting with family curses, blackwood trees and orts. Then there's the bloody Coven that hates me. I'm about to ask him if we can chat about this tomorrow when Belinda bursts into the kitchen and throws her bags down in a rage. Ink doesn't bother trying to say hello. We all hold our breath.

'He's an absolute shit,' she says, holding her bump.

We wait.

'For the past couple of days we've been getting on like we used to. That woman moved out of our house. Which helped. We've met for coffee a few times. Had some chats on the phone. It was going well.'

She caresses her bump, and I can see the baby kicking. I want to reach out and touch the new life, but best not to when Belinda is in a prickly mood.

Jason gives her a glass of water. She takes a few gulps. 'Honestly, I thought we had a chance. We were making plans for us to move back in over half term.' She throws the rest of the water in the sink with a splash. 'Then he said…' She holds the edge of the sink. Knuckles white. 'He said we— *We* can get the baby adopted. Because obviously this child might look different from the rest of us.' Belinda turns to face us. A serene smile on her pretty face. 'So I told him to fuck off.'

'Well done, love.'

'Can't spend the rest of my life apologising. I'm not giving up my boy,' she says.

'It's a boy?'

'Yes. I wasn't going to say. But on the last scan. Well, there he was.'

Amy wanders into the kitchen half asleep, clutching a rag doll. 'We're going to call him Willy Wonka,' she says.

Chapter Forty-Six

I lie in my single bed with Ink squashed beside me. The curtains and window are open to let in some air on this hot summer night. Owls call in the Blackwood and I worry about everything. Walter. My kids. The twins. Barry and whether the police will come knocking again when

Edward discovers the body is missing from the casket. Should I tell Jason and Belinda that their mother is a witch? A witch with problems.

From the bed, I touch the wall where the secret closet is. Where Bethany rests inside a leather suitcase. Strange that sleeping so near a dead body does not bother me. If anything, I'm comforted she's here. Home at last. Just not sure what to do with her for the best.

I sleep but wake early. Around me, the house is quiet. Saturday morning no-rush quiet. I pull on a sack dress and sneak outside, gathering a few things I need along the way: a tin of flapjacks, my wand and a pair of Turkish slippers. 'Come on, Ink, it's time we paid Mouse a visit.'

The birds sing as I follow Ink into the Blackwood. Now and then she stops and sniffs the air. Then she turns off onto a narrow path among the bracken. Another ten minutes and we reach a small clearing where a dwelling of sorts sits between a pair of beech trees. I wait on the edge where there is the slight coldness of a protection barrier. I could easily counter the spell, but it seems rude. Like entering someone's house without knocking. Ink noses beneath a door flap made from an old rug, and Mouse appears.

'Lilly!' he cries, waving a hand at the barrier. I step into the clearing.

'Are you alright?' I ask. 'So sorry I haven't visited sooner.' I hand him the slippers, feeling ridiculous. Does a man camping in magical woods need slippers? Probably not. On the contrary, he's delighted. He kicks off his shoes and puts them on then prizes off the tin lid and smiles at the flapjacks.

He ushers me to a log seat and I watch while he lights a fire and hangs a kettle to boil. He looks different: tanned and healthy, not so thin and stooped. He's still tiny, but now he's vibrant and his orts shine silver – no longer the pale smoke they were in the library. Once he's settled Ink on a blanket, he sits opposite, beady eyes gleaming.

'I thought I'd come and tell you what's been happening,' I say.

'I saw you on the news.' He taps a phone peeping from his top pocket. Something else that's new – he never had a phone before.

'Not sure I did the right thing, stealing her.'

'Her?'

I explain the whole crazy business. When I've finished, the kettle is boiling. Mouse goes into his dwelling and returns with two tin mugs and a jar of expensive instant coffee. 'Sorry. Run out of milk. Doesn't keep in the heat.' He makes the drinks and we eat flapjacks, both of us thinking.

'Barry Rutherford is a bad man,' he says at length.

I nod, too busy chewing to reply.

'He's not a powerful witch. Not really. Most of his strength is stolen – and I should know.' Mouse flinches at the memory.

'I think he wants Bethany to enhance his abilities,' I say, wiping crumbs off my chin.

'True,' he says, adding more sugar to his coffee. 'Barry is

driven by one thing: power. He's definitely planning to use the body for his own ends. There's a lot of latent magic in a dead witch. Even one who's been dead for hundreds of years.'

'I've tried to tell him she needs to be laid to rest in order to lift the curse on our two families. But he's not bothered about that, I'm sure.'

Mouse drains his mug and sets it on the moss. 'You've got a few options. Give her to him and hope the curse on your family does not return.'

'No!'

He smiles faintly. 'Give her back to Lord Edward on the proviso that he uses a lot of security – enough to keep Barry out.'

'No. I'm not letting her be on display for tourists to gawk at.'

'Bury her here in the woods, or your garden, and hope your protection spells stay put when he involves the Coven. And he will involve them.'

I know he's right.

'Or bury her in the churchyard and hope the magic that protects the other witches there will keep her safe.'

'How can I be sure she'll be safe there?'

'Put a hex on her. Something dangerous. Or better yet, hex him.'

'I'm not sure about dangerous?'

'You've got the power.'

'Yes,' I say, surprised by my own confidence. 'But I'm not that kind of witch.'

Mouse presses his lips together and looks at the ground. 'I've suffered for years at that man's hands.' He shivers. Poor Mouse. I feel guilty for coming here with all my problems. 'There are two more options.'

'Okay.'

'Do nothing. Deal with whatever dark magic comes your way as it happens. He will come, Lilly.'

'Or?'

'There's an old bit of magic known as the mortsafe spell.'

'Mortsafe?'

'Yes. It was popular when grave robbing was rife. Many known witches were often tasked with casting this spell on the graves of loved ones to keep out intruders. It's a difficult bit of magic to learn, but not impossible. It's kept me more or less safe all these years.'

'Really?'

'Yes really. It's a long story. The gist is that Barry Rutherford tried to steal all my power, but my mother had set this spell on me as a child, so he couldn't. It doesn't have to be cast upon a dead body. His revenge was locking me in the library, starving me of sugar and stealing a little of my energy when he could. Then you came along.' He smiles properly. His little face lights up, making him impish and cheeky. I can't help grinning back.

'And it's safe – this spell? I don't want to cause anyone any harm. Even that bastard Barry.'

'It's safe. But it's an old and difficult spell to master.'

'Can you teach me?'

'No. I can't do it...' He fetches a huge book, which he places on my lap. 'It's in here. This was my mother's. I'd like it back one day.'

'Yes, of course,' I say, opening the cover for a peek. Like my spell book, it doesn't have a contents page. 'Could you show me where the spell is?'

'It's in that book.'

'Yes, but where exactly?'

'It's the entire book. There's a reason these old spells went out of fashion. Too time consuming for the modern generation.'

He's looking at his pocket watch as if he has somewhere to be. Ink is waiting by the path. 'Thanks,' I say, getting up.

'No trouble, Lilith Blackwood.' He checks the time again.

'If you need anything, just come to the cottage.' I'm thinking of a shower – although he looks clean.

'I've got more than I need. In fact, I'm just going to collect my grocery delivery,' he says. We walk along the path, then he turns off toward the road. I stand for a while holding the book and watch him trot through the trees in his Turkish slippers.

Ink, keen to get home to her breakfast, streaks ahead, stopping now and then for me to catch up. The book is heavy and I'm glad when I reach the cottage.

Hilda leans on the gate.

Chapter Forty-Seven

S omething must have happened to Walter! With the book under my arm, I run along the path, boobs wobbling. I wasn't built for speed. Middle age has accentuated this fact. 'He's fine,' says Hilda, holding up a meaty hand so I don't crash into her. She helps Walter from the car.

'Amazing what a bit of de-hexing can do,' calls Walter as he grapples with a Zimmer frame.

In the kitchen I try to persuade Hilda to have some breakfast. She smiles and returns to the Bentley. I gather up cereal bowls and hide the huge book under a mound of clean laundry at one end of the table.

'So,' says Walter, stirring his tea, 'you must have tackled Barry Rutherford.'

Above us there is the sound of running feet and a few squeals. I lower my voice. 'Saw him at the hospital. We had words,' I say.

More squeals and shouts. 'You're going to have to tell them the truth about yourself eventually,' he says, looking at the ceiling.

'They've got enough on their plates,' I say as Belinda sails into the kitchen with the twins and, after a bit more chaos – lost shoes and a misplaced birthday gift – they leave.

'Ahh the young – so many parties to go to,' says Walter. I make us a fresh pot and tell him everything. When I've finished, he drags the spell book in front of him and lifts the cover. 'Yes, I've heard of the mortsafe spell.'

'And?'

'Never knew anyone who could do it.' He thumbs the pages. 'It's going to take a fair while to learn this.'

'I'm going to give it my best shot.'

Mid Witch Three

'That's my girl. But it's grand magic and you'll need seven magical adults to cast the spell. More if possible.'

I get a notepad and make a list of names. 'Mouse. I think he'd come. I thought I might ask Elaine Waters.'

'Me,' he says. I write 'Dad', which makes him smile. 'Hilda, you can always count on her. And Joan. She only has a trace of magic, but it will do.'

I write, 'Hilda, Joan'.

'Still need one more,' I say, looking at him expectantly.

'Can't help you. At my age, people are dead or they've gone gently crackers.' He looks tired, so I usher him into the sitting room and snug him up in the easy chair. 'You could ask that man of yours.'

Claudia appears. That cat has a sixth sense when it comes to available laps.

'Who?' I say, although I know bloody well who he means.

'Young Rutherford,' says Walter, smoothing Claudia's black fur.

'He's not my man.'

'He is.'

I open my mouth to protest, but Walter is already asleep. I slide off his specs and put them on the table, then take Hilda a mug of tea and a blueberry muffin. Because I'm an optimist, I check for eggs: still no luck.

Jason surfaces – all dressed up carrying a small holdall. 'I'm going to London for a couple of days.'

'What about your magazine job?'

'Packed it in. Can't do everything,' he says. A car picks him up in the lane before I can protest.

I put some blankets under the apple tree and take the book and a mug of tea. 'Might as well start now,' I say to Ink as she settles herself beside me and throws her head over my legs. After one page, I give up.

When Walter wakes, I have not got anywhere with the spell but the kids' uniforms are on the line and I've made Mrs Tingle's red velvet cake and decorated it with sugared violas from the garden. Walter and I eat quiche and salad in the kitchen. The door is open to keep us cool, and we can see Hilda standing by the car eating the thick slice I've taken her. 'I did ask her in... Doesn't she ever pee?'

Walter laughs. 'I've never known it happen.'

'Can't you let her go and do something instead of hanging around?'

'I used to try that. But she won't leave me.'

I watch her. She's finished eating and is passing a duster over the already gleaming car. Walter turns in his chair. 'Who needs familiars when you've got Hilda?'

'How's Atlas?'

'Asleep in the car. He likes the car.'

We talk about the weather for a while and then he pulls the Zimmer frame closer.

'You could always stay here.'

'I know,' he says, patting my hand. 'But I have nice people taking care of me.'

'I made you this when you were asleep,' I say, passing him

a protection charm. He takes the small cloth bag, pops it into his pocket, gives it a pat, then hobbles to the gate where Hilda is waiting. When he's safely tucked into the back seat, he holds out his hand and I take it.

'That old curse will never be completely lifted until Bethany is at rest with the others,' he says, squeezing me.

'I felt it lift a bit, though. The curse.'

'It eased. Your kids seem free from what you've told me. But what about you and love, Lilly?'

'I'll be okay...'

'Never too late for love. Work on the mortsafe spell. If not for yourself, then to keep Barry away. He's a bastard, Lilly. Be careful.'

After the car drives away, I stand in the lane. It's cool under the trees, but I'm hot. The older I get, the more I long for summer to end. I need autumn.

Chapter Forty-Eight

Mary and John's wedding vow ceremony is the hottest day of the year. Even with every window open on the bus to Market Forrington everyone is boiled alive. Sophie and Amy are delighted with their frilly purple frocks. I have plaited their hair and tied lilac bows onto their freshly polished school shoes. They sit next to each other holding huge circlets of purple silk roses like kids in a Victorian painting. I have also tied a large purple bow around Ink's neck. The invitation omitted to mention plus ones being human. I'm wearing my best frock, which is red and flowery and comfortable, but ugly sandals. Big Bag is stuffed with things to keep the kids amused and plenty of snacks for Ink.

The bus pulls up in the middle of the high street and we get off and walk quickly along a side street to the church. My plan was to get here nice and early. So of course we're late. As I hurry the kids into the churchyard, I can see Mary – a vision in a tight fitting, strapless lilac gown with a long train – waiting in the porch.

'Oh!' she says, glaring at the twins. 'The flowers are for their hair, and where are their ballet slippers?'

'Sorry, no money for extra shoes,' I say, putting a circlet onto Amy's head.

'It's too scratchy,' she says, whipping it straight off.

'Now come along, girls. Put them on or you won't be perfect,' says Mary, just as Brian appears sweating in a three-piece suit with a lilac waistcoat. We don't acknowledge each other. The twins give their dad a hug.

'And you will need your hands free for this.' Mary gives them a basket filled with rose petals and plonks the circlets on their heads while they are distracted.

'It's too hot!' says Sophie, taking it off. Amy copies her sister, and they stand with their arms folded.

'Now, girls. These were very expensive, and if you don't wear them we won't all look the same.' Mary crouches and I'm sure I hear the dress creak. She pats her own silk flowers and attempts a winning smile. Never easy with that much Botox.

'But we don't want to look like you,' says Amy.

'Flower hats are silly,' says Sophie.

'Mum, don't worry,' says Brian. 'Just let them carry the flowers. It won't matter.'

Mary sighs irritably.

'Come on, Mum. The vicar's getting twitchy.'

'That dog isn't coming in!' she says, pointing at Ink, who is stretched out on the cool stone flags of the porch.

From inside the church, an organ starts to play. 'Now, children, you know what to do,' says Mary, ushering them through the door. She hands them the basket, which is a little too large, especially as they are also holding the 'flower hats'.

The packed church turns to watch. Amy and Sophie are like rabbits caught in the glare of headlights and are near to tears. I kneel beside them and speak quietly. 'It's okay, girls. Really easy job. You've just got to walk to Grandpa John.' I give John a little wave and he waves back and gives the girls a thumbs-up.

'Can't we walk behind Grandma?' says Sophie.

'Why do we have to go first?' says Amy.

'Didn't you bring them for a rehearsal?' says Mary.

'Shall I take them, hold their hands and carry the basket?'

'Dressed like that!' says Mary, baring her teeth at me. 'You'll spoil the whole thing in that ghastly red.'

Brian is too busy mopping his sweaty brow to help. The music stops, and the organist turns around, sees that no one has walked down the aisle and begins again.

Mary takes Brian's handkerchief and dabs her makeup. She's nearly in tears and I don't want to spoil her special day even if I think she's a prat.

'Ink,' I say, 'come and help.'

Ink gets up, has a good stretch and wanders over. 'Inky dog, can you carry this and take the twins to John?' I say.

Ink takes the handle in her mouth.

'You'll be alright, girls. Ink's coming with you. Give me your flowers.'

Before Mary can protest, I position the twins on each side of the big black greyhound. 'Here, put your hands on her back, that's it. Well done.'

As the dog and the twins step into the church, there is a collective 'ahhh'. Ink walks solemnly along as if we have practiced, and the girls make it to Grandpa John, who is all smiles. They don't scatter any rose petals, but you can't have everything.

In my awful red frock, I wait at the back of the church. Ink stays with the kids and they all sit on the floor at the vicar's feet. They look angelic. The two sweet little girls and the big sleek black dog. When the service is over and we are once again in the sunshine, it's all anybody can talk about. A crowd of admirers take their picture. Mary huffs (she can't frown) as the girls stand beside Ink and smile for photographs.

The official photographer is so busy taking pictures of the twins tossing petals into the air while Ink obediently holds the basket, Mary has to remind him of his duties.

After church there is a reception at Forrington Manor, a short walk away. I follow behind, so as not to be a red blot on the purple landscape of this re-wedding.

The function room, predictably, is a cloud of lilac. The guests, also in shades of purple, waft about drinking champagne. I hide behind a fake tree festooned with plastic roses and watch Brian and his girlfriend each holding one of the twin's hands.

'Is that your dog?' says a member of staff. His badge clearly states Manager, so why does he look like he's on work experience from college? I must be getting old. Ink is standing on a sofa in reception.

'Yes,' I say.

'We don't allow dogs on the premises, Madam.'

'She's part of the wedding vow party,' I say blithely as Ink digs frantically at the cushions.

'May I suggest you take it outside?'

'No. She has to stay with me.'

Before he can argue, Mary comes in from the garden with John and the photographer, all of them sweating. John accepts a glass of champagne and goes off to mingle. Mary has stern words with the Manager. She points at me and he points at Ink, who is circling for a nap.

Mid Witch Three

The guests are taking their seats on flimsy chairs that have a lilac net bow tied onto them. I'm just wondering whose job it is to tie bows on the back of chairs and if you can pick any colour when I hear a familiar laugh. Edward is guffawing with a slim woman in a purple trouser suit and spectacular heels. I shrink back behind the fake roses. But in this dress, I'm easy to spot. Edward strides over, clenching his fists and scowling.

'Lilly, we need to talk,' he says.

Has he realised the casket is empty? I wait.

'Please take your seats for the wedding vow breakfast!' says someone over a microphone.

'The dog, Madam.' The young Manager is back. 'I've spoken with the Manager, and he says it's company policy...'

'I thought you were the Manager,' I say.

'I'm the Deputy Manager. Anyway, the dog—' He looks behind at the sofa where moments ago Ink was stretched out for a long hound nap.

'Ahh, it's outside?'

Who knows?

I smile and he slides away to apply his expertise where it's needed.

'Lilly,' says Edward, moving out of the way of a group come to sit at a table behind him.

'I'm sorry,' I lie.

'Even so, I don't think I can trust you now.'

I almost laugh. He needs to formally end the relationship.

I hang my head in pretend shame to hide my relief. He doesn't know I've still got Bethany.

'It's over, Lilly,' he says, shaking his head and walking slowly away. The nearby table of guests is weirdly silent. Obviously heard the whole thing. Maybe I should weep dramatically, so they really have something to gossip about. Then Brian appears with Amy and Sophie.

'Why can't we stay with you?' says Amy.

'I thought there would be cake,' says Sophie.

'I've told you, this is a grownup party,' he says. 'There's a special room just for you.'

'Shall I just take them home?' I say. Brian has gone.

Chapter Forty-Nine

Life gets in the way of anything I want to do for myself. It's a constant theme. I think it's the same for most women. The kids break up for the summer holidays and Belinda hunts for a flat so she can make a new start. Jason spends a lot of time in London. I'm not sure what he's up to, but he seems happy, so I don't pry. Jason is a problem for another day. Between looking after the twins, baking and running the house, there is little time or energy for learning long and complicated spells. I fall into bed exhausted and promise myself that tomorrow I will get some magical learning done. Tricky when the cottage is full of kids who don't know you're a witch.

It's a strange state of affairs because on the one hand I'm delighted to spend time with my grandkids and I'm aware that soon they will be gone, and I won't see them every day. On the other hand, I have a magical responsibility to keep Barry from getting hold of Bethany, who is still hidden in my bedroom. I press on with the endless jobs and childcare, telling myself that in September they will be back at school, and I'll have more time. Walter says the best spell day is Halloween. Which gives me two months to get my act together.

It's a rainy day, so I've got the girls in the kitchen decorating biscuits. The radio is playing Classic FM, and Ink and Claudia are snoozing beside the range. Maud is in the apple tree pecking apples. I'm pressing out scones when Belinda returns from her morning house hunt.

'Found it!' she says, plonking a bag of groceries onto a kitchen chair.

I pop the scones in the oven.

'Perfect little flat in Marswickham. Just off the high street and near the bus,' she says, smiling at her daughters. 'When you're old enough, you can get the bus and visit Lillymar,' says Belinda brightly. 'And, if we get this flat, you can still go to Foxbeck Primary!'

'We like it here,' says Sophie, smearing a blob of pink icing on the table. Amy begins to cry.

'Wait till you see it!' says Belinda.

The rain has stopped, so I pull on wellies and check for eggs so Belinda can persuade them. Since the house hunting began, the twins have been adamant that they want to stay here.

Outside, the wet garden smells fresh and I detect a slight twang of autumn in the air. The chickens come out of their coop now it's dry. They are delightful. I love to see them fluffing and pecking around the garden, even if they help themselves to the veg patch and never lay eggs. Cocksure struts out and ruffles his feathers. Stretching his wings, he fixes me with a malevolent stare.

'Don't start your nonsense, Cocky,' I warn. He'd like to argue, but he knows it's no use with me. I hum a few notes of the soothing song. He folds his wings, blinks and potters off to check on his hens. I lift the lid on the nesting box. Nothing. Perhaps I'm feeding them the wrong food. I'll get in touch with Mr Richards. Ask him to give me some advice.

'Mum! Come on! It's getting cold!'

In the kitchen Belinda is slicing a ready-made pizza. It smells delicious. Even Ink has got out of bed, lured by the smell of cheese.

'Small celebration,' she says, pouring fizzy lemonade. The twins are in a better mood. 'I think we should drive over and see it after lunch,' she announces as she slaps juicy triangles onto our plates. I get the scones out of the oven, then take my place. Like the kids, I enjoy the pizza, but I'm worried about Belinda leaving when the baby is due in a few weeks, even though I understand her need for her own space.

After we've cleared up, we cram into Belinda's small car. It's a bit of a squash. Even without Ink, who I've left behind to guard the dead body in my secret closet. Marswickham is not too busy. We drive halfway along the high street and then turn off, navigating a maze of side roads to a modern building.

'The good thing is it's already empty, so no wait,' she says as we jump out of the car. A young man in narrow grey trousers and pointy shoes waits by the front door. 'Hi, Timothy,' says Belinda. 'This is my mum, Lilly, and my kids, Sophie and Amy.'

'Yes,' says Amy when Timothy looks at them, 'we're twins.'

Sophie pats her mother's tummy and says, 'And this is Marmaduke.'

The flat is ideal. It's on the ground floor, which will be easy for prams and pushchairs. There are three bedrooms, a bathroom, a small kitchen and a large living room. It's a pity there is no garden except for a little patch at the front. But I don't say anything.

'The bedrooms have built-in cupboards,' she says. 'I thought I'd take this small room so the girls can share the big room. Could easily fit two beds in there.'

Mid Witch Three

'And then Wellington can go in here,' says Sophie, standing in the doorway.

'Wellington?'

Belinda shrugs.

'Will Daddy be able to find us?' Amy is crying again. It's very loud in the empty flat.

'Why don't I leave you to it, Ms, er?'

'Blackwood,' says Belinda.

'Ms Blackwood. Yes. Take the key and drop it into the office and we can sort out the paperwork there.'

Belinda takes the keys. 'What do you think, Mum?'

'Seems fine, love.'

'Thought I'd have a chat with them and then take them to the park,' she says.

I can understand she needs a bit of time with her kids. 'I'll walk into town.'

'Great. We'll meet you there later.'

The walk into town takes me twenty minutes. It was only five minutes in the car. I can't think when I last had a look around Marswickham. That's the trouble with not driving; it's easier to buy things online than get the bus. I decide that the best use of my time is to purchase the stuff that's impossible to get right online: underwear. Middle-aged underwear, to be exact. As luck would have it, Marswickham has Bramptons, a large, old-fashioned department store. I take the rickety lift to the lingerie department.

Winter is just around the corner, and I need warm tights. They have a good selection. A bit of secretive packet unwrapping to judge the size of the waistband and leg length would be helpful, but a shop assistant is guarding the display like a magpie does her treasure. And I should know. I choose size extra-large in black– because I'd rather the tights be roomy and comfortable and they'll probably shrink, anyway. A red pair on sale catches my eye. Half price. The only size is large, which is probably too small. I can't resist a bargain. Into my basket they go.

I need a comfortable, non-scratchy bra. Luckily these are on display, and I can have a good feel. The ones I like and can afford come in a bargain pack of three. The colours are awful. Orange with pineapples, a weird shade of pale green with an ice lolly motive and the last is plain beige. Nobody is likely to see them unless they are on the washing line, so I put them in my basket and move on to the knicker display – the silky, lacy sort that are purchased individually. What I need is a multi-pack of the large and comfortable variety.

I'm trying to find them among the thongs and G-strings when a golden shimmer flickers in my peripheral vision. I turn. GFR is perusing the nightwear section. I can't help staring. He's gorgeous in a navy shirt with the sleeves turned back and slightly faded jeans. And his orts – they're glowing.

A shop assistant shimmies over all smiles and charm. She holds up pale grey silk pyjamas. They go toward the pay desk, and I duck out of sight. Good, he's going, and he hasn't seen me. Little miss flirty is keeping him occupied.

Back to my knicker selection. Tricky job when all the models on the packets are bone thin. I can't imagine the thongs, high legs and mini briefs coping with my fat arse and mottled, middle-aged thighs. And why is everything in garish colours? What's wrong with a nice navy blue? What I want is school knickers – in a middle-aged size. There is an array of panty-shorts that look less likely to cause permanent damage to my privates. I'd very much like to undo the cellophane and shake a pair out to see if they'd fit. No chance. Mrs Eagle-eyes is still watching me. Damn.

As I edge along the display, I notice packets labelled 'full panties'. The model is still a twenty-something size ten, but the shape looks comfortable. Now the only question is, what size? Petite, small, medium, large, extra-large or extra-extra-large. Just how big do I need these knickers to be?

I have that strange sense I'm being watched. When I glance at the pay desk, Grant is looking right at me. Now he's walking over. Fuck. I drop the big knicker packet, and as I walk toward him I snatch a packet of something else. We meet beside a mannequin wearing a black negligee.

'Lilith,' he says, staring at the packet of knickers in my hand. Animal print thongs. Size S. He raises an eyebrow. The spell bind over his face looks tighter somehow. But apart from that, the man is positively glowing.

We stand there like idiots. Then I blurt out, 'I'm learning a spell to keep her safe.'

Grant nods. I lower my voice and lean closer. 'It's grand magic. I need seven witches. Will you come?'

'I can't,' he says. Before I can persuade him, he's walking away. I almost throw the thongs at him.

Eagle-eyes is straightening the knicker selection while giving me a hard stare. In her hand is the packet I dropped. I snatch them and thrust the thongs at her.

'Well, really!' she harrumphs as I head for the pay desk.

Unfortunately, the desk is not manned. The shop assistants have gone for a tea break. A small queue forms, and Mrs Eagle-eyes has to serve me. 'We have a no returns policy for these purchases,' she says. She rings up the items after she loudly checks the sizes with me. 'Full size panties size extra-large?'

'Yes.'

'Easy fit washable brassiere three pack, D cup?'

'Yes.'

'Moisture wicking winter tights extra-large.'

'Indeed.'

By the time everyone in the queue knows the size of all my intimate garments, my fingers are tingling.

'Would you like a bag?'

'Got one.' I rummage in Big Bag, grasp the first pocket shopping bag that my fingers find, put it on the counter and step back, making it clear I expect her to pack. She purses her lips and shakes out the banana-cock bag. Quickly stuffs in my purchases and pushes it toward me as if it's on fire. Someone behind me snort-laughs.

Chapter Fifty

I n the high street, I check my phone. I have four missed calls and several texts from Belinda, saying things like 'Where are you?' and 'Call me back?'
I call her back.
'Oh god, Mum!'

'Where are you? What's happened?'

'The baby's happening.' She groans and I can hear the twins fussing in the background. 'I don't know where I am. We came to the park and went for a walk on a public footpath. There's nobody here. Oh shit!'

'Belinda!'

'My waters just broke.'

'Hang on. Did you call the ambulance?'

Another groan. 'Of course I phoned the bloody ambulance!' She hangs up.

I stand in shock for about thirty seconds. Then I hit the emergency call button on my phone. Grant answers on the first ring. 'I'm not doing it, Lilly. You'll have to find someone else,' he says gruffly.

'It's not about that. I need your help. Belinda's having the baby. Right now in the fucking park. Or near the park.'

'Where are you?'

'Outside Bramptons.'

Then I see him running along the street. He grabs my hand. 'The car's not far,' he says as we hurry down a side street. 'Where's your bloody dog?'

'Guarding a dead witch in my cottage,' I pant.

'You should never leave home without her!' He clicks the key fob, and we get into the vehicle. We arrive at the park gates in record time. He abandons his car on a verge, and we rush in. Rain patters on the path. The park is empty. I call Belinda.

'She's not answering.'

The park is huge with a great swathe of green. 'She probably played with the twins, then walked from there,' I say, pointing to the swings at the far end. We run over. Several paths lead off in different directions. 'Fuck!' I say.

'Take the crow,' he says.

'What?'

'The crow, Lilly. Get in its head and search for her. You can do it with your magpie!'

A large crow stands on the grass. Can I do this?

'Don't think. Just do,' he says.

I drop to my knees and put my hands in the wet grass, and the earth's energy greets me. I breathe in. The crow looks directly at me, tilting her head to one side, and spreads her wings to fly away in a panic, so I hum the calming song I use on Cocksure, push the energy toward her and close my eyes. When I open them, I'm inside the crow looking back at us. The crow wants to get out of the rain, but I need her to fly above the treetops in the gathering storm.

Up we go. The rain is heavy on her wings. She hates it, but she does my bidding. Back and forth we follow one footpath and then another. It is hard to judge how far Belinda and the twins might have walked. Perhaps the medics found them. At last, I see a flash of red and green. The twins' raincoats. Belinda won't be far away.

I drag myself back from the bird with difficulty. 'This way,' I say.

Grant runs ahead and I wobble behind. We find them on

a grassy verge beneath a maple tree. I'm on my knees beside Belinda. She's crying and gasping.

Grant goes to the twins. 'Come on, girls, help me look for the ambulance people.' He takes them by the hand and heads off. I do what I can to make my girl comfortable, but what can you do for your daughter when she's giving birth outside, in the pouring rain? I hold her hand, promise help is coming and sing the soothing song in the hope it will take away some of her fear as I cover her with a gorilla-themed rain poncho.

What seems like hours later – but is only ten minutes – Grant reappears with a pair of paramedics and a stretcher.

The paramedics are perfectly calm and absolutely brilliant. In seconds, they have the situation under control. The beautiful baby boy is delivered in the open air. Rain patters on the leaves of the maple tree where the crow sits. Grant has the twins wrapped inside his coat. It's an extraordinary moment as I sit beside my daughter, admiring the baby boy. I'm beyond tears.

'What are you going to name him?' one paramedic asks.

'William,' says Sophie.

Belinda laughs. 'Yes. That will do. William it is.'

After a night in hospital, Belinda and baby William come back to North Star Cottage. It's a busy yet happy few weeks. Walter visits often and declares he will gift Jason and Belinda some money so they can get on the property ladder. I'm a little taken back by this, but he insists, telling us he has no other relatives who he can spoil. Belinda finds an end of terrace in Marswickham with a garden and more space, and

Mid Witch Three

Jason? Jason carries on playing video games and absconding to London every five minutes. I resolve to have a proper, sit-down, 'What are you doing with your life?' talk just as soon as Bel and the kids leave. I'm worried that he will use the money Walter has given him to become a professional layabout.

The first week in October, Any-Job-Steve arrives with his van and Hilda with her own car, which turns out to be a large Volvo. They help with removals. Apart from clothes, toys and a few bits of furniture I have given Belinda, there is not much. Something else I will need to do is tackle Brian; he thinks he's got the moral high ground, but that doesn't mean he gets to keep all my daughter's stuff.

Jason returns from London and is a great help with the twins while we organise Belinda's little house. I mostly coo over William, who is the most cheerful baby. Any-Job-Steve is in his element – he really can do anything. He hangs curtains, assembles flat packs and plumbs in a new kitchen sink. We have fish and chips for dinner, and even Hilda stays to eat with us before driving Jason and I back to the cottage.

I'm glad Jason's home so I can have that 'chat' with him. But as soon as we're back, he's off out and doesn't return until the small hours. I'm making toast for my lunch when he finally shows up in the kitchen in a dressing gown and odd socks. He sits at the table and I give him my tea and toast, cut more bread and boil the kettle again. Best let him eat first. I'm not a complete monster.

We munch away in happy silence for a bit, and then

Jason pushes his plate to one side. 'Mum,' he says, taking a swig of tea.

I'm expecting him to tell me he's buying a sports car or something ridiculous. I wait. 'You know that video game I've been working on?'

Working seems a bit of a stretch. I nod.

'I've been talking to a few companies in London who like the idea.'

'Idea?'

'For my video game. Anyway, yesterday I got an offer for Rainbow Dragon.'

'You've been creating a video game?'.

'Yeah. Trouble is, it all seems great when you're sitting with these people in a chic Bistro in London. But who fucking knows?' He pulls a fancy navy folder from the chair beside him. 'Do you think Walter, or someone from his office, could check this over for me?'

'He'd be delighted.'

'Turns out I can draw cute dragons and programme a video game, but this legal shit is beyond me.'

'I'd love to see some of the game,' I say.

Jason grins, fetches his iPad and shows me Rainbow Dragon.

'I think it's amazing,' I say and mean it.

'It'll be more impactful when there's music and stuff. This is just a concept. But you get the idea.'

I pat his hand and wipe away a tear. We hug and I push

away a pang of guilt for thinking he was just mucking about all this time.

'Keep meaning to show you this,' he says, getting a social media channel up and scrolling until he finds a picture of a slice of cake. 'What do you reckon?'

'Yes, lovely. Nice photo and nice cake,' I say, peering at the screen.

Jason scrolls this person's account. Lots of cakes beautifully photographed by someone calling themselves Sylvia Cakelove. Slowly, the truth dawns.

'Those are mine. My cakes!'

'I thought so too. I wasn't sure at first – because they're all cut into slices and look...' He clicks onto the Sylvia Cakelove website, where you can buy cake by the slice.

'How much!' I cry. 'She's charging half the price of the cake for one slice!'

'Do you remember who bought these cakes?'

'Yes, I bloody do!'

Chapter Fifty-One

I n another week, Jason moves into a flat in Barrington because it's easy to get the train for London there. He's renting while he sells Rainbow Dragon. Turns out Walter has an entire team who specialise in digital intellectual property. They've found him an agent, turned down the original offer and there is now a bidding war. Turns out my son is a quiet genius.

I give the cottage a good clean and have a sort out. Move myself back into the big bedroom. Drag the charity bags full of Jason's childhood clothes to the top of the stairs. Dig over the vegetable patch. Make some jam. Anything to keep busy in my suddenly too quiet home. Ink follows me about and keeps sighing. I think she misses the kids too.

The giant spell book sits on the kitchen table unopened, so I take it up to my witchy attic room in the hope it will help me focus. After months of neglect, my den is covered in dust, so I clean and sort. Eventually, I light some candles, sit at the table with a notebook and give my specs a rub with a little cloth. From the round window, I have a view of the woods. It's October and the leaves are changing. Time is running out. This is by far the most complicated magic I've ever attempted, and there is much to prepare beforehand. I should have started months ago.

I read until I hear a familiar call. 'Ting-a-ling!' I don't hurry to meet Mrs Tingle calling from the garden gate. Cocksure has chased her so many times she's too scared to come in.

'Oh, isn't it ready?' she says, seeing I'm empty handed. She taps her watch. 'I'm on a bit of a schedule here. Will it be long?'

I'm fiddling with my phone, finding Sylvia Cakelove. I show her the screen.

She peers at a slice of Bakewell Tart on her website and feigns complete innocence.

'Is this you?' I ask.

'Me? No.'

I grasp her by the arm. 'Mrs Tingle, you've been selling my bakes as your own for a pretty profit.'

'No. Lilly, I would never do such a thing. It must be someone else,' she gasps, all wide-eyed innocence, but the lie is a dark stain seeping into my hand. I grip her more tightly as Cocksure flies onto the gatepost and stands tall in the October sunshine.

I pull her closer and whisper in her ear. 'I have the uncanny ability to sense when a person lies, Mrs T. And you are a deceitful old bag.'

'Never have I been so insulted in all my life!'

Another lie.

'You're going to close your false business venture and find something legal to do.' We are almost nose to nose. 'Or I will take you to court. My father's a solicitor.'

She blinks. 'It was only a bit of fun. I didn't think they'd sell. They're not that great, your cakes.'

Another lie. I let her go. She staggers back, into the pothole. The muddy water reaches her ankles.

'Look what you've done!' she shrieks, stepping out and shaking her feet. I fold my arms as she squelches to her car. 'They say you're a witch. That's what they say in the village – witch.'

'At least I'm not a cheat and a liar.'

Over the next few weeks, I work on the mortsafe spell. I collect herbs on moonlit nights and hang them to dry over the

Mid Witch Three

range. I crush yew tree roots and mix them with beach sand and dust from the cottage. I sandpaper my wand – just a little – and add the wood dust to moon-blest water. Getting my mother's big black cauldron from behind the old stables, I scrub it clean and boil up a potion with strands of my hair and those of my familiars, even seeking the green-eyed fox for a few clumps of her fur. And every chance I get, I chant the words I must say.

With the basics of the spell organised, my next problem is the need for seven magicals so I can cast grand magic. I post a letter to Elaine at Poorbrook House. It seems the safest way to contact her. She doesn't reply, but I think she will turn up. Mouse agrees – obviously. I have Hilda and Walter and Joan. I still need another, and as Elaine does not get in touch with any suggestions, that leaves GFR. Not ideal.

I've not seen him since Belinda gave birth to William – or Baby Bill, as we call him – in the park. It was a surreal experience; I can't blame him for staying away. I'm going to have to ask him again and insist he helps or, at the least, suggests somebody else.

October is flying by. Every day I resolve to contact him and then bottle out. I'm on my hands and knees under a hedge searching for empty snail shells when a car pulls up in the lane. From Ink's reaction, it's somebody she likes. She's skipping about like a puppy. No wonder – it's Grant. I stand and attempt to brush mud and leaves from my old jeans.

'You left this in my car,' he says, holding up my banana-cock shopping bag. I'd forgotten all about my underwear. I hope he hasn't looked.

'Tea?' I ask as I take the bag.

He stands outside until I ask him in and then brushes his fingertips on the doorstep star. On the stove a small pan simmers. I drop in the empty snail shells and then wash my hands.

'You've started the spell work, then.'

'Long job. But I'm almost there. Just a few more tasks and I'll be ready for Halloween.' He sits at the table and pets Ink as I make tea and lift a chocolate gateau from the fridge.

'My god, that looks delicious.' He grins.

'Made it for someone who didn't collect. Might as well eat it now,' I say, getting plates and forks.

'Who was it?'

'Not entirely sure. But I have a good idea.' I move the banana bag off the table and tell him about Mrs Tingle. I bet she was behind this cake order. Sitting together is oddly weird and strangely cosy. This man has given me cunnilingus in a field. He's witnessed the birth of my grandson. And I'm worried about asking for his help.

'I need seven. To cast the mortsafe spell effectively.'

He nods as he squashes the last of the crumbs onto the back of his fork.

'Still need one more. You could stand to one side or something – keep yourself hidden.'

'No!' he shouts. Ink hops off her blankets and stares at

him. 'Sorry,' he says quietly and holds out his hand for her to sniff. 'Not me, Lilly. You know why.'

The bind around his mouth appears to tighten. I reach out my hand to free him. He shrinks back as if I hold a flame to his face. 'Let me,' I say, softly.

'Why can't you just be content with a bit of normal fucking friendship? It's got to always come down to this. I've bloody told you. I'm hardly going to give up my family for you! Not today, and certainly not on Halloween.'

He snatches his jacket from the back of the door and shrugs it on. *Mrs Beeton* wriggles to the edge of the shelf. I hold up my hand to stop the book's evil intent.

'Just stay out of my life! You're nothing but trouble,' he yells.

Ink barks.

'You came here,' I say. 'Prick.'

'Whenever I see you, I wish I hadn't!'

I lower my hand and flick. *Mrs Beeton* flies from the shelf and whacks him in the stomach. He bends double, and the gateau hits him in the face. Disbelieving eyes peer out from a layer of chocolate. I'd laugh if I wasn't grabbing a lump of cheese from the fridge. 'Why don't you fuck off?' I say.

Off he bloody well fucks, and I throw the piece of cheese into the long grass. Ink harrumphs, but she goes after it, giving me the chance to clean up the mess. Even magical dogs must not eat chocolate.

Chapter Fifty-Two

As it's such a quiet, still night, I walk to the church with a basket on my hip. Ink mooches a few paces ahead. At the lychgate, I expect to see Bethany. It seems so strange without her. In the graveyard, Ink and I go to the family graves.

Mid Witch Three

A breeze rustles leaves along the path and a huge harvest moon rises behind the ancient yew trees. In a few days, on Halloween, the moon will be full. St Gutheridge and All Angels squats among the crooked gravestones. One window flickers with light. Then it's dark. I watch. The old church is hardly used, so it's unlikely a candle going out. 'Probably just the moonlight,' I say to Ink. She's not bothered, snuffling about in the long grass.

Another problem: when I inter Bethany, she'll need a headstone. Something to worry about tomorrow. I put my basket down and get my garden trowel; I need soil from the graves of all my sister witches for the mortsafe spell.

The task takes longer than expected. Grave soil must not be mixed, apparently. So I have labelled jam jars in my basket. The spell book doesn't state how much soil, so I'm opting for a good scoop. Bethany Blackwood is the last and oldest grave. She was the first author of my family grimoire and daughter of the burnt witch of the same name. There is more power than the other graves as I dig. A tingling in my fingertips, a beating of my heart. It's true what they say: there is a lot of magical energy even in an ancient dead witch.

Each grave gave freely, but not this one. Despite the recent rain, the soil is stone. Ink puts her snoot in the way and has a good sniff. I'm tired and cold and could do with a deep bath and a mug of hot chocolate. But I need this grave's soil probably more than any of the others, and I grasp at the weeds beside the ivy-covered headstone. 'It's me, Lilith Blackwood, the midwitch of North Star Cottage!' I say. The soil softens, and I put a good scoop into my jar. 'Right, that's it,' I say to Ink, standing and brushing off my knees.

Drat, I have forgotten to take some from my mother's grave. She kept her magic secret, so I don't think of her as a witch. I chat to her as I dig. 'I'm learning a spell to lay Bethany safely to rest. It should lift the curse for good.' My breath is a cloud in the moonlight, and I wonder if she foresaw this.

My basket is heavy; even a small amount of soil weighs a lot. I should have brought a wheelbarrow. I glance at the church as I struggle past.

Light flickers at the window.

I stop. Ink presses against my leg. I put a hand on the back of her neck where her hackles rise. Curiosity killed the witch, but I can't help myself. I creep around the side of the building to where a low side door stands ajar, casting a thin bar of light over the frosty grass.

If I'd any sense, I would take heed of Ink's response. She's on the path, head down, tail between her legs. Not pushing her long snoot through the door to see what's happening. I imagine a kindly priest at his evening prayers.

'Come on, Ink,' I say, ducking inside. I'm in a back room stacked with chairs and tables. Dusty boxes and hymn books line the shelves. I walk toward the light through a door and into the church where candles burn on the altar. It's quiet and still. 'Hello. Anybody there?' My words thunder. I step closer and stand in the middle of the aisle. The pews are empty. The main doors are closed. At a rustle behind, I turn, expecting Ink. Instead, there's a man in a long robe with the hood pulled over his face. Dark orts seep across the stone floor. I don't need to see his face to recognise who it is.

'Barry Rutherford,' I say.

'I thought you'd never get here,' he says, as if we had an engagement.

Then everything goes blank.

Chapter Fifty-Three

I don't know how long it is until I wake. My mouth is dry, I need to pee and my head throbs. It's dark. Completely dark. No chink of light or hint of shadow. I'm lying on my side on cold stone, my hands and feet tied behind my back. Somewhere someone softly cries.

Mid Witch Three

'Who's there?' I say into the blackness.

The sniffling continues and then, 'I'm so sorry, Lilly.'

'Mouse?'

More crying, louder this time.

'It's going to be okay. Just give me a minute,' I say, trying to sound reassuring. I mutter an unbinding spell. It takes two tries, but the rope loosens enough to free my hands. I sit up and snap my fingers for a flame to see by. Shadows jump across the vaulted ceiling and over the tombs. I say the unbinding spell again, more confidently this time, and the ropes on my ankles flee.

'Mouse, where are you?' I hold my flame high and the shadows leap.

'Over here...'

I find him behind a stone sarcophagus. He's not even tied up, but he's injured. Curled in a ball and crying like a child.

'What did he do to you?' I ask.

Mouse shakes his head. He's terrified. 'Just wait there,' I say, as if the poor bloke can move. I wander through the crypt. It's not that large – maybe half the size of the small church above. I came down here once as a child with my mother. Can't remember the reason now. There's a niche by the door with a wooden angel in it and candle stubs. I light the largest with my witchflame and carry it back to Mouse. Now I can see him properly, I can ease his discomfort.

He is bound by a spell more harsh than the one that holds Grant in thrall. This one hurts. Barbed lines dig into his fading orts. I kneel beside him, ready to remove it.

'Don't, don't touch me. I'll die!' He's hysterical, poor man.

'Mouse, you have to trust me. If I leave you like this, you will die.'

He's shaking, and I put my hand gently on his shoulder and sing the soothing song. From my pocket I take my wand and wind the threads of the hex onto it. So many jagged lines that don't want to let go, but I make them leave, twisting my wand until Mouse is free. I slide the bundle off my wand and throw it into the candle flame, where it burns with dark smoke and angry hisses. Mouse sleeps, so I cover him with my coat to make him more comfortable. Then I wander around the crypt. There are no ghosts. Even if there were, I don't think I'd be worried. I read inscriptions on the tombs and run my hand over an empty wooden coffin propped against the wall. There is a stack of slate roof tiles, a weeping plaster angel and a headstone. It is old but not weathered and the inscription is clear.

Here lies Bethany Edith
Witch of the Blackwood
Whose life was taken in the eighteenth year of her age.

A tree and a star are etched beneath the date.

I've always known she was young, but the truth of it brings me to my knees. For a long time I kneel there in the candlelight, my resolve to cast the mortsafe spell stronger than ever.

At the door I try an unlocking spell, to no avail. Then I listen to the quiet and sense Ink is out there somewhere – and Maud. I close my eyes. Maud perches on the church roof,

Mid Witch Three

preening herself in the moonlight. It's easy to settle inside her and look about.

The graveyard is peaceful. Ink hides behind Sir Galahad's tomb, her old tartan coat blending with the ivy. A cloud covers the moon, and light from the church windows flickers and is gone. In the new dark, the side door creaks open.

Voices!

I hop down the roof and perch on the back of a pig-shaped gargoyle. Barry comes out, whispering to someone. I'm interested to find out who hit me over the head. Ida Carmichael-Grey steps onto the path. She's stronger than she looks. My head is throbbing.

They murmur to each other as they lock the door, and I'd like to fly near to listen but they'd easily recognise Maud for what she is. Ida stops before they go under the lychgate and casts a hex on the church. I'm not worried; I've been catching her useless hexes in jars for months. I hop back onto the roof to watch them walk along the lane toward Fox Green. They must have parked their car there, so I wouldn't see it.

When they are out of sight, I shake my feathers and come back to myself. Mouse is waking. He rubs his eyes with his fists and sits up, blinking in the candlelight.

'How are you?' I say.

'Sorry. Very sorry. He made me tell him.'

'It's fine. Don't worry. He's a horrid man.' I pat his arm. 'It's not your fault. But I'd like you to tell me what you told him,' I say as kindly as I can.

'Everything. He knows everything. About the mortsafe

spell. That you're going to cast it on All Hallows. He knows you have the burnt witch hidden at North Star Cottage.'

'Any idea what he's planning?'

Mouse pulls out a large spotted handkerchief and blows his nose with a honk. 'I heard him and her talking.' He lowers his voice as if he thinks we might be overheard. 'She's bringing the Coven – the "Inner Coven" – on the night.' I lean close to hear. 'They were talking about a sacrifice for the burnt witch's power. It's dark magic, Lilly.' His stomach rumbles loudly and I still need a pee.

'How long have you been in here?'

'Not sure. Couple of days?'

No wonder he's in such a state. Locked in the dark and damp with no food or water. Not to mention the hex.

'Come on, it's time to go,' I say.

'It's no good. I've tried to find a way out. The door's spelled shut.'

'It's going to be ok. Ink's out there, and she can open most doors.' I put my fingers to my lips and whistle in a loud, arcing loop. Dogs have very good hearing. I just hope my magical dog's is better than most. With the candle, I lead us to the low door and whistle again. We wait. Mouse wrings his hands. Can she hear me? Then the door opens, and Ink greets us with her skinny wriggle dance.

We follow Ink up winding steps and through the dark church. Outside, I search for my basket. 'What have you lost?' says Mouse, hugging himself.

'I was taking soil from my family graves – for the spell.'

Mid Witch Three

'Barry has probably been waiting for you to do this.'

'I didn't notice anything watching. I'd realise if a bird was his familiar,' I say.

'They don't come to people who steal magic,' says Mouse with a shudder.

'Why don't you wait for me under the lychgate while I search for my things?' I say. Mouse is too weak to argue.

As soon as he's gone, I dodge behind Sir Galahad's memorial and squat for that much needed pee. Ironic that the older I get, the more I need to pee – and yet, if caught short in the countryside, squatting low enough so that I don't piddle on the back of my jeans is proving more difficult. I hold the ivy on Sir Galahad's memorial to steady myself and hope Barry doesn't return and catch me with my pants down. As I stand and make the all-important sidestep, my knee creaks painfully. By the time I've righted myself, fastened my jeans and cursed my knees, a large clump of ivy has come away, revealing my basket. A wave of relief floods over me that Barry has not got hold of the grave soil. I thank the ivy.

Poor Mouse looks cold and hungry sitting in the lychgate, so we go home. After I've fed him beans on toast and a large slice of chocolate gateau, I insist he stays.

'I don't like doors,' he wails. 'I want to see the sky!'

'It's not safe in the wood, Mouse. You need to stay here with me. Just until...' I take him by the elbow and steer him up the stairs and into the bathroom. He stands there like a forlorn child, his dirty face streaked with tears. He's wearing the Turkish slippers. They're covered in mud. I give him a towel and drag in one of the charity bags that live on my landing. 'Have a nice bath. See if you can find something in here to wear and I'll make you some hot chocolate.' His face lights up. Mouse is easily distracted by sugar.

Later, when he's tucked up in Belinda's room with hot chocolate, a stack of shortbread and Claudia for company, I sneak outside.

The beautiful moon has gone, and the clouds have gathered. A misty rain falls on this still night as I renew the protection spells around my boundary. 'Should have done this around the church and wood,' I say to Ink. Thankfully witches' familiars are like normal dogs in that they love you unconditionally even if you are an incompetent witch.

She follows me into the woods, where I cast more protection spells and gather blackwood leaves for magical strength.

Back at the cottage, I wash the Turkish slippers and put them on the range to dry. Then I spend the night on the easy chair with my clothes on and my wand in my hand.

Chapter Fifty-Four

Rain on the window wakes me early. In the kitchen, I make tea and toast, check my emails and write a to-do list. I have orders for two lemon drizzle cakes and a dozen iced buns in pink and white. I press on with the jobs and message Walter to let me know when he can chat.

It's only 8.30am when he video calls me. Walter, spritely in a yellow tartan dressing gown, is eating breakfast in bed.

'Hold on, my darling,' he says, 'let me prop you against the toast rack. That's better. Right oh. Let's hear your news.' He cuts the top off his boiled egg with a fancy silver gadget.

'Barry locked me in the church crypt last night...' I begin.

Walter happily eats while I tell him the whole story, occasionally raising his eyebrows and nodding. 'Well,' – he dabs his mouth with a linen napkin – 'sounds like you've had quite a night.'

Halloween is only two days away and so Walter decides the best course of action is to gather the others in readiness. He will arrive tomorrow with Joan and Hilda. Mouse is already here (I'm not to let him leave) and Joan has had a secret word with Elaine.

'So we just need one more person,' says Walter, peering at me over the top of his specs.

'I can't think of anyone. I thought you'd know someone?'

'No, my dear. There's just the one fellow and you've got two days to sort him out.'

Mouse ambles into the kitchen in Jason's old Spiderman dressing gown.

'Mouse is here,' I say, turning the phone around.

'Ahh, if it isn't young Master Kregalle!' cries Walter.

Mouse peers at the phone, takes a bow and says, 'Mr Cranford! How are you?'

Mid Witch Three

I give Mouse the phone so they can have a chat and go upstairs for a shower. An hour later, they're still talking about old times.

'Lilly, you know what must be done,' says Walter when Mouse returns my phone with a bow.

'No,' I hiss. 'I don't know. He's made it very plain where his loyalties lie. We need another to make the numbers.'

'Male pride is a complicated thing, but at the end of the day, everyone wants to be rescued.' He winks and ends the video call.

Mouse stands at the kitchen window looking toward the woods with longing on his face. I touch his elbow. 'As soon as this is sorted out, we'll get you somewhere to stay.'

'I like it. The woods are where I came from. Where we all came from. It was a long time ago…'

My phone chirps, which I ignore. 'You're welcome to stay in the Blackwood if that's what you want. But it might be cold in the winter.'

'I'm free?'

'Yes, of course. But can you stay in the cottage until it's safe? And I need…'

'Witches for the spell. Yes. Be better to have more than seven,' he says, looking at the woods again.

'Much better,' I say and try not to worry that I might only have six. Ink comes in from the garden, closes the door behind her with a nudge of her snoot and leans against me. I pat her sleek head. Would a magical familiar count?

'Why don't you get dressed and I'll make us some pancakes. We could have maple syrup.'

I tell Mouse to help himself from the charity bags while I get on with icing the buns. I keep two for the twins just in case Belinda drops in on the school run and box the rest ready for collection. Then I crack an egg (not one from my own hens) and make pancake batter.

Mouse arrives in the kitchen wearing pink jeans with ripped knees and an orange fluffy sweater with a sparkly unicorn. And the Turkish slippers. He seems quite happy with his attire, so I make no comment. He enjoys his pancakes with a lot of maple syrup then helps with the washing up. I tell him that Walter, Ellaine, Hilda and Joan will be staying, and he's delighted. 'A proper witch party!' he says, drying a cake tin.

'I'm not sure where everyone is going to sleep.'

'You'll need to fetch Mr Grant.'

'I don't think he wants to come to this witch party.'

'He does.' Mouse nods vigorously. 'He does.'

I ignore this and set about making up beds. I have a few sunbeds in the stables, and I do what I can. 'Everyone will have to decide for themselves where they want to sleep,' I say, looking at a bed I've made on the sofa.

'You should go now. Before it gets dark,' says Mouse, trying on a knitted blanket.

'Where?'

'Mr Grant's.'

I force a laugh. 'No idea where he'd be?'

Mid Witch Three

Mouse closes his eyes. Takes a deep breath. 'He's at his flat in town. I'll show you.' He places his cold little hands over my eyes. With a jolt, I can see Grant. He's sitting at a desk in tracksuit bottoms and a t-shirt.

'Bloody hell. How do you do that?' I gasp.

Mouse smiles. 'I can do a lot of things with freedom and sugar.' He chortles. Then he's serious again. 'You need to get him.'

'But I need to get Bethany's headstone from the crypt, and I don't know where he lives.' I'm still making excuses.

'That's easy,' he says. 'I will fetch the headstone, and I'll bring your fox to keep me safe, and I'll show you where he lives.' I expect another bit of witchery. Mouse finds a pen and paper in the kitchen and writes the address.

Chapter Fifty-Five

When I call Any-Job-Steve for a lift he says he'll be forty-five minutes so I go upstairs to change. What do you wear to persuade a man to help with the biggest spell of your life?

The banana bag is on the floor in my bedroom. I haven't

Mid Witch Three

unpacked it because of some mad idea about organising my knicker drawer and throwing old stuff out before adding the new. I empty the banana bag onto the bed and stare. This isn't my shopping. Well, some of it is: packet of comfy full knickers; warm tights; budget bras pack of three. But there's more: a matching set of red satin briefs and a plunge bra; sheer stockings and a suspender belt; a short silk dressing gown in pale pink with matching bed shorts and a camisole top.

He must have put his own shopping in my bag. These can only be for Rebecca. Putting them to one side, I open the knickers and select red ones with a leaf design and a bra from the three pack – pale green with ice lollies. My reflection in the long mirror is ghastly, but the underwear is comfortable and affordable. Good choice.

Next on, the warm black tights. They are soft and woolly, and I sit on the end of the bed and pull them on and on and on. When my legs are covered, I still have a handful of material left. I'm not tall, but how tall was the person in mind when they designed these tights? I pull the waistband up. Somehow the top of the tights are not long enough to cover my bum. I'm cut off mid buttock. I ease the waistband down so it's under my stomach and under my bum at the back. Nope. Off they come. If any woman is that shape – two metre legs with a short narrow waist – I'd like to see her.

I open the bargain red woolly tights. They are a nice cherry red and I pull them on. They don't have overlong legs, and the waist is generous and reaches all the way over my boobs to my armpits.

Any-Job-Steve's van pulls up in the lane. Drat, he's early. I wrestle the waistband under my boobs. I look ridiculous, like I'm going to do a mime about a chicken. The only clean dress is a denim pinafore. I put on a red t-shirt and the dress and hurry downstairs – and nearly break my neck! The tights have a foot shape. An enormous, twice-the-length-of-my-actual-foot shape. Whose genius idea was this? Who did the designer know with short legs, big feet and a very long body? I'd laugh if I wasn't so bloody cross.

'Come on, Inky dog. Get your coat,' I say, finding my boots. I can't pull the tights higher or I'll have a heel shape in the back of my leg, so I tuck the extra footage under my toes and squash my boots on.

Ink gets out of bed and stretches. Mouse is sitting at the kitchen table with a teaspoon and a bag of sugar. Grabbing Big Bag, the banana bag with Rebecca's presents and my phone, I throw on a cardigan and a duffle coat. Ink shakes, and now she's wearing a coat – not the old tartan one but the new one I made her, which makes me smile.

'Don't eat all the sugar!' I call. 'I've got cakes to bake tomorrow.'

The drive to Barrington takes ages. The traffic is awful and there are three lots of road works. I hold my phone on my lap while Steve chats about his grandkids. Should I text GFR and tell him I'm on my way? I don't want to turn up and find him gone. Then again, if I text, he's bound to guess why I'm visiting and decide to avoid me.

'What time shall I collect you?' asks Steve as he pulls up outside a glossy apartment block.

'Oh, staying the night with a pal,' I say, holding up Big Bag.

'Ahh, right you are then!'

I pay and wait until he drives away. Then I get the bit of paper with the address on from my pocket. Yes, this is the correct building. I push the large glass door. No going back now.

A doorman greets me from behind a marble desk. 'How may I help?' he asks pleasantly.

'Visiting a friend,' I say, wishing I knew the flat number. All I have is Barrington Towers.

'Are they coming down?' he says, nodding to a 'sorry dogs not allowed' sign.

'She's not a sorry dog,' I say, twitching Ink's lead in the hope she gets the hint.

Ink steps forward and wags her tail. She's now wearing a service dog harness. The doorman doesn't pet her. 'I've never seen a greyhound service dog,' he says, eyeing her suspiciously.

'They're very good. Nice and calm.'

'What can she do?'

'Oh, she's in training.'

'Aren't they supposed to pick stuff up if you drop it? Open doors and things for people in wheelchairs?'

'Yes, that's it.'

Ink stretches out on the thick carpet and starts dragging herself along for a nice carpet scratch. 'Not exactly highly trained behaviour,' he says.

'Well. Like I say. Work in progress.' I scowl at Ink, who carries on scooting the side of her face along the carpet with a big doggy grin.

An old-fashioned telephone rings loudly on the desk. Startled, Ink jumps up and barks.

'Oh, good girl. Is the telephone ringing? Well done,' I cry, finding a dog biscuit in my pocket.

The doorman answers the phone. 'Yes, of course, Mrs Lamington. I'll be right up.'

Ink sits in front of me, ears up as I continue to praise her. She leans her long neck forward for the biscuit. I give her the treat, which she nibbles a little at a time, making a huge crumby mess.

'She's going to be a hearing dog?' he says.

'Early days. But yes,' I say.

'I had an uncle who was deaf. Who are you visiting?' He picks up the telephone.

'Grant Rutherford.'

'Who shall I say is calling?'

'Rebecca.'

Chapter Fifty-Six

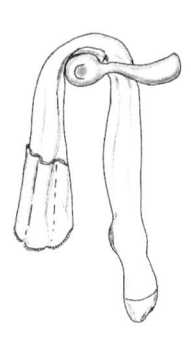

O f course, GFR lives in the penthouse on the top floor. I step out of the lift and into a hallway.

'Have you come to suck my dick?' calls Grant through the open door.

I wonder what Rebecca's response would be.

Get me a cushion for my knees?

Yes?

It'll cost you?

Ink wags her tail. She's already ditched her disguise and lead and trots inside. I wish I was as enthusiastic and stand on the threshold. A long mirror shows me how unlike the glamorous Rebecca I am in my funny old pinafore dress and red tights.

I unzip my muddy boots and step inside, red feet flapping.

'Be there in a minute, honey,' he calls. I can hear water running. Is that his response when she visits? Jump in the shower? Probably.

From outside, I expected his place to be modern and clinical. On the contrary, it's all bookshelves, pictures and comfy chairs, wood floors and thick rugs in earthy tones. It's cosy and warm and I wonder how long he's lived here.

Grant strides into the living room with a white towel around his waist. Ink scoots about excitedly, and I try not to stare at his bare chest and shimmering golden orts. He looks fit, both magically and physically.

'It's you?!' he says, patting Ink.

'Yeah, just me. Better put some clothes on. I haven't got time for a blow job.'

'Why are you here, Lilly?'

'I'll make some tea while you get dressed.' I turn away. Definitely can't concentrate with half-naked, tattooed and hot-as-shit Grant.

Ink settles in an easy chair with a contented sigh. She's been here before then. I flop-flap in the ridiculous tights to a door that I hope is the kitchen. It is.

Masculine, yet homely. Wooden butcher's block. Green cabinets with brass fittings. Black-and-white tiled floor and a large pine table and six vintage metal chairs. The kitchen window is the length of the room, and city lights glow far below.

By the time I've made two mugs of tea, he's back wearing jeans and a black t-shirt.

'How's Belinda and baby William?' he says, sitting at the table.

'Doing fine, thanks. She's moved into an end of terrace in Marswickham. They seem to be settling down.'

'That's great,' he says, taking the lid off a sugar bowl and putting two spoonsful into his tea.

'What do you want, Lilly?' he asks it softly.

'I need your help with the mortsafe spell.'

He sighs and stirs his tea. 'There's nothing I can do.' He doesn't meet my gaze.

'I've been thinking. About your predicament. Maybe I could release your binds, you make up the seven for the spell and then, when it's done, I'll put them back on you. If that's what you want.'

Grant laughs without humour. 'How's that going to work, Lilith? You think my brother won't recognise me? You realise he'll be there to stop you, and he won't be alone.'

'You're on his side, then?'

'I'm on no one's side. I've made it clear I'm not getting mixed up in this and he respects my wishes. He's my brother.' He lifts his tea and puts it down again. 'If you'd had siblings, you'd understand. I can't just turn my back on him. He's family. You can't choose family.'

'You realise your brother is a total bastard?'

'Was there anything else?' He stands, indicating I should go. I stay put.

'Coward,' I say quietly.

'What?'

'You're a coward. It's easier to ignore your brother's wrongdoings. Easier than doing the right thing.'

'I've had a rough week, Lilith. Nothing you can say is going to change my mind.' He holds the door open.

'You understand this affects us all? If I don't get Bethany peacefully interred with the other witches, the curse goes on ruining our lives and those of our children.'

As soon as I say this, I remember he and his brother haven't got kids. No wonder they don't care. 'That baby boy you saw being born, Grant! Doesn't he deserve love?'

I say nothing about not wanting Barry to use Bethany for his own nefarious ends.

On the wall, an intercom buzzes. Grant presses a button. 'Mr Barry is here to see you, sir.'

'Thanks, Mack,' says Grant. He's gone pale and his orts are strange. 'No back door,' he says, stating the obvious.

'I'll hide.' But where?

'Might be safer to say you dropped in and leave as he arrives. I'll tell him I turned you down – which I have.'

We're in the sitting room now, and I'm shoving Ink out of the easy chair and straightening the cushions. 'There's a problem with that plan. Barry locked me in the church crypt last night. With Mouse.'

He opens his mouth to say something, but there's no time.

'He thinks Rebecca's up here – that's what I told the doorman. Do you think he said something to Barry?'

'Probably.'

'Good. I'll be Rebecca. In the shower.'

'Right,' he says.

He gets my things from beside the door and shoves them in my arms. 'Through there. There's a shower in the ensuite. Ink, come.'

The bedroom is more cosy, masculine chic. I muss up the bed and draw the curtains. Taking the red bra and knickers from the banana bag, I drape them over the bed, throw a stocking over the door handle for good measure and turn on the shower. Soft music plays. Of course, he has speakers in the bathroom. This must be Rebecca's lurve playlist. Yuck.

'We've got to be quiet,' I whisper to Ink, trying to settle her on the bathmat and wrapping a towel around her to keep her cosy. Ink won't lie down. She sits bolt upright, ears pricked, and when we hear voices, she curls her lip.

I sit with my arm around her and listen, but I can't make out what they're saying over the shower and the music. Ink's hackles rise and, like her, I sense Barry and it's not good. When I saw him in the church, I was the superior witch. As I watch his murky brown orts swirl under the bathroom door, that is no longer true. Whose magic has he stolen to make him stronger than me?

They argue and I wait, wondering how long I should leave the water running before it looks suspicious. Then Grant is back. 'Nice touch,' he says, holding up the stocking. He turns the shower off. Even in the steam, I can see his orts are diminished.

I get up from the floor and try not to grunt. Ink saunters into the bedroom with the towel on her back, jumps into the bed, circles and settles herself for a proper nap. Grant pets Ink and tucks her in. But those orts... I don't like the look of those orts.

He pats Ink's head as the soft and sexy music plays. 'You should try this on,' he says, tossing the bra at me. He's giving me his sexy-as-fuck smile, but I'm not fooled. GFR is afraid. Away from the bathroom steam, I can see his dark green orts clearly. What's worse is that they are not fading back to his usual golden glow. I've read that book Mouse loaned me and learnt what the colours mean. This is a bone-deep fear of a particular person.

Grant sits on the edge of the bed, hooks the knickers with a finger and lifts an eyebrow. 'Thought the colour would suit you.' I step closer and he snakes an arm around my waist. Even with the sexual tension between us, those orts are still a horrible green.

'Are you afraid of Barry?' I say.

Mid Witch Three

The question catches him off guard. He hesitates and forces a laugh. 'He's my brother.'

Truth.

'Answer the question. Are you afraid of him?'

'Of course not.'

Lie.

His eyes widen as he remembers I can tell the difference between truth and lie as easily as black and white. He doesn't move. We stay locked in the stare. And somewhere deep inside of me, I know he wants to be saved.

I pluck the binding spell from his face like a spider's web. There are more tendrils than last time. I have to pull and wind and speak aloud the witch words. The web changes to ropes in my hands, heavy and laden with slime and muck. My physical self wants to drop them with revulsion. Witch me knows they are another of Barry's illusions. I grasp them tighter and pull. When the last is free and I whisper a counter curse, they shrivel and fizzle away.

Grant rubs his face with his hands. He starts to get up but I'm not finished yet. This time I'm going all the way. 'Be still!' I command. Grant is frozen and unblinking. 'Show me what binds you.'

He cannot disobey and holds out his arm. I grasp his wrist. The Coven's mark of a black feather is not out of place among his other ink. I lean in to scrutinise it then brush my fingertips over the design to judge the magical power within.

'Wait there,' I say, even though he can't move until I release him from the bind.

In the kitchen, I find a small jar of anchovies and tip the contents into a bowl. GFR cannot move. He's still holding out his arm. Ink puts her long snoot on his shoulder, as if to reassure him. She thumps her tail as I approach, jar and wand in hand.

He's so still and silent. This terrifies me. I've never used my power to take someone's free will. I'm not that kind of witch. His orts are a strange mist, and it's clear he's full of trepidation. If I worry, I won't go through with this, and I'll never know if I should have set him free. Making someone do something against their will is not the witch I want to be, but what if he can't be free unless I free him? What if his only chance is if I take the initiative?

I don't look at his face for fear of seeing regret. 'I can reverse all this – if that's what you want,' I say. Although I'm unsure how. My hands shake as I hold my wand over the Coven's mark and close my eyes to centre my magic. Acknowledging the power within myself, strong and pure, I call it forth. My stumpy yew wand is the focus of my strength; with a flick, the feather peels away. Its magical claws are deep, and I pull hard to drag it from him. At last, it is a curling, struggling thing that hangs on wisps of smoke at the end of my wand. I hold the jar beneath it. The black feather writhes and wriggles toward Grant. I speak stern witch words to get it into the jar and keep it there while I screw on the lid. Then I snap my fingers to release him from my thrall and step back.

Will he be angry?

Chapter Fifty-Seven

Hard to be angry when a greyhound is licking your ear. Grant flops onto the bed and lies there while Ink wags her tail and stands on his chest. I'm not sure what to do. Is he okay?

'You're too heavy. Get off, you mad dog,' he says, getting

up. He pets her while she does her skinny wriggle dance. I get it. Grant is back to normal, and Ink knows it.

Ink and I follow him to the kitchen and watch while he drinks a pint of water. 'I guess I'm on your side now,' he says, wiping his mouth with the back of his hand. His orts still look a bit iffy.

I don't have time to process exactly what he means. Grant is across the floor and is kissing me. Proper, full on squeezing me tight and tongues. No messing. When we come up for air, he holds me close, cradling my head against his chest. 'I want to fuck you, Lilly. But we should talk.'

Truth.

He lets me go and I move away, only to stumble and fall headlong onto the rug. 'Oops!' says Grant, helping me up and trying to keep a straight face. 'I think I might have been standing on one of your, er...' He's laughing at my ridiculous chicken feet.

I sit at the kitchen table while he makes tea. His orts have returned to a gentle golden glow. They're not as bright as I've seen them, but he's okay.

'Tell me about being locked in the crypt,' he says.

I tell him the whole story.

'Ida's was there,' he says.

'I can't believe Barry has convinced the Coven to get so involved.'

'You'd be surprised.'

'Why are they helping with something that will just make him more powerful? I mean, what have they got to gain?'

'Barry has convinced them that the burnt witch will make them all stronger.'

'How?'

Grant shrugs. 'Not sure. I'm not exactly on the management committee.'

I hear a door slide open and I reach for my wand.

'It's ok. Just Ink letting herself out for a pee on the roof garden.'

'She knows her way about then?'

'Yeah. Had this flat for ages.'

'What about the "no sorry dogs" policy?'

'I used to sneak her in by the service lift from the underground car park.'

Ink wanders into the kitchen, and Grant puts a bowl of water down for her.

'I should go,' I say, standing.

'No. You should stay. Barry thinks you're safely locked away. Mouse will keep a low profile. I told my brother I'm not leaving the flat until November the first. He thinks he's got everything sorted.'

'I don't understand?'

'You can't risk being seen.'

'What I don't understand is how does Barry think he's going to get his hands on Bethany if I'm shut in the crypt and not about to take her out of hiding and cast my protection spell on Halloween?'

'Barry plans to use the special powers Halloween bestows to break into North Star Cottage and steal her.'

I'm already walking to the bedroom to retrieve Big Bag and leave. Grant pulls me into an embrace in the doorway. 'Don't worry about Mouse. He's a powerful witch if he gets enough sugar.'

'He was eating a bag of demerara when I left,' I say.

'Stay. I promise this will work out. You've got the seven. We just need to keep low.' He taps a message into his phone and shows me. It's to Elaine and simply says, 'Free. See you tomorrow night.' He presses send.

A response pings back. He shows me the thumbs up.

'Anyway, you have no excuse not to stay. It's not as if you don't have a change of underwear.'

'Rebecca's underwear.'

'What makes you think that? I bought it for you. It's your size.' He holds imaginary large boobs, and I have to laugh. 'And I think the stockings would be much safer than the, er...' He's laughing at my feet again.

'Okay, I'll stay.' I text Walter to let him know where I am and that they should all make themselves at home. A part of me worries what they will all eat. As if reading my thoughts, Walter sends a picture of everyone at the kitchen table eating fish and chips from the paper.

In the living room, Grant picks up the anchovy jar and peers at the feather inside. 'What do I do with this?' he says, switching on a lamp for a closer look.

From around my neck, I lift the ribbon with the little pouch tied to it, take out the sea glass and hand it to him.

'Where did you get this?'

Mid Witch Three

'My mother's Coven mark. Remember that day Ink dug it up from the grave?'

'It just looked like a muddy stone.'

'It keeps the Coven's hexes away if you keep it close.'

'She was a clever witch, your mum.'

'She was.'

'Make yourself at home.'

'You look exhausted.'

'Yeah, and grubby. Think I'll have a soak in the bath.' He rubs his face and heads to the bathroom. I sit on the sofa with Ink. Then I get up and put a hex on the front door so no one can get in. Just in case brother Barry comes back.

'Lilly! Any chance of a back scrub?'

I debate whether I should ignore him or shout no. Then I think, fuck it, why not?

Chapter Fifty-Eight

T he bathroom is exactly that: a room with a bath. A large circular bath set before a tall window. I stare at the view of the city. The moving lights of cars on the roads. Windows glowing yellow. I prefer the countryside, but this is still pretty.

'Is there a curtain?' I'm not sure I want to get naked in public.

'It's one-way glass. We can see out, but the good people of Barrington can't see in,' he says.

He's lit candles – the expensive kind that have three wicks and smell amazing. I'm not the first woman he's seduced with his bathroom. No doubt Rebecca flings off her clothes so he can get an eyeful of her designer underwear. I wriggle out of the ridiculous tights and my huge knickers and unclip my bra so I can remove everything in one go, including the sea glass pouch, which I put on a shelf by the sink where white towels are neatly rolled. Does he do that, or does he have a cleaner? Next to the towels is a small basket of spare toiletries. I unwrap a toothbrush and clean my teeth. Might as well.

Grant moves his legs to one side as I step into the bath. I sink into the hot water, glad there are lots of bubbles so I can hide.

'Absolute bliss. I never have a nice soak.'

'That's the trouble with you. You don't make time for yourself.'

'I suppose you're always in here bathing by candlelight.'

'It's not unknown.'

'Alone?' I open one eye.

'Not always.'

At least he's honest. He slides his leg over so he's touching mine. His touch excites me. I can't think of anything else – I'm totally focused on where our skin meets. It's ridiculous really; he's only resting his leg. Then again, we are naked and, well, wet.

'You can't see the view over there,' he says, nudging me.

Grant is the view as far as I'm concerned. He holds out a hand, which I take, and he slides me across, somehow twizzling me about until I'm settled between his legs. He kisses the back of my neck, which is bliss. His erection presses against me as his fingers find the sweet spot between my legs. Grant's good with his fingers, not too rough or too light. Pleasure pulses through me and I wriggle. I'm no sex goddess. Truth is, I'm slightly embarrassed to let myself go.

'I've got you, Lilith,' he mumbles in my ear and wraps his free arm around me, holding me gently yet firmly in place. 'Come for me, Lilith, because I'm not going to fuck you until you do.' His deep voice shivers through me.

His fingers are still working my clitoris. He picks up the pace and increases the pressure just enough. I'm undone and make a strange yelp then grab his wrist because I can't take anymore. When I've got my breath back, I reach behind for his hard cock. I'm not quick enough. Grant gets out of the bath, water falling off his dark skin. He's gorgeous and I can't take my eyes off him. No wonder my specs have steamed up.

'Twenty years ago, I would have shagged you in the bath. These days my knees can't take it. Come on, there's a comfy bed where I can give you a good seeing to.'

We don't stop to dry ourselves. I pad wetly after him like an eager puppy. In the bedroom, he pulls the covers off the bed and takes lubricant from a bedside drawer. After he's applied some to his cock, he pushes me onto the mattress, where I bounce and giggle, legs open with abandon. He's on top of me, gazing at my face, grinning his sexy grin, but his eyes say that this is more than us having fun. He edges nearer so the tip of his cock nudges my vagina. I need him inside me and hook my legs over him. He holds back, kissing me into an impatient frenzy. Then he enters me, long and slow and we find a steady rhythm. Grant is nice, more than nice. I like the muscles in his back and shoulders and the scent of his wet skin.

When he pulls a pillow under my hips, the new angle is a game changer. I was enjoying it before. Now I'm moaning like a porn star who can't act. When he speeds up and pumps me harder, nothing else matters. I'm not making to-do lists in my head or wondering if the kids are okay. I'm breathless and having a silent orgasm. This man knows how to fuck me into oblivion.

A few manly grunts and he comes, dipping his head into the curve of my neck. We stay locked together for a bit. Then he reaches for the bedside drawer and fishes out a box of tissues. Man-sized – what else?

Much later, after we've had a nap, I hear him in the kitchen feeding Ink a tin of tuna. Dressed in one of his t-shirts and woolly socks, I stand in the doorway.

'Warm enough?' he asks.

'Yeah, I'm fine.'

'Made some pasta. Thought I'd better use up the

anchovies. Hope it's not too spicy.' He dishes up onto hot bowls and we sit at the kitchen table.

It's delicious, tomatoey and fiery. 'What's this called?' I ask.

'Tart's spaghetti,' he chuckles.

I refrain from asking if he makes this for Rebecca. He passes me the parmesan. Not the rubbish stuff that comes in a tub and smells of old socks. He has an actual lump and a special grater thing.

When we've eaten, I rinse the plates and he stacks the dishwasher. Music plays softly in the background. We're in a post-sex bubble, pretending tomorrow is not Halloween.

We mooch into the sitting room and snug up with blankets and Ink. He flicks through the TV and finds a film. Afterward, we go to bed and I take my HRT with a sense of relief. Good job I keep a few spare doses in Big Bag; the last thing I need is a hot flush tomorrow mid spell.

Mike was not a cuddler – unless he wanted something. Grant spoons me from behind and promptly falls asleep. I wait for the much-needed soporific effect of the hormone dose. It's the unsung benefit of HRT, the fact that it helps you sleep. Knackered middle-aged women across the country breathe a silent thankyou as sleep arrives. We all wake about four hours later when the drug wears off, our heads full of to-do lists – but that's life.

Surprisingly, I don't wake and instead have a long deep sleep, which I put down to the sex. Lucky me. I wake alone to a grey dawn. Grant's penthouse is empty, and he's left me a note by the kettle: 'Gone for supplies. Taken Ink. GX.'

I shower and put on the red bra and knickers. He's got my size exactly and they look nice. Seems a shame to plonk on an old t-shirt and my faded denim pinafore, but hey ho. I make the bed, tidy the sitting room and sit with the notes app on my phone, trying to think how best to tackle the day.

Grant returns with a paper bag of baked goods, artisan coffee, dog food and a gleaming shovel, which he props by the door. 'Somebody is going to have to dig that grave,' he says.

'I've got spades and stuff.'

'Yes, but this one's sharp.'

I don't argue.

We eat and drink, lost in thought, then start speaking at once. 'I've been thinking,' says Grant after I've encouraged him to talk first. 'Why not go to the churchyard now, this morning. Everyone is at the cottage, even Elaine. She messaged me. My brother won't expect it. He'll be going there tonight.'

'But what about the moonlight – Halloween moonlight.'

'I think it's minimal, the effect. You've got the spell ready, so do it now. It's still the thirty-first.'

He's right, it would be an elegant solution. And it would certainly catch Barry and the Coven out. But I have a vision for this spell. A witch's vision. I pat Grant's hand.

'You have to trust me on this. It's got to be tonight.'

Chapter Fifty-Nine

North Star Cottage looks empty and still when Grant pulls up his car in Church Lane. No light at the windows or curl of smoke from the chimneys. Not a chicken in sight. Grant and I exchange a glance as we walk to the kitchen door.

As far as I can tell, my protection spells are all in place. So why is everything off? I pull my wand from Big Bag too late.

Grant smacks into an unseen wall. 'Fuck!' He staggers back, clutching his nose.

Ink barks.

Mouse opens the kitchen door, a big grin on his face. 'Lilly! We weren't expecting you until tonight.' He waves an arm. The air shimmers and he beckons us inside.

'I thought it best to add extra precautions,' he says, standing on the step and reinstating the barrier, which looks like a shield of ice from this side. The kitchen is full. Walter and Joan are squashed together at the end of the table, Elaine is stirring a pot of stew on the range and Hilda is making tea. Ink scoots about, greeting everyone.

'Thank you,' I say. 'Thank you for coming.'

They mumble variously that it is no trouble and they are happy to be here.

'Where's Maud?'

'On lookout at the church with Oscar,' says Elaine, referring to her black cat familiar. My own cat, Claudia, is curled asleep on top of a stack of old magazines on the kitchen table.

There is a party atmosphere, and as everyone chats I sip my tea and lean on the sink. Grant settles Ink on her blanket nest, his golden glow surrounding him. He looks well. So does Walter, his silver orts a healthy shimmer. Atlas the rat sits on his shoulder twitching his whiskers. Elaine's orts are pink wisps at her feet as she stirs the pot. Joan and Hilda only have a faint glow. Mouse's are the brightest in the room; they are now iridescent and, like my own, multicoloured. He sits cross-legged on the worktop, wearing a Spiderman tracksuit and sucking a lollipop. He must have found the sweet jar I keep for the twins.

'I'm sorry, Lilly,' he says quietly. 'I've eaten all the sugar.'

'Don't worry. I'll get you some more.'

'Last night I went to the church for the headstone.'

'That's great. Thank you.'

I can't stop staring at him. He looks so different. He's still tiny, though. Still Mouse.

'You look great,' I say.

Mouse smiles at his Turkish slippers. 'My clan are here. I need more than sugar for magical energy. I need to be happy.'

'I'm glad you're happy,' I say.

'Is there anything else you need?' he says.

'I think everything's prepared. Except Bethany. I should have got her a coffin.'

'We thought of that.' He hops down, and I follow him into the sitting room, where a small wicker coffin rests between two chairs. The lid is decorated with fruited ivy, rose hips, dahlias and autumn leaves.

'It's beautiful,' I say, staring at the coffin even though I have a sense that others are in the room. Coloured orts sparkle in the air.

'Who's here?' I ask quietly.

Mouse goes behind the sofa and speaks a few words in a language I don't recognise. A woman even smaller than him creeps out, and he tucks her under his arm. 'This is my wife,' he says.

She steps forward and grasps the edge of my dress. 'We remember Bethany,' she says.

Mouse lifts the lid to show me Bethany safe inside.

'We, er, we thought we'd best get everything organised in case you got held up,' his wife says.

'It's perfect. Thank you. How old are you?'

Mouse grins. 'Old. May I make a suggestion?'

'Of course.'

'You should go into the woods and cleanse yourself. Renew your energy. We will have everything ready for you as the moon rises.'

Mouse's wife leads me by the skirt to the front door – the one that's permanently locked and out of use. Mouse opens it and we stand in the porch. A narrow road leads into the woods.

'I hardly ever use this door,' I say, staring at the road where people walk. 'Who are they?'

'Magical friends, Lilly. They're going to the church. We'll all help put Bethany safely to rest.'

'What about Barry?'

'There's nothing he can do against all of us and a midwitch. Go.' He gives me a little shove.

In the woods, the green-eyed fox joins me, and we wander among the blackwood trees. There is nowhere I'd rather be than here in nature as the season turns. I am at peace among the falling leaves as the trees sigh and begin their winter rest. No wonder they call this the Season of the Witch.

Hooded figures step into my path. Dark orts twist over the dry ground as they surround me, joining their hands in a circle of hate. My heart beats fast.

'Everyone warned me you'd come,' I say.

Barry throws back his hood, his grin ecstatic, his eyes wild. 'You should have listened.'

Beside me, the green-eyed fox shows her fangs and Barry laughs. 'I don't think your woodland creature will save you this time, Lilith Blackwood.' Around us, the forest is empty where moments ago allies walked. He must have made a barrier so no one can see us. Beyond it, unseen, Ink howls.

From his cloak he brings a candle, and the circle of witches do the same. One snaps her fingers for a flame, lights her candle and passes it on. They each ignite their candle from this one and begin a chant. The witch words flow and fill me with dread. They are summoning fire.

'It's time you met the fate of your ancestor,' shrieks Barry as they pace around me, holding their flames aloft. The green-eyed fox whimpers, her ears flat to her head. Poor creature. All animals are afraid of fire. I put my hand on her back to steady her as I kneel.

The witches are still. The chant complete. The spell almost executed.

'Let this witch burn and the woods with her.' Barry laughs and drops his candle onto the dry leaves. The others

Mid Witch Three

do likewise, and a wall of fire flares up as the Coven witches step back.

Pushing my hands beneath the leaves and into the moss and soil, I close my eyes the better to feel the power of the Blackwood. A forest should be afraid of fire – it's only natural. But not these trees, which have avoided the ravages of axes and burning over many centuries. All the Blackwood needs is one good witch to harness its power. And that good witch is me.

In the witch language, I ask the earth for water. Underground brooks combine and soon a torrent is brought forth, sprouting from every dry crack on the parched ground until all that is left of the witch fire is smoke. As soon as the fire is quenched, the green-eyed fox leaps at Barry, sending him falling into the undergrowth. With a flick of my hand, the barriers hiding us disappear. Ink comes to my side and many hands reach for Barry and his mob. There is no escape.

When the full moon rises, I find the ancient road – now revealed – to St Gutheridge and All Angels. The road cuts through the fields and I enter the churchyard through a side gate. The crowd parts. So many people. Some wear conical hats and long capes. Most look ordinary – like me. Ghosts hover unseen among the living.

Grant leans on his new shovel next to the grave he's dug. Through the lychgate, Mouse and some of his clan carry the wicker coffin with a slow, steady pace and hum a haunting tune. The folk they pass pick up the melody until we all make this strange music. The coffin is gently lowered into the freshly dug earth.

I hold my wand to the moon. 'Behold the earthly remains of my sister witch. A life taken too early and with cruelty. Lost and now returned to rest with her family who ever missed her, even in the afterlife. I cast this spell that she can remain here for eternity, unmolested and magically intact.'

At my feet, the spell supplies are laid on a cloth. I summon each ingredient into my hand and sprinkle them onto the coffin. 'I give grave soil from the witches in her bloodline. Herbs from the ground we all have walked.'

The last is a cloth pouch full of fine dust – the contents varied and complex. It's taken me weeks to concoct, and I hope I got it right. In my left hand, I snap a flame and let it grow tall. I switch to the witch tongue and speak the spell words as I tip the dust into the flame. It burns in the air with a thousand specs of light while the words flow out of me loud and clear.

This last act could not be practised. It's the part of the spell I worried most about, but I trust my strength. Here on All Hallows in the full moon's silver light, I am a powerful midwitch, strong and pure.

'This is my essence. Let it seal the magic within forever.' I spit to give the water element and then kneel, cut my palm with my cleansed athame and drip my blood into the grave.

'All elements are called to seal this grave.' I breathe in, pulling my magical energy from the ground up, and then I blow out a long breath. Wind whips around the churchyard, shaking the branches of the trees and rattling leaves along the paths. The ancient yew trees creak.

'Whosoever wishes to add their own essence for the safety of this witch's soul, let them come forth,' I say.

I'm weak from the effort. Grant stands behind me so I can lean on him while these kind strangers take a handful of soil, add blood or hair or charm bags and drop them into the grave. Then Grant solemnly shovels in the soil, and I kneel with my hand in the earth to make the grass grow and a few tendrils of ivy thread over the headstone where Maud perches.

Now the mortsafe spell is cast, and there is nothing more for me to do.

Barry and the mob of Coven members are brought from the crypt. There is much booing and cursing. Too exhausted to care, I don't get involved.

Barry runs bollock naked along Church Lane covered in pumpkin juice and feathers. 'Please don't hurt me!' he wails as Ink hounds him, snapping at his bare arse.

Walter puts Michaelmas daisies on my mother's grave for her birthday. There is a bonfire in the field and lots of eating, drinking and dancing in the moonlight.

Grant and I sleep in the wood.

⁓

The following week is busy. A lot of magical people want to meet me. It's weird being a kind of celebrity, and I hope they're not disappointed when they discover I'm so ordinary.

There is a general holiday atmosphere, but slowly folk return to their normal lives and I am left to get on with mine.

Mouse and his clan wait outside the kitchen one frosty morning.

'We've come to say goodbye,' he says, presenting me with a fragrant wreath of evergreens from the woods.

'That's beautiful,' I say. 'But you're welcome to stay.'

'That's kind. But my family—' He looks over his shoulder at the raggle-taggle bunch. 'After all this time, they're ready for a change.'

His little wife steps forward. 'Thank you for the eggs,' she chirps.

Eggs?

'What about your books?' I ask Mouse.

'We'll be back. The Blackwood is our home.'

'Really?'

'Lilly, we've always been here. You just never realised.'

I have so many questions, but Mouse is already following his family to my garden gate. As they leave, a wave of sadness engulfs me. 'Come back soon,' I cry.

In the morning, I'm delighted to find six brown eggs. 'I suppose you knew about this,' I say to Maud as I carry them in my apron back to the kitchen.

Then I have a tidy up, wash the kitchen floor – a constant occupation this time of year – put together a stew for supper and make a malt loaf and a batch of cheese and chive scones. Kitchen jobs bossed, I brew a pot of tea, chuck a rug over the step and sit in the winter sunshine.

Mid Witch Three

Grant and Ink return from a walk to Fox Green shops to fetch supplies. He puts the milk in the fridge then sits beside me. We watch Ink and Claudia drinking the moon-blest water from the birdbath. Cocksure struts up to them and then changes his mind, nonchalantly pecking at a windfall. We laugh and Maud ruffles her feathers in the bare branches of the apple tree.

Grant puts his arm around me, and I scoot a little closer. Multi-coloured and golden orts mingle on the path. He kisses the top of my head, pulls an autumn leaf out of my hair and tosses it onto the path, where it skitters through the colours of our magic. So pretty in the sunlight.

'I love you, Lilith.'

Truth.

Afterword

Thank you for reading Mid Witch Three. If you can take a moment to leave a review I'd be very grateful as this really helps the books visibility.

Also, why not join my mailing list for updates on the progress of the next Mid Witch book.

www.djbowmansmith.com

Acknowledgments

Grateful thanks to my husband and daughters for their constant support and encouragement.

And my editor, Anna Sharples, for her endless patience, insight and knowledge. Find her here:

www.sharpsightedgrammar.co.uk

About the Author

DJ Bowman-Smith writes witchy paranormal women's fiction. She's passionate about giving mature female protagonists the strong voices they deserve.

She lives with her husband on England's south coast and has two grown-up daughters. When she's not conjuring up magical mayhem on the page, you'll find her creating her own artwork (because apparently one creative obsession wasn't enough) or baking because her husband loves cake.

Much of her inspiration is found in the everyday: overheard conversations, people watching and walking Evie whippet on the beach. She says magic is everywhere, if you know where to look.

Deborah loves connecting with readers who share her passion for stories with grown up protagonists and midlife humour, so don't be shy about finding her on social media or joining her mailing list—she'd love to connect.

www.djbowmansmith.com

Printed in Dunstable, United Kingdom